P9-DMO-749

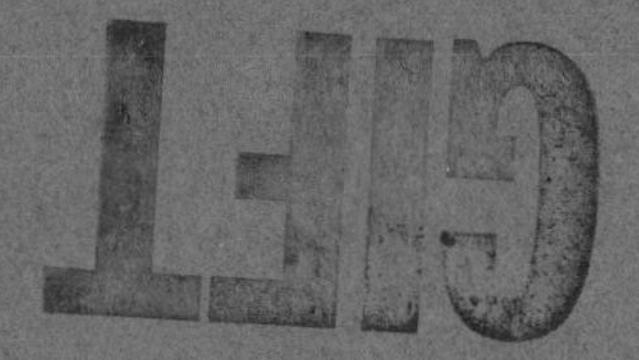

UNDERTOW

A NOVEL BY

LYNN STEGNER

This book is a work of fiction. Names, characters, places and incidents are either the product of the author's imagination or are used fictitiously. Any resemblance to actual events or locales or persons, living or dead, is entirely coincidental.

BASKERVILLE Publishers, Inc.
7540 LBJ Freeway/Suite 125, Dallas TX 75251-1008

Library of Congress Catalog Card Number: 92-074927
ISBN: 1-880909-02-2

Manufactured in the United States of America
First Printing

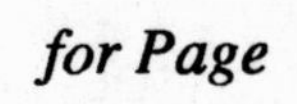

for Page

PROLOGUE

Driving north on Coast Highway 1, the cars ahead suddenly halt on a bridge over a wide river bed, and as you sit waiting for the light to change, you notice the timid little sign that tells you it is the Salsipuedes River. Hot, maybe bored, you open the window and look for the river trickling over the hardpan between the summer sand bars, though if it is winter or spring you have no trouble finding it beneath the bridge – a muddy seaward rush, bank to bank. And if it is the winter of '83 you watch the water froth beneath a continuous downpour, whole eucalyptus trees bobbing along, their whitish trunks through the brown water like the half-buried bones of ancient animals.

The light changes and the highway, temporarily routed through the town of Santa Lucia, becomes Ventana Way in its urban disguise, a five mile constriction of rumbling eighteen wheelers, suburbanites darting in and out of traffic as they pursue their list of errands, fuming wrecks you know must belong to students attending the University on the west side of town, and people like you just heading north, just wanting to get back to the coast. Past stucco bungalows and primly painted Victorians, surf shops, pizza parlors, an old corner market, the ubiquitous box of free puppies and a dusty, sad-

eyed girl behind it, cradling a furry ball. Somewhere embedded in every block there is a real estate office which reminds you that California is always for sale, particularly along its coast. You wonder if you should stop for gas. You consider a burrito or a burger. Maybe you'll pick up a six pack and some chips; it is 75 miles to San Francisco. But you don't because there is too much traffic and you just want to get out, and by now you're beginning to think you missed a sign. By now you figure you are lost. Stealing glances to the left, you search for that yellow-gray light, that suggestion of space, of emptiness, that the ocean casts upwards against the clouds like a vast reverse shadow.

Abruptly you are out of it, accelerating as the road unfurls itself like a long, white ribbon through fields of Brussels sprouts and lettuce and artichokes, and continues northward past Davenport and the landing where whalers used to tow their great catches. You light a cigarette, wish you had that beer, and because you feel free you decide you may never stop. As long as the road goes on, so shall you. Now you are rolling within earshot of the deep, trumpeting vocalization of the elephant seals languishing in the sands of Año Nuevo. Onward. North. Up the continent. To the left, white beaches, sheer cliffs, black rocks nesting in sea foam, and the blue relief of the Pacific lying forever west toward the band of purple called the horizon. And to the right the California foothills, in the summer as soft and yellow as cake batter, in the spring as green as New England.

But if you are here in January of 1983 the fields are sodden black islands amid standing pools, and you can't hear the elephant seals over the roar of the gale force winds. The road is just the widest course of water between flowing ditches. A few cars pass; there is a serious, purposeful quality about them – jeeps, pickup trucks, vans, equipment crowded against their windows, emblems on doors, heavy treads. The radio says that a mud slide south of Big Sur near Nacimiento Road has closed the coast route, and people stranded in the villages be-

yond the slide are being helicoptered out. In the opposite direction, at Trinidad Head, a first growth redwood falls across the road, its trunk diameter over 25 feet, and there are reports that the locals are already at it with Alaskan chain saws, cannibalizing the old giant.

January 27th, 1983. The year is important because it is the year the strongest El Niño *of the century is recorded. A meteorological-oceanographic event,* El Niño, *but event is far too small a word; "little boy" too sweet a translation. Once, maybe twice every 100 years something of this magnitude occurs. It cannot be predicted. From Alaska to Chile, the Pacific Ocean changes . . . the ocean changes. Temperature and sea level rise; upwellings of colder, nutrient rich waters slow or cease; the warm waters bring heavy rainfall, flooding, land erosion; storm tracks move southward to desertic regions; coastal winds intensify. And the marine life, the seals and guano birds, the cod, mackerel, squid and anchovies, the whole, interdependent chain is thrown into confusion as species emigrate to colder, deeper, further waters, emigrate to adapt. To survive.*

The month is important because on Año Nuevo Island the pinnipeds are there, hundreds of female elephant seals crowded onto the point beach to give birth, to nurse their pups, and to reconceive. The date, too, is important because the 27th is the first day in a violent, three-day storm that thrashes the California coast; the time is important because 8:00 a.m. marks the onset of high tide, the highest tide of the year.

At 7:00 a.m. on the 27th day of January, 1983, three marine biologists huddle in the grainy dawn light under the eaves of the State Reserve office, a weathered barn left over from the Flora Steele ranch built at the turn of the century. The ranger is inside finishing paper work while they wait for the helicopter he has coaxed the Coast Guard to send to Año Nuevo during the worst storm of the season in order to take three crazy biologists out to the island. For the elephant seals.

In the interests of science. The ranger shakes his head and signs the forms. Maybe the job is making him a little soft.

At 7:30 a.m. they fly the half mile from the mainland point to the island; the pilot agrees with these apologetic scientists that they could not have made an ocean crossing even in the best of boats, with the most experienced navigator. The usually discernible pattern of wave convection around the island has been obliterated by the storm. From the south and northwest great walls of breakers collide mid-channel, demolishing each other. Beneath the El Niño *tides, and the massive, wind-whipped surf, and the pounding rain, the shape of Año Nuevo is hardly recognizable from the air. Dark, amoebic, somehow more alive even as it is being beaten under, parts of the island vanish, then reappear, parts are simply inundated, rocks and reefs and jagged juts of sandstone are devoured by the incoming waves, spit out, devoured again and, when the tide reaches its peak, are swallowed completely.*

Maybe the members of the expedition already know what this means for the island's inhabitants. Maybe the chief scientist guesses but maintains his investigative distance. Maybe his assistant was around during the big storms of '79, and has already seen what can happen, and maybe she is now wondering if once again she will have to fight the urge to interfere, to help, even while she knows that there is no helping.

The pilot sets the helicopter down on a dense patch of ice plant: the sand is too wet and too unstable in the wind. Hitching up their packs and equipment, the trio head over the rounded spine of the island toward the point beach on the leeward shore. It is 8:00 a.m.. There are over a thousand seals in the rookery, mostly pregnant and nursing females. For three hours the tide rises, the massive waves break further and further inland, the seals press toward higher ground. Eventually the cliff is too steep, and the inland seals, clinging to its base, turn on those in retreat; turn, biting and snarling, and fight them back into the raging surf. By 11:00 a.m., the point beach is reduced to one tenth its normal size and the rookery has been torn apart. Rent from their mothers, pups are sucked out to sea by the powerful undertow, then pitched back, along with driftwood and rocks and the bodies of those who have preceded them, to be crushed against the cliffs. Out in the seething water, females struggle in the surge, calling to their lost offspring.

A winter of '83 is not to be expected; neither is the kind of exquisite and awful timing that can bring about disasters like the destruction of the elephant seals. Seldom do events converge so precisely, and when they do you sense there will be changes, irreversible changes at the nethermost levels, in the substrata, changes that claim new directions. No, the winter of '83 was a freak. Today when you pass Año Nuevo State Reserve the sun overhead is uninhibited, the sky and sea compete for the blue, and from a distance the island off the point is as flat as a stepping stone. Then it is behind you. A salty breeze curls over the cliffs, rustles up across the fields. Resting your elbow on the open window sill, you breathe in deeply. Highway 1 twines on toward San Francisco, points north. At Half Moon Bay you have a choice to make – turn inland toward the Interstates, toward the tidy advance of the suburbs and the computer firms and the chain restaurants, or go straight where the coast road takes you along a narrow rift beneath Devil's Slide, a steep rocky incline on which nothing can be built and very little grows, a place where no horizontal peace will ever be found. Straight, you decide. Forward. Full tilt. Through San Francisco, crossing the Golden Gate, you jog northwest and break for Bodega Bay, Point Arena, Mendocino, and other quaint seaside hamlets. Then Highway 1 merges with 101, but it is the same two lane road up to Arcata, Crescent City, Oregon, Washington and the Olympic Peninsula. There it doubles back on itself and retraces the edge of the continent, untroubled, it seems, by the ocean pounding up from below and the winter storms beating it apart. Every year sections of the road crack and sag and finally let loose, plunging 500 feet into the cold chaos of water.

And you keep coming back to Coast Highway 1. You stand on a promontory, looking north and south at the faint scratch it makes in the almost vertical backs of the hills as they scramble out of the water, you stand and feel its insignificance, its bravery. You know that a great part of its beauty lies beneath you in the Pacific, in the future. Because it is the ocean's purpose to make of the edge of the continent, of every cove and point, every bight, every spur and spit, to make of the endless deviations a straight line. It is your job to bear witness, to keep coming back.

ONE

A quiet, sunny, Friday afternoon. The acacia trees drooped with blossoms, yellow puffs, honey sweet and alive with bees, and the sky had gone distant, a deepening blue. The air, hazy with pollen, still held out a wintry keenness, though it was early May and time for yielding. A flock of cedar waxwings, attracted by the hedges of pyracantha berries around Elliot Newhouse's yard, lit in the branches of the magnolia, their yellow bellies and black masks a brilliant flashing as they dive-bombed the bushes, some of them already drunk and crashing into the windows. Elliot dragged Holmes onto the porch where, deprived of access to the stunned birds dropping below the sills, he whimpered and groveled out his ardor for the hunt.

The Newhouse kitchen. The Newhouse house – a three story Victorian with a corner turret and a grand entrance, beveled windows, pocket doors and pass-throughs, a curving balustrade that ended in a magnificent oaken comma, delicate floral wallpapers, a bidet in the commodious upstairs bathroom, and everything arranged just so – hat rack, umbrella stand, settee, 'art' furniture, oriental rugs, a leather chesterfield in the back parlor, a fainting couch on the second story landing – like the set of a period piece. Off the kitchen, beyond the glassed-in porch and pantry, the stoop had been expanded into a deck which faced southwest over the neighbor's shake roof and the foothills and across the bay toward a spur of the smoky blue Santa Lucia Mountains.

Jill Newhouse was out of town, attending an architecture convention in Chicago, and Elliot had been instructed to water the plants at least twice in her absence. Which he did now, finally, because they were looking a little peaked, because Jill would be returning the next afternoon, and because it gave him something to do.

In that place Elliot Newhouse and Anne McBain waited. She had had the test in the morning and was told she could call after three o'clock for the results. In the hour and the weather, in the occasional admonitions to the thwarted Holmes, in the wine they sipped, the topics they pursued, there was a casualness that jarred. It irritated her when Elliot sat back and began skimming an article containing the mortality figures from the Año Nuevo rookery. Nevertheless, she asked him what the final toll was.

"683 out of 975. Dead."

"All pups?"

"Yeah."

"And all drowned," she said, making a face.

"Some. Some the sharks got." He poured himself some more wine. "Most died of starvation."

"How could that happen when you didn't lose any females?"

"The beach had been ripped away. A lot of females gave up trying to find their pups, and abandoned the island for the mainland."

"Well, it's over now," she said. "*El Niño*, the winter."

"Not the effects. Who knows how many years we'll be dealing with this." Elliot looked at his watch. "I guess you can try now," he said.

"It's just three. I'll wait a few minutes."

"You can always call back."

She went to the phone and dialed Dr. Havenstein's office. The nurse's voice was so hesitant that Anne was not sure she meant what she said. Nowadays they never know which answer a woman wants, she thought, responding with a bright "Thank you" to put the nurse at ease. Though she did not feel bright or airy; she felt that something giant had just lowered about them, like a bank of winter clouds, and she wanted help looking at it, it was so obviously beyond her control. Turning, she found Elliot's eyes and said, "Positive."

He was standing in the corner of the kitchen reading her face as the word reached him, and she knew he perceived instantly the importance of his first response. For less than a moment he sagged, like someone who has had his wind knocked out, and his expression – so brief it might have been subliminal – was pure alarm. Then it was gone. It hardly seemed to have happened at all. And he did what he always did. He stalled. Pouring himself some more wine, smiling now, his face loose and indulgent, leery around the eyes, he said, "You're kidding." And in that unforgivable delay she knew his fear.

She knew also that there was no real doubt what he wanted her to do.

When they went to dinner that night and she refrained from drinking, he pretended it amused him, it was cute. And in bed he floated his hand above her stomach, widened his blue eyes, made his ears go up, wearing an imbecilic grin and rocking his head back and forth, Stanley measuring Olly for a new suit. "*Thi*s big?" he teased.

She squirmed, not wanting to be silly, wanting to wonder at being his woman with their child, to be close and quiet and. . . *reverent*. The window was open and moonlight pooled around the room, lending a photo negative quality to the walls and furniture. Holmes was at the foot of the bed, paws straining against the carpet, body twisted as he snarfed at a flea. The sweet fragrance of jasmine lilted through the window, dreamy and paradisiacal.

Anne rolled over, laying her head on his shoulder, and his arm curled automatically around her. She moved the palm of her hand lightly over his chest hair as if to divine the future.

"Can't you ever be serious?" she said.

"Only during football season."

"Elliot," she said, tugging at one of his hairs.

"Hey, hey . . . okay. What do you want me to say?"

"I don't know. Not that. I'm scared. Why do you have to kid around?"

"That's what I do when I don't know what to do."

"It's not good tonight. I need you to be with me."

"I am here, sweetie, don't worry, we'll figure something out." He pulled her in closer so that her face touched his beard. She closed her eyes.

"The jasmine's strong," she murmured.

"Yeah, it smells like the Woolworth perfume counter."

"No, it's nice, especially at night, so exotic and unexpected. It doesn't seem real." A few minutes passed, and as hard as her fears fought back the question that might invite what she was unprepared to hear that night, or imagine doing one day, there was a larger part of her that hoped, that saw their love as a kind of eminent domain and her pregnancy a significant enough event to override ordinary concerns, standard rules of conduct. It's strong enough, she thought, it could force a decision. That a life was at stake, she did not honestly feel. The thing germinating inside her was an idea, and had not time or size yet to *be*, to spill out over the rim of thought and become real. For now, only they were at stake.

Maybe what she saw in his eyes that afternoon had not been alarm, only surprise. He was entitled to that. That and more. And at dinner, if he had been amused by her not drinking, by her gearing to the new course, he had also been solicitous, as if he had given her not a baby but a case of flu. Maybe after living with the idea for a couple of days, he would begin to see a kind of beauty in the timing, an excuse to do sooner what he wanted to do anyway.

For the last year she had been unhappy, had told Elliot that if he did not make a decision by the end of summer she would have to leave. It wasn't clear he believed her. She wasn't sure she had convinced herself. Intellectually, at least, it was obvious: she would have to move on. An elusive guilt drifted between her thoughts, the scent of something with which she was almost familiar. But guilt about what? What had she done? It would be ludicrous to think this anything but an accident, especially now when she was considering a future without Elliot. Yet she did not completely trust herself and wondered as she lay against his solid chest if she was subconsciously capable of so crude a ploy, and if the possibility occurring to her did not *ipso facto* condemn her. In which case she deserved his caution.

In the moonlight the room lost color; the red comforter went dark gray, her hand on Elliot's chest a lighter shade, the schefflera in the far corner a black, Rorschach dappling creased and reversed where the walls met, and on the back of the door the mirror resolved itself into an empty gleam. Elliot's warmth began to penetrate her bare skin, and the jasmine breeze cooled their faces. Down below the house in the open fields she heard the almost human squeals of coyotes.

No. It was an accident. As much as she did not want to have to leave him, as much as she knew he wanted to be with her, this was too desperate an act. She would not have forced the issue with a baby. But I am pregnant, she told herself, and forced the issue seems to be.

Change. It occurred to her that there would have to be a change, soon now. The thought of it, the promise of relief, even though she had grown used to things, was vaguely exciting.

"What are we going to do, Elliot?"

There was a silence, like a hole opening up.

"The timing's not exactly the best," he said.

She kept smoothing his hair as if nothing was approaching,

as if they were engaged in a rational conversation about a solvable subject. A sea anemone poked with a stick will withdraw in a sudden, silent spasm of tentacles caving inward; Elliot, likewise, had a habit of closing up when faced with disapproval or danger, or a question that probed too deeply. "No, not the best," she said.

Encouraged, he said, "If this mess with Jill was settled and if I didn't think my leaving now would cause a breakdown of some kind, it would be different." He shook his head gently. "It's still hard for me to believe."

"You mean there would be a time when it would be okay? If I was pregnant?"

"Sure."

"That's nice news." She tried to make her voice calm, her attitude pliant. Where he really stood in all of this, his naked reaction . . . that was what she wanted to see. She would have to try very hard now to hold herself in so that he would come out.

"I've got a lick or two left in me," Elliot said. "Even old farts can change. Sure I want to reproduce us. We both want to reproduce us. Only under conditions that are favorable to a new life. And I wouldn't call these favorable conditions. I'd call this bad timing."

"It isn't exactly happening now. It takes nine months to have a baby."

"Well, we can't just wait for the little nipper to introduce himself at the breakfast table someday. We have to do something now."

"Yes. I am pregnant." Half a minute passed as she drank in the jasmine, and tried to block out the sound of the coyotes and the memory of Elliot's description of them when she first heard their eerie call as the sound of babies being slaughtered. "Can't we change the conditions?" she asked.

"I don't know that there's time, sweetie, even though this really cranks up the heat. I'm trying to bring about a separation that won't tear everybody and everything in pieces, and I just don't know how long it will take."

She didn't want to hear about everybody, or how long things would take. Their future . . . he was talking about a future. "I'm glad you want to have a child with me. I never thought I'd hear you say that."

He cleared his throat. "Well, you know that I mean 'have a child' in the grand sense. I mean it without practical considerations. I mean it aesthetically as a portrait of you and me, a genetic statement of what you mean to me." Fumbling for the glass of wine on the nightstand, Elliot paused, tucked in his chin, and took a sip; then, reaching to put it back, he changed his mind and finished it off. "I know what you're thinking," he said, swallowing. "But having mixed emotions doesn't cancel or devalue the 'I want.'"

"No, it doesn't, but it just might qualify it out of existence."

His face in the shadows was broad and expressionless, his arm around her almost rigid, so wary was he, it seemed, of betraying himself.

"What do you want to do?" he asked.

"I guess that depends on your intentions."

"Well, what would you do if I was out of the picture, if I didn't exist?"

"But you're not."

"Hypothetically, Anne."

"What are my options?"

"You know them as well as I do."

"Not really."

"What are you talking about? Not really?"

"Not as stated by you."

"Come on, Anne." Abruptly he sat up and flipped on his reading light.

"You want me to have an abortion because the timing is bad."

"Typically you reduce my argument. You snag one word I happen to use and hoist me with it. You know what I mean by timing."

"The timing is the timing, Elliot. The world can't always adjust to your practical considerations. It might have a plan of its own. The world might not want to come to Mohammed."

"I'm not asking it to adjust. You can do whatever you damn well please. I am simply saying that I can't make any promises at this time because I am allowing those dreary practical considerations that you find cautious and unmanly to emerge."

"I don't find them unmanly. I find them questionable. Why can't you make promises? Not for my sake, or even Jill's. It's because you don't want to make any decisions, you don't want to be the first to commit. You'd rather wait and see how it all shakes down before you make your move. Practical considerations . . . what's that? What's *im*-practical about not wanting to abort our child's life when, according to you, you're 'working on' a separation and in nine months we could very well be together?"

"How can I make promises, Anne? Look, I know you dismiss my, ah, shall we say, *conservatism* as just more covering my ass – which it's not. My ass is pretty uncovered at the moment and my nerve ends are pretty frazzled. How can I make promises? What if I said, 'Have the baby, Anne, someday I'll marry you and we'll raise the kid together?'"

"Why can't you say that? What does it take for you to make a stand?"

"It takes something less speculative. Because what if I didn't make it, what if I wasn't free in nine months or two years or ten years, how would you feel about me then? No. I won't make a stand, not if it means destroying other people's lives in the rush. And as much as I want to guarantee my presence in your life, I won't. Not this way. I love you, Anne. We have always been brutally honest with each other, and this is no time to start making assurances that may spring a leak."

"Brutal honesty isn't necessarily a virtue. It doesn't absolve you from responsibility," she said, and sat up, drawing the sheet over her breasts, thinking *brutal honesty . . . what bullshit.* "Just because you're announcing a hands off attitude doesn't mean your hands are any cleaner – they can get just as dirty doing nothing, Elliot. They can be just as dirty."

"Yes, well, I'm not shirking my responsibilities. I have others too, you forget. People who didn't choose to have their lives blown apart."

"If you think I *chose* this . . . "

"It's a consequence of one of your choices, as well as mine," he said.

"And still you won't make any guarantees. You won't change even for this."

"I'm not in a position to. I never have been. You knew that from the beginning."

She was making him say things he would have rather postponed. He would have held her, and told her not to worry, and the next day he would have come up with the soft words. But tonight, tomorrow, the words would mean the same, and if he was going to say them, she wanted them hard. She wanted him to feel bad. "Oh yes. You were always careful to remind me of that," she said bitterly, then weakening, "but I guess I never really listened, maybe, because I felt so strongly that we had found a . . . a home in each other." Voice quavering, will diminished by the hour and the argument and the magnitude of her predicament, she looked back and found nothing and no one to blame but herself. She had not been smart. She had not even guessed accurately, though she had waited long enough, it seemed, for any reasonable wager to pay off. She was a fool, a fool surviving on intermittent reinforcement and a pathetic, dog-eared scrap of hope, the wanting him so extravagant she had no funds left to satisfy the terms. Now here it came, the fine print swelling to bold face indignities. You are not his wife. You have no rights. You are on your own.

She was shivering. Elliot hauled the comforter up to her neck and tucked it behind her shoulders. "We *have* found a home," he said. "We just haven't paid for it yet."

I'm paying for it now, she thought, I've *been* paying for it. Of course I had no business being with him in the first place. It was a bad thing to do, falling in love, letting myself fall in love. It was not kind. If I had been stronger, if I hadn't thought all happiness lay with Elliot . . . romantic delusions. Telling myself that I wasn't spoiling anything that wasn't already spoiled and making it worse for everyone, spoiling it more. The waste is beginning to show. I'm twenty seven and the waste . . .

Elliot settled down against the pillows. In the late night silence, the pain was a presence beating between them. Stiffly they sat as if they had just met. Across the room the window divided their image between the outside and inside, the two of them translucent in the glass, uncertain, side by side, the reading lamp casting a cone of yellow light over their heads while they peered nearsightedly from the outside in, and from the bed at themselves out in the moonlight among the sooty shadows.

"If I have the child," she said, "whether or not you participate in its upbringing, will you help financially?"

"Of course." Tapping his finger tips together, he turned his face and examined her expression; she made a point of voiding it of emotion except for a faint, glassy-eyed impression of overloaded circuits. "Is that what you want to do?" he asked, still watching her.

"I don't know. It's one of the options." She felt tired and bruised. All that seemed worth knowing was the minimum he would do; everything else was hurting too much. "You know how I feel about abortion," she said.

"Being Catholic?"

"I'm not much of a Catholic anymore. A little of that maybe, residually, and a basic repugnance to abortion – probably women feel that more because they have fewer opportunities to pass on their genes. Some of it is biological. Some of it isn't. Maybe if it wasn't you . . . I've always wanted to have your child."

"I know."

"I wouldn't be here if my mother had gone that way. And at the same time I know how much she resented being tied to my father because of me, how disappointed she must have been when he never married her. Every time she looked at me there was a certain grain of pure anger that my presence wasn't enough to hold him. And you know, even if I wasn't a failed ploy, even if she just wanted to have a baby, she must have looked at me and seen him and remembered her unhappy life and felt hate. I don't want that to happen to me or my child."

Turning the reading light off, Elliot drew her against him, trailing his fingers around her back in reassuring patterns.

"Maybe it doesn't matter," she said. "Maybe seeing makes no difference, you go where you're going to go because of where you started and you're stuck having the same old accidents on the same old road and the most you can ever learn is how to prolong the time between crashes. Or stop moving, stop living."

"Like your mother?"

"In some ways, yes."

"I don't subscribe to that gloomy view and I don't think you really do, either."

"Maybe not. It seems that way now. I don't feel very smart. Because you're right, everything you said makes perfect sense, it always does. I don't want broken promises. I don't want anyone's life destroyed on my account, including my own."

"That's what I'm trying to avoid," he said. "Our lives undone by guilt."

"Of course," she said. "Your fears are perfectly legitimate, and there's nothing wrong with your feelings and intentions, they're perfectly reasonable. In a way, I'm sorry for that."

The moon disappeared above the window, illuminating the outside in a dull, pewter glow and removing from the inside the sharp black and white shapes of reality. She stared into the grainy space. To what had they come? Where were they now? Before her eyes the grains swirled, losing depth the longer she looked until a flat, suffocating grayness pressed down at her. Elliot's body, though it touched hers, seemed separated by the same grayness, and his voice came loose, like a sudden memory that did not belong anywhere, a memory without bearings. She tried but could not picture his face. It frightened her.

"What you feel is more important. It's your decision," he was saying. "And as circumstance allows, I'll be there no matter what you choose."

"No matter what I choose . . . "

"I love you," he said.

"I know," she said, but there was no life in her voice, and conscious of it, she added, "I love you too."

Squeezing her brusquely as if to revive her, he tipped up her chin and kissed her. "It's late, let's forget it tonight. Tomorrow we'll pull up our socks and figure something out."

Anne sank limply down into the crook of his arm. "I don't think we can win this one, Elliot." The admission made her cry.

"Ah, come on, we've been through so much. You're the one who's always telling me to see things positively. Sleep now. It won't be so bad in the morning."

"Okay," she murmured, and later, "You were right about the jasmine." But she felt that his body had loosened, heard his breathing lengthen and even out, and she supposed he could not hear her.

Down in the moonlit fields the coyotes had stopped their plaintive yelps, while the heavy, rolling bass of the surf went on, *legato*, below the brink of land. She did sleep finally, taking comfort in the rise and fall of Elliot's chest and in his presence for the night, for the moment.

TWO

The coffee grinder. Smiling drowsily, Anne blinked in the hazy light, arched her back, and sank back down into the warm chaos of sheets and pillows and comforter. "Elliot," she sighed.

At home, she rose abruptly and made the bed, erasing the impression her body had left, showered, dressed, and shut the bedroom door. The day began with things to do, and if there was any transition from the state of sleep to alertness it was as sudden and as complete as the sun clearing the rim of a deep crater. But this morning they were together. They would linger, and the metamorphosis would be a languid passage, like the first hours of a holiday in which everything has been instantly forgotten, and time becomes an arbitrary thing.

In her mind, she ticked off the activities narrated by the sounds straying up the stairs – the zing of the juicer, the twin clicks of glasses placed on the breakfast tray, the bell on the toaster oven announcing what? muffins, bagels – it didn't matter, she felt unusually hungry – the utensil drawer clattering open, then bare feet thumping softly away, squeaking on the hardwood, the front door, a rubber band snapped, the newspaper shaken out, and another sound not from the east end of the house but from the south, through the window adjacent to the bed, a playful growl. Anne pushed over to see what Holmes was up to, but the sudden ache in her breasts reminded her, and she dropped her face into the pillow, drawing in her elbows to support her weight. "I'm pregnant," she whispered, listening to the size of the word. "I'm pregnant," she said again, louder, and Holmes' funny little murmuring growl and her own quickened heart beat acknowledged the fact.

If he had been pleased for a few minutes, for the first night, one night . . . If he had given her *some small joy* in the idea – a hug, a wondering shake of his head, a little softness around the eyes – before the wheels of caution came trundling, like a juggernaut, over her dreams. He could have lied, even, could have pretended that there were no words too ugly to say.

"Pregnant," she said. "Me."

Again Holmes grumbled.

Lifting her head, she squinted out the window at the deck, steamy and ablaze in the first light. There lay Holmes, her dog, and between the north and south rows of his teeth, delicately, as if he had no teeth, was a cedar waxwing.

"Breakfast is served, my pet," Elliot said, as he swung into the room and around the bed to the nightstand where he set the tray.

"Holmes has a bird. It's still alive," she said.

"I know. I can't get it away from him. He caught it." Elliot shrugged. "It's his, I guess."

"Why doesn't he just kill it? Why does he have to play with it?"

"He's not hungry, I fed him when I got up. He's a predator," Elliot said, running his hand along her calf. "And he doesn't get many opportunities to hone his skills."

"Torture."

"Nature red in tooth and claw," Elliot sang. He began riffling through the newspaper for the sports section.

She went to the window, pushed it up, and leaned out toward the dog. "Get out of here, Holmes," she shouted.

Confused, Holmes stopped his tender mauling and clamped down on the waxwing, as if he was afraid it would be taken from him. From the side of his muzzle several long, yellow-tipped feathers poked out. "Go on, get out." He rose then and slunk off, casting an injured look at Anne. She was naked, and the morning air sent a chill up her spine as she closed the window.

Though for over a month she had marked time by the approach of their week in May together, she wanted it to end now. She wanted to be home, to clean the house, read a book, go to bed early. A cool, shiny Saturday. A day that was still relatively empty, retrievable even, a day in which she could take a bearing or two. She would unplug the phone and close the gate at the end of the gravel drive that led to her house, and no one could reach her, no one could touch her. Elliot would be picking Jill up at the airport that afternoon, so there would not be his call to wait for. There would not be this place to come to where small things were dying. And no one cared.

Cradling her breasts, she padded down the hall and into the bathroom.

"Your muffin's getting cold," he said.

"I'll be right back."

She slumped onto the toilet, and in the opposite mirror, examined herself – not too horrible, under the circumstances, though a little water and a comb would improve things. She turned on the hot water tap and let it warm up while she rummaged through her toiletry kit for the bar of clear brown face soap. Behind the kit on the counter stood the mysterious bottles and jars belonging to Elliot's wife, the milk cleansers and astringents, the avocado eye cream, the Norwegian facial masks, the French powders – all so worldly, so adult. In comparison, the contents of Anne's kit seemed childish and crude. She picked up one of the jars of cream, unscrewed it, sniffed, wondering if Elliot liked the scent, if he and his wife were close enough anymore for him to notice it. Steam was rising from the sink. She wrapped her hair up in a towel. Several times she doused her face, then with a wash cloth, she rubbed the soap into her skin using circular motions, and rinsed it with warm, then cold water. Again, she examined herself in the mirror. Better. The skin was pink, the eyes brighter, and even with her hair hidden, without it to soften her features in the morning light, it was still a striking face, and for that she was grateful. People forgave faces like hers. Elliot always said that she looked like one of Picasso's women, with the classic Greek nose (though there was no Greek in her history), and the large, lidded eyes. But the face was not oval, it was broad, and the lips were full, not pressed in like a bud, and the cheek bones were as high as a squaw girl's. She ran her fingertip over the two reddish marks: any amount of sun left color where her cheek bones rose beneath the skin, so that she often looked flushed and healthy. Letting her hair down, she brushed it back from her forehead and watched the caramel-colored waves move down below her shoulders. After a month or two of the dry summer heat when her swimming schedule increased, the upper layers would dry and blond. Elliot seemed to like it best in the summer.

She pulled on Elliot's plaid robe which was hanging underneath a long, cool, slippery thing, salmon pink and trimmed with lace. The sight of Jill's robe luxuriating down the back of the door, awaiting Mrs. Newhouse's return, Mrs. Newhouse's body, seemed to reduce Anne to a grubby, back street accident that a little cash and a bus ticket could remedy.

Maybe that's what it is, she thought, exactly what it is.

Elliot put the paper down when she returned. "Come and eat," he said.

She found herself watching his hands as he passed the orange juice and plate of muffins. How confident they were, imperial almost, the backs honey tanned, the white palms studded with four perfect calluses, fingers long and intelligent, their movements, as if choreographed, fluent expressions of everything Elliot Newhouse was about – natural grace, studied precision, a history of work enjoyed, of recognition duly achieved. The good life. So why was she here with this man in need of nothing? Was he honing his skills? She decided to let Elliot bring up the night before.

"Look at this," he said, handing her the newspaper. He tapped the bottom of the page.

The headline read, "Found: 15 million year old whale skeleton."

"I thought you weren't going to leak it out," she said.

"Impossible not to. Anyway, it might attract funding, funding we could quietly divert." Crinkling one eyebrow, he tried to look roguish. Dr. Newhouse was known among his colleagues as a master at enticing stray funds from the thicket of bureaucracy. Elliot liked to win, especially on someone else's dime.

Anne shot him a disapproving smile, and read on. "Dr. Elliot Newhouse, director of Marine Biology at the University, and head of the research team working with northern elephant seals on Año Nuevo Island was standing on a cliff Wednesday when the ledge gave way, and he slid, uninjured, down to the beach thirty feet below. He glanced back up at the newly exposed cliff face and noticed, he said, embedded in the ancient sandstone, what looked to be a massive jawbone. 'So far all we can say is that it is a baleen, or toothless whale, between 12 and 15 million years old,' Newhouse said. The California Gray Whale which annually migrates north and south along the Pacific Coast is also a baleen whale. 'This is much smaller,' Newhouse said. 'Maybe an ancestor, maybe an extinct species, it's just too soon to tell. We have to wait for the fellows with the picks and shovels and toothbrushes to show up, which given the apparent age of this thing, won't be long.'"

"How long?" she asked.

He drew in one corner of his mouth. "Sunday. I'm taking five out in the afternoon. One guy – Borovich – is the real thing, a paleozoologist from Florida with a long trail of books and articles; the others are groupies."

"Is there room for one more?"

Elliot hesitated. Instantly she wished she had not asked. Because she was a would-be, a research assistant four days a week at the marine lab across the bay while she worked as she could on her Ph.D. thesis, and to support the weight of that dream, a part-time waitress at a local dinner house. It was possible he did not want her there among the dignitaries; it was easy to see how he might prefer to be exclusively Dr. Newhouse with them, not a man with a dewy-eyed young woman on his arm. Her presence might very well act as an alloy in an otherwise pure scientific event. Maybe now especially. She had become a problem, to be separated out, to be escaped from. He had yet to raise the fact of her pregnancy that morning. Still, cetaceans were her thing.

"Sure there's room," he said.

"Really?"

"You bet. You've got the right credentials. It might be disappointing, though. There's not much to see because it's buried about three feet under. You have to stand on the beach and look up at the face of the cliff, and then it's just a 12-inch length of bone. Look, I was going to drop these guys off at the site, then we can hike over to the other side of the island. One of my females we put a depth recorder on hasn't returned yet, and I thought I'd see if she's hauled out in the last two days. Or maybe she just didn't make it." Elliot frowned into the black hole of his coffee cup. "That'd be a 2500 dollar piece of equipment measuring the last dive of a decomposing elephant seal. Damn." He gulped down the coffee. "But maybe we can find her. So meet me at the security gate. We need to talk, anyway," he said, patting her stomach. He wore a light expression, no smile, and no perceptible ticks of concern around his sea-blue eyes, as if what they had to discuss could be simply addressed on Sunday and fixed on Monday. Not to worry, not to wallow in it, he seemed to say. Which was, of course, what Anne would do until then, operating on the theory that to wallow was to understand. To obsess was to see.

To be kind, he waited until she left, but as she drove away she saw him through the window with the vacuum cleaner, already ridding the house of her presence, her prints.

THREE

The coast highway might clear her head. In her mind Anne saw the road on the edge of the continent on a Saturday morning, still deserted, and wondered how far north she could get by nightfall, how long it would take for Elliot to discover she was gone. She wondered if she had whatever it took to run. At the stop light opposite Bea's Market, she rolled down the window to let some of the wet morning air in, took a deep breath, sighed. *Oh, Elliot. What am I going to do?*

Except for a garbage truck lumbering up the coast to the county dump, and a VW bus with a couple of surfboards lashed to its roof, the road was deserted. When the light went green, she squeezed the accelerator, the rear wheels spun a moment before the pavement caught them, then the old blue pickup lurched forward and bounced along at an even 60. A veil of clouds dulled the morning sky, and under it the Pacific flattened out, twinkling faintly yellow along the sun's path. Thin, bluish-gray ripples writhed indecisively across the surface, like dark veins in a vast slab of marble. Except for salmon season, local fishing boats trolled the outer bay waters; this was too far north. From the cliffs to the horizon, the ocean was dawn-of-time empty. And she did not want to run north up the coast road, tracing the edge of nothingness. She wanted to be home in a house, surrounded by small, neat, man-made objects. She wanted to be held in, to be safely contained.

Ten miles out of Santa Lucia, she swung east onto the Grade, and wound into the hills toward the scattered, unincorporated community of Refugio where, for the last five years, she had rented a cottage on a ten acre piece from a stock broker and his wife. They lived in San Francisco, had built the place as a summer home, but the kids had grown up and, though getting away from it all was the point, Refugio might have brought that aim too close to the mark. It was a half hour drive to the things money could buy. And because of the way the house was situated on a bluff facing southwest over a deep canyon, and backed up to an acre of madrone and Douglas fir and tan oak, the only visible lights were those winking along the strand of the peninsula clear across the bay. The isolation worked on the psyche; it came incessantly and bored, like the surf, into the weak spots, eroding the architecture of sanity. To Anne it seemed that along the back roads of Refugio there were more 'for sale' signs than anywhere else in the county, the dream homes of young couples who, within a year, filed for divorce and sold out. The inability to live in a place like Refugio was an inner weakness, she believed; it was what came of being weaned on city fumes and city time, on the jangly, speeded-up, immediately gratified, kaleidoscopic vision of the good life in which every minute was consumed, every pool of silence drained off, every space filled.

Not in Refugio. If you liked yourself well enough, something good and strong might come of days passed in the high hills – or so she had reminded herself during those early months when the loneliness milled around the house, a sullen company of ghosts.

At the thousand foot level, the road switched abruptly north then east past a bank of eucalyptus planted a century ago as a windbreak. Their trunks were as smooth and yellow as ancient Greek columns. For the next mile – always *that* mile – the air warmed a good ten degrees. In the winter it cooled by the same amount, in the same place. On up another four miles, and the pickup rocked onto the Nelson's rutted driveway. George Nelson had been a vineyardist in Refugio for over thirty-five years, his wife, Donna, a weaver. Anne met them at the voting polls one year. They were good neighbors; they picked up her mail when she was gone. No one was in evidence – she realized she was relieved. Back to the kitchen, gathering up her mail, she then hiked into the vineyard. Holmes dashed by and out of sight.

Long, leafy shoots followed the cordon wires; underneath the foliage the berries had already set, the embryonic clusters with their hard, green nubs like plastic replicas from which some child had plucked the grapes. In four months they would be a dusty yellow, and so plump that one ruptured grape could provide a home for a metropolis of wild yeasts.

"Holmes. Come on. Come on, boy," she called, following the tractor road that bordered the vineyard.

Last September, we made Chardonnay from these grapes, she thought. Good Chardonnay – big, rich, full of character, but lacking structure, backbone. The fruit had been too ripe, and the wine probably would not live long. She stopped, reaching along a shoot, and ran her fingers over the baby cluster. What about this vintage? So many variables had to be factored in, and any one of them down the road might beget a flaw. What of this year? she wondered.

George Nelson had sold them a ton of fruit for half price because it became clear he could not get all of it off in time: the temperature had shot to 98 and stuck for three days, the sugars were climbing dangerously high – 24, 25 brix – and there were not enough pickers to go around. Someone even stole onto his property one morning, and hired two workers out from under him. A couple of home winemakers willing to harvest was the best George would do with that last bottom acre. So they borrowed an old apple press, bought six plastic garbage cans from the hardware store, and showed up at eight Saturday morning with a jug of lemonade and small pruning clippers.

George shook his head. "Take you all day with those." He held out a grape knife, its sickle blade as thin and sharp as paper, and demonstrated the quick, wrist movement, the back of his hand pushing up under the foliage, the blade finding the main stem at the top of the cluster, the left hand cradling each bunch as it let loose. "It'll cut down on the MOG, too," he said. (Material other than grapes, they later learned.) "But you gotta watch your fingers. We had to fish the end of Tomas' pinky out of a bin of Grenache last year, and it wasn't easy. They're about the same color." Elliot had laughed.

All morning in the heat they picked. The sticky juice covered their hands, and the bees followed them from vine to vine, and their backs very soon declared themselves. The vineyard had been sulphured over a week before, and the fine white powder and the fine dry dirt mingled with the sweat on their necks and faces, forming a gritty paste, and whenever Elliot wiped his forehead, or Anne brushed her cheek, it would smear, like war paint. A terrifyingly sweet day, Anne remembered. She could still hear their voices in the hot stillness, drifting across the rows as they planned their winemaking strategy – number of hours on the skin, variety of oak, cooperage time, racking frequency – information which they scavenged from conversations with George, from the Encyclopedia Britannica, and from a pamphlet provided by a local winery's tasting room. She could still feel the fellowship even as they raced each other to fill the last two garbage cans, Elliot jogging back to the truck with the white bucket held atop his head, like a Masai warrior carrying a pot of curdled milk, tipping the grapes gently over and glancing at the level of her can, then dashing back to his row. And she could still see him kneeling in the trough at the base of a vine, the sickle knife poised, and the happy, tired, sunburned face of the man she loved peeking at her through the jungle of leaves, a bunch of yellow grapes dangling in his curls, and his expression as giddy as young Bacchus spying a virgin.

"I don't trust you," she said.

"Neither do I."

And later, when the springs under the truck went flat, and the sugary juice slopped and cooked on the hot metal, they leaned over the tailgate to take in what they had done. "We work well together," she said.

"We do," he said thoughtfully. "We do."

The winemaking project had the double virtue of being based at Refugio, at her place, which reduced the number of town meetings where they had to be furtive. And it was solely theirs – by which Anne meant it was something he did and had only done with her. Inviolate. They tended and tasted and tinkered with it until one March afternoon Elliot hauled a hand-cranked bottling device out from the back of his van. The bottles were sterilized, the clear, gold liquid siphoned from the barrels, the cases stacked up on the kitchen floor.

"To the future," Elliot had said.

"The future."

"Come on, Holmes. Where are you?" Appearing at the top of the vineyard, the young Australian Shepherd paused, then launched himself down the furrows, and in thirty seconds skidded up to Anne's shoes, his tailless hind end throwing his entire body side to side. "Let's go home."

Holmes was a confident, well-mannered dog, and he rode in the truck with the dignified ease of someone accustomed to being chauffeured. His one blue eye and one brown eye surveyed the road ahead. Now and then he twitched his nose imperially. When he walked he pranced, and when he ran he leaped, and all gaits in between seemed elevated to an effortless glide. His coat was gray flashed with orange and white, and these colors against the dark, hardwood floor were as lovely as a clot of autumn leaves floating on a shaded pond. It was Holmes' arrival that prompted the move to Refugio. She might be still dwindling away in that gloomy apartment with its one window gaping at the parking lot and its thin walls reporting the solitude of her life. The solitude continued, but in Refugio it had a certain ascetic dignity.

Elliot encouraged her to get a dog for company, and one winter he watched the pet columns in the local paper. Because she had read somewhere that they were loyal, one-man dogs, and because she liked their harlequin looks, she decided on an Aussie. Finally someone across the bay offered a litter. They drove down together. Half a dozen puppies swarmed their feet, all except Holmes who stood diffidently off under a cypress tree, inspecting the visitors.

"Why do you like him?" Elliot asked.

"Well, look. He's being cautious." Absently, she lifted the fattest pup tugging at her shoelace, and held him so that his white paws dangled limply over the back of her hand. "He shows discretion."

"Maybe he's just unfriendly. Or weird. Now this one . . ." he said, picking up a squirming bundle.

She released the pup. "Doesn't he look lonely? Poor thing." Slowly, she walked to the cypress tree and sat down in the grass next to him. "Are you just shy, little fella? Is that it?" She stroked his downy head. The pup kept watching his siblings almost as if he was embarrassed by them, by their playing up to prospective owners. He would have no part of that.

"Look at this one's tongue, Anne. It looks sewn on."

Shaking himself, the young Holmes dropped his haunches and laid his muzzle on Anne's knee. Take me away from here, he said.

"Well?" Elliot asked.

"I don't know. Maybe I should find a place first. The manager would give me no more than the required thirty days, then boot me out."

"At the strangest moments, you can be as practical as stone," he said. He was disappointed, and in a funny way hurt.

"I'll think about it."

Late that night, Elliot cracked open her apartment door and in pranced Holmes, whose first act was to sleep against her neck where he could feel the reassuring beat of her heart. Both winning moves.

With some urgency, Holmes went off to his favorite trees and posts to reinstate local territorial laws; he, too, had been absent a week and had matters to tend to.

The phone was ringing as Anne unlocked the front door. Elliot she hoped, calling to say he missed her, or to talk about their time together as they often did, like tired lovers trying to preserve a few moments of ecstasy by holding each other a little longer, postponing the immeasurably desolate business of sleep. Dumping the bag of groceries on the counter, she picked up the receiver. It was not Elliot. It was Marlene, her father's third wife.

"I hate this kind of thing. I just hate it," Marlene said.

Almost shrinking from the phone, Anne waited. Marlene never called her. Occasionally, when Anne tried to reach her father, she got Marlene, and they would converse pleasantly and superficially of things neither cared about. Because for over a dozen years, their relationship had been inert. It was not anger or contempt. It was reticence of sudden exposure, the way two people, staring at each other across a room, and seeing things not meant to be seen, or hearing things not meant to be divulged, will swerve away. Except that she and Marlene had known each other, known and come too close, two planets in the same orbit. The relationship did not survive the collision, and now they were worlds apart, the orbit disintegrated, the memory painful.

"Mal died Thursday. Your father."

"Thursday?" Anne repeated, trying to remember what she had done that day. Vaguely, she groped for a chair.

"It was quick."

"Oh, good," Anne murmured, as if in a dream. Nothing

said had bearing yet; she rummaged her mind for any rules or forms of etiquette governing the situation.

"I guess you'll want all the details. Most people do."

"Yes," she said. She did. Details were sound. They could be touched, turned over, leaned upon.

"I'm not good at this. Your father would've done better. He had a knack for drama." Marlene snorted cynically into the phone. "He's been rehearsing this one for years. Poor Mal."

"It's too bad. It's all too bad." Anne pushed her fingers through the week's accumulation of dust on the bookshelf, and took in the rest of the furniture, the details of the respectfully quiet assembly, the chair anticipating her body, the table awaiting her meal, the floor missing the warmth of her feet. Beyond the glass doors, she let her eyes rest on the sunny field of treetops, and beyond to the dark canyon where a small, undistinguished creek found its way west to the ocean. "You're not alone, are you, Marlene?"

"My sister's here. We're working on a bottle of gin."

"Can you hold the line, Marlene?" Anne went to the refrigerator and removed a tray of ice. She held it under the faucet for a moment, then flexed it against the counter top until several cubes rattled out. These she dropped in a tumbler, replacing the tray before she fetched the whiskey from the liquor cabinet. She poured until the ice cubes floated up from the bottom of the glass, set the bottle next to the phone, took a sip, then another. Whiskey in one hand – it was trembling, she noticed – she picked up the receiver and slid down to the floor, thinking as she did so that the pregnancy would simply have to yield to circumstances, that there was nothing for it but to have a drink when someone had just told you that your father was dead. "Okay. Well, I'll just take the facts. You know how I feel about the rest when it comes to Dad."

Again, the cynical snort. "It's not very interesting," Marlene said. "Not up to his usual heroic standards."

In a chaise longue in Palm Springs on Thursday afternoon Malcolm Kroeger McBain had died of a heart attack while working on his tan. He was wearing a pair of blue Hawaiian trunks, a watch, and a tiger's eye ring. Twenty five years ago on his birthday Nellie Gallagher, Anne's mother, had given him the ring because it was heavy, primitive looking, and big enough not to embarrass his enormous hand: the band was a half inch of hammered gold and, carved on the square of tiger's eye twice that width, was the sightless face of a Polynesian idol. Next to the chaise longue lay a tube of suntan lotion and a market appraisal for a proposed shopping center in Long Beach. His glasses were never found though he was virtually blind without them and could not possibly have read the appraisal unaided. A ten year old girl who was swimming in the far end of the pool said that she saw him wiggling and waving his hands, said she thought it was a bee, there were a lot of bees around the pool because of the water. Marlene had been napping in the room and, when it began to get dark, she went down to the patio to fetch him for cocktails. She said she knew from a distance that he was dead from the relaxed, sprawling attitude of his body, and the fact that he was still lying on his back. He always tanned his front first, then his back, because if he ran out of time, or it got too hot, at least the part that people saw through his open shirt would look good. The medical examiner's report was standard except for a brief notation at the bottom of the page: *unusually large muscular development about the heart possibly due to intense exercise during a period of the victim's life followed by extended relative inactivity.*

Extended relative inactivity, Anne repeated to herself. Yes.

"Are you there?" Marlene asked.

"Here, yes."

She was sitting cross-legged on the kitchen floor concentrating on Marlene's cool, husky voice, always easy to listen to; her words were unadorned, her manner laconic. Marlene had a small, attractive figure, lively eyes, a wit as pert and natural as the snap of a summer sail, and a smile like a wink between old chums. Never assuming a maternal distance, she had behaved as an older friend, and they got on well during summer visits when Anne was a young girl – so well that Mal McBain called his daughter 'the shadow' because she followed Marlene around. They played cards, went shopping, smoked cigarettes in restaurants (though at home it was forbidden), enjoyed swimming at the club, going to the zoo. And they talked about Mal McBain. At first her affection for her father's wife jostled Anne's sense of loyalty to her own mother, but in the end she felt no great conflict. She liked Marlene too much to accept her mother's deprecations – their meanness had a canceling out effect. "She's dumb; she's only after his money; I hear she has a lot of wrinkles." From someone who had never met Marlene, it seemed unallowable. But for the sake of peace and her mother's satisfaction that Mal McBain had made the wrong choice and would suffer for it the rest of his life, Anne offered evasive agreement, and went on liking her father's wife.

"He wanted to be cremated," Marlene was saying.

Anne's head bobbed up out of the past. "What?"

"Wants his ashes scattered on Orcas Island."

"I can't believe that, it's so out of character."

"Why?" Simple. Point-blank. Slicing deep.

Then remembering, the oblique shift. "I don't know. He was always so obsessed with his . . . I mean he took such good care of himself – weightlifting and hair implants and *tanning* – to want to be burned up . . . " Since those three days in August that final summer when they had been excruciatingly open with each other, Anne and Marlene had never spoken directly about certain matters, never used certain words. Their current relationship survived as it could by near misses and deep allusions and a mutual unwillingness to give in to the alienation of knowing too much about the other. Also, there were the two inescapable facts: Marlene did not leave Malcolm McBain that summer, and Malcolm McBain was irreversibly Anne's father.

"I wonder if it's so out of character," Marlene remarked.

"He wanted you to scatter them."

"God." Anne shut her eyes, trying to beat back the idea, to eclipse the image in her mind of him sitting in his briefs at his desk early some morning, as she had seen him so many times during summer visits, the opening stock report run out on the carpet, a cup of black coffee sloshing over his left hand as he penned away his many belongings. Probably the task moved him. Crying came easily to Malcolm McBain and, because outwardly he was anything but tender, it was also surprisingly effective. At some point he must have realized that, Anne figured, because the older he got the more he wept, the more often he assumed the victim's role. So probably out of habit he squeezed out a few self-conscious tears and, with childish confidence, entered in his last will a last blasphemous wish. "God, that's pitiful," Anne said.

"If you ask me, it's weird." In the tone was that old look of ennui (eyes rolled upwards, lip curled somewhere between worn-out disgust and stale fascination) that was as vivid to Anne as if Marlene had been sitting across the linoleum painting her nails. "Anyway, will you?" Marlene asked.

"Will I what?"

"Go to Orcas. Personally, I don't see what difference it makes now. He'll never know one way or the other."

"I still can't fathom why he wanted me to do it."

"He probably had some ulterior motive." She gave arch emphasis to the word 'ulterior.'

"I'll think about it," Anne said. She flicked her head sideways, and made a wry face, thinking *of course there really isn't any question, is there?*

"If you go, I'll send the urn up after the service on Monday."

"Oh, the service," Anne said. In the thought of people gathering without him, she suddenly felt some small reality to her father's death. "I guess the whole family will be there," she said.

"All the relatives fit to mint. I have an idea there's more

somewhere." It wasn't clear whether she meant more relatives or more money. "You didn't want to go to the service, did you?" Marlene's questions automatically exposed the correct answer and embarrassed any inclinations to the contrary.

"No. I don't think I could sit through the eulogy."

"You won't miss much." Anne could hear her light up a cigarette. "I didn't think you'd be all broken up about this," she added.

With her father's wife knowing everything, it was not possible for Anne to show more than a seemly concern for Malcolm McBain. Because Marlene could not have understood anything but a gesture from her after what he had done. She would not understand that an old feeling, an earlier affection could be stranded and surrounded, flooded by its opposite and left like an island. To feel but one, cold, uncomplicated thing would have been, in fact, a relief. No, where genuine affection ended, practical considerations began for Marlene. "I'm too old to start over," she once told Anne. She was cutting her losses.

Anne was not all broken up, as Marlene put it, but she could feel that island moving under her feet, and there seemed to be no place to run. Hesitating, she said, "I guess I feel a little bad, something I'll . . . miss. Maybe just knowing he was out there. Thursday morning he was *among us*. And Thursday afternoon he was gone. And there's no chance of anything else."

"Did you ever think there was? Did you think he could've changed?"

"Maybe I hoped." Anne shifted uneasily on the hard kitchen floor. She felt like a disappointed child confessing, after all the presents had been opened, to a ridiculous, unrequited birthday wish. "It did stop," she added. "And after awhile, we tried to be friends, because there was the whole rest of our lives ahead . . . my life . . . and it seemed important not to feel that I had punished him to the grave. Maybe there wasn't enough time. But it *did* stop."

"Phooey."

"Pardon me?"

"It stopped because he was afraid. I went to a lawyer that summer just to get some information. You know, see what my options were. But in the end I didn't feel like going through the hassle."

With all her heart Anne wanted to stop Marlene. She opened her mouth, but nothing happened, and Marlene stomped on through the muddy bottom of the past.

"Mal said your mother must not have believed you, or else she would've taken some action. He wrote letters to her. All soft soap. He was afraid of her. I have an idea he hinted maybe they could get back together if she lost some weight."

"My mother?"

"After you left he started denying all of it, said you were psychotic, that you were trying to destroy him. He rationalized himself into believing he didn't do anything. I notice he didn't try to deny it when you were still here."

"No."

"And there were girlfriends, you know. I found motel receipts with the name changed – McBee, McBeth – for two people. Two. He *kep*t the receipts. Can you believe that? For his taxes. He wasn't going to lose the deduction. No sir, he deducted his women. The long distance sections of some of the phone bills were missing, too. And he had a post office box, I found out. He lied about everything. Everything. Lies. And the really sick part is that I think he *believed* the lies."

A precarious silence. Was it over? Was she finished?

Then, in a voice tired of itself, tired of disgust: "He must have really hurt inside. Do you think he did?"

To Anne, the question seemed desperately idle. It tolled – hopefully, and yet knowingly in vain – like church bells across a deserted village. "I don't know," she said. Her ears were ringing, her face stinging hot, her heart crowding her chest. Why? How could he?

A trail of muddy prints led from the front door to the

kitchen sink, back and around the bookcases into the dining room. Forgetting Marlene, Anne began to count them, wondering where she had stepped in mud – it had been a dry month – and why only now she was noticing them.

"Anne?" Marlene asked.

"I thought by not mentioning it," Anne said, confused, frowning at a muddy print turning the corner and leaving the kitchen, "by letting it go . . .he's not stupid, he's very smart. . . he would at least feel sorry . . . I thought that was one of the reasons we left it behind. And with what survived, we went on, even if it was formal. That seemed important. As awkward as it was, it seemed important to go on . . . somehow. He was my father, after all."

"I don't guess he knew how to be sorry." Marlene's voice pinched off as she tugged on her cigarette, then, exhaling, it opened and loosened low into a cool, matter-of-fact synopsis. "He didn't want any trouble. You grew up. The opportunities disappeared. And he had to act like everything was dandy normal. He had to be nice and go on. Formal, you said. Right. Formally your father."

Anne swallowed some whiskey. "It was better than the other, and better than nothing," she said. "To believe he cared was my right. If he didn't, if he didn't know how, so? I had the right to pretend, too." She was almost angry, almost crying. He had just died, and if not deserving polite applause, at least plain silence was his due before the critics had their bloody say. Though Marlene had not described anything that sounded off-key or out of character – Malcolm McBain was fully capable of devious self-preservation – it was not a variation Anne wanted to hear. Maybe Marlene needed a little solace, too. Behind that tough, life-weary tone, a small voice might be asking, a small voice might be wishing that things had been different.

"Are you okay? How do you feel?" Anne said.

"Nothing new," she said. "Isn't that weird? I don't feel anything new. It's like I've been through this before with him.

Death." She cleared her throat, dismissing the subject. "I'll leave it for you to call your mother."

"I may not do that right away."

"S'up to you."

They said their good-byes, and when Anne hung up the phone she felt a pang of sadness for Marlene, for her friendly bearing, her fine, light wit moldering down and flattening out into an impassiveness from which escaped here and there, like a vapor, the caustic by-products of resignation.

FOUR

At a certain point in Anne's life it became awkward for her to address her own mother as mom, or mommy, or even mother. Nellie was how she thought of her, Nellie Gallagher. The business with her father – that was what deformed things.

For years she had expected her mother would figure out what was happening and come to her rescue, putting an end to it as mothers magically did when you were too young to say no. But she never did figure it out, despite evidence that seemed to Anne obvious, despite telltale signs that, in an age when almost everyone was psychologically conversant, bordered on the vernacular. So the years went by. Expectation dwindled to hope, hope gave way to desperation and, at age fourteen, with singular apathy toward the consequences, Anne was obliged to save herself. After which, mother and daughter became unnatural peers.

Nellie slid easily into the role of an equal with her daughter. Not because she forgot who she was supposed to be or (having failed its most elementary charge) had given up being a mother. Somehow, it just seemed inappropriate. In terms of needs, daughter had effectively changed places with mother. It had been Anne who had been forced to act, to explain and, when Nellie refused to believe, it was Anne who reviewed the chronology and presented the proof, convicting all three of them.

"I always had my memories, you know. I thought I had memories of him, at least . . . to make up for his leaving, and for the empty years. Good memories of Mal . . . they were all I had. Now even those are gone. You've ruined my memories of him," Nellie had cried.

And apologizing, it was the girl who offered comfort to the woman.

"Mal," Nellie said, when referring (post disclosure) to Anne's father.

Nellie, Anne thought, when talking with her mother.

Mother's Days were uncomfortable exercises in selective nostalgia, some of the memories even invented for the other's benefit. Usually Anne drove home afterward feeling vaguely depressed, vaguely angry, as if they had staged a play for an empty house. They were in full collusion, and reality was their adversary. This Mother's Day in particular would be difficult, because on this sunny May morning there were real things to discuss – a pregnancy they might have celebrated, and a death from which they might have drawn conclusions, a specter from which they might have been released, together. Both subjects would have been absolutely appropriate for a mother and a daughter, absolutely natural. And absolutely impossible.

Still in her nightgown, Anne sat on the deck with a cup of coffee and gazed south over the coastal foothills. Soft white fog had seeped inland, pooling in the low spots and trickling along the creases. On the coast, beneath the greatest body of fog was the town of Santa Lucia and in it, the seaside restaurant where Anne worked three nights a week, and where she and Nellie would soon share Mother's Day brunch, toasting each other with cheap sparkling wine. There would be Nellie's endless flow of words, and Anne would bite her nails, and the waitress would take too long. In the end, out in the parking lot, squinting over the hot, steel roofs, someone would have to say 'let's get together . . .' or 'I'll call you . . .' Someone would have to hoist up the lie, and hope that the other pledged allegiance.

Of course it wasn't all a lie. Anne loved her mother . . . or rather, she felt for her. Maybe that was love enough.

From the bright surface of the fog, a wild dove erupted, arcing up over the snags of a dead fir, circling round it once, twice, then swooping up, it perched on the uppermost limb. Below the branch its long tail feathers flicked, balancing its almost weightless weight. *Coo-ooh, coo, coo-coo*, it called, the sad notes declining as if uttered by someone who had all but given up the search. She was sure it was the same mourning dove she had identified in March at the beginning of their breeding season, and probably the same one who had used that tree last year from which to attract a mate. Still alone, she thought. The dove, as if ashamed, suddenly dropped from the limb and plunged back into the fog.

Anne will never marry, she overheard Nellie say to Uncle Bernard, the hushed voices of conspiracy and doom still painful after three years. Nellie had been making one of her many pilgrimages to Vancouver and The Family, Anne in tow. Why didn't they just move there? Anne wondered, move back to the northwest?

She got up and went into the house. As she slid the glass door up to the jam, she decided to let neither piece of news – her pregnancy, her father's death – break cover that day.

The restaurant was a Spanish villa built a hundred years ago on a sandstone cliff above the place where the Salsipuedes River died in the Pacific Ocean. Along the inside of the faded, pink adobe walls grew some of the largest cacti in California, most of them in full flower. The patio itself – brick laid in a sandy dirt – resisted horizontal rules of conduct: many of the wrought-iron tables had been made level with the help of small, wooden shims jammed under one or two of their legs. The chair cushions were a pink and green print, the tablecloths were white, and the champagne flutes began to sparkle as the fog burned off.

Anne was glad she was not working this morning – Mother's Day brunch, a rough shift. At eleven o'clock, the hostess stepped up to the podium, and the crowd pushed forward. Fortunately, it was her friend, Georgia, who presided over a waiting list and the milling impatience before her as if she was the emcee at an awards ceremony.

"Better add my name to the list, Georgia."

"Anne, you're playing the guest. What fun. How many will there be?"

"Just two." A twinge of embarrassment.

"I haven't many deuces today." Georgia made a visual tour of the patio. "Almost everything's been set up for families. But there's a young couple in the corner, I think they've had a tiff," she winked. "They won't be here long."

"I'll wait in reception."

Twenty years ago when the old villa was refurbished and the additions designed, the architects had had the foresight to divide the lobby and parlor into east and west wings, the east wing adjoining the porte-cochère being constructed of the original adobe with small, deep windows, thick rugs, and an altogether intimate and comforting assembly of heavy, Spanish furniture in which to lose oneself, and amber lights to soothe the eyes and expunge the passage of time. The west wing began without transition, the ceilings vaulting abruptly thirty feet up, the south and west walls replaced by banks of windows which gazed out over the patio and the ocean.

Except for two people behind the reservation desk, the east parlor was empty. Anne dropped down onto a couch. Her mother was supposed to meet her there at 11:30, but she would be late, and that was okay. She took off her glasses, she glanced at her watch: 11:35. One of the young men behind the reservation desk crossed the parlor and flipped on the television set, apparently for Anne's benefit because, as he adjusted the volume, he nodded back at her, his smile the merest twitch of servility.

"Thank you," she said, wishing he had not turned it on.

On the television screen, four women and a young girl, all wearing identical blue dresses, sat on a bench across from a man in a seersucker suit. The man was speaking into a microphone and gesturing toward the bench. The shrunken, white-haired woman on the far left – obviously the eldest – had been made up for the occasion, and the gory, red rounds on her hollowed cheeks were excruciatingly perfect in shape, as if all efforts to apply the makeup in a natural manner had been abandoned for the symbolic. The old woman had been elevated to art. She looked startled, Anne thought.

A family walked through the reception area toward the Bella Vista patio. Peripherally, Anne noticed pastel colors, a camera bag, held hands. A woman said, " . . . in the morning," and giggled. Petty talk. Disappearing froth on a wave. Rounding her shoulders, she stared at the amber haze behind the parchment lampshades, mentally throwing up a barrier around herself and the end of the couch in which she had taken refuge. The unspeakable pregnancy, the unnegotiable death of her father seemed to remove her, to push her beyond the trivial act of sitting, waiting to have brunch on a warm, May day in Santa Lucia.

On the television, the old woman was tilted stiffly back, like a propped doll. Slowly her head descended. One of the white petals nesting in her hair spun down to her lap where a trough had formed in the taffeta between her legs. When her chin was about to meet her breast, her head jerked up and wobbled in place as she blinked at the world seemingly for the first time.

"Mrs. Wiggins, how does it feel to have four generations of daughters with you here on Mother's Day?" said the man in the seersucker suit.

"You don't know," said Mrs. Wiggins, ruffling the petals in

her lap. "Young man, you don't know that I'm beside myself, I'm beside myself . . . "

Anne found herself wondering what the old woman was trying to say to her – beside herself with joy? overcome by a sense of fulfillment? or was she beside herself, having an out-of-body experience? A batty old broad, Elliot would have said. He would have laughed at Anne's ruminations, too, and it would not have bothered her at all. She liked his amused deprecations, found herself in fact relying upon him to untangle the lines of conjecture she felt driven to spin. Lighten up, he would say, and at once she would feel lighter. You think too much; forget it, he would say.

Closing her eyes, she took a deep breath and let time pass.

"You're not watching TV, are you? On a day like this?" Nellie was impeccably fashionable, wearing a peach and beige plaid on white linen skirt that fell softly to the middle of her calves, a white silk blouse set off by a string of coral beads, and a loose-fitting, silk blazer of the same color. Her two-tone pumps – beige on white – tied in nicely the speckled, shell earrings Anne had given her one year. The pageboy cut was the same – neat and modestly turned under at the bottom so that the rolls were as smooth and golden as baked meringue. She was removing a small, ribboned panama hat angled smartly across the brow, and when she looked up, her eyes in the dusk of the east parlor were greenish points of light.

"Just waiting for you," Anne said. "Happy Mother's Day," she added.

Nellie ignored the wish. "You've always been so patient, haven't you? And I've always been late," she said, not sounding the least bit sorry. She was straightening the ribbons on her hat.

Anne rose from the couch. Should she embrace her? Or would that fluster Nellie? It was Mother's Day, after all. Reaching out, she pulled her mother to her, saying again, "Happy Mother's Day," and at once she sensed Nellie going rigid inside.

"Yes, well, thank you, dear, that's nice."

From the podium Georgia held up two menus, raised her eyebrows, and beamed over the crowd at them. Their table was ready. A man opposite Georgia handed Nellie a red rose – all the mothers were given one – and Nellie smiled and thanked him, looking as giddy as a debutante. Georgia seated them next to the plexiglas walls separating the patio from the edge of the cliff where they could look out over the ocean.

"What a gaudy woman," Nellie said, when Georgia was out of hearing range. "Those colors . . . I'm surprised the management allows it."

Georgia had her black hair cropped close and feathered, and in her bright, bohemian outfits she looked like an exotic bird.

"Does she always dress like that?" Nellie asked.

"I don't know. I only see her here." Anne stared intently at the ocean, hoping that Georgia would not notice Nellie inspecting her. "She's a nice person."

Nellie owned a clothing boutique across the bay in a wealthy, seaside resort. It catered exclusively to the silk and cashmere crowd – lots of pleats, subdued colors, natty hats, mostly Republicans, and mostly retired. In that set, Georgia would have been as out of place as mallow in a bed of lilies, something wild and purplish, something to be weeded out.

"Well, after all, she's just a hostess." Nellie made a point of smiling so that the effort showed. "You look pretty . . . the perfect, hour glass figure. Most women would be green with envy." Anne was wearing an oversized, teal cotton blouse cinched in at the waist with a wide leather belt, a pair of straw-colored twills that tapered to her ankles, and huaraches. "Still not using makeup?"

Under the table, Anne began to pick at her nails. "No."

"How about a little lipstick? Would you do that for me?" Nellie rummaged through her purse.

"Mom."

"We both know that your lips tend to look blue, especially when you haven't had much sun, and it won't hurt just to touch them up some. Here. Try this one." She handed Anne a tube of cherry-red lipstick.

"I'd really rather not, mom. It's the, the taste. I don't like how it tastes."

"You'll get used to it. All women do," Nellie said. "It's like wearing high heels."

"Thanks, but it makes me feel nauseated." She tried to smile and look sick at the same time. "Really."

"Fine," said Nellie, as she accepted the tube Anne held out for her. Saying in effect, 'if you're going to behave like that, let's get this over with,' Nellie picked up her menu so that all Anne could see were the painted teardrops of her fingernails – cameo pink was the color she had always worn – and her smooth, smug pate, not a hair out of order, looming above the page.

Nellie Gallagher probably should have had a son, probably would have preferred one. She used to tease Anne that they had given her the wrong baby at the hospital, and it wasn't until Anne was old enough to notice similarities in their features – the straight line of the nose, the flat feet, the way of laughing that started high and descended to the chest, the smile that half closed one eye – that she was truly convinced her mother was only kidding. Still, it had been an upsetting notion. What if one day Nellie decided that they *had* given her the wrong baby, what if Anne misbehaved and her mother just walked off with a shrug, because it had never been certain that she owed Anne anything more than what was owed the victim of a cruel mistake? Sometimes she would imagine another mother up there in Seattle raising Nellie's beautiful baby boy, and she would feel not only her own inferiority and Nellie's terrible loss, but a gratitude frantic and immense for the food she put on the table, the clothes she bought for Anne, the turquoise bicycle, the chocolate bunny placed secretly on the bedstead the night before Easter, even for the punishments which Nellie said she inflicted because she cared. Rarely did she imagine another mother longing for a little girl like Anne.

When she entered puberty, the sport of the wrong-baby was abandoned for a far more disturbing tack. Then, Nellie was a disturbing person. Especially angered, she wished aloud that she had listened to the doctors and put Anne up for adoption. Having uttered it once, it became easier the next time, and thereafter part of their dialect. "She's a healthy baby," the doctor said. "We'll have no problem finding a suitable family." Implying the obvious – that Nellie and her circumstances were unsuitable. To pitch a child into the precarious and unforgiving world of illegitimacy, single-parenthood and poverty, he told her, would be selfish beyond words. And Mal, having failed to persuade her early on to abort the pregnancy, agreed with the doctor. Nellie balked even more. "It was you and me against the world," she told Anne. "I wouldn't let them take you away from me." Invariably these depositions elicited (as they were meant to), hugs and thank you's and many assurances that she had done the right thing.

So, what to some might have seemed an abnormal tradition, was to Anne and Nellie perfectly natural. On Anne's ninth birthday, she rode her bike down to the drugstore to buy the lady's manicure set she had seen in the window case. Anne had had to steal part of the money from her father's bill clip during his last visit, but about that she felt small remorse, because as her mother was always telling her, he had a lot of money and he didn't send them enough of it. For giving birth and providing life, for not putting her up for adoption, for the years of sacrifice, Anne presented the manicure set to Nellie on the appropriate occasion – Anne's birthday. Nellie accepted the gift as if it was a token from a house guest – something *pro forma* and, next to Nellie's gifts, comparatively meager. From that year on, a present for Nellie on Anne's birthday. They understood each other: Anne considered herself to be perpetually in debt, and no attempt to veil this fact was made by either.

No, Nellie Gallagher should have had a boy. A son, she might have forgiven, but a female child became for her a relentless reminder.

The waiter arrived with the champagne and, apologizing for the wait, took their order – a couple of eggs and hash browns for Anne, a strawberry waffle for Nellie, signaling to Anne that her mother was angry with her. Nellie's weight was as unstable as her moods: Anne could not say which was cause and which effect, but she had long correlated Nellie's penchant for sweets with retaliation. When Anne provoked her, Nellie would shove a wad of money at her, and send her to the store for a handful of candy bars, thereby assigning the breach in her diet (she was always on a diet) to Anne's insolence. In general, during her slim periods Nellie's posture improved, her manner became businesslike, her wit savage, and her vanity conspicuous, as if she hadn't quite convinced herself.

Inevitably, the vanity turned on itself. Gaining weight tended to subdue her, the layers of fat serving as a form of padding around the sharp edges of false esteem. She would slump into sentimental maundering punctuated by painfully bright outbursts in which her happiness was betrayed by the shrillness of its insistence: she became a child play-acting for visiting relatives. It left Anne with schizoid memories. There was the Nellie in her ultra-suede jetting off to Paris for the spring fashion shows, or having her colors done, or tooling up to the city with the top down and a long, white scarf tied around her hair, its tail end skipping on the wind, to have lunch with a friend, to take in a musical (she loved musicals), or the Nellie who left all the doors and windows open and turned on the radio and painted yellow daisies on the cupboard doors.

And there was Nellie of the darkness, not leaving her bedroom, staying under the comforter for days surrounded by discarded newspapers, magazines and letters, dirty plates, empty bags of candy and cans of pop, the TV murmuring to her from in front of the dresser mirror where she placed it to eclipse her own face, a red blanket hanging over the curtains to obscure the world, a sickly light leaking through it, the air in the room stale, the door always closed. Stains mottled the carpet next to the side of the bed where she lay. She used a bath towel as a napkin. Every few hours she'd call for Anne to take something away, to bring her something to eat, to go to the store and buy her peanut butter and french bread, or just to sit and listen to her talk. One day when Nellie was obliged to emerge from her cave because Anne did not hear her, Anne went to the hardware store and bought a little bell, and set it there on Nellie's dresser so that she would no longer have to suffer the indignity of hollering.

Eventually, a week, ten days, sometimes longer, the door would open and Nellie would shuffle down the hall, pale and puffy, squinting in the light. In her hand would be a comb, because by then her fine, dry hair was so matted that she could not work it out herself. Almost in tears, almost dreading the happiness she was reaching for, she would ask Anne. And trying to be perky and upbeat about it, Anne would have her sit on the couch, and for the next two hours would chatter about school, about the house work, about her friend's new puppy, while her fingers separated and pulled at the pathetic mats. Now and then she would wince with shame for what her mother had done to herself.

"I saw Elliot's name in the paper yesterday," Nellie said.

"The whale skeleton, yes."

"That's quite a find. He'll be credited with it, I assume." Ever since Anne told her mother about her relationship with Elliot Newhouse, she had been an avid follower of his career, though she evinced no great interest in Anne's similar work. Her attitude was somewhat like an art critic's politely dismissive nod toward the talentless efforts of a dilettante. She used to try, it seemed to Anne, to appear supportive, but apparently even that became too difficult. A look of pain would cross Nellie's face whenever Anne spoke of her work at the marine lab, or of her unfinished dissertation; she might have been a cripple describing her attempts to get up on a horse. She could almost hear her mother imploring her, 'Just give it up, dear, you're embarrassing yourself. After all, you're female. Musn't forget that.' Anne no longer brought up the lab, though the fact that she also waitressed seemed perfectly acceptable to Nellie. In general, the subject of Anne's living was not a frequent one. Elliot's, however, was.

"Will he be the only one working on the dig? That's what it's called, isn't it? A dig?" Nellie asked.

"I suppose so. It's not really Elliot's field, paleozoology, but I'm sure he'll be involved. It's buried right in the middle of his elephant seal population, his study area, and anyone who wants to get out to the island has to get his permission. There's a group going out this afternoon, in fact. Bone brains, Elliot calls them. I'm going along to help him try to find one of his females who hasn't hauled out yet. She's carrying a time-depth recorder, a very expensive instrument." Anne took a sip of champagne. "But I'll also take a look at the whale, what there is to see."

"How exciting," Nellie said.

"Yeah, I thought so too. And the weather's perfect. It'll be fun." For a third of a second, Anne wanted to tell her mother about being pregnant. But there was Nellie, lowering her head, catching and holding Anne's eyes with her own.

"So things are fine with you two?" she asked, coveting the truth now, insisting on it as if Anne would lie, and at the same time clearly unreceptive to anything but an affirmative.

The brief desire to let Nellie in vanished. "Yeah, sure," she said faintly.

"Good, good." Nellie peered out over the cliff at the waves shattering against the rocks below. "Elliot seems like the right man for you."

On one level Anne appreciated her mother's support of Elliot – none of her friends supported him, except for Loretta. But on another level, it was disturbing. Mothers were not supposed to encourage relationships with married men. So she liked Elliot. Elliot was a likable fellow. That shouldn't mitigate a mother's duty to at least frown upon such affairs and, in Nellie's case, to point to her own history as proof that it was a losing proposition. But she never did, not with Elliot, not even with the ones before him. Her own mother.

Watching a woman at the next table reprimand a little girl, Anne sipped her champagne. None of Nellie's reactions have ever been particularly maternal, she thought.

When Anne was a child, Nellie would commission her to ask Mal for money ("because he's angry with me," she would say, "and he can't resist you, you're his princess"), as she delivered Anne to his hotel room so that they could share some 'special time' together – usually have dinner, spend the night, and go shopping the next day for new school dresses (which had been preselected by Nellie). But there were moments when Anne supposed her mother knew what was happening. The thought was unbearable, and Anne expelled it from her mind. Once, Mal forgot to muss the empty bed and, when Nellie arrived the next morning to pick up Anne, there was one obviously slept-in bed, one perfectly made. On the way home in the car, Nellie asked if he had given her any money. Anne gave her the check. A silence, then, "By the way, I think you're a little old to be sleeping with your father." That was it. That was all she said, and she said it as if she *had* to say it, wanting only to get the words out of the way, as if complying reluctantly with convention. No anger or concern. No questions. No curiosity. She might have been reciting a meaningless lesson – 'Thou shalt not . . . ' And Nellie was known to get excited about Anne washing her hair too often.

The lunch servers at the Bella Vista tended to be young, single, student types, less refined and less in need of money than the dinner crew who had families and mortgages to support. Management usually awarded dinner shifts to the more stable applicants – career servers – while the luncheon shift, because of the smaller tips, suffered the vicissitudes of youth, inexperience and high turnover. The sub-adult male now presenting their brunch was no exception. His white-blond hair, cocoa butter tan, and long body fixed him as a member of the local surf-bum clan. After he placed Anne's meal in front of her, he paused to consider Nellie's – a waffle from which rose a mountain of whipped cream studded with giant, red strawberries – before relinquishing it. He shook his head once. He pursed his lips. He raised his eyebrows and peered over the summit of the whipped cream at Nellie who was clearly perplexed by his little act, but willing to be amused once the punch line and her waffle had been delivered. She had always enjoyed the attention of handsome young men. This one was probably bucking for a good tip.

"Lot of Btu's in this baby," he said, clearly pleased with the play of his wit. He was waiting for the inevitable question.

Anne groaned inwardly, shifting her attention to her plate where the two yellow eyes of her eggs stared back at her. Because of the long hours spent waiting for the next killer set in the cold Pacific, surfers were obsessed with the number of thermal units or calories in the food they consumed. But this was the wrong quip and the wrong person.

"Pardon?" said Nellie.

Anne shoved a forkful of hash browns in her mouth, hoping to encourage him to *put the damn plate down*.

"Heat," the surfing waiter exclaimed, as he landed Nellie's waffle. "Sucker's loaded with calories. Have to jog a few extra to off this one." Still grinning, he adjusted the miniature pitcher of maple syrup so that the handle pointed accusingly at Nellie, then traipsed off to fetch them some more champagne.

Nellie looked stunned. She kept her face down when he returned and, once departed, picked up her fork, poked at the whipped cream, flattening it as best she could, then she stared glumly at the rose lying next to her plate. Softly, "He wasn't very nice."

The old protective feelings welled up. "No, he wasn't. He

was out of line." Though Anne was certain the waiter meant no harm, and couldn't possibly have guessed Nellie's sensitivity to her weight, especially since she was enjoying a spell of relative thinness, his overly familiar manner and his loutish sense of humor belonged at the local sprout house, not at the Bella Vista. She half suspected he'd been drinking, and followed him as he rolled around the room, ducked into the busing station where – *yes*, he *was* drinking – she could see the top of his head over the screen, flinging back once, then again, longer, and he swung out of the station, wiping his lips with the back of his hand, tugging on the tips of his vest. He slid his eyes in Georgia's direction. He flashed her a cocky grin and saluted. Within seconds, Georgia had him by the elbow and was escorting him through the breezeway into the kitchen.

Still wounded, Nellie smiled bravely across the table. "I've been a good girl, lately."

"You look great, mom."

"You know how I love strawberries, and this morning I thought 'it's Mother's Day and no matter what, I'm going to treat myself.'" She threw her jaw out and popped a strawberry in her mouth. "I mean if you couldn't come, if you were too busy or something, I was still going to celebrate, because we made it, didn't we? And it wasn't easy, all those years without help, trying to be both a mother and a father to you, but we made it without him, didn't we?"

"Yes."

"So what's wrong with a few strawberries? Don't I deserve strawberries?"

"Sure you do."

"My beautiful daughter." Nellie put on a warm face. "You were always such a bubbly girl."

"Was I?"

Nellie's body jerked, as if someone had struck her in the back. "Of course you were. Don't you remember?" Frowning, she pushed her head at Anne. "Don't you remember coming home from school with your papers, gold stars all over them, and the, the valentines you made for me, and the drives, how about the drives we used to take up the coast . . . they were fun. We used to get so silly, stopping at roadside stands. Of course you remember that." She sat up straight, waiting for an answer, afraid that Anne would not corroborate her version of history, and needing it at that moment because of the waiter.

"I guess so, sure. The drives were nice. I remember the big orange stands," Anne said, asking herself, *why bother? It's Mother's Day, and why disappoint her, why confess that it's not how you remember those years? Sure, the spasms of manic happiness – they happened – but they did not offset the long, low times.*

Nellie was still staring at her. 'Don't dare hurt me,' said her hard, green eyes.

"I wasn't much aware of how I was feeling. Kids are, well, they just live, you know, without paying attention to how things are affecting them." The everyday atrocities were, in fact, what Anne remembered.

Clearly relieved, Nellie picked up her fork and carved off a piece of waffle, her perfect, pink fingernails glossy under the noon hour sun.

Those fingernails. The everyday atrocities. Those flawless fingernails, pointing at the toilet bowl. "Didn't I tell you to use my bathroom?" "But mom, you were still asleep." Pink nails sparkling, sparkling like chips of colored glass. "It's broken. I told you to use the other bathroom until I got it fixed." "I'm sorry. I didn't want to wake you." "Did you have to do *that*?" Pointing at it, there in the toilet bowl. "Yes." "Well if you couldn't flush it, where the hell did you think it was going to go?" "I don't know." "You assumed I would take care of it, I would clean up after you." "I thought you'd be mad if I waked you up." "I've got news for you. You did it . . . " index finger jabbing in the direction of the toilet bowl . . . "You're going to clean it up." Anne staring blankly at the thing floating on the water, waiting for directions. "Well?" "What, uh, should I go get a bucket?" It is a particularly large stool, and she is overcome with shame. "Just pick it up," her mother says dryly, "and carry it to the other bathroom." Anne starts to cry. "Now you're going to blubber because you don't want to dirty your hands." Her mother grabbing the soap dish – a fan shell – and dumping the bar out. "If you had any idea how many times I've cleaned up your messes, you'd cry for me. Not yourself." Kneeling next to the toilet bowl. "Put your hands out." With the fan shell, her mother scoops up the stool – her face wrinkled in disgust – and lets it roll across Anne's fingertips until it settles precariously across her palms, a fecal bridge spanning the immeasurably brief distance between dark and light. Carrying it down the hallway, wanting to hurry but afraid that if she does, if she bobbles it, it will fall onto the carpet, she stares at this thing that belongs to her, that is her, this thing that disgusts her mother and makes her mad, this that she did, nasty and foul-smelling, and she understands for the first time something about their relationship.

Georgia swept toward them like a great, magenta bird, folded in her arms, and landed lightly before them. The patio breeze played across the silky fabric of her gown, the winged sleeves trembling as if weary from her flight, her black hair feathering as she cocked her head. "May I bring you some more champagne, or coffee?"

"No, thank you," Nellie said. "Just the check."

To Anne: "Mr. Smithers has been called away . . . " One of her beloved dramatic pauses, "Permanently."

For the first time that day Anne laughed. "And now we have you. A much happier ending."

A delicate bow, then she withdrew, leaving, Anne fancied, a Cheshire grin and the trace of a sweet, ethereal scent on the air.

"She *is* strange," Nellie said.

"I don't think so. Georgia's just trying to be herself." Anne looked challengingly at her mother, trying to soften her voice.

Again, Georgia faded in, delivered the check, and faded

out.

"Anyway," Anne continued, "I admire Georgia. At some point in her life, she must have imagined who she wanted to be and she stuck to it. She's happy. Who can argue with that?"

Nellie pushed her chair away from the table, saying as she straightened, "I didn't know she was such a close friend."

"That doesn't have anything to do with it." Anne saw Nellie glancing at the check on the table. "I'll pay," she said.

As they were walking toward the porte-cochère, Nellie said, "Even your friend Georgia wears makeup, dear."

FIVE

A recent high tide had left the narrow, cliff bottom beach knee-deep in kelp and rotting jellyfish, but it was the mainland terminus for the only safe channel between the island and the point – a distance of less than a mile – and all boats had to be launched from it.

Elliot high-stepped over to the bank to help her down. The fresh air and his kind hands – so uncomplicated – were a relief after brunch with her mother. She felt a surge of gratitude for him, as if he had rescued her from a dimly lit, airless room, and carried her here to the edge of the ocean to set her free. He was so easy and even-keeled and straightforward. Where she had been seemed not to matter to him. He did not ask about her morning with Nellie.

"I brought a bottle of wine," Anne said, dropping into the spongy tangle of seaweed. "Chilled."

"Girl of my dreams," he said.

"Yup." She gave him a big hug and kissed the side of his neck. "Mmm . . . you're salty."

"I hit a baby breaker."

"You did? It looks so calm today." Though in Santa Lucia the great, blue wedge of sky and sea had been brilliant earlier that morning, twenty miles north up the coast the fog was late burning off, and the sea beneath the thinning mist was a restful mauve. From the northwest and the south the swells pushed in around the tiny island in the usual crescent patterns, meeting just left of mid-channel where they formed what Elliot liked to call the ducktail-do – a line of opposing, cresting waves. Not a good place to be, and not predictable, either: the area tended to shift depending upon the season and tides, and those rooster-tails (as they were generally known) could easily swamp a boat.

The Zodiac suffered mysterious leaks and had to be topped-off before each crossing. While his shoulders rose and fell over the pump, Elliot talked. "It is calm, but there's an ebb tide and it's pulling north. I drifted out of the channel and hung up on a rock."

"With passengers?"

"And no shortage of suggestions. Borovich likes to play captain. He says running the channel is *exactly* like putting around the Keys on a summer day."

She laughed. "I hope he drops by this winter."

Breathing hard now, he nodded and reached over to press one of the gray tubes. "Good enough," he said, closing the valve.

Anne started loading the gear which was strewn about the beach, except for one red bag lying two feet from a dozing female elephant seal. Who would toss their pack that close? she wondered. She was tempted to leave it. There were, in fact, several molting females in the vicinity, along with one bull sound asleep in a salt chuck puddle inland from the launching beach, a 5500-pound living island whose skin rippled from the end of his overhung proboscis to his hindquarters.

Creeping toward the bag, her approach was detected. The seal threw her head around, bared her canine teeth, and barked irately.

"Here, use an oar," Elliot said.

Hooking the bag with the oar, she swung it around and

dropped it into the raft, then climbed in after. Elliot pushed them off.

Año Nuevo Island probably separated from the mainland no more than 350 years ago, and the watery breach between the two was a shallow crossing over ancient marine terraces and rocky reefs almost completely exposed at low tide. The channel between the southern reefs and the big breakers rolling in from the northwest was the deepest, though during an ebbing tide it was common to run up on rocks. Twice Anne pushed the Zodiac off with the oar while Elliot handled the outboard and kept his eye on the wall of breakers. From the water they looked like distant ranks of blue, snow-capped mountains, almost Japanese in their layering effect, and very much alive, and roaring, and moving diagonally toward them, just glancing past the channel. It did seem calm today: still, neither spoke. If you knew better – and Elliot did, having watched one of his associates drown a few years back – calm didn't count here. Calm was no more benign than an idling chain saw.

They neared the sandy bight on the eastern side of the island where a man wearing the torso half of a red wet suit stood in the center of the beach, his arms crossed over his chest, his chin dipped down and sideways in an attitude of scrutiny, his khaki baseball hat speckled white. Frowning, Anne glanced back at Elliot.

"That'd be Captain Borovich," he said under his breath. "Brand new wet suit. He was concerned about the cold water . . . coming from Florida."

"Is that bird shit on his hat?"

"I hope so." Elliot throttled down, pausing just behind the place where the waves curled over, and waited for the raft to rise as the next swell drove landward. Then, sliding off its back, he scuttled in after it, careful to let it break just ahead of the bow as they rode the frothy carpet onto the sand. It was a small beach, but Borovich would not step aside – he seemed unaware of anyone but Elliot. As Elliot tipped the props up out of the shallows, Borovich concentrated on his back. Anne was forced to pull the dinghy diagonally past him where the beach dropped abruptly off, a maneuver which rendered the task doubly strenuous. Tying off to a heavy piece of drift wood, she trotted back to help with the gear.

"How goes it?" Elliot called to Borovich.

"That's my bag," Borovich said, pointing to the red pack.

Smiling broadly, Elliot tossed it to him. "Wasn't critical, was it Frank? 'Cause I wouldn't've stopped to have lunch if I'd known you needed it."

Frank Borovich turned, marched head down toward the cliff, and bumped into Anne. She stuck out her hand. "Hello, I'm Anne McBain." For a moment he looked nonplused, as if she was a figment of someone else's imagination suddenly incarnating in his, then, recovering, his face took on the poignancy of someone pleading for his life. Dropping the red pack, he placed her hand between both of his, and told her in all earnestness, "My dear, you are truly lovely, and it shines from the inside out. Why are you here?"

She lowered her eyes and smiled, checking peripherally Elliot's activities – he was still assembling his gear – and answered that she was here to assist Elliot, though she had hoped to glimpse the whale skeleton sometime during the afternoon – she had done some work with killer whales, she explained – and would he, Dr. Borovich, very much mind if she wandered over at some point, provided she did not interfere with his work. He had given her the upper hand, but she would let him think otherwise.

"Yes, yes, that would be fine. Its posture in the sandstone presents an interesting problem." Cocking his head curiously, he added, "It's a baleen, you know."

"Yes," she said. "I'd still like to see it."

He ran the palm of his hand over his near bald pate, as if he had forgotten where he was going. It seemed Frank Borovich had been wrecked, had had, as it were, a collision which had reduced the hard, bright, challenging stance of the man on the beach to a skew-eyed heap of desire which, Anne noticed, Elliot was about to tow away.

"After you, Frank," he said. Borovich was Anne's height, stocky, barrel-chested and muscular – not the ideal body type for scrambling up the 15 foot cliff face, reaching spider-legged from hand hold to toe hold – but with agility and without help, he was the first to clear the ledge – in order, it seemed, to be in position to pull Anne over the lip.

"We might poke around the site later, when there's more to see," Elliot said.

Borovich nodded and continued to examine the sea gull guano on his hat. Then he covered his head and turned toward the west side of the island where the whale skeleton was buried.

Elliot and Anne headed over to the southeast beach where most of the molting females would be lounging about.

"What did you do to him?" Elliot asked, passing her a sideways leer as they walked.

"Nothing. He bumped into me. That seemed to be enough."

"It was for me."

"That's all it took?" She raised a disapproving eyebrow.

"To get my attention, yes. To keep it, not on your life. No, I was suckered by your rapier wit and your vpl."

"My what?"

"Visible panty line."

"Funny."

As they approached the top of the island, the gull activity increased, and Elliot pulled her under the fallen light tower whose upper platform, now half submerged in the sand, formed a kind of lean-to shelter. Of the seven or more species of gulls migrating through the area each spring, the large Western Gull was the only one to nest on Año Nuevo. There were around a hundred pairs on the tiny island, which meant that every few feet in the dunes above the tidal flats lay a clutch of up to three mottled, moss green eggs, four when there was a shortage of males and two females banded together to raise the fledglings, thereby increasing reproductive success. Many of the gulls had used sheaths of molted elephant seal pelage to feather their nests, along with bits of dried seaweed, fishing line and yellowed grasses.

"Did you bring a jacket?" Elliot asked.

She held up a pile pullover, shrugging.

"It'll be ruined." From his backpack, he pulled a green windbreaker with a hood. "Here, use this."

"What about you?"

There was no answer. Elliot was most gallant when no one expected him to be, or when the gallantry wouldn't be pointed out. Once, on the Rio Grande, when she was learning to run rapids, he concealed his good will inside a casual, laissez faire attitude. They had come to a long, Class IV rapid with a couple of serious technical moves, not beyond her ability but certainly beyond her composure. It was the hundred mile section of the Rio Grande with a Wild and Scenic designation, and they hadn't seen another raft in days. Of the six people, she and Elliot were the only two who knew anything about river running. When they stopped to scout the rapids her mouth went dry. It looked bad. There were a couple of places where the consequences would be disastrous if she screwed up. They discussed his running it, then hiking back up river and taking her raft through, but the canyon was steep, it was questionable he could get back without hiking inland. A minute or so passed as they watched the water and calculated the best route. "Hell," he finally said, "you can run it. All you have to do is miss that hole at the top, which'll be easy. Keep your stern against the right boulder and don't stop pulling. After that, take it as it comes and, if you're going to hit a rock, just remember not to hit it sideways, right?"

Anne nodded, though her stomach seemed to collapse inward with fear. He was right: she could read the water, she knew how to run it. She just didn't want to. It scared her to the marrow.

"Wait until I'm out of the chute," he told her. "Then start."

Elliot put the two strongest men in her raft, taking the woman and an older man in his, presumably in case she flipped and they would be forced to swim, though he never said this; he just did it as if it was simply time to shuffle passengers. He would not let her make eye contact. He moved about the rafts, cinching this, lashing down that, chatting about eddying out for lunch in a mile or two, about the half pound of smoked oysters he planned to consume. He would not let her betray her fear: there was no point in it. She had no choice. Fake it, he seemed to say. Fake it to me, too, for your sake. Don't recognize it, don't say the words. He slapped her fanny. "You'll have a great run, kiddo. Make you feel like a million bucks."

The upper half of the rapids was the worst stretch, and was separated visually from the lower half by a house-sized boulder mid-river which they had to skirt. Elliot was beyond this boulder by the time she hit the chute, so she did not have his example to copy – she had to run it herself. And she did – perfectly. She felt indeed like a million bucks, shouting as she drifted past Elliot who was waiting in an eddy at the bottom, "Did you see that pivot? Did you see my pivot?" In answer, he shook his head and smiled to say, 'You see, of course you could run it.' Later, one of the passengers in Elliot's raft reported that while he was still negotiating the rapids and was unable to look back, he asked repeatedly, "Can you see her yet? Can you see her?"

Jogging across the dunes sent the gulls into panicked flight, which naturally prompted random defecation, though from below the bombings seemed not the least bit unaimed. Breathless, they ducked into the instrument shed situated on a small rise just above the beach where most of the molting females and juveniles had hauled out. Instantly Elliot announced, "She's here." Anne peered through the dusky air at the strip chart to which a radio receiver had been attached: it measured within the nearest hour when any of the elephant seals carrying a time depth recorder arrived on the island. On the strip chart the straight line rose abruptly to form three uneven peaks, then flattened, rose again within a few inches and continued off the chart in a range of jagged ink.

"Since Friday," he beamed, as he knelt on the floor of the shed, rummaging through his packs. "And it looks like I have everything we'll need."

"Why does the line go flat in the middle of the recordings?" she asked.

"She probably hauled out briefly, drifted around the shelf area for some last minute foraging, then hauled out for the duration. She'll be here about a month."

The shed was closet-sized, with one sandblasted window looking out on the point beach, several shelves for instruments, hooks for wet suits and such, and a single, rickety stool from which to survey some of the winter breeding activities when it was raining. Because the dunes seasonally shifted, the building had been perched up on five foot piers and, as Anne sat on the stool regarding the hundred or more molting elephant seals through which they would have to search for Elliot's missing female and the valuable recorder, she could hear the onshore breeze whistling like a siren under the loose floorboards. The sun had successfully burned through the fog, the island warmed, its colors going from murky gray to a bleached white, while the sea, still untroubled, seemed to ripen with the afternoon to a romantic, lavender blue. The quality of light, the sense of remoteness, the soft, salty air lent a Mediterranean ambiance to the island. They might have been happily stranded. They might have nothing to consider but themselves, she thought, nothing but what the rest of the mammals on this island concerned themselves with – reproduction.

"*Coito ergo sum.*" Elliot's favorite quote. To a biologist, reproduction is the most important thing any animal does. And Año Nuevo, because it was removed from the mainland and therefore protected from terrestrial predators, and because of its sloping rocks and sandy beaches, had become a breeding sanctum sanctorum for harbor seals, Steller sea lions, and northern elephant seals. That didn't count the gulls, cormorants, pigeon guillemots, and black oystercatchers, or the California sea lions who, though not breeding on Año Nuevo, used the island as a home base. In terms of biomass alone, those twelve acres of cherty shale, graded reefs, and sparsely vegetated dunes supported a staggering weight. What difference would two more mammals make?

But our species has other things on its mind, she thought, staring at a male Steller sea lion from whose mouth hung an eight inch salmon flasher. Our species enjoys sport fishing, wants a career, and has been observed to prefer not to contribute to the gene pool, has in fact terminated viable pregnancies. Our species has heaven on its mind. In one way or another.

Elliot distributed his gear about the shed in no apparent order, including his bespattered shirt, then paused to consider her. His face was excited, but she could tell that he was making a momentary effort to reign in before he committed himself – and her – to the job at hand. In his yellow, patagonia shorts, blue undershirt, and nylon flip-flops, with his dark gold curls windblown, boyishly disheveled, and his ten-day stubble – he was growing a beard again, at her insistence – Elliot was to Anne the picture of virility. The right combination of youth and age, of easy excitement and restraint, of willfulness and compromise, of an endearing innocence and ability that bred trust. Typically, he arrived at social functions late, underdressed, and slightly drunk, yet he could argue politics with more authority, or describe operas with more passion than any of his most erudite cronies, though he often didn't. He listened and he was reticent, (not shy) – a powerful mixture. A man's man. His broad, big-boned shoulders seemed to span the width of the shed. His tan, like a living source of light, glowed in the dimness. She felt that he was too much for her, and at the same time she wanted to be with him, only

Elliot, and alone. In elephant seal terms, he was an alpha male.

"Look Anne, I know this was supposed to be a Sunday excursion, and that we need to talk, but this is really important."

"I know, and it's fine."

"She's been here two days already, and I'm worried about the recorder. I'd like to get it off her before she rolls on it, or it's somehow damaged. Can we talk about things tomorrow?"

"Tomorrow's fine, really." She shrugged. "Anyway, it might be good to give it a rest." To reassure him, she picked up one of his packs and pushed open the door, raising her eyebrows to ask if he was coming before she turned and went down the steps.

She had not told him about her father's death, or that probably she would be heading up to Washington on Tuesday or Wednesday. So far Malcolm McBain's departure from the fold had not animated any of the standard sentiments – loss, grief, anger, fear – and it was disconcerting, even vaguely embarrassing. How could she tell Elliot? How could she allow him to console her? Gee, uh, thanks anyway, Elliot, but I really don't miss him anymore. I stopped missing him years ago and actually, Elliot, I hate to say this, but I don't seem to be feeling much of anything. There was, also, the possibility that that information delivered at the right moment might soften his attitude toward the pregnancy. How many deaths could she be expected to bear, after all? No, she wouldn't tell him and have the afternoon ruined by pretense.

She looked out across the empty sea. The wind shoved past her as if she was in the way.

Elliot caught up with her, and together they started across the dunes. Maybe it would not have been all pretense, she thought, if she told Elliot and he was comforting; maybe she felt something . . . a little more tired, more alone. She and her father had shared a certain weight, they could remember the same events, doubtless not in any similar manner, but still . . . the time, the smells, the way the light fell against the wall that summer, as if yielding, as if dying there in the room just as places inside her were going dark, the moist heat of a Texas storm, the black crickets, and every sound, every breath of movement beyond the door – these things could not be altered by desire, or loathing, or even forgiveness. They left marks, had become part of the final cast. He was gone now. His memory of her, too, and of the events – all gone. There remained only Anne for the remembering, the weight hers alone. Such a strange heaviness, too, such harmless things pulling down – the weight of the hibiscus, a poignant red, and the gray belly of clouds above, the thunder shower like a spasm that shred the sky, and the rain beating down on the red petals in big, spattering drops, sultry air coming in through the open window, coming in and not leaving, not ever leaving it seemed, and the wet leafy palms slapping against the window, and the devils that dusk conceived. It was all hers now. For the remembering.

Elliot squeezed her waist as they veered toward the point beach. He was happiest when there was a purpose from which he might deviate: a day devoted to leisure undid him, a day of work brought out the rebel. And she wanted him to be happy with her today, to be reminded. She wanted to be the girl he fell in love with, the thought he looked about for when casting into the depths of the future, a quick, shimmering movement, a possibility. So they would find the seal, and retrieve the recorder, and then settle against a warm bank to drink the bottle of wine, and be at home together. They would enjoy each other for the afternoon. Tomorrow they would talk about things. Tomorrow. She didn't want to lose him, though there were times when that seemed inevitable, part of a plan she had forgotten that was now self-realizing.

The point beach was roughly shaped in a triangle with two sides bordering on the water and a third lying against a sandstone bank about five feet high. Elliot figured that they would find her near the water's edge on the periphery of the harem (if they were lucky) because she had recently hauled out. Her name was Gina. She was twelve years old, a large female, about 1300 pounds, and she had been one of Elliot's most reliable subjects since she weaned her first pup over nine years ago. She had been involved in studies concerning the energetics of lactation, feeding habits, competition among females and currently, free-ranging dive patterns. Elliot harbored a certain affection for Gina, Anne knew. He often spoke of her as if she represented (in terms of reproductive success) the consummate female elephant seal. Some of his colleagues had accused him of anthropomorphizing, and Anne noticed that at least with her he did not deny it.

Depending upon how near they drew, the molting females yawned, honked, or trumpeted, being, unlike most pinnipeds, utterly unafraid of human beings. Here and there arcs of sand erupted among the languishing seals as they flipped the cooling grains across their backs. Peelings of molted skin littered the beach, the seals themselves looking leprous at this point, the old skin a light brown, the new a bluish gray. Abandoned and helpless, a few late departing weaners were wandering through the harem searching for their mothers, long gone – the weaners would be five months old by now and should have left the rookery a month ago. And it was not unusual to see some males on Año Nuevo during the spring molt for females, though for the most part they were sub-adults sparring in the surf, or resting a day or two from their seasonal foraging.

Elliot caught her arm. "Watch this guy," he said. A large male was moving crossways through the harem toward the surf, scattering a pair of weaners and leaving a path of angry, head-rearing females.

"He's huge."

"That's Donovan. I wouldn't be surprised if he challenged old Lear next winter. It's about time for a change of guard."

They watched him plunge into the surf. Obliquely Anne noticed a female lying in the wet sand who did not raise her head as Donovan passed. "Hey," she said, pointing. Elliot followed her arm. A glint of metal. It was Gina.

He hung back as they approached her. There was something wrong. Her body was oddly contorted. Moving in from the surf side, Anne stopped when she was about three yards away from Gina. "Oh God," she cried, her fist going to her mouth. She could feel Elliot standing behind her, off to the side, and she forced herself not to look at him.

"Shark," Elliot said.

There was a large, oval wound in Gina's flank, pink near its outer edges, bloody in the center where the bite was deepest, and a loose flap of flesh hanging from the wound. The jagged serrations indicated the work of a Great White.

"Still bleeding. Probably happened within the last 24 hours," he said. His eyes fixed on the wound, he seemed to be in a daze.

"She'll survive it. They do, don't they, usually?" She stepped back to stand beside him. The low surf swirled around their ankles, rushed backwards, digging holes behind their heels as the water drained away.

"Depends." Dropping his head, he watched his feet disappear under a wave and reappear as the water slid back out. "Damn sharks hang out there above the continental shelf, cruising the shallows, waiting for the seals to return to the rookery. And the seals, they have to swim across to get here. They have to." He seemed to be talking mostly to himself. Part of Elliot's hypothesis developed from data gathered with the time depth recorders suggested predator avoidance as one of the functions of the high rate of deep diving in elephant seals. Once they cleared the shelf, they plunged to depths of 800, 900 meters, and even while crossing the shelf area, they dove repeatedly until reaching deep water, in that way reducing surface time and proximity to the White sharks feeding in waters above 100 meters. At the wrong moment and in the wrong place Gina had had to surface.

Elliot pulled his feet from the sand and moved up to the hard ground where he dropped his packs and fished a tape measure from one of them. Eyeing him suspiciously as he crept toward her, Gina finally let out a weary half-bark, half-growl. He stood perfectly still behind her. Within four or five minutes, she lost interest and turned away, blinking sleepily. Though it was encrusted with the sand she habitually flipped across her back, the wound was not infected and would probably remain clean if she stayed near the water's edge and took a dip now and then in the salt water. Leaning over, Elliot held the tape above the oval bite, measured its longest and widest diameters, and checked her for other wounds. Just behind her shoulders there was an old propeller bite, a perfectly round shallow hole about the size of a tennis ball, but it was well healed; and she was blind in one eye – otherwise Gina appeared unscathed. Backing off, Elliot sat down next to Anne on a mound of sand, entered the measurements in his journal, and dropped the book between his knees. "I don't know," he said. "It's a nasty bite."

To their right, the yellow sun behind him like stage lighting, Borovich came stomping through the shallow foam to stand before them, loud and huffing and near-naked without his wet suit. "This is a good time for you to come over," he said, looking exclusively at Anne. "I'm about to begin extracting some of the pieces from the sandstone."

"We haven't really finished here yet," she said, though she did want to see the bones as they lay, before removal.

Borovich frowned. He watched Elliot spreading out his instruments on a towel.

"Actually, Frank, we haven't started," Elliot said. He was screwing together the flat pads attached to each leg of the tripod from which they would suspend Gina to weigh her, and he was purposely not pausing in his labors to make eye contact.

His hands on his hips now, Frank's pectoral muscles began to twitch as he considered his options. He had what most women would consider a handsome physique. "Say, why don't I give you a hand?" Obviously he perceived that in order to have time to squire the young lady about his old bones, he might have to assist Newhouse, odious as that must have seemed to him. And obviously he had not perceived that the young lady assistant and the marine mammalogist maintained something more than a professional relationship.

Elliot didn't answer. Anne smiled wanly in Frank's direction. It would be interesting to see the whale skeleton. Mostly though, she realized, she wanted to get the recorder off Gina so that she and Elliot could sit in the sand and drink the bottle of wine. If Frank Borovich was helping, especially with the weighing procedure – ordinarily a three man job – it would, in fact, go a lot faster. Anyway, she appreciated Borovich's attentions, because she felt Elliot needed to be reminded now and then that other men of his caliber (intellectually, at least) found her desirable.

Frank nodded at the gleaming depth recorder. "What's there to do? Knock her out, and get your recorder back, right? What's that? Thirty minutes?"

"And weigh her. And take some blood."

"So add ten." His tone was all impatience trying to sound perky, his words sharp staccato notes against Elliot's slow and indecisive movements.

"Thanks anyway, Frank. Wouldn't want to impose." Elliot stood up, turning his back to Borovich, and began to erect the dynamometer tripod. Clearly he was in no hurry.

Anne caught Borovich watching her as she rose to help Elliot.

"No imposition, Newhouse. I gave the crew a break." A lie, Anne figured. He bent down, picked up the CO2 pistol with his left hand, while his right hand rattled through the pack for the vials of ketamine and diazapam, and dispatched Elliot an insipidly challenging grin, so convinced was he that there was now nothing standing in his way but outright rudeness.

"What're you doing?" Elliot shouted. He tried to grab the pistol from Frank, but the stocky man, his head flushing pink, staggered backwards, unwittingly aiming the empty dart gun at his assailant. Elliot had to shut down a smile before talking. "Look Borovich, I haven't even decided if I'm going to sedate her. She's got a bite out of her flank the size of a Christmas ham, and she might not survive the ketamine on top of that."

Dropping his arm, Frank glanced over at Gina. "Then why are you setting up the tripod?"

"I'm thinking about it. I'm just thinking about it."

The paleozoologist was genuinely confused. "What about your data, man?" Frank said 'man' in a Dickensian way, as in 'My good man, have you taken leave of your senses?'

Elliot didn't answer.

"You mean you'd sacrifice your data and your, your recorder . . . what's that cost, two, three thousand . . . on the *chance* that she couldn't take it." The dart gun hung limply from his hand. The surf swirled in around his short, knotty calves as an incredulous smirk crossed his face. "What is this . . . new-age sensitivity? animal rights? or is it just that in California the animals have to be *consulted*, their *feelings* considered?"

"She's twelve years old," Elliot quietly said. He was untangling the lashing on the sling, still taking his time. "Gina's been a reliable animal. Losing her could handicap other projects."

"Gina?" Borovich's taut regard abruptly went slack. He seemed to think he had won something, because he marched up the sand in the spirit of good sportsmanship, placed the gun on the towel, and touched Elliot's back with the flat of his hand, a gesture both avuncular and patronizing. Elliot stiffened. "If she's twelve, then she's not going to live much longer. And if that bite is as bad as you say it is, and you don't get the instrument off her, you'll lose her anyway, and your data. And if she is a reliable animal, then she's been through the ketamine many times before, she's been immobilized and handled, and she's not going to go into shock, or apnea, wound or no wound. Forgive me if I presume, Elliot, but it's my understanding that it's only male elephant seals who respond badly to immobilization, males who occasionally die of shock as it were." At the end of his lecture he made a point of surveying the sea of elephant seals – mostly female – behind Elliot, his head moving slowly left to right 180 degrees to indicate that there were many more Ginas where Gina came from.

"You left out one thing." Elliot shoved his face down toward Frank's highly satisfied mug. "It's none of your business."

Borovich swung around and tramped back up the beach, his heels kicking up mini spouts of sand.

"I guess he won't be adding you to his Christmas list," Anne said.

"What an ass. He oughta stick to bones and leave living animals to people who care."

She stood off and watched Elliot's profile as he tared the equipment. His tone, she noticed, was the same as it had been the other night when they were arguing about her pregnancy – put-upon, self-righteous, trying-to-think-of-everyone-and-not-getting-credit-for-it. And she could hear the words . . . *my leaving now would cause a breakdown . . . not if it means destroying other people's lives . . . I can't make any promises . . . our lives undone by guilt* . . . He didn't think Jill could handle the truth, not now, not all at once; he was going to dole it out in bite-sized bits. And he was willing to risk losing Anne (just as he was willing to forfeit his data), and jeopardize a future she knew he wanted to avoid the pain today. It wasn't clear to Anne who couldn't handle it: Jill and Gina, or Elliot.

"I think Borovich cares," she said. "In a different way. He cares about the data, about a larger goal."

"He cares about your sweet ass."

"Seriously, Elliot."

He stopped his tinkering, glanced at Gina's wound, tipped his head sideways, inspected his hands. He looked boyish and uncertain. "Well then, what would you do?" His eyes went to her face. "What do you think?"

"I think the odds are in Gina's favor. I think you should retrieve the recorder and your data. You need to keep working toward completing the species profile, and I know you know that. I think you need to stop underestimating the females in your life." Elliot smiled broadly at her, and she smiled self-consciously back. "I think," she went on, still smiling, "you may in fact be projecting."

"Jill is not an elephant seal," he said, not angry.

"Neither are you," she said. "You know, one man, one woman?"

"You got me there." He was loading the CO2 pistol. "Okay. We'll try it."

Elliot fired two ketamine darts into the flank opposite the wound. Gina flinched, then almost immediately relaxed. They settled on the mound of sand to wait for the drug to take its full effect.

Up the beach on the damp sand near the water's edge sat the male Steller sea lion Anne had seen from the instrument shed. His eyes closed, he pointed his nose up toward the heavens, as if asking a question; his brassy mane widened from his neck to his shoulders, like an inverted horn; from his mouth the salmon flasher hung, an eight by four inch flat of metal, and somewhere embedded in the lining of his throat or his stomach was a triple hook that once belonged to a man gone fishing, probably mad about losing his rig. On the seaward side of the island, on the rocks slanting up from the surf, the rest of the male Steller sea lions had begun staking out their breeding territories before the females showed up later in the month. Over the sandy spine of Año Nuevo Island Anne could hear their hypnotic barking, could imagine their busy preparations for creation, jousting for this rock, that ledge, puffing up their fatty necks in challenge, baring their fangs. But not this old fellow. Probably he was dying. The flasher caught the sun; she blinked and turned away.

Fifteen minutes passed. Elliot approached Gina. She was

quiet. With a screwdriver, he loosened the hose clamps that held the time depth recorder and the radiotransmitter to the epoxy mount which was glued above her shoulders to her dorsal midline. Within two weeks when she molted the mount would fall off. He placed the instruments in one of his packs. "Might as well get a syringe ready," he said.

Anne started measuring out the ketamine, this time with some added diazapam. It was often necessary to administer more injections if the animal was not, or did not remain fully sedated, though Gina appeared to be utterly oblivious to their activities, even to Elliot's probing in her jagged wound.

"No infection," he said. "There's some muscle missing along with about 5 inches of blubber. Body cavity not violated."

"Hmm."

"That syringe ready?" He stared at the back of Gina's head, then laid the flat of his hand against her pelage to feel for movement. With each heartbeat, the flesh quivered faintly.

"Never mind," Elliot said. "I guess we don't need it."

She *was* calm. And Anne couldn't have been more satisfied, because now he would realize that he had been underestimating Gina, just as he was probably not giving Jill enough credit. Any woman would want to know the truth, and would survive it, too, because it was the truth. Now Elliot could have his data, and Gina would go on, and they would soon be drinking that bottle of wine, talking about the future.

Elliot drew three tubes of blood, then placed them in foam slots inside a hard plastic case, which was in turn wrapped with blue ice and buried at the bottom of one of his packs. Laying the nylon sling along Gina's downside, they rolled her onto it, brought the bars together, and clipped on the carabiners. The tripod was positioned over Gina. One of its aluminum legs would be subject to licks of foam if a good-sized wave spilled in, so Elliot trotted over to a nearby rocky ledge and returned with a piece of loose shale which he jammed up against the flat foot of the tripod to prevent it from slipping. Using a come-along, they winched her up. A wave rushed toward them and, as it retreated, pulled the sand out from around and under the flat of shale. She danced into the surf to steady the leg. Creaking, the sling shifted heavily her direction as it suspended all ten feet of Gina no more than an inch or two above the Pacific. Elliot centered it, then read the weight.

"You've lost a few pounds, old girl," he said, squatting to look at Gina's face. She saw Elliot's knees rock forward into the sand as he stared intently at the seal, at her face, at her flesh, at her one good eye. Eventually, a long sigh diminished his chest.

"What?" She was still bracing her body against the tripod leg, unable to move until Gina was lowered. Something was coming, and she wanted to leave, but she had to hear it because it was Elliot there kneeling in the sand, Elliot who loved her. Inside there was a click, a sound as familiar as her own front door closing behind her, familiar and cold and lonely at once, as if she had returned home and found that all her furniture had been removed, and there was a strange smell, too, lingering in the darkness on the hollow air, the smell of something, and she was fascinated by the meaninglessness, the power of what might have happened, of what was coming. "What is it? What?"

Elliot paused as if he thought there might be a way not to answer. "Well . . . what it is is she's dead. God *damn* it."

They packed up everything and headed for the shed. Tomorrow he would come back with some men, and they would cut Gina open to take measurements and samples, test this and that, and Gina would be for the last time a most reliable animal.

Borovich and his crew would not be ready to leave until 6:00. They had an hour to wait, and it was clear that Elliot did not want to stay on the southeast end of the island with the elephant seals. They carried his packs to the launching beach, except for the one containing the bottle of wine in which he expressed faint but grim interest, then walked up over the crest of Año Nuevo toward the seaward ledges and the old foghorn house. It was likely he blamed himself for Gina's death, and just as likely that Anne's role in persuading him to sedate her despite her recent trauma did not cross his mind. Or so it seemed. If all had gone well, he would likewise not have credited Anne with the success. Or so she hoped.

Not pausing, they passed the excavation site. Frank trotted after them, caught her arm, frowned. Elliot kept walking.

"Didn't you want to see the whale?" he asked.

She watched Elliot move away, his solemn gait, his tired shoulders. "No time," she lied. "Have to a make some notes with Elliot." She lifted the pack to indicate it was full of journals and books instead of a bottle of Chardonnay, and started to leave.

"Say," he said, "I wonder if I might . . . call you sometime."

"No," she cried, and ran after Elliot. They had been in collusion, this foolish, puffed up toad and she, and the shame she felt was doubled by her having enjoyed his attentions for Elliot's benefit. And at Gina's expense.

In the early seventies the old foghorn house had been converted to bunking quarters for scientists come to work on the island. It was perched on a seaward jut of sandstone and, having taken the brunt of Pacific storms for over half a century, its clapboard walls were brittle and pocked, its windows virtually opaque, its floor rotting through. When she entered, Elliot was standing in front of the potbelly stove, as if remembering a warm fire. They climbed up to a sunny niche at the west end of the loft. There was an iron bed supporting a shredded mattress, a wooden box covered with candle drippings, and one small window facing west. The window was like the others down below – so sandblasted it was opaque. On the bed, leaning against the wall, they drank the wine. Elliot was mostly silent, and she felt in that a great kindness. Every now and then he surfaced from his thoughts and patted her leg. "It happens," he said. "It happens."

They stared at the little blind window facing west. It bothered her, not being able to see out. Below and beyond the square of impervious light were rocks and waves, ocean, horizon, the earth curving down, black space. She could smell his skin, sweet and salty, and she wanted to be folded up in his arms and inhale that living scent forever. But he was away within himself. She thought about her father dying, and about Gina, about the baby growing inside her and how amazing it was that it would keep growing, that it was growing at this very moment with death just before and death to come, sooner or later, maybe even before it felt the sun on its face, or smelled the sweet salty smell of a father's skin.

Elliot filled her cup a second time. Suddenly the window went dark. Outside there was a sound, a vast rustling.

A black sky; hundreds of thousands of sooty shearwaters flapped overhead. She slipped her hand in Elliot's and together they watched the flock, miles long, glide over the water toward the horizon, like a great funereal veil drawn westward. Here and there, the wind caught the veil, black gyres of birds spun up into blue hollows, settled back down, and continued west. In time they began to see the end. Their two long shadows crossed a patch of yellow light, the sun was a disc again, the air quieted. The pall of shearwaters moved away.

"Time to go," Elliot said.

SIX

"There's only one thing you can do." They were the same words, the same tone Loretta used when a storm had blown out Anne's refrigerator last winter.

Anne stared back. "Right." She had not the faintest idea which one thing that was.

"Get rid of it *tout de suite*." She threw her head sideways in a matter-of-fact way. A trim brunette, Loretta was shorter than Anne, not particularly athletic, but immensely disciplined, the kind of woman who made everything count.

The vigor of Loretta's pronouncement had a dazing effect. In the morning light of the lab offices Anne felt herself twirling languidly off, a speck of dust on disturbed air. What Loretta had said, the way that she said it, seemed incontestable, and to think otherwise, to consider even for a moment having the baby, even to pause, would have been tantamount to lunacy.

Loretta was a good friend. They had been students together at the University, had kept in touch during the two years when Loretta went east to be with an old lover, and when it became clear the romance had not survived the time apart, the first thing she did was get on a plane and fly back to California where she secured a job in a bank less than an hour's drive from Anne. Loretta might have been disappointed in Elliot's inflexible stance, but she had great patience, great sympathy for the predicament their affection created, caring for Anne without preaching the obvious. She was no fool. Anne would not have left Elliot, and within those limits Anne knew that Loretta had always kept her best interests at heart. Plus, she liked Elliot Newhouse, though they seldom encountered each other. She liked what Anne made of him, and she gave her friend a lot of credit. So it was never the affair she supported; it was her relationship with Anne. When Anne was unhappy, Loretta's measures were swift, not curative. They would go out, anywhere – a movie, lunch, to the city – providing a stop-gap that addressed symptoms. The affliction itself was too massive, too far gone. During the last year Anne had begun to wonder aloud if the affliction was not herself.

In the silence following her ruling Loretta cocked her head – a tender warning to make no resistance.

Anne dropped her eyes to the desk blotter. Its borders were an inky motif of doodles she had penned in distraction during her two years of employment at the lab. In their knotty, repetitive shapes she could find no answers, only recriminations for the same messy, unconscious mistakes, and now this harshest of echoes, this pregnancy. "Abortion," she said, the word tasting of metal, of the tools that would work their way into her womb.

Leaning over from her perch on the near desk, Loretta squeezed Anne's shoulder. Good girl, she seemed to say. Anne would not look at her. In her terrible sensible presence she felt ashamed. And there was furtiveness in her answer, because she felt that Loretta had betrayed her. Wasn't she a woman, couldn't she understand?

After all, this was *abortion*. The accident of the uneducated, the stuff of news specials on life in the inner cities, of paperbacks and B movies, clinic bombings, old rattlings in high families, of pernicious whisperings at late-night parties.

How had it come to this? How, after all the years, had they been so careless, so casual? How was it that the one thing Anne McBain had most wanted to avoid, the most potent, most telling symbol of her mother's unhappy life – a life she must not duplicate – how was it that it now stood on her doorstep, flashing a sadistic grin, the debt collector who had finally caught up with her?

Fellow lab workers began trickling in. Loretta stood to leave. "No one needs to know," she whispered. "It'll be easier to put it behind that way."

"Okay," said Anne.

"Don't do anything yet."

"No."

"There's plenty of time. I'll go with you."

The walls of the lab offices had been gradually shelved in, some of the boards rough-hewn, and not one matching another. It was obvious that the first carpenter had begun at desk level opposite the window and, like the effects of a stone dropped in a placid pool, the rest of the shelves had radiated out, up, down, and around, lining the entire room. They supported primarily boxes and jars of organisms which followed no particular system of order and which, having secured berths on the shelves, were not disturbed again. Beginning at the topmost shelf, Anne let her eyes zigzag down until they came to a gallon-sized jar containing the preserved remains of an embryonic elephant seal, an ashen pink comma with shriveled flipper arms and fleshed-over bulges where the eyes would have been. At its early stage of development it was not visibly different from a human embryo. "Did I tell you that Gina died?" Anne asked.

"Gina?"

"One of Elliot's females, his oldest."

Loretta's smooth white brow creased. "That's too bad," she said cautiously.

"It was an accident."

"Tell him I'm sorry."

"Yes, I will. I'll tell him about the abortion and that we're all very sorry about Gina. It was an accident. But I can put some things back the way they were. There's time, I'll tell him."

"Are you okay?" Loretta said.

Now all seemed far away – Loretta, the lab workers glancing curiously in at them, the abortion, Gina, even Elliot – peacefully far away, as if she had retreated from her own life and was standing behind it, behind herself, listening and watching, agreeably indifferent. Abortion? Okay.

"Maybe you should take the day off."

"Okay." From her safe distance Loretta's pleated brow struck Anne as ridiculously serious. She grinned broadly. It was the worst thing she might have done and somehow it seemed that that was why she did it. Normal behavior was not only impossible, it was monstrously out of place, the talk of abortion over Monday morning coffee having thrown them into another world where the rules were different, where all was not as it appeared, a world where mothers murdered their own.

Loretta's expression wavered between concern and the example of brave resolve she wished to set for Anne, the former prevailing when Anne grinned like an imbecile. "You're scaring me. Do you want me to stay with you today?"

"I'm fine," Anne said. She was not trying to sound convincing until the thought that Loretta might actually call the bank with some excuse to take off and be with her broke her state of indifference and produced instead annoyance. Because she did want to be alone, even though she sensed that there was something dangerous in that. "I was just thinking that Elliot wished me a Happy Mother's Day. Isn't that funny?"

Loretta winced. "Forget it." She took Anne by the shoulders. "You're a beautiful woman. Beautiful. You've got everything going for you. And to let him . . . to let yourself get sentimental at all, to let this wreck your future, and I'm talking about your future with Elliot, too, and the Ph.D., everything . . . well don't. Just don't."

"It's hard."

"Try not to think about it. Take the day off and do something you enjoy. I'll call you tonight."

Anne spent the morning running a statistical analysis of data on zonation and characteristic algae distribution in the tidal regions of the bay, quiet movements of numbers and Latinized words, oddly soothing she found, as the numbers sorted out neatly, accumulated and became entities with meaning, while the Latin did not change, could not evolve – reliably dead. At the end, she looked over the figures on the page: they were very small and very precise, not her usual irregular flourishes that jumped the lines. She wondered if Allan Willets, her supervisor, who was down at Buck's slough observing snowy egrets for the day, would know that it was her work. The handwriting did not in any way resemble hers. It seemed desperately orderly, as if written by someone on the brink of madness, some mousy little nobody. She shoved the paper away from her, but her eyes fell on it again. They frightened her, those shrunken symbols, because it seemed that they could not bring themselves to stand up any longer; they were collapsing inward, apologizing for being even as they diminished.

I should leave, she thought. Take the rest of the day off, or . . . stay another hour, type it into the computer, and run it out on the laser printer where it will emerge devoid of the personal, of me. And no one will know what had been.

A couple of biologists strolled into the lab office with their lunch sacks. They were talking about the new sushi bar down the road. One of them tossed his bottle cap into her wastebasket. It hit the edge and clattered to the bottom. "Two points," was all she could think of to say. They smiled in her direction, their faces lumpy with food. She buried the analysis in the file folder, laid it on Allan's desk along with a note explaining that she was ill, and walked out of the lab.

There was only one woman in Dr. Havenstein's office – a pregnant woman – and the possibility that Anne could get them to do it right away seemed promising, especially if she told them that she had to leave town. A simple procedure, she had heard, using a suction device, a kind of mini-vacuum cleaner. There would be a slight tug, a few cramps, the sound of the machine – no more than five minutes. Then she would climb in her truck and drive down the road, and no one seeing her would know what she had done, or could say that she was anything but alone.

"We cannot terminate a pregnancy until you are far enough along to avoid an incomplete abortion," Dr. Havenstein's receptionist told Anne. She was a young, baby-voiced blond, and Anne couldn't help picturing her with a pink paper wedge in her hair, scooping ice cream at the county fair.

"I have to wait?"

"Six weeks." The receptionist paused in her bookkeeping duties to look with her innocent face at Anne. "We don't want to leave any viable tissue."

"Viable tissue?" Anne imagined an angry, mutilated creature writhing toward birth. *Viable tissue* . . . is this what they had come to?

"There has to be enough there, of size," the receptionist explained, "for doctor to eliminate."

"Oh." So she would have to let it grow inside her. She would have to let it *b*e before it could not be. What a horror, this business. She did not want to know anymore, and yet she could not leave the office without having settled the matter, without committing herself. It would be a small feat – she could not bring herself to call it courageous, that was much too fine a word, even though it seemed to require something like courage. To go back to Elliot, or to Loretta for that matter, without a voucher of intent would not do. "Can I make the appointment anyway?"

Dr. Havenstein's receptionist studied the calendar, her lips pursing around the numbers as she silently counted, then she penciled out a card for Anne. "Bring two hundred dollars in cash on the day of your appointment."

"Cash?"

"Yes."

"But I'm a regular patient of Dr. Havenstein's. He's my *regular* gynecologist."

An indulgent smile. "Therapeutic abortions must be paid for cash in advance. Policy, you understand."

She did not understand. She did not want to understand.

The receptionist was looking for a discreet show of comprehension, but the blank suspense Anne felt was apparently all her face could deliver, because the receptionist tried again. "Some of the women who make this choice are new patients, that is we . . . they don't return after the procedure."

Coughing conspicuously, the pregnant woman seated in the waiting room leveled her eyes at Anne, and began to stare blatantly at her. She was wearing a yellow jumper with a bunny patch sewn into the front panel, and for some reason the bunny made her a little easier to ignore.

Anne dropped her voice. "It's not the money. This is the first time, and I'm a regular . . . "

"Yes," she interrupted, her voice sticky with the effort, as she dismissed the debate by handing Anne a packet of information on the procedure, and a form releasing Dr. Havenstein and the clinic from responsibility for complications or patient death.

So. She had been assigned to a caste of wanton, murdering welshers. That was, after all, what was implied. Oh sure, they would do the dirty work, they would clean up your mess for you, cash in advance. In a room occupied by a mother-to-be and a sweet-young-thing there was nothing left for Anne except shame. Her ears flushed, her palms prickled with sweat. They couldn't imagine how it might happen to a responsible person, a nice girl. *She* had been a sweet-young-thing, and she wanted more than anything to be a mother, too. *Oh*, and that perky, patronizing 'yes,' the officious shuffling of triplicate forms which would excuse them from their mistakes while correcting hers, those bright, pure, unbreakable eyes that said, 'I have more important things to do, virtuous people to attend to, pregnant women keeping their babies' . . . it was too much.

Turning, the receptionist went to the back wall and replaced Anne's file. Her hair was cut in what was known as a 'bob,' a favorite among phys-ed instructors, and it jiggled gayly as she moved. Watching it, Anne felt utterly squalid. The receptionist returned, leaned forward over the window counter, and peered past Anne. "Debbie," she called.

The pregnant woman rose.

Anne understood that as her baby would be, she, too, had been terminated. Managing a limp 'thank you,' she slouched away, dodging the advancing Debbie. As the office door shut, she heard Debbie say, "I felt the baby move," and the receptionist squeaking her approval.

The afternoon had warmed. On her left she was approaching a bank of eucalyptus trees planted as a windbreak on the cliff above Mariah State Beach, their strong scent already filling the cab. It was a scent she associated with summer in California. On impulse she turned off the highway. Loretta had said to do something she enjoyed, and a swim on a weekday when the beaches were not crowded sounded nice. Cleansing. She slipped into her suit in the cab of the truck, and started across the parking lot toward the sand. As she passed the fish stand, she noticed an empty phone booth, and stopped to call Marlene and tell her that she would take her father's ashes to Orcas Island, to go ahead and send the urn. But there was no answer. She would try again after her swim.

Down near the surf sat a trio of mothers watching their young children waddle after retreating waves. The women were wearing straw hats. They were laughing, too, the sound floating above the roar of the surf and coming to Anne as a soft, bird-like trill. So that's what they do when hubby's off to work, she thought. Sunbathe. Watch the kiddies. Talk about recipes and watercolors. She could hear the snideness in her thoughts, but considered it basically Pavlovian, a response single, working women felt when exposed to housewives, a response not deserving much attention. Because these women were beautiful, sitting there on the empty beach, like figures in an impressionist painting. Beyond them a veil of fine salt spray shimmered off the water, while the sun seemed to pause above the three straw hats as if eavesdropping, or, like Anne, simply enjoying the prettiness of the scene. Anne let her steps angle away. But she kept watching, for there was a sweet lastingness about them, and she couldn't help feeling lifted up. It was right for them to sit on the sand; it was good that they were here minding their children as they sparred with the Pacific Ocean, while at the farthest end of the beach a lone bum rummaged through a garbage can. They were keeping it going, even while parts were breaking down.

Mariah State Beach lay between the jetty the Army Corps of Engineers erected to create a yacht harbor, and the sandstone wall at the south end of Main Beach. A half-mile stretch of perfectly straight shoreline without undertow or rip tides, it was the only good beach in the county for the serious lap swimmer.

Diving through a wave, she tucked into the trough behind the breakers, and began to swim parallel to the shore. Whenever an incoming swell bobbed her up above the white mane of the breakers, she could glimpse the three straw hats and the toddlers; when she neared the other end of the beach, she could see the transient fishing returnable bottles from the green barrels the Park Service provided. Her hands sliced in, and the cold water pulled along her body. The initial ache in her shoulders subsided. A whirlpool of voices and clips of events swirled about her mind, pulling her down faster until she was seeing and hearing everything at once, then a small gap of nothing, more words, pictures, nothing again – she was listening to the air rush in, then bubble out underwater. Lungs fully expanded, she settled into the rhythm of breathing, and for the next twenty minutes was untroubled by thoughts.

Eventually the muscles along either side of her spine went numb. She waited for a low swell, one that would not break in a head-to-toe crash but dissipate smoothly across the sand, and rode the wave in. The women were gone, but here came the transient with his sack of bottles. She toweled off, hoping he would pass. Many of the transients around Santa Lucia had been patients at mental facilities before federal funding dried up, and were here because of the climate – they could sleep outdoors most of the year – and because of the liberal attitudes, which were confined, like the warm weather, to the north side of the bay. This fellow, apparently wearing everything he owned including a wool overcoat, shuffled right up to her. She draped the towel over her wet suit.

"Here," he said, and he held out a straw hat.

Anne stared at it, then at his face, youngish and sleepy-looking.

"It blow'd up the beach," he said. "I caught it."

"Thank you," said Anne, and smiling, tipping her head deferentially, she added, "Thank you very much."

He shrugged and walked off.

The hat fit. Under its brim the sunlight filtered through in tiny, diamond flecks, and she found that she did not have to squint.

Stopping again at the pay phone, she dialed her father's number. The thought that he would not answer, and that she would not have to steel herself for those first lifeless words, frozen in time – *Hi daddy* – was more than a relief; it was a kind of amnesty. Her heart was not pounding. She felt calm and confident. Maybe it was the happy fatigue of the swim. Maybe it was the new hat.

"How was the wake?" she asked her father's widow.

"Fine."

"I've decided to take the urn to Orcas. There's a job I'd like to interview for in Vancouver, so it'll work in." Once again she heard herself camouflaging what residual affection she felt for her father. A job interview . . . why would Marlene care? What difference did it make now?

"It's already on its way," Marlene was saying. She cleared her throat. "I took a chance."

Not a very big one, Anne thought. "Good," she said. From there the conversation trickled off. There was no outpouring of regrets or recriminations, no shared flood of emotion. Neither, Anne noted, even offered a cool condolence. She realized that this was likely the last time they would have anything to say to each other.

Anne climbed into the old blue pick-up. In the rearview mirror she examined herself wearing the straw hat. She tried a serene smile for the famous impressionist, his paint brush poised above the empty canvas. I would like purple hair, she told him, and bee-stung lips, and a babe with a sea-green gaze. I could be one of them, couldn't I, sitting on a white beach? Or I could get the job in Vancouver where it rains and rains, and that'd be the end of it. Because painters do not paint childless, hatless, career women whose faces have turned to stone.

SEVEN

Elliot had received the news of her father's death, and of the trip to Orcas with his usual wary caution, casting his response in the mold of her attitude, which was, to say the least, without many contours. She had not told him about the job interview. She wanted to spare him the uncertainty while she was out of town. Then if they did actually offer her the job she would tell him, and he would realize finally that she was serious about the deadline, and could not be put off any longer. But for now, she did not want him to think that she was looking at other options, because maybe she really wasn't, maybe she was just kidding herself. And maybe, too, he would take it as a sign that her love was not as strong as it used to be, and his love would slacken in response, to protect himself.

For a Tuesday afternoon the airport was crowded, mostly with business commuters. Anne stopped at the Western Union window to wire Joe Sanborn, her father's oldest friend who was still living on the island, to tell him that she would be arriving on the late ferry, and to ask if he would join her for dinner. That there would be someone she knew waiting for her, even a partially deaf old man with a penchant for apple butter and Coors, was comforting in the extreme. Just someone there, at the other end.

Beside her, Elliot listened as the woman read back the wire. "Why don't you just call?" he said, handing her the box with the urn.

"I don't think he has a phone, or if he does, it's not listed."

"He might not be alive, Anne."

He said this, she knew, to prepare her. Elliot was always pointing out the downside and in his case, it truly was a gesture of kindness. "I'll just wait and see," she said.

They wove through the crowd to gate 19 and placed her carry-on, purse, and the box onto the conveyor belt. A young, overweight, black woman wearing owl-shaped glasses and a security uniform watched the screen as the articles passed under the x-ray camera. When the contents of the box were displayed, she stopped the belt. Elliot shoved his hands into his jeans pockets, glanced around, and audibly *ahemed* to the back of Anne's neck. Over her shoulder she threw him a silencing frown: he needn't always behave as if they had something to conceal, she thought.

"What's in the jar?" the woman asked, her voice unctuous, bored. Over the rim of the glasses, her eyes bobbed up like a couple of search lights to observe Anne's reaction. Her head, however, remained canted toward the screen, in case the contents of the jar tried to escape.

"Ashes. It's an urn."

The search lights brightened. "You'll have to open it." Meaning what? It looks like blasting powder? Cocaine?

At which point another security officer, noticing the stalled line, ambled over to regard the screen on the opposite side of the conveyor belt.

"It's an urn," Anne repeated solemnly.

Elliot was now nibbling on his finger, as if he would consume his very presence. Behind him, a line of craning necks had developed. A baby started to bawl. Anne wanted to wheel around, to explain that it was her father, her father's ashes, but the urge snapped as a wave of fatigue and embarrassment overcame her. Here she was – imagine it – defending her father's ashes. Shamed, somehow culpable, (because they were his, and she was his seed), she appealed to the second security officer. "Really sir, it would be, uh . . . indelicate, don't you think? to poke through someone's ashes." He was the one with the badge; he could overrule the woman.

Almost imperceptibly he dropped his head, glanced at the line, then reached under the screen and flipped a switch. The belt whirred alive. His smile was officially apologetic; it seemed to confide that he numbered himself among the cognoscenti of urns and of The Correct. As Anne passed under the metal detector arches she heard him whisper to the woman (still staring reproachfully at the screen), "of someone dead."

They found two seats in front of the windows and collapsed into them. Elliot squeezed her hand, released it. Sorry for all that, he meant. Or maybe, brave girl. She leaned against him. They had a half an hour to wait.

Someone dead. Dead. My father is dead, she told herself.

For days she tried the words, each time emphasizing a different one. She recited them as a mantra, emphasizing nothing, just listening to the flow of sounds. She tried to slip them into her heart by whispering, to drive them into her brain by announcing, "My father is dead." But the words and the ways in which they were uttered cast no spell of sorrow, opened no window to meaning, enlightened no dim corners of their history together. In her mind she heard them sounded in the dull, mechanical tones of a recorded telephone message – 'is not in service at this time and there is no referral.' My father is dead and there is no referral. She might have been informed that Einstein's theory of relativity had been changed, that time and space were once again absolute and independent realities, that her life was no longer relative to her father's because his had stopped. His world with its peculiar frame of reference had ceased to move, while her life continued to spin forward relative to what now? Itself? It seemed to Anne the fitting theoretical conclusion to what had become a hypothetical figure.

Until that hot August afternoon when she told Marlene, Malcolm McBain was real. He had fingers like roots, and he snored when he drank too much, and he desired. He was a human being she tried to understand and, understanding, tried to resist. Failing that, she exorcised him. That summer Malcolm McBain was transferred from the real to the safe realm of the abstract. He was simply *out there*, a distant planet.

To Anne, he became my father the developer; my father the world traveler; my father the millionaire, the hunter, the brilliant mathematician, the *bon vivant*; my father who loved dogs; my father who overcame polio by hiking ten miles every day, who could hook a derby salmon in a swimming pool on a bet; who 'could'a been a contender' if he hadn't killed a man in the ring, and quit, he said, heeding the voice of conscience. He was her father who, sporting a dark tan in the middle of winter, would wink naughtily, explaining that as the great, great grandson of a Confederate general, a little molasses might have dappled the cream. He was all of these, but he was never and would never again be just her father.

They seldom saw each other in the years following that summer. A cousin's wedding was the last time she encountered him, but he did something so strange, and to this day utterly inexplicable, that she silently vowed to restrict their contact to phone calls and letters. He sat on her lap. A 230 pound man. Not drunk. Not mentally deficient. Not anything but clearly taken with her presence, and proud of her, proud of their connection, and finally so giddy just to be there talking with her that there was nothing for it apparently but to sit in her lap. Peering around his great back, Anne spotted Marlene maneuvering swiftly through the crowd toward them, while those nearby, looking confused, pretended to have missed the joke, and let their attention and their feet drift awkwardly toward the champagne. "What are you doing? Get off her," said

Marlene. Giggling like a child, not knowing really what he had done, he rose, and his wife towed him directly to the other side of the reception hall.

For the most part, Anne hardly recognized what he had done then and in the years before as being connected to her. It seemed to belong to someone else. More probably than anyone knew of the man Malcolm McBain, she knew, yet still she understood very little. He was intimately foreign to her. So theirs became a theoretical relationship, as fragile as a paper maché piñata which one good whack of reality would have caved in, releasing . . . what? she wondered. Not anger, though it seemed to her she ought to feel angry; pity maybe, but to such a wan degree she could not finally claim that; hurt? no, he loved her, it seemed, as he could; releasing nothing perhaps except a pair of small, twisted hopes – his, that she would be for him what she had been, and her hope that he would be what he had not been.

Now Malcolm Kroeger McBain was dead of a poolside heart attack. Gone too were the irreconcilable hopes.

Between his ashes and Elliot, Anne sat looking out the windows at the gaping cargo doors of Alaska Airlines flight 10 to Seattle. Two men wearing earphones were tossing suitcases onto a belt that ran up into the hold. The last thing she wanted to do was board that plane but she felt she had to, compelled by a new voice, clear and cold, a voice that, because of the recent movement of events, only now she was able to hear.

In the fields between the runways a hot wind set off dust devils that twisted up into a bleached out sky. There was a vacancy about the day, a sense of waste and overexposure. She felt she was seeing too much, none of it in focus. The air in the waiting room was tense and that added to the gin and tonics she and Elliot had consumed at lunch produced in her a woozy, lost sensation. She asked herself, leaning into Elliot's shoulder, if the alcohol meant that she had subconsciously decided to go ahead with the abortion. Pregnant women did not drink.

One drink, half finished: ambivalence? It's your decision, Elliot had said Friday night. Was it her decision because he did not want to be blamed one way or the other, or because by some primordial whim it was inside her body, not his? And last night when she told him about Dr. Havenstein's – *I want you to do what you want to do.* What did that mean? How was she supposed to interpret that, how was she to deal with that piece of doublethink when what she wanted included him? His attitude was a wind that blew straight down her bow, testing her, watching to see if she would fall off or come about. She closed her eyes. What difference did it make, the talking, the watching? Each knew what each wanted, and wanting to please, too, she had made the appointment at Dr. Havenstein's. And Elliot, with shining, downcast eyes and apology crumbling behind his words, asked her about the procedure and reminded her not to do it on his account.

"I'll try not to," she had said, wishing he would stop her, wishing he would go to the phone and tell Dr. Havenstein and his do-good receptionist to forget it, this one's a keeper.

"How are you doing?" Elliot's beautiful long fingers combed through her hair, jiggling into the tangles until they let loose.

"I'm fine."

He cocked an eyebrow.

"I guess I'm tired."

"I don't know why you're doing this. You don't owe him a thing." The little he knew was enough.

"It's too late. The urn's here." Another baggage cart pulled up underneath the wing, and the men with the earphones continued the loading procedure, the suitcases tumbling through the black opening into the belly of the plane. "Anyway, I need to get away. I can't see anything anymore, and maybe a little distance . . . "

"Maybe," he said. "I still wish you weren't going."

She nodded. "I keep wondering what it'll do to us, if I go through with it, what it would do to any couple. It's making me clingy."

In a tone that was meant to lighten things up, he said, "Clingy is fine with me." Elliot hated heavy departure scenes. At that moment, however, he struck Anne as a little too unconcerned, too blithe.

"Everything's fine with you. Nothing's fine with you. What's the difference?"

He took off his glasses. "Let's not get into it. Not now."

"Then when? When are we going to get into it so that we can get out of it?" She paused, glancing around to see if anyone was listening, then lowered her voice. "You know, you used to commit to everyone, thereby, I realize now, committing to no one. Now you've told Jill all bets are off, and you've reminded me, daily it seems, that there are no guarantees. We are all in suspended animation, don't you see that Elliot? Don't you love either of us enough to say no?"

"You can say no, Anne. Anytime. You've got your deadline. But don't expect me to walk away leaving a wreckage, because Jill deserves time. She needs to understand."

"If it's permission you're waiting for, forget it. Because for Jill to understand, she'd have to admit there's something wrong with your marriage, and that would be signing its death warrant. She's not stupid."

"No."

"You know, Elliot, you remind me a lot of male killer whales . . . you don't leave mom unless there's a reproductive female in the area, and when you've done *that*, you swim on back home to mom."

"Jill is not my mother."

"No? She gives you *carte blanche*, in effect, by never asking the dangerous questions. Sounds like mom to me."

Elliot tipped his head. He looked calmly angry. "That's always been the problem with your research, Anne, the way you interpret cetacean behavior by anthropomorphizing it."

"Maybe so. Sometimes the parallels are too blatant to resist. But I'm willing to leave marine mammals out of it. I just want to know why, given the *fact* of our relationship, what it says about your marriage, why you're still there."

"Because I was not unhappy with my marriage when you came along. I am simply happier with you."

"Oh Elliot," she moaned. "There isn't enough of anything there to produce a real live decision."

"Maybe not fast enough to meet your deadline." From the way he said 'deadline,' as if he was being erroneously and hastily sentenced, she realized for the first time that it was not just the prospect, but the *idea* of the deadline that hurt him. How could she fix a date on which they would do the impossible? he seemed to ask. Elliot turned, regarded her face. "Has it ever occurred to you that resolution may not be subject to your kind of accounting?"

"Maybe it's not, but I do think that action shapes thought as much as the reverse, that a man who behaves as a, a thief say, after awhile would be a thief. He would begin to think like a thief. It's not in me to leave you, I don't want that because it's not how I feel . . . absolutely opposes how I feel. It would be so much easier for me to wait some more and hope for enlightenment and deal with the bad days as they come. I know how to do that. It's who I am now, I've become that person . . . a mistress. I get up every morning and pour my dreams through a sieve, waiting for the day those dreams grow big enough to hold onto, or the holes close up. That, by the way, was your job, you were the vessel, and I put everything into you." She paused, took a deep breath, let it go. "Maybe I expected too much, and at the same time maybe I didn't expect enough . . . not of you, I mean of life." A young woman laden with baggage staggered to a seat near them and, leaning against the heap of effects, closed her eyes. Her mouth fell open, and she appeared to be trying to scream.

"I'm just tired," Anne said. "Leaving you will be pure

make-believe. The trouble is, I can imagine it, and until now that wasn't possible. It scares me to death. So the deadline's for me, Elliot. Not you. I'm the one who has to stick to it because I'm simply more unhappy than you are. I must be. You've never adjusted your pace to anyone else's. It was foolish to wish that you would. And now even this, even this isn't enough." She felt a sudden surge of anger, and without fully realizing what the words meant, heard herself say, "Actually, Elliot, it'd be a good idea if you made up your mind now, while I'm out of town. The deadline has just been moved up."

Elliot made no answer.

What she had said, and his silence scared her; she didn't know how to explain herself, but began to speak, as if to haul up from a dark well the meaning without knowing in advance what it was at the end of the line. "I just can't do this anymore. Whatever I would have done, I would have still been waiting around for you to make up your mind, as a single woman or a single parent, and in either case, I would have given up too much to live with the situation as it stands. If we were together, it would be different, there would be forgiveness, there would be hope. And even if we weren't together, there would be some hope."

"There's plenty of hope, I don't know what you're saying," he said.

"But not waiting, no Elliot. I'm not going to wait anymore. Not with abortion on the table."

In the past whenever she bottomed out Elliot usually kept quiet, offering no defense, no brighter sides, no promises things would get better. Sometimes he suggested she should leave him (and seemed to want it for the relief alone) but the words were so frightening they scurried back, like cubs straying too far from the den. The time it took for him to drive to town, to get to a pay phone – that was about as long as it ever went – twenty minutes of sheer desolation. But now they were looking at those words and in a serious way venturing into them, into the wilds of solitude. And this time he could not keep entirely silent. This time it must have been too real.

"You don't have to do that," he said.

"Don't I?"

"Of course not."

"But the other is worse. If I don't know about us for sure, I can't have the baby. I can't. For me, it'd be suicide."

"Okay, I understand that," he said, touching her hand. "I do. And Jill and I are talking."

"Talk, yes," she said, feeling the keener edge on her impatience. "But you're not talking about the real issues. She probably thinks these conversations are supposed to repair your marriage, when in fact what you're doing is trying to persuade her that the marriage is in the dumps and that she ought to leave. Which would handily relieve you of yet another odious decision." Looking directly at him, she added, "You've talked before."

"That's right, we've talked before, we're still talking. Seventeen years of marriage can't be understood and written off in a few chats. It takes time. She doesn't want to hear it."

"Neither do I." Again, the uncontrollable words.

Elliot stared at her. "Meaning?"

"Meaning every time I get fed up, you promise to talk to Jill about the inadequacies in your marriage, then I retreat, full of renewed hope, and you stop talking."

"That isn't exactly accurate."

"Isn't it?"

"No. We don't stop talking. But I do stop pushing so hard. It strikes me as unkind and unproductive."

She bent over, resting her forehead in the palms of her hands. "The whole thing is unkind and unproductive, for everyone." Near them the sleeping woman opened her eyes and glanced blankly around the room. Anne sat up and examined Elliot's profile, mentally holding herself in, and when she spoke finally, her voice was as level and as steady as a final chord, pedal down. "When I get back from the island, it has to be finished, one way or another. It has to, Elliot."

"I guess that's up to you, sweetie."

"You'd like that, if someone else decided."

"No, I wouldn't." His face was puffed and blotchy from the heat, or maybe from last night's whiskey – he had, as he put it that morning when he picked her up, over-served himself. He looked as tired as she had seen him. He was hunched over on the plastic airport chair, grasping his glasses between his knees as he tried to adjust the safety pin that had held them together for the last year. Elliot Newhouse was a patcher. Seldom would he admit that something – a broken plate, an ill-founded conclusion, a collection of data tainted by missing entries, a pair of glasses – was a total loss. Anne found herself wondering now if she was not just another broken thing he was holding together, or fixing up. There was something glorious in that kind of willfulness. And scary, too, for him, she thought. Because what was going to happen when he failed? What would it cost him? Cost her?

His shirt was wrinkled and hiked up his side, and she could see his skin through a tear in his undershirt. For that she loved him. And for the safety pin, and the freesias he kept on his desk, the doctoral degree wadded up in the back of a drawer behind a guide to the Owyhee Mountains, along with the blue tipped matches he whittled down and poked at his teeth with during more contemplative moods, some homemade flies, the cassette the hypnotist had given him to help him quit smoking, a broken depth recorder, his boatman's pliers, a letter she had written him from Swift Current, Saskatchewan. No obvious order, no clear-cut ranking of interests. He was attracted to many things in seemingly equal measure. Among his favorite sayings was 'A little too much of everything will be just enough for me.' And he could handle it, usually.

He was staring at his topsiders, the worn brown leather moving whenever he wiggled his toes. His eyes flicked up her direction, then fell back, but she had caught that same lost, vaguely astonished quality that was there on Sunday when Gina died. Heading off the instinct to comfort, or to confess as she always had in the past that she would wait a little longer, that it was worth it, that she loved him and had no other choice, Anne meant to say gently, "I'm just trying to like myself," but the words struck out, and to soften them she added, "That's all."

"You should. You have every reason to." He slid his glasses back on, and looked out the windows. "It may be too late for me, though."

"I can't wait anymore."

"Won't."

"That's right. Won't wait."

"I don't blame you," he said.

"Oh Elliot . . . I'm pregnant."

He lifted her hand and placed it atop his knee, then covered it with his own. She could feel his warmth. She could feel, too, the unyielding calluses at the base of each finger.

"If you could just tell me . . . " she said. "If you know . . . you do know in your heart of hearts who you're going to be with, tell me now, don't let this happen."

"I can't."

The waiting room had emptied through the glass doors opening onto the runway. Near them, a woman stooped to put her arms around a boy and a girl. They waved to daddy who with his briefcase and garment bag was climbing up the stairs into the plane. They belonged to another world in which Anne would never be granted membership. Their days were light, their faces smooth, even their sadness was a small and charming thing, like a keepsake to remind them they were alive.

"Well . . . " Elliot started. They rose and hugged each other, her eyes dampening his neck.

She said, "I love you," listened to his worried echo, then she repeated it.

"I know," he said.

"Do you?"

"You're going to miss your flight."

She collected her things and backed up to leave.

"Don't forget me," he whispered.

Anne smiled. "That's my line."

"Not anymore."

Was that pride in his voice, had she done something, passed some mark he had set for her? His hair disheveled, shirt hanging out, cuffs pooling on his laces, Elliot stood there looking like a retiring coach at his last game.

"Get going," he said, lifting his chin.

Reluctant, afraid, she took a few steps backwards, then stopped. Under one arm was the urn containing her father's ashes; under the other a purse in which could be found pieces of paper revealing who she was, what she belonged to, even some of the places she had been. There was the résumé listing what she had done, a birth certificate for crossing the border. In the carry-on suitcase, the clothes reflected her taste, a book her education, a couple of magazines some of her interests. Yet she would have erased it all, or made it over to stay, because it was in Elliot Newhouse she saw the world, and in him she had found a home. What did it matter who she was? Being with him was all that was important. She would change, if only not to leave him. And this trip to the island, this interview . . . what silliness. She gazed into his eyes, trying to find herself there, still cherished, not forgotten.

"Three days," Elliot mouthed, then he grabbed her and pulled her hard against his chest. "You look like a waif, damn it."

"I'm a girl in trouble."

"Three days it is then, fair enough Anne. I guess it is time to clean house."

She was afraid to speak, afraid of breaking his resolve. And the last thing she wanted to do was imply that she might soften. "Can I call you tonight?" she said. A safe, habitual question.

"I'm counting on it."

At the top of the stairs she raised her hand up into the hot wind, then let it fall to her side. Standing apart, his eyes cast down, shoulders hitched up, and hands buried in his pockets, Elliot was the picture of predicament. She saw him turn, recede into the crowd. And in that instant she felt a profound sense of loneliness for him that was as physical as a craving for a drug that had been abruptly taken away. As she walked through the plane, she had to concentrate on the aisle carpet to keep from crying. Hers was the only seat left on the flight.

So to Orcas Island.

The plane climbed above the south bay metropolitan area, and she scanned the tangled ribbons of highway, as if to catch one last glimpse of Elliot's gray van heading west over the mountains to the sea. Somewhere among the multitude he moved, this man who said he loved her. She was leaving him to sow her father's ashes from which she would reap a dubious harvest, it seemed. And there was the question she would have to address with (theoretically) the clarifying benefits of separation, a question miserably similar to the one her own mother answered over a quarter of a century ago when she was a girl in trouble. Matters of death and of life, in their ultimate conditions and in measurable quantities – good enough reasons to run, she thought.

How did she end up here? Surely, surely the explanations for her behavior, her 'history' as Elliot put it, as if it was a disease in remission, were more interesting than the standard ingredient list – Fate, Freud, Self-fulfilling prophecy. Although in the early days when Elliot had seemed nervous about her 'history,' she had had to acknowledge it, even with a certain perverse pride – the accidents and illnesses, the old bones, the bad mistakes – point to and grant each as it slouched past. Yup. Shrug. That was me. And that, too. 'Fraid so.

But what difference did it make now that they were here? So what if Elliot Newhouse happened to represent the last of her relationships with older, unavailable men? Okay, married men. Impossible men. She had told him about the ones before. He was aware. And he stayed. Because what was important was that they loved each other and they were here now. That the old currents of her history might have swept them together she could not deny. But to extrapolate from that a definition of who they were, what they meant to each other . . . no. No. Even if losing had been part of the formula, and knowing how to accommodate loss had created a certain anticipation for it, even if in darker moments she conceded this, she would not accept it now. She wanted to win this time. The measures were new. They had alchemized, she and Elliot Newhouse. This was the Grand Passion, he was fond of saying.

The pregnancy would be their acid test. It was natural for a woman to think so, a biological truism: a man should want his woman's child, and if he did not, then there was something wrong, something missing. The circumstances might comprehend much more than the life of a child, but she could bring herself to feel this. And what if she had the abortion? Would he then find a reason to get out before something worse happened?

Gently, she raised the tips of her black leather pumps, then eased them back against the box containing the urn tucked beneath the seat in front of her. Ashes. To ashes. The last physical remains of Malcolm McBain were providing as his final deed a foot rest: a fitting although uncharacteristically humble deed. While in her womb, the earliest shapes of life were stirring, and even as she sat there, elaborating two upon one, four upon two, until one day there would emerge a highly ordered mass of details, eons old, and protesting – a baby. Their baby. At this point the small ambition inside her, and the ashes at her feet probably weighed about the same. The living and the dead.

EIGHT

The rental car looked like a giant white shoe box with a pair of red vinyl slippers inside – tuck'n'roll buckets – and it reeked of cigarette ashes, and it chattered on a minute or so after it had been shut off, but it satisfied Anne's peculiar brand of thrift which was both selective and Catholic, and when she launched it onto the Interstate for the hour and a half drive to the Anacortes ferry landing, she did so with guilt-free confidence.

The shoe box fell apart around Marysville. A blown water pump. Luckily, she pulled off when she first heard the ominous growling, because soon enough the pump would have disengaged, sending the fan spinning through the radiator, which would have likewise required replacement – according to the kid at the gas station who went off to hunt for a new pump.

Anne walked down to the cafe next to the tracks to wait. White stucco, blue striped awnings, red flowers in the window boxes – outwardly nothing had changed at the pie place. They used to take her here on weekend outings for a wedge of coconut or banana cream, the six-inch hat of meringue the main attraction. Not for him. He didn't have a sweet tooth, her mother said, as Anne did. *Which tooth*, she would ask, trying to be cute for them. No, he drank coffee cooled with ice cubes which he fingered periodically from his water glass, while mother and daughter explored the sweet wonders of the Marysville Cafe. And they talked the way adults did when there wasn't anymore reason to stay, when the pie was long gone.

One of their trysting spots, Anne realized now. A do-nothing town on the periphery of the Tulalip Indian reservation, 40 minutes north of Seattle where it was unlikely they would run into anyone they knew, a town too close to the city of Everett to attract any but illicit lovers or stranded travelers. Ideal. She was not unaware of the geographical requirements special to such relationships, and for the first time in a long time, she felt genuine shame. Her obsession with Elliot had buried too many natural feelings. Too many.

At the counter she ordered a slice of rhubarb pie and a cup of coffee. She had grown away from cream fillings and meringue, just as Nellie Gallagher and Malcolm McBain had grown away from each other. The weekend outings belonged to another country, and the people who enjoyed them were characters in a storybook, not to be seen or known now beyond the thinning pages of memory, not to be touched by the present. In a corner booth Anne imagined the three of them, but the faces were blank, the words inaudible, as if they were still keeping secrets from her. There was only the fluffy white meringue before her, and the tiny squares of ice floating atop the coffee, disappearing into the black. There were her parents talking indecipherably above her head. And there was the long, long wait for the future. Always the future, where things would get better, where they would be together.

The rhubarb was tangy, the crust dry and flaky with a buttery, background flavor. Elliot would like it . . . and he would like the place with its swivel stools, stacks of newspapers, bottomless cup of coffee, and the 'what'll it be' greeting. He was a great fan of the no-nonsense approach. He drank his whiskey neat. He had worn Levis for the last 30 years on virtually every occasion, and to suggest that he might try a pair of khakis or cords would have been the same as asking him to change the color of his skin. He avoided restaurants where the waiter was introduced by the maitre d' – first name only – and whose intention plainly was to become a cherished friend by the end of the meal, restaurants where one was invited to "experience" the salad bar.

Vaguely, she considered calling him to tell him about the car trouble, and that she missed him already. But the man in the shiny green suit using the pay phone was obviously cutting some kind of deal – real estate or insurance, she guessed – because he kept gesturing with the edge of his hand to make each selling point, and he seemed ignorant of the possibility that there might be other customers needing the phone. In the end she was glad. She wanted Elliot to have time to think things over, too. The thousand miles of terrain between them might act as a persuasive premonition. So far, it had with her.

"I used to come here over twenty years ago," Anne told the waitress at the cash register.

"Yuh, me too," she said. Her name tag read 'Pearl.' "Everyday. And I've got the veins to prove it." She swung a doughy leg out from behind the candy case. Her veins were like blue cords that had been twisted so tight that they curled and doubled back on themselves, the swollen knots painful to look at; at any moment it seemed they might burst.

"I'm sorry," Anne said.

Pearl made a sound, short and high-pitched, that meant either 'what do you care,' or 'what do I care.' Then she pivoted about, slid a meringue pie off of the wire rack, plunged a knife into it, and made the sound again.

By the time Anne reached route 20 west to Anacortes, she wished she had not left California. Fragile and lost, she felt that there were now no stones that did not wobble under her feet. Everything – Elliot, her father, the baby, her own motives, the job in Vancouver, even the car she had rented, even

Joe Sanborn, the old guru, alive or dead, with whom she hoped to dine that night – everything was in question. Worse, she had the queasy sense that she was becoming a stranger to herself, that the hard questions were stones against which facets of her character were being rubbed, reshaped, obliterated. It was not a pleasant sensation. She caught her eyes in the rearview mirror; startled, they fled to the windshield and the road ahead.

Above the Skagit River valley the sky hung like a vast scar, very smooth and impermeable, from which fell neither rain nor mist but the phlegmatic drizzle of her youth. The flashy squalls that beat into the California coast moved quickly east, leaving in their wakes true blue skies and a countryside sparkling with the promise of a scrubbed, repentant child – it'll never happen again, it beamed. But this was stolid weather, real in a day-in-day-out way. She remembered – it was more the memory of a feeling – this light everywhere the same expectant matt-gray against which green amplified, and the pinks and reds of the rhododendrons seemed almost frantic.

At the landing eight lanes funnelled down toward the dock, and she chose lane 5 of the two designated 'Orcas,' then shut off the engine. It coughed a few times, shuddering into a deathlike silence. Beside her, a teal Porsche purred to a stop. The man inside – slender, self contained, on the rise, probably a commuter going home to a placid smile and a Cuisinart, maybe a blue-eyed boy who could beat his dad at video games – shook out the *Post Intelligencer* and disappeared between its pages. How she envied him his normality. She saw him greeting people, ordering lunch, and how she hated him for that paper, for caring about the news.

She tried the radio. It squawked back at her, dispersing across the bands. Dumb static. Never mind; in fifteen minutes the ferry would arrive and she would leave the mainland world behind.

The sky brightened tentatively, the drizzle eased up.

Tugging on her rain coat, she glanced over at the box with the urn sitting upright in the passenger seat. There sat Malcolm McBain, waiting for the ferry that would carry him home. Once again, she thought, I am party to one of his whims. It was just a box, ashes, a handful of lightweight chemical compounds; still, he seemed to be watching her, like a shrewd hunter anticipating her last fateful move. She pushed the box onto the floor under the dashboard where it was dark. Just a box. Just ash. Ashes can't burn.

There was a picnic deck cantilevered over the water next to the enormous pilings, and she zigzagged between the cars toward it. People were relaxing in their cars, doors ajar, snacking, reading, talking; children skimmed along the beach like pebbles across still water; two lovers held hands on the quay. It keeps on, she told herself. But she felt no more a part of the festivities, of the happy waiters, the world busy living, the world *just busy*, not thinking, not paying attention, no more related or welcome than if she had been a curse uttered in church.

At the edge of the deck a pay phone hung inside the recesses of an egg-shaped metal box. Glancing at the empty bench, she went to the phone and dialed Elliot's office number. No answer. She tried the steno pool. One of the secretaries told her that he was in class.

"Is it urgent?" the secretary asked.

She paused. "Yes, it is." While she waited, she read the carvings on the back of the picnic bench: Mark+Julie '80; killroy was here; DJ+MT tru luv.

"Hello?" Elliot's voice, concerned, questioning.

"It's me," she said.

"What's wrong?"

"Nothing. I just had to call you."

"Are you sure you're all right?"

"I'm fine, really." She laughed a little laugh. "I feel like an addict. There was this lonely phone and I couldn't resist. I hope it's okay."

A small silence. "Weren't you going to call tonight?"

"I couldn't wait. I know it's silly. I was just missing you. I'm at the ferry landing in Anacortes, and it's been raining, and there's this bench everyone's carved hearts and true love on, and . . . tonight seemed so far away."

"I miss you too," he said.

"You seem so far away."

"It's only three days," he said.

She did not say anything.

"Look Anne, sorry if I sounded abrupt. I'm in the middle of class."

She surveyed the waiting lanes for her rental car. She spotted the teal Porsche, the driver's door hanging ajar, and on its opposite side the white station wagon she had rented. Another dozen or so vehicles had pulled in behind it; now the only way out was into the ferry. "Maybe it won't be three days," she said. There was a silence at his end of the line.

"What are you talking about?"

"I don't know."

She heard Elliot say something to someone, but his words were muffled. Then, as if he was moving the phone, a few rattlings accompanied by the percussions of his palm pressing and lifting off the mouth piece. "What the hell's going on?" he asked in a loud whisper.

"Nothing. I guess I need to figure things out, too."

"I thought we talked before you left, about things. Maybe I should come up."

"No. It's better I'm alone."

Elliot let out an exasperated huff. "I don't think so."

"Maybe it's the best time for me to do this, while I'm away from you. Maybe it won't happen otherwise."

"What won't happen? I told you that I would . . . look, I'll try to get a flight out of here tomorrow afternoon, okay?"

"Don't do that, Elliot."

"I don't know what's . . . Christ. Will you call me tonight? Because I can't really get into things right now."

"Your class."

"Yes, I have a class, I can't help that. And it isn't very private here. You'll call tonight? I'll be waiting," he said.

"I'll call, unless I can't get to a phone," she said, pausing, then, "I love you, Elliot."

"Well I do too. I just don't understand what's . . . "

"We'll talk tonight."

She took the middle of the bench to discourage company. Below, the water frothed around the ranks of tarred pilings opening into Guemes Channel. That smell . . . still alive . . . she breathed deeply. More than any other, the smell of those blackened timbers standing in salt water, and spiced with the barnacles encrusting the eight foot wide signature of tides, the seaweed hanging like a torn skirt where the waters had retreated, sharp and pungent – more than any one smell that salty blend pitched her backwards to childhood. That it was still the same after all the years was comforting. Was wonderful. I haven't changed, I can remember you, it seemed to say. In your blue sailor dress, I remember you, and the dark eyes too big for the face, the smile like a half-moon rising in a pink sky, and your body swaying side to side, giddy with its own newness, one hand woven through your mother's silky fingers, the other buried in your father's mitt. You are remembered. You are.

Think of daddy. He had big hands. He was gone. Nothing could be altered, and it was safe now.

Below her the water swelled in against the pilings, the seaweed swam up to the surface and dropped lifelessly as the wave slid back down. A lacy white V of foam disintegrated before the next wave rushed in.

No, it was over. He could not change, what happened could never change. If the occasional memory disturbed her, it was only phantom pain. It had no reality now. There was only the wondering why. That too would never change.

Try to think of him before it started. After all, he was dead, and from the living death exacted clemency. Though she had done that . . . thought of him before it started, often . . . and that might have been part of the problem. He had been given too much mercy. The line was too slack.

Still, sitting on the bench, watching the waters of Guemes Channel tear away at the old pilings, and smelling those smells, she went back. She went back past the New York time even, where the first tiny rift occurred. That earliest memory was fragmented. Some vital thing had exploded and no one had seen. When Anne unearthed the shards of the event that might have warned someone, it was too late, because it was the repetition of the event that reminded her, that sent her digging through the layers of memory for the missed sign. It seemed to Anne now that she must have blinked the way children will do when what is happening is too big. The imprint remained on the insides of her eyelids, a dark and darkly shimmering negative.

Don't think.

The cold waters of Guemes Channel pushed up between the pilings, roiled around under the dock, withdrew. Overhead, flapping, hovering, necks twisting down this and that way, sea gulls surveyed the landing area for a stray morsel. The young ones were a mottled gray and more restless, more frantic about food. The older gulls, the pure white ones, displayed a bright red dot, like a single drop of blood, on their beaks. The water shoved in and folded back down. In front of the next swell a ragged piece of flesh buoyed up and, when the water shrank away, it hung just below the surface, pale and mossy. Fish bait, she thought. Almost immediately the gulls spotted it. Half a dozen careened down to the water, *screaking* furiously at each other. A young gull dipped under and brought it up, while the next two arrivals grabbed a hold and, below a cloud of anxious latecomers, the three of them yanked deliriously at the fish. It was a small rock cod, orange and black with a fan of spines just behind its gills.

Anne had hooked rock cod before. Deep water fish. If they surfaced too quickly, their stomachs ballooned. One on the line had no choice. The tip of her pole would flutter slightly as its viscera exploded, and from then on she reeled in dead weight. A day of trolling for salmon without luck usually drove her father to rock cod, despite the difficulty in cleaning them, and the fact that he did not regard them as very good eating. He would not quit empty-handed. She let her line out as he did, down to the bottom, so deep she hardly knew when she had one, and they would haul up dead fish until her arms ached. She could still hear him as he cleaned them on the dock planks, cursing their poisonous spines, and their bony bodies, and most of all the fact that they were not salmon. While at home Anne was blamed for the rock cod. "I know it's not sporting, but she had to catch something, didn't she? She's just a kid." And into the freezer it would go, along with the venison and geese and ducks and elk they would never eat.

When was it all good? Where was the man who made her dizzy with joy? The house in Seattle? It had nice memories, didn't it? And she wanted to miss him, damn it, she was supposed to miss him, she wanted to return to a good green place, even if later some of the happy days would vaporize, like a mirage, when the debt came due. Back before it started. She closed her eyes, letting her mind follow the traces back to that good green country.

NINE

The brick house was perched halfway up a steep hillside on the outskirts of the city. Thirty-three flagstone steps climbed up from the street, switching back and forth through dogwood, ivy and ferns, arriving finally on a wide, cement porch surrounded on two sides by the house and on the third by the blue and green falling tapestry of Seattle, the lakes, and Puget Sound beyond. It was the weekend. Anne was home from the Convent and they were all briefly together. Even her father, who couldn't live with them because you could only have one marriage at a time and he already had one (over the mountains where it was yellow and hot) – even he would be here this weekend.

Overhead, cumulus clouds sailed eastward, tacking around the snowy, hovering cone of Mount Rainier. In the mornings when she lay awake, anxious for her mother to rise, she stared outside her bedroom window at the mountain, sometimes flushed pink, sometimes as white as light. And on the clearest mornings she made animals of the dark patches and gave them names. The mountain was always there. She talked to it when she was sad.

Saturday morning. Her mother was inside frying chicken

for the picnic. The radio crooning from atop the refrigerator told Anne she was in a pretty mood. Out on the porch Anne bounced the blue ball, one for the first step, two for how many days she would be home, three he's on the third step, four, five how old she was, six, seven, two bounces for eight because it was a long step, nine, ten. She caught the ball and trotted over to the railing. But he was not on the tenth step, his long, white car not parked next to the curb. She counted ten steps in from the railing so that she would not be tempted to peek, and started over. This time she made it to twenty, not including the extra bounce for the eighth step, before anticipation overcame her. He *had* to be there on the twentieth step, looking up for her, and she had better hurry. She ran to the railing and, as she leaned over it, the ball somehow squirted from her arms, arched down across the empty steps, tapping two, three, then in magnificent, slow-motion leaps, the blue ball gamboled down the street and disappeared around the corner into another world. Gone. Terribly gone.

It never occurred to her to go after it. She was not allowed down the steps. And there was no question that her mother, even though she knew what happened around the corner, would not find it for her. She had been warned about the ball and the porch. There was nothing that could be done. Still, she cried. The ball had looked so happy bouncing down the street. It was a mean thing to do. Blue was her favorite color. And her mother would be mad.

She went inside, crawled into the rocker, and from a distance watched her mother move around the kitchen.

"You lost it, didn't you?" Nellie said. She was turning the chicken over, but the grease was spitting back at her and she had to lean away, working the tongs at arm's length.

The rocker stopped. They always knew, you never had to tell unless they wanted you to say it so that your face got hot and you couldn't keep your eyes up because something heavy in them pushed down. She rolled in her lips and focused on her mother's pedal pushers. They were white with lavender rosebuds below which flared two shapely calves, like twin vases.

"You didn't listen to me, did you?"

"It jumped away way down the street."

"Yes," she said without interest. "Have you learned a lesson?"

She looked up at her mother's face – calm, all-knowing, untouched by the loss. "To not play with my ball on the porch."

"No. To listen to me, honey. You don't have a ball anymore," she said from behind a cupboard door.

"I don't have one anymore," Anne echoed. She began to rock again, repeating to herself *listen listen*, forward back, *listen listen*.

"No, you don't," her mother said suddenly, sharply. "And I'm sorry I gave it to you. Maybe another little girl will find it and take better care of it. Maybe you just aren't ready to have nice things. When your cousin Deirdre was here she listened to me."

The thought of someone else with her ball made her cry again. "I don't like Deirdre," she said.

"Straighten up young lady. Your father will be here any minute and he doesn't like whiners."

Snuffling, Anne rubbed her eyes and rocked in bruised silence. It was not true that she did not like her cousin. Deirdre was a quiet, pretty girl about two years older. The last time she came to visit she gave Anne a small Eskimo doll with real seal skin boots, but when she had gone her mother told Anne the doll was too nice to play with, that she could set it on her dresser and look at it.

Behind the rocker the screen door opened. And the thing she had not taken care of, the thing she was not ready to have and did not deserve suddenly floated down like a great blue bubble, plopped in her lap, then rolled over her knees and down her legs out across the kitchen floor and came to a stop at her mother's feet. Anne was horrified.

"Daddy!" Up into his arms she fled.

"Hello princess. Did you send your ball out to meet me?"

"You weren't there, I counted, I did."

"Well, it went a-huntin," he said. "And it bagged a bear, a *hungry* bear." He tried to nibble on her neck.

From the kitchen her mother stood watching, a chicken wing dangling from the tongs. "We've just been discussing her negligence," she said.

"Her what?"

Nellie Gallagher ignored his question. Instead, she picked up the ball, went to the hall closet and stuffed it in an empty hat box where it stayed until Anne forgot about it.

Mal McBain arranged his daughter in the rocker. "Any coffee left?" he asked.

"Why are you late?"

"Huh . . . had some things to go over with my lawyer."

"On Saturday?"

"What difference does it make, you're not even ready?" He dropped a scrap of chicken in his mouth and grabbed Nellie's waist. "Come on, give me a hug, gorgeous."

Not seeming to want to, she draped her arms over his shoulders. "Anne's been anxious. She doesn't understand your working, especially when it's her day with you."

At the mention of her name, Anne leapt out of the chair and, squeezing her body between the two of them, insisted she be picked up again. Mal McBain chuckled, launching a search and tickle mission that sent her into squealing wiggles. Her mother moved back to the counter and began packing the picnic basket.

"Her hair needs combing," Nellie said.

Now he was here and it did not matter, even her mother being quiet, making the air in the room hard to breathe, did not matter. They were going for a picnic out in the boat and she would wear the orange pillows and fill her pail with white clams.

Seating herself in one of the high-backed maple chairs,

Nellie raised her eyebrows at Anne, who understood she was to fetch the comb from the bathroom. When she returned, she positioned her body facing out between the flowered pedal pushers, holding her head straight, watching her father sip coffee.

"Stop moving."

Anne took one nervous step back, but her scalp stung.

"If you stopped pulling away from me it wouldn't hurt."

"It hurts a little, mommy," she said tightly. It was hard to keep her head still. There was something wrong. It wasn't usually like this. She clutched the sides of her sun dress.

"It can't hurt, I'm holding it at the top."

Down through her heavy chestnut hair the comb yanked, as if coerced by something outside them, by an old, dark force. Her head felt sore and hot.

"Ease up, Nellie."

"This is how I comb my hair. See, I've got it at the roots."

"You're hurting her." He set his cup aside.

"Is she crying? Because you're here, that's why."

The tears would get her in trouble, she knew. She braced herself, but they popped out like warm little fish racing two by two down her cheeks. Her mother was hurrying and rough now, on purpose, because he told her not to, because he was late.

"Here, let me do it."

"Fine, if that'll stop her whining."

He lifted her to his lap and she felt the weight of his big, soft hand on the back of her head, the other one loosening the tangles at the bottom, working gently up until her head cooled and her hair fell in smooth wavelets.

"I'll get the Mae Wests," he said, setting Anne back on her feet.

When he had left the room, Nellie narrowed her eyes. "We've had enough of your little act. Enough." Her lips were hard and white.

Anne climbed in the rocker, determined to be quiet. It was

so much nicer when her mother wasn't mad, when she talked fast and squeezed Anne's hand for no reason. It would be best now to be quiet.

Mal burst up through the basement hatch and tossed the life jackets on top of Anne. Pushing an orange panel aside, she saw that he had made big 'Os' of his eyes and mouth. "I didn't see you," he whispered. She beamed back at him and wiggled her fingers to wave.

The kitchen was a mess, but the basket was packed and Nellie was hanging her apron on the back of the pantry door. "I'm ready. I guess we'd better call the harbor office and check on the weather."

"Nel!" He threw an arm around her and led her to the window. "Have you looked outside? Does that look like anything but spring fever and a few more freckles?"

Nellie blushed. "No freckles. I'm getting a hat." She broke away and headed for the closet. "You're sure about the weather?"

"Huh . . . well, if you don't trust me, Nellie . . . " There was the suggestion of a warning in his tone. Anne heard it and avoided her mother's eyes. They couldn't fight, not now. They were going for a picnic, out in the boat. Her mother could get mad, turn around and be happy, but not him, not her daddy. He would stay mad. He would stay mad till it was too late.

Nellie's lips parted, she seemed about to say something, changed her mind and murmured, "Oh Bear," (he liked that nickname), "of course I do. It's just that *I* don't know, and there's no harm in asking." She paused, glanced at Anne nesting among the life jackets, made a quick dispelling gesture with her hand, saying, "But you're right. It's a beautiful day."

They drove over to Mukilteo where he moored the *Molly*, an eighteen foot outboard named for his favorite hunting dog whom he had shot accidentally when she leapt from a point in front of the barrel. Outside the harbor mouth the *Molly* cut a white gash deep into the blue space as she headed for a cove on the east coast of Whidbey Island where at low tide the butter clams bubbled, like sweat on the sand. The bow flung itself up and down as if the *Molly* was that old Labrador, unleashed, tracking a fresh scent over the rolling hills of eastern Washington where he hunted in the fall. There was wind out of the west and clouds, too, steady-going but broken up, nothing solid, nothing organized, and the cold waters of the Sound glittered back, hard and defiant.

Anne sat with her back to her father, hypnotized by the wake surging up in clean, white plumes, fanning out, softening, the water sewing itself up miraculously until even the seam of foam was gone and what the *Molly* did to the water disappeared. Where they had been she could no longer make out.

After a while, the water had its usual suggestive effect.

"I have to go," she told her mother.

"Anne." There was irritation in her voice. "Can't you wait?"

"Take the wheel, Nel. Here, princess," and he took her hand. "Go off the back of the boat like I do."

Confused, she peered over the stern at the churning props.

"I can't," she said.

"Why not?" Winking back at Nellie, his face quizzical, he said, "I do."

The girl looked up at the V of black hair on his chest. She wanted to keep away from his smile. It made her uncomfortable. It reminded her of a boy at school who told her a word and snickered when she repeated it for his friends. But to please him, to give the right answer was all that she wished. She appealed to her mother's hair rolled in like a sea shell on the back of her head. Nellie was busy driving the boat. The engine was loud. A high, bright sun made her squint, and turned the water to the blackest blue. She really had to go. "'Cause I have to sit," she tried.

"Oh? Now why is that?"

There was something he wanted, something funny she did not know how to say, and she blinked up at him, a small, contrite smile trembling on her lips. She sensed she was disappointing him, but felt helpless to fix it. For the first time his teasing was not fun. She did not understand it. It made her feel bad. *Molly* bounced on across the water and Anne squeezed her father's hand to steady herself. "Daddy! I'll fall into the water."

"Here," he barked, shoving a bail bucket at her just as the boat lurched against another swell. "I'll hold you."

Even through the cool, salty air she could smell his after-shave lotion. In the mornings when he was there with them she would station herself on the toilet lid, fascinated by the neat, pink roads cutting up and down through the white foam, the hot water rinses and finally, sifting out of the steam, the after-shave lotion – as sharp and spicy as a winter blossom. Now though, it seemed too close, too much.

Anne pulled down her panties and squatted over the bucket. So that she could not see him watching her, she shut her eyes and focused on the reassuring drone of the engine. His big fingers pressed into her shoulders. When it was over, he emptied the contents of the bucket over the side, rinsed it out, and rejoined Nellie. From the back of the boat Anne heard them laughing and her mother's singsong "Oh Mal," which meant he had said something naughty. Suddenly chilled, Anne hunched inside her Mae West.

Diagonal gusts beat eastward. Everywhere islands rose out of the water. The sun seemed to pivot directly overhead before it started down the western sky. Her back to her parents, she sat admiring the vast, watery garden. She felt very small and live.

The wake began to curve gradually. Around the next rocky point *Molly* slowed, her putt-putting conspicuous in the quiet cove, and bringing to mind her mother's shoes clicking down the long hallway at the Convent. Except for an apron of sand at one end, the banks of the cove rose steeply, forming a solemn green gallery of Douglas fir. The water inside was as smooth as a slab of jade.

"Tide's really out. Could be a minus tide. We'll have to keep our eyes on the boat," her father said, cutting the engine and letting her drift in. Gasoline fumes wafted back over them. Anne was watching the surface of the water for the moment it became transparent. When it did, rocks appeared cankered with barnacles and seaweed.

Mal McBain hauled up the motor, went forward and jumped in the water with the bow line, towing the boat in until the water dropped to his knees. Nellie touched up her lipstick while they waited for him to find a suitable anchor rock. Last summer he lost the anchor when he tossed it overboard without tying it down. They had been mooching for sockeye off Point No Point when they found themselves drifting too fast with the current, so her father threw out the anchor. Neither of his buddies would volunteer to dive for it, even though he said it could not be very deep. And her father could not swim; he said his muscles made him sink. "Rock's just as good," he had declared, dismissing his mistake.

There he was, plunging his hand into the water, groping around for a rock light enough to budge (so that he could get the line under it) and heavy enough to hold the *Molly*. Anne was growing impatient.

"Okay," he puffed, straightening, wading back to the boat. "Got your pail, princess? I see a lot of dimples in the sand."

"Yup. My pail and my shovel and my Mae West."

"Leave your shoes here," her mother said.

"But the rocks . . . " She looked at her mother's face, the implacable smile, the raised eyebrows that said 'do not question me, do not make a scene, you cannot win.'

"You'll ruin them if you get them wet."

"Nellie, they're tennis shoes. The barnacles are sharp," her father said.

Nellie shrugged. "She wanted to wear her new ones. I can't afford to keep replacing them."

"I'll pay for them, all right?"

Nellie shrugged again.

As he carried Anne to the beach he told her, "We'll just keep an old pair in the boat from now on."

Nellie let her pretty calves down into the water. "Ooooh, it's cold," she squealed.

"Cold as a whore's heart," he muttered.

As she wobbled through the water, she stared at his back. "What does that mean?"

"Huh? Nothing. It's a saying."

She seemed to debate that silently as he spread out the plaid blanket; then in a quick, high voice, a voice so happy it made Anne flinch, Nellie said, "Let's eat now while we still have the beach," sliding a sideways glance at Mal, "then we'll find that patch of grass."

His eyes went big, clowning eagerness. "What do you say, princess? Are you hungry?"

Anne nodded. Her mother wanted to eat now, so they would eat now.

While *Molly* rocked lazily in the shallow water, the three lounged on the blanket eating fried chicken and the carrot salad her mother had prepared late the night before, dipping their fingers into a jar of sweet pickles, tearing off hunks of french bread. Her father ate both heels because they made his teeth strong, he said, and to prove it, he crunched down some of the smaller chicken bones to Anne's delighted objections.

Before them the receding tide had exposed a litter of briny driftwood, rocks furry with moss, barnacles, red starfish, sea cucumbers, bruised looking mussels, little greenish crabs and all kinds of seaweed strewn like the entrails of a prehistoric monster – a great, glistening sea feast bubbling and snapping and hissing in the sunlight.

Anne and her mother reached out for the same piece of chicken and snatching her hand back, Anne smiled appealingly. Her mother was so pretty in her lavender blouse and the big white hat with the purple ribbon tied in a bow under her chin, her green eyes and freckled cheeks and the way she had of looking excited just because you were, even though you knew she wasn't really, she was just trying to be nice. She was looking that way now as she handed the piece of chicken to her. "So you're going to get us some clams for dinner? Do you think you can fill the pail?"

"Yes. I'm gonna look for the dimples."

Her father stood up to slap the sand off his damp khakis. The basket was re-packed, the blanket shaken out and folded over Nellie's arm. "We're going for a walk, honey," her mother said.

Anne looked up from the hole she was digging. Her mother was smiling softly at her.

"I have something for you." It was a box of Cracker Jacks, her favorite.

"Thank you, mommy. Can I go too?"

"We need you to watch *Molly*," her father said, and he picked up a stick, walked to the edge of the beach and drew a line in the sand. "If the water reaches this line, call us. We won't be far, just up that hill a ways."

Then they were climbing up the muddy bank and into the trees. For awhile she could see her father's white shirt flickering behind branches, disappearing into the greenwood. Anne dropped to the sand and shook out the caramel coated popcorn into the skirt of her sundress; it was the prize she wanted first, down at the bottom of the box – this time, a yellow, plastic ring with a tiny white ball for a gem. She thrust her arm out, hand limp for the kiss of an imaginary suitor.

"I'm the princess," she announced. Out in the cove *Molly* bobbed in agreement. "Don't go over the line," she warned the water. "If you go over the line, you're a monster and I'll call my daddy." One by one, she ate the Cracker Jacks.

Around the abandoned pail the cold water swirled, fell back, rushed up again, retreated, draining through the tangle of seaweed with a long, tired hiss. The tide was moving in. She dropped the Cracker Jacks box and went to the rescue of her pail which was burrowing into the sand. Whenever a wave fell back, she quickly surveyed the soggiest stretches for the teeny dimples that meant a clam was trying to escape. She kept only the small ones, the white shelled butter clams, tossing the horse clams into the surf because, though her father did not care – he ate anything – biting into those big, gritty stomachs that popped like a balloon under water made her shiver. Each clam was rinsed off and placed, not dropped, into the bucket so that its shell did not crack. They were then anointed with handfuls of water to keep them fresh.

Overhead, clouds blotted out the sun intermittently, piling into the blue hollows until the sky seemed to sag darkly in places and the cove went gray and the wind scooted across the water as if someone was chasing it. The tide surged up and slid down, retreating a little less each time. The seaweed and starfish, the barnacled rocks, sea cucumbers, purple mussels, and baby green crabs were now completely submerged. She dragged the bucket backwards and a half hour later dragged it back again, but the soggy boundary gave up fewer and fewer clams. It seemed to her that a lot of time had passed since they had left. Her feet had become numb and remote. But the pail was almost full and when it was, she told herself, when it was just full, they would appear, they would be happy about the clams. Then obliquely she noticed color darting beyond her on the receding tide. The Cracker Jacks box. Dropping her shovel, she ran after it, but her feet were awkwardly stiff and she stopped when she saw a wave bend over the box. It surfaced behind, and she could just make out the smiling blue sailor on the package still saluting as he floated toward the boat and out to sea. The boat.

Molly was tugging wildly on her leash. Anne looked for the line her father had drawn in the sand. It was gone. The beach had shrunk to a thin, sodden band at the foot of an abrupt slope. When had it happened? Why hadn't she seen it? She stood at the bottom calling for them, twisting the plastic ring around her finger as she listened for an answer, for a sound; calling again, the water crawling toward her feet. *Hurry, hurry*, it said, *I'm coming to get you.* Glancing over her shoulder, she stared at *Molly*, now forever away from her and going crazy in the chop, jerking at the bow line. A wet gust shoved past her, catching up above in the heavy boughs of Douglas fir. They reeled slowly, like giant dancers. Another gust and another until there wasn't any separation between them; it was a steady blast. The cove seemed to swell alive. Everything was moving. She screamed and begged and whispered for them to come back. She grabbed the picnic basket and the bucket of clams and pushed them up the slope behind a tree trunk to keep them from sliding down.

It started to rain. She tried to calm herself. She thought of the radio in the kitchen that morning and the blue ball going away and coming back and her mother telling her to *listen listen* and the feel of her father's hand covering the whole back of her head. It was hard to be calm, she was shivering so. Then, as if they were in the next room, she summoned her mother and father again, and the sound of her own questioning voice venturing out, small and clear and hers, into the roaring cove, to be torn apart instantly, as if she had not said a word, only imagined she had, as if she and *Molly* and where her parents were did not matter, the sound of her brief living voice made of the trembling inside her a strange braveness.

Half standing, half sitting against the slope, her arms hugging the front panels of her Mae West, she watched the rain come down crazy on the water, slashing one way then another. The wind was everywhere, a booming that seemed to erase the parts of things. It was funny, she thought, how the noise made everything wash together, even her mind began to drift about until everything seemed in some way the same. It was scary and wonderful, the way the wind was to *Molly*, to the water, to the big clouds and tall trees, and to her too.

Beyond the mouth of the cove white caps dotted the gray water. The rain was powerful and steady and suddenly had a weight to it that sent her scrambling up the muddy slope to crouch under the Douglas fir with the picnic basket and pail of clams. Her hair hung in wet, pointed ropes. Her pink legs and hands against the dark earth scared her. Time went by in chunks, like a dream that kept waking her up. Wasn't it raining where they were? Weren't they tired, didn't they miss her?

She heard her own name flap by on the wind – her mother's voice – and Anne twisted around and saw her skidding down through the trees followed by her father, whose black hair made a wild slash across his forehead. She had never seen him so mussed up and she knew then that this was serious, that she had better be quiet and grown up.

"Are you all right, honey?" Her mother pulled her against her stomach. "We were very lost." She took her daughter's face between her hands and looked into her eyes. "But we're going home now, we're going to go get warm and dry and I'm sorry we were gone so long. It was scary, wasn't it? Did you call very long?"

"No," she lied.

"You did just right. You stayed put."

"If she'd kept calling we might have found her," her father said as he slid past them. "Christ. The bow line's slack."

"What?"

"The boat's loose." He was standing in the rain in the low surf, his shirt open to his broad, hairy chest, his face ruddy and warped in anger. "Tide might push her in, but we can't wait." Not looking back, he waved his arm and his voice went tame. "Come on over here, princess."

"What?" Nellie stammered, then, comprehending, she cried, "No."

"She has a life jacket. She knows how to swim, she swims like a fish."

"Not in this . . ." Nellie was trembling, "this storm. She's a child, Mal, no."

"Nellie," he yelled, his big arm gesturing, snapping out and back like a boxer's jab, "neither one of us can swim. We don't have life jackets. Why am I paying for swimming lessons at that fancy place, huh?"

"Not for this." She squeezed her daughter to her side.

Trying to be persuasive, he lowered his voice, but it stayed taut, and even Anne wondered. She would have done anything he wanted but he wanted it so much it scared her a little. "All she has to do," he was saying, "is swim out, grab the bow line, and swim back with it."

"It's too far and too rough. What if the bow line won't reach?"

"It'll reach, Nellie. I promise you, it'll reach."

"No. We can wait for someone to come along."

"In this? Who? Who's going to come along?" He glanced sharply in her direction, his expression a mixture of disgust and rage. Anne watched his hands at his sides opening and closing as if he was trying to hold on to something that kept slipping away. A second later, the sight of them too much for him to bear, he tore off his glasses and tossed them at Nellie. "I'll be damned if I'll let a thirty thousand dollar Chriscraft break up on the rocks. I'll be damned if *I'll* wait," and he plowed out into the cold water.

The girl and her mother watched the pale moon on the back of his head as it bobbed away from them, every now and then going under, appearing beyond the next wave smaller and more cherished and less real in the growing distance. Just moments before he had been there in front of them, with them, big, red-faced and alive, now floating far off like the blue ball, maybe out of the cove and around the point into another world. Because her mother would not let her swim. His muscles make him sink, he said. And oh, who could bring *him* back? Anne stared at his vacant glasses lying in the sand at the foot of the slope. All by themselves, she thought, all alone out there with his muscles, and he would sink. I could have swum, she thought, he said I could have. I don't have any muscles. And oh, *what* could bring him back?

But he reached the boat and they saw him fold his body over the side, heard the engine start up, watched him jerk in the bow line – there was an empty loop at its end – and, still standing, aim the boat at them. Gathering up the picnic basket, clams and blanket, the girl and her mother jumped down off the bank to wait in the shallows. Anne picked up his glasses and rinsed them in the water. Nellie, apparently, was not surprised he had made it.

"Not the clams," she said. "Pour them out."

"But mommy . . ." She stuck her hand in the bucket, palming one of the little white clams, let it go, swished around for another. They were hers. Cool, pebbly, abundant, they swam around her fingers. She had dug a long time. And when her feet hurt from the cold, she had kept digging. Why couldn't she keep them? What had she done wrong? "They're the good kind," she said.

"Don't argue with me now, Anne. We have to wade out and they're too heavy to fuss with. Pour them out."

Mournful, confused, she looked up at her mother's profile, then back at the pail, selected a few clams and dropped them one by one into the surf, but sensing peripherally her mother's leveled eyes, she emptied the pail at once.

Over the chop *Molly* leapt toward them, careened left, throwing up a fan of cold salt water, and stopped within arm's reach. Nellie yanked Anne backwards.

"Well don't stand there gawping. You didn't want to swim, right?" he hollered.

To Anne gazing up, his stance, his presence was king-size – legs braced apart, one hand on his hip, the other on the wheel, his chest heaving and the white shirt snapping at his back, his hair whipped up, his forehead as imposing as a stone wall, his gray eyes flashing while the rain pounded down and the wind ran relentlessly at them.

Nellie tossed the things over the side and pushed herself up into the boat. With one arm Mal reached over and plucked Anne from the surf, shoving her down into the bow compartment where the fishing tackle and gas cans were stored. "Stay there. You too," he said, grabbing Nellie's arm. "Get down there."

"No, I'm staying up here with you." Her face was set, her

lips puckered in defiance. The boat pitched awkwardly in the crosscurrents. She clamped both hands over the back of the seat.

"Suit yourself," he said, and the boat squirted around and headed for the mouth of the cove.

When they cleared the opening, *Molly* slowed suddenly, smashing into a hill-sized swell that rolled underneath like the back of a huge sea beast, humped behind them, the boat then plunging down, slamming again into the next swell, Anne's body jarred each time. Through her shoulders and hips she felt the danger, the bad waters on the other side of the floor. Very soon the smell of gasoline and old fish bait and the lurching up and down convulsed her stomach. She tightened her throat but the warm bile rose and spilled when the bow dropped and sent another shock through her bones.

From her dark hole she could see them hanging onto the windshield, their faces blotchy and worried, popping up and down in front of the clouds, like carnival targets. Her mother turned, wobbled two steps over, clutched his arm, and kissed him full on the mouth. For a moment, his hawk-eyed intensity relaxed. A wave broke over the stern. And even though he had to shout above the wind and engine, Anne could tell that he was not mad anymore. "Gotta hit 'em straight on, but I just can't figure the damn crosscurrents in the Sound."

Nellie glanced nervously at the sloshing water.

"High tide makes it worse," he continued. "Pumps everything up."

The boat slid down the trough and was climbing up the next swell when a starboard wave jostled them and they rocked sideways over the crest, taking on more water.

"Should I bail?" she quivered out.

"Not yet. Just hang on." He was very excited. He seemed to be actually enjoying himself. He reached over and patted Nellie's fanny. "*Almost* as wild a ride," he said, his eyes gleaming.

Then the engine gasped, sputtered, and stopped. The wind

boomed up into the void.

"Great timing." Her father bent down to where she lay, grimacing at the smell of her vomit, and hauled up the red gas can. "Take the wheel," he said to Nellie. "When I get it hooked up, throttle down and straighten her out head on, then open her up. Remember, *head on*."

Anne watched him weave back to the engine, drop to his knees, yank lose and re-attach the black, rubber hose to the new can and, as he eyed the pressure gauge, begin squeezing the bulb. His arm was wet and shiny so that each time he squeezed the bulb she could see the thick muscle curving across his upper arm ridge, flatten out, then again, ridge and go flat. Behind him an iron gray wall was piling up as *Molly* drifted down another swell. Anne was so seasick and weak she stopped caring what happened. Her eyes wandered from the lavender rosebuds on her mother's pedal pushers to the mounds of waves with the lacy tufts to her father's jerky movements with the pull starter, the stern dipping water onto him, kindly, almost as if he was hot and wanted cooling off, and she thought how silly he looked and instantly felt bad. But the not caring crowded back in behind a rush of nausea. She closed her eyes. The floor boards shuddered against her.

The engine coughed, gurgled bravely, choked off, coughed again, began bleating like a stray kid, finally ripped out a steady wail.

"Throttle down, throttle down and straighten her out . . . down Nel, down," he screamed. The boat veered sharply, burying half the stern. She saw him grab for the side of the boat, miss, and grab again, this time catching an aluminum pole that was part of the canopy frame. "*Now* gun her," he was yelling. "Now." When they had straightened out he crawled back to the seats. Breathing hard, staring at her face as if he saw something he hadn't recognized before, something that frightened him, because it was fear Anne heard in his voice when he said, "You almost dumped me overboard," a dazed, plaintive, childlike fear.

"I didn't know which wave to aim at. You said the cross-currents . . . "

"The biggest one," he interrupted. "Christ, Nel," his expression still confused, frowning into a kind of pleading question. "The big one, Nellie, you have to aim at the biggest because they can bury you. They can kill you."

They were two hours getting back to Mukilteo, a run that normally took less than an hour. No one spoke. The *Molly* settled into a strained rhythm as she negotiated the storm, cutting northeast finally around the bottom of Whidbey Island and up across Saratoga Passage. A man in yellow foulies met them at the slip, caught the lines, and tied the boat off while Nellie threw the bumpers over the side. Mal McBain jumped onto the dock, smiling and shaking his head at the man. "Thanks," he said. For the moment it had stopped raining but his clothes were plastered to his skin. The wind pushed up hard off the water.

"How's it around the point?" the man in the yellow slicker asked. His eyes were the same gray as the water, only faded and set inside identical creased fans. Red and brown spots mottled his face.

"Not pretty," Mal McBain said. "Twelve foot swells and heavy chop and tide rips half a mile long."

"Happen to see a blue gurdy rig name *Lost Legacy?*"

"No, didn't see anyone. I left a brand new anchor up in Patrick's Cove and nearly lost my life trying to catch her," he said, indicating *Molly*. "From that point on, I didn't see anything but the next one off the bow."

The fisherman gazed past Mal McBain out beyond the harbor mouth where the gray waves crashed into each other. "She's got a temperamental pump," he murmured. "Hope my boys had sense enough to duck into the canal and wait it out."

"I would've done the same myself except for them," he said, nodding at Nellie and Anne. "The girl's sick," he added. Then, "I could use a drink. How about a short one?"

The man in the yellow slicker glanced over at the woman

and girl, eyeing them for a moment with a mixture of tenderness and resentment as if they were somehow disabled, cogitating while he cupped a match and lit a cigarette and took quick stock of them whose weakness forced this man and his boat through a storm he had no business trying to weather, then blinking, the remoteness came back and he declined.

Still seasick, Anne staggered behind her mother up to the car. Half an hour later her father emerged from the Sea Horse Tavern relaxed and talkative, but her mother's low voice shot back and they argued into a jagged silence on the way home.

Curled up in the back seat, Anne wondered at that morning. How far away it seemed. How different everything now looked. Some small thing had come undone, some connection come loose, and to think about it made her head hurt the way it did at school when she had to read. Why did he tell the man in the yellow slicker it was a new anchor when it was a rock? Why did he say she could swim and her mother say no? And why did they get lost? They were not supposed to do that. They were supposed to hear her when she called. And they did not.

The inside did not feel like the outside anymore. It was true she was safe, her daddy was here and they were going home, the three of them. There would be light and food and he would snuggle her up into his arms. But she did not feel safe. She did not feel happy. She did not want to be held. For the first time in her life doubt had crept up to awareness, but she had no words for what caused it. The more she thought about it, the more she feared something was about to fall apart. But what?

Holding onto herself tightly, she let a dulling isolation envelope her. She stared at the bald spot on the back of her father's head; there were no meticulously combed strands hiding it anymore. It was a surprisingly perfect pink hole in the middle of his hair.

How she wished her mother had not argued, not said it was his fault. Yet she sensed obliquely that he was wrong, that she would not have been sick, her mother not scared, not angry now, that maybe if he had listened and taken better care as she should have with the blue ball that morning, things would not be all broken. How she wished her mother was not crying.

The windshield wipers slapped rhythmically back and forth as the car swished along the wet roads toward the house with thirty-three steps. Around them the dusk thickened. City lights spilled across the darkening streets, bleeding water colors into each other. Anne rolled over, faced the seat back – she did not want to see his bald spot, it was naked and ugly – and with her finger, printed her name on the leather until sleep released her.

TEN

The Washington State Ferry slipped past Shannon Point undetected and, turning, issued suddenly from out of the mist like a ghostly hotel, announcing its arrival with a monotonic bellow, followed by three impertinent blats. Lined with cars, its jaws seemed to widen as the boat drew closer and, when it reached the outermost pilings, the engines reversed, churning up the water so that the ferry appeared to be foaming at the mouth as it slid between the timbers up to the landing. There were no spectators behind the tiers of windows; they were all crowded against the railing on the second deck. Anacortes was the beginning and end of the ferry boat's run, and it would be completely emptied.

Anne jogged back to her car. The man in the teal Porsche was revving his engine. From the cracked window cigarette smoke curled up over the roof, and a faint scent of cloves lingered on the damp air. She made a mental note to check his plates when they boarded: he couldn't be from Washington, least of all the islands.

The unloading process did not take long, she remembered, yet she felt impatient. Then, maybe the plunging sensation in her gut was not impatience but dread, since by any reasonable account she was headed for a wall of endings. All aflutter for the blow. Shivering, she started the motor and flipped on the heat. Well, then, let's get it over with, she thought.

The cars ahead of her began to inch forward, though they had no place to go yet. She lifted her foot off the brake and closed the gap. The ferrymen wrestled with the vehicle ramp, hauling it left, right, shoving it back toward the boat, finally bouncing on one corner of it to flatten it against the concrete. The driver of the pickup to her right, a middle-aged man wearing a Mariners baseball hat, stuck his head out his window and waved to her. When it was clear he had her attention, he raised his eyebrows and pointed to the nonexistent space between her car and the next. She nodded back: go ahead.

When Anne met Elliot she remembered feeling immensely relieved that she had found someone with whom she could happily spend her life, that now she would not have to bother with the time-consuming and slightly demeaning search in which people of her age were obliged to engage. She felt the same way about marine mammalogy. It suited her. It would be a long-lived interest. And the two together – meeting Elliot, having a calling – seemed to put her ahead.

At the top of the windshield a collection of drizzle points finally grew big enough for gravity to notice.

Anne sighed. There was a certain predictability about risk taking after awhile. How risky could it be if you knew what was going to happen? I'll handle it, she told herself. I'll scatter the ashes on Orcas Island. And when I get back to California, *if* I get back to California, I'll just grit my teeth and have the abortion. Do my job, make new friends, change the house around – that would help. Simplify. Live a quiet, boring life. Without Elliot. Without any man, for a long while.

The iron ramp was adjusted, the great chain drawn aside. Up on the highest deck in the pilot house, a tall figure in white stood watching. The captain. Anne lifted the box with the urn from the floor and set it on the passenger seat. Sorry, she whispered, then checked herself. Ashes, that's all. She looked up for the white figure; it was gone.

From out of the mouth of the ferry, cars squirted two by two, the buses and big trailers laboring past and, streaming down from the upper decks came the foot traffic, people with bicycles, backpacks, suitcases, an old man with a birdcage, the whole bustling outflow orchestrated by three young ferrymen in yellow jackets and plastic covered caps. When the last car clanked off the ramp, the ferrymen turned around, beckoned the waiting lanes down according to island, taking tickets and swinging arms toward designated parking lanes. They were friendly, officious, and reassuring; they had the ferry loaded again in fifteen minutes.

It's still . . . *fun*, she thought – the comings and goings. What a wonder. And that she cared . . . how nice. The minute she had left California, she felt herself separating from the rest of the world, her life splitting off and free falling. But this place and these moments were exhilarating, and there was something blessed about that. For the first time that day she was not missing Elliot.

She ended up in the cavernous midsection, a bus in back and a family wagon in front. One car honked, another answered, several more joined in – crazy hoots ricocheting off the steel walls like trapped birds. She dropped her head, embarrassed. Next to her an older couple sidestepped out of their car and, while they locked it up, Anne waited, frowning at the noise, then she slid out and headed for the stairs that led up to the lounge and promenade decks. Three cars back she noticed that the man in the teal Porsche was one of the horn honkers. Yahoo, she said under her breath, and cut over to the stairs.

The ferry shuddered. Its great engines rumbled up, enveloping Anne and the rest of the passengers ascending the stairs. When she came out into the lounge and the door to the stairwell whished shut behind her, the roar instantly retreated to the background against which the early evening sounds of the passengers loosened and warmed. The lounge windows were steamy, the booths beneath them crowded. Except for a trio of boys chasing around the decks and a woman in rubber boots tossing bread to the flock of trailing gulls, everyone had settled inside. Making a complete tour, Anne took a seat up front in the observation area facing a row of windows that curved back along both sides of the ferry. Directly behind was the cafeteria; a line had already formed. One of the trio burst through a door to her right, sending a blast of wet air across the seats. There would be two more after him. She felt chilled. And the smell of food . . . she couldn't decide if she was hungry or queasy.

Through the gray mist across the gray water the ferry moved, making a soft port turn into Rosario Strait where just beyond at its western perimeter they would enter Thatcher Pass, they would enter the part of the archipelago known as the maze.

A couple holding hands drifted up to the windows and the woman, smiling politely at Anne, tugged her man to the side, out of Anne's line of view. They were eating hotdogs, and Anne decided that she very much wanted one, a burnt hotdog with mustard and relish, the bun toasted and butter melting into it, she could practically taste it, tangy and juicy and meat-sweet. Even as her stomach twisted in rejection, her mouth watered. A craving.

If Elliot was with her now, she thought, he would get up and fetch her as many hotdogs as she could eat, presenting them with a loving smile, gifts in which it seemed he would know the greater satisfaction. And six weeks later he would drive her to Dr. Havenstein's to keep her crummy appointment and put things back the way they were. He could do that – juggle the irreconcilable. It was getting harder, she realized, impossible maybe, not to translate his attitude into the rough language of worth. Where was the bottom line? How much *did* she rate?

Not enough, she thought.

Outside the rain streaked windows Cypress Island rose in a mountainous green blur. At the shoreline, as if someone had taken a cleaver and squared it, was a wall of sheer cliffs. Here and there plumes of surf erupted against the walls, slid back down into the sea, reached up again. The ferry pushed on toward Thatcher Pass, leaving Cypress as it fell off to the starboard and became part of where they had been, part of the past. The movement and the leaving behind relaxed her: the further from the mainland she was, it seemed, the safer she would be. She felt a great longing to be alone and extravagantly miserable, to be like one of the smaller islands that disappeared at high tide, nameless and unwitnessed except by a few old timers with dislocated memories. Like Joe Sanborn. But within that isolation a small panic flared up, a lick of fire on the gray flats, and the thought of calling Elliot as soon as they docked on Orcas, to hear him tell her he loved her, not to worry, *courage*, became for awhile obsessive.

It was nearly 5:30 by the ship's brass clock. Anne got up and wandered into the cafeteria. At the head of the line stood some teenaged girls, a couple of businessmen behind them. She stared at the dark wall their backs created.

She bought a hotdog and to put it out, a glass of milk. Her seat in the observation area had been taken, but she found another two rows back, and flopped down in it, mentally shrugging. Maybe it was not a craving. Maybe she was just plain hungry. And anyway, if he could do it, she, too, could learn to juggle the irreconcilable, could feed the life she would later extinguish, like a bad case of indigestion.

Ahead to port, the small, twin humps of James Island – two green turtles kissing in perpetuity. Behind James was Decatur lurking low in the mist, and forming the southern gatepost of Thatcher Pass through which in five or ten minutes the ferry would carefully slip. Then they would be deep inside the archipelago, unable to see the mainland in the east where they had begun. Though that morning in California, and just a few moments ago as they crossed Rosario Strait, the idea – of leaving behind, of hiding – had been appealing, the prospect of it now bothered her. In space, Elliot Newhouse was a thousand miles away. The physical separation seemed only to encourage the emotional distance that was opening up between them. It was a terrible feeling, a kind of partial death.

If there were no ferries or airplanes, if this was the year her father was born, and she would have to wait for quiet seas, use a dugout or skiff to reach the mainland, then start walking south along the coast, she could be months getting back to Elliot, by which time the question of the baby would have been decided and, lean or round, incarnating on his doorstep, she would have been still looking for a smile.

Of course, regardless, Elliot would smile, she thought. He was easy that way. In the end, if no other choice remained, he was at worst accepting, and at best an amiable proponent of his side of the fence. Elliot would not run away, or seek solitude, or want to remake himself. He liked where he was, he liked being around people who spoke the same language. And in fundamental ways he thought who Elliot Newhouse was, was just fine. True, he had fallen in love with a woman to whom he could not commit, but he was making that relationship fit within the contours of his life, he was dressing the lawless up in laws.

His drinking had increased. It used to be when they would have a few days together Elliot would linger in bed. He would flip on the morning news, have a cup or two of coffee, maybe read while Anne showered. Making mental lists, he established a consciousness before entering the day as one would a reputation in a field before delivering an opinion. With Elliot, thought truly preceded action. He plodded. He hated to lose.

But lately he was either up and already outside splitting wood, tinkering with one thing or another, cooking breakfast, or he was dozing, because he had been awake, long before dawn; he had lain beside her, staring at the light fixture in the middle of the ceiling, tapping his fingertips together. He seemed like a man who could not quite believe that his original calculations had been off, who went over and over them silently, not conceding error yet, not until he had found the simple, obvious, correctable flaw. At these moments he was seldom aware that Anne, too, was awake and watching him, sensing his frustration and wanting to help, but not helping, not lately. She hoped he would give up trying to make it all work. It was getting to be too hard. Every time he left the house in Refugio, and she stood out in the gravel hanging onto Holmes as she watched Elliot disappear before a cloud of dust, another point of light inside her seemed to burn itself out. She longed for a decision, any decision.

No, Elliot was not one to run. He had the ego to think he could figure it out, or fix it up. Unlike Nellie Gallagher, Anne thought. Twenty years ago she fled, trying to obliterate the past and invent a new life away from Seattle where it had got so that she could not stand people knowing who she was, what she had done. Unlike Elliot, Nellie did not like being around people who knew her; it was too restricting. Once Mal's divorce had been settled, he was to follow, and they would pretend that they had been married all along. Anne would have his name. A happy little family. None of their new friends and associates would have witnessed the disruption in their past. Moving south, it would vanish into the depths, like the wake of the ferry trembling now beneath Anne.

She was still hungry . . . maybe another hotdog . . . oh, forget it. Forget it. They weren't good for you anyway.

Portland had been the plan. It was far enough away from Seattle, but similar to the evergreen state, and Nellie no doubt figured that that would make it a more comfortable change for Mal. Probably it was raining when she drove into the city. Probably the stench from the pulp mills along the Columbia River reminded her too much of Puget Sound. She claimed to have found nothing suitable for them. She said she thought she saw someone they knew in a market near the city limits. Keeping south, away from the wet, rotting Northwest, away from the life which itself had begun to rot, Nellie finally stopped at a fruit stand on a hot dry day in the Santa Clara Valley. They were selling cherries and she loved cherries. In

California. The golden state. She checked into a Holiday Inn, called a real estate office, and for the next three weeks, drove around in a white convertible with a Mr. Kent Jarvis who was slim, silver-haired, and wore a beige cashmere sweater over button-down collars, and who knew exactly what Nellie was looking for: a ranch style house in a new tract surrounded by orchards. The neighbors were rosy-faced young families who stopped by when they saw the Bekins truck and invited them to a block party. Nellie painted her bedroom lavender, enrolled Anne in the local school, and waited.

Of course he never came. Soon enough, the money began to arrive, the checks signed and dispatched once a month by his lawyer. Oh, he called, he made assurances, he talked about a big deal he was putting together in New York City. But it was clear that his interest in her had dwindled, and that in fleeing the scene Nellie had allowed her lover to give in to new inclinations without her and the child's presence to cloud his conscience, or get in the way. He was going through with the divorce and if Nellie was angered, if she perceived that she was to be likewise cast off, she might have fouled things up for him financially. So far his wife and her lawyer were unaware of the other relationship.

Nellie and Anne, waiting a thousand miles south in California became a kind of business obligation. Hush money. And as the months went by, Nellie withdrew until it ceased to concern Anne when she came home from school to find the bedroom door shut, to hear her mother crying; it no longer bothered her to warm up a can of beef stew or macaroni, and eat it on the coffee table, the TV turned down low so that her mother would not think that while she was unbearably miserable, Anne was enjoying herself. And even though they needed the money, somehow the checks the lawyer sent made Nellie feel worse, because Mal had not even troubled to write them himself: he had the hired hand shoot the lame horse.

And there was Anne, her very presence a condemnation, a daily reminder that Nellie had made irreparable mistakes.

Coming to California was supposed to erase them. Here was Nellie with Anne in California. Where was Mal?

Down in the bowels of the ferry, Anne thought, going to the place he came from to lie down for good. Nellie's Mal who never came. My father. Where? In the clay pot down below, a little heap of cold ash in the passenger seat of a rented car, going back. Mal McBain. Down below and going back.

"The world is dirty," Nellie used to say. "People don't take responsibility for their own crap like they used to, and sometimes you have to muck around in their mess."

The messes belonged to Anne's father, or to the other people in the office where Nellie eventually got a job, or often to Anne. Invariably they came about because Anne was negligent, because Anne didn't think about anyone but herself, because Anne didn't care about her own mother.

Nellie decided that the best way to teach her daughter about responsibility was to give her a pet that would need to be fed and cleaned and trained, just as Nellie looked after Anne. Not a dog. A dog was too much trouble. A cat could be left. So on a Saturday afternoon they drove to the pet store, and Anne picked out a long-haired orange kitten who kept sliding her paw down the window as if looking for a way out.

"Why don't you like that Siamese?" Nellie pointed to the blue-eyed cat mewing petulantly by itself in the back of the glass case. It was older than the orange one, thin and nervous looking. The tip of one ear was ragged. "I bet it's pedigreed," Nellie said. "The other one is a mix. It can't be worth anything."

"I like it best," Anne said.

The owner of the pet store agreed to give them the orange kitten provided they bought the Siamese, which, it turned out, had been returned by the original buyers. "Terrible people," the little man said. A band of dun-colored hair that ran from the top of one ear around the back of his head to the other ear had been permed to give it more "volume," as the ads said. He looked like a dandelion that hadn't been blown on hard enough. "Didn't know a thing about good breeding," he went on. "No appreciation, none at all."

Nellie shook her head, clucked her tongue.

"Last few years I get people who don't care." The little man sucked in one corner of his mouth. "Cute. That's all it takes anymore. Cute."

"It's obviously a valuable cat," Nellie said.

The pet store owner beamed. "There's still a few of us left, I guess." He lifted the Siamese from the case and placed it in a cardboard carrier. The orange kitten he handed directly to Anne, winking at Nellie as he did so as if to say that bad taste was acceptable in a child so long as mother was maintaining the standards.

According to the pedigree, the Siamese's name was Cassandra's Pride, but Nellie agreed that that was too long for everyday use and dubbed her Cass, taking no interest in the naming of the other cat. Anne called her Orange and she became the favorite. She slept on the book shelves, paws and tail dripping over the edge. Slow-moving, peaceful to watch, she came as a dog would have when summoned, enjoyed attention if it was offered, but otherwise seemed content off by herself, tending her own concerns. At a certain point she rejected the litter box for the soft, black dirt on the north side of the house. Cass was entirely different. Always in a lap, or under foot, or rubbing against a leg, meowing her endless needs. She skittered from one place to another, pausing to stare, and in her blue eyes was a kind of dumb worry, as if she thought she was missing out on something but couldn't figure out what. Anne liked her well enough. And there were those papers that said she was valuable. *She* would not be neutered. But it was Orange she loved.

Cass rarely went outside. She preferred the litter box to do her business, the pile of warm clothes just out of the dryer for her naps, someone's swinging foot to pounce upon. Orange, if it was a sunny day, would disappear for hours. It was Anne's job to keep the litter box clean, to wash out the cat food dishes so the ants stayed away, to check each animal for ticks and mites and fleas, to train them not to sharpen their claws on the upholstery.

Sometimes Anne forgot about the litter box. It was kept in the garage under the steps, and if she wasn't specifically looking for it, it was easily neglected. Which is what happened that day about a year after the cats came to live with them. She went off to school, she forgot about the litter box. And according to Nellie it was full. According to Nellie, Orange got into it and mucked around, then she hopped onto the pile of warm clothes and left her feces prints all over them. On a sunny day when Orange was likely not there. In the litter box which she never used. The litter box, Anne's responsibility. So Nellie had Orange put to sleep before Anne came home from school. To teach her a lesson.

"You understand that I'm not blaming Orange. It was your responsibility to keep that box clean."

No, Malcolm McBain never came to live with them in California, and Nellie's plan that the three of them would start over with happy lives and sanitized pasts backfired in the worst way. That he did not come, that she had miscalculated, and that she was stuck with Anne, with her mistake in a strange place, were like whips driving her into the past. Because Nellie Gallagher remembered. Though she was not very good at it. She left out a lot of things. And the present went on, unrecorded, hardly noticed. Anne grew up. From the day they left Seattle to the day twelve years later she and Nellie met for coffee after Anne had moved out, not one picture of Anne was taken. A gap, a ghost, a mysterious ache, not often noted, not fondly remembered, not pasted in an album and saved for the slow years. Not until Anne was gone, of course, gone into the past where she would be recast into someone Nellie could say she enjoyed. Even loved. "Let's have the waiter take our picture," said Nellie. There they stood, mother and daughter, Anne's arm around Nellie's shoulder, Nellie smiling self-consciously at the waiter, the two of them trying to act related, like tourists who had just met in a foreign land.

The mist immediately around the ferry was thin and gray – a scotch mist – swirling softly, too light to fall. But ahead between Decatur and Blakely Islands, from Thatcher Pass a finger of thick white fog emerged, ominous and otherworldly. In moments, the ferry would burrow into it, and anyone in another boat passing north or south through the Strait could watch its yellow glow disappear, like the face of someone beloved into a crowd of strangers.

Maybe, Anne thought, you could not start over, you could not erase the tablets, you could not even run and hide from it the way Nellie had tried to do by going to California, and maybe Anne, too, with this job in Vancouver, this reverse flight. Because it was all inside you – where you had been, what you had done, who you had known – you were the sum. And the mind, or a child, or a pattern of living would haunt. You could not escape your own skin. And responsibility . . . what did that really mean? It was not enough to say 'yes, I did that, and I will live with it.' Because was Nellie alive those years? Did she ever forgive herself? Or was Mal's moving to California supposed to do that? Would that have made it all right? Would he have provided the proper pedigree? Sired by McBain, Nellie's pride.

No, maybe the best you could do was go on to the next page, say that you had made mistakes. That too was your right.

The rows of seats in the observation area had filled in. Most of the passengers had finished their snacks and coffee, and were settling down with newspapers or books or private thoughts for the rest of the ride. The woman seated directly in front of Anne slammed down her paperback and reached back to nab her son who was playing tag across the aisles with two other boys. "Zeke," she snapped, hauling him over the seat. "This isn't the place. You're disturbing other people," and she smiled apologetically at the handsome man sitting next to her. In spite of Zeke's transgression, she was obviously proud of him, a scrawny, dark-haired boy with big teeth and skin the color of custard; the handsome man's chuckle was all the approval she seemed to need. Patting Zeke's leg, she picked up her book. Shortly, Zeke twisted around, a desperately jealous glint in his eyes as he watched the other two boys, still free, still at the chase. Then the man leaned back, and Anne saw that it was the driver of the teal Porsche, and she witnessed also, as if it might have been meant for her, the almost lurid wink he sent the boy. Zeke whipped back around, making himself small by scrunching down against his mother, and seemed to compose himself by meditating on his left tennis shoe swinging up and back near the butt of the passenger in front.

That man can't be from the islands, Anne thought. He just can't be.

ELEVEN

The warning light on Fauntleroy Point flashed every four seconds. Anne counted seven intervals as the ferry left it to port and moved through Thatcher Pass. Midway, another light flashed a warning from the shoals off the southern tip of Blakely Island. Giving it wide berth, the ferry swung north for the run up Harney Channel which was strangely, suddenly devoid of fog. Anne went up to the bow windows. Except for the smaller coves and narrow passes at the perimeter of the San Juans, the archipelago – at least its interior – was exposed. The inner sanctum. There was a high ceiling of clouds, but nothing low-lying or oppressive, and she could not help feeling that she was entering a secret garden and had all the time in the world to explore it.

The ferry cruised on. There was Frost Island – she had been waiting for it – the lily pad floating in the shadow of Lopez and, between the two islands, the sand spit shaped like a bent arm, Spencer Spit where she and Elliot had gone for the oysters. On their last night. Elliot's skin, sunburn on tan, had looked like a ripe peach, she remembered, on the longest day of the year. June 21st. A slack tide. They had chartered a 38 foot sailboat out of Port Townsend on the Olympic Peninsula, she and Elliot and two other researchers, and were on their way back south from the Queen Charlotte Strait, having spent the month working through the islands and inlets between mainland British Columbia and Vancouver Island. It was almost three years ago.

She could remember their last night as if it were, indeed, only last night. The sun was casting a languid, apricot glow across the water as the four of them lounged on deck drinking gin and tonics, watching the reflection of the mainmast wriggling away from the side of the boat. The sailboat had been a bad idea. No one had anticipated how often they would end up becalmed in the lee of islands, no one knew how crazy the wind currents were inside the islands. A lot of the time they motored. And Sid trolled. Sid was a tide pool specialist when he wasn't fishing or bragging about fishing, though the seven pound salmon he had hooked in Upright Channel was not, in Anne's view, a grand enough reason to brag given the average size of Chinook.

On a teak platter the fish lay spine down, balanced by the flaps of heavy, pink flesh. It looked sensuous, its long body spread open, its color shocking in the late light. Sid was going to stuff it.

Slightly drunk, Elliot danced around the deck with a camera, snapping pictures of Sid and his salmon and the rest of them – tanned, healthy, full of boozy goodwill – convening in the cockpit. It was the first time she had seen him with a camera. She tried to not look at him, at it, but she could feel her heart, and in the end she let a shy, excited smile escape. She was Elliot's phantom. They had always been very careful about leaving any evidence, a record, a photograph.

"Your teeth are so white," he told her, as he peered through the viewfinder.

"They're supposed to be white. Teeth are white," she said, still self-conscious.

"No, no, they're really white." He shot the group, then pulled her up from the bench and posed her alone against the mainmast. "Come on, smile for me, chicken." One eye closed, Elliot's face popped up above the camera. "God, they're white. White white."

"The picture," she giggled.

"Ira," he called. "Take a look at this."

Ira struggled up out of the cockpit with his gin and tonic, a wary face aimed at Elliot. Ira found everything fascinating. It had become a standing joke during the trip to invite him over for a look-see either at some piece of banal phenomena or at something they had fabricated themselves. Yesterday Sid had planted an osprey talon in the mantle cavity of a Diodora for Ira's inspection. Ira would not bite. But tonight he was playing along.

"What do you make of this?" Elliot used the camera as a pointer.

"Hard to say, m'man. Hard to say." Behind his pince-nez Ira's small, bright, boyish eyes squinted theatrically.

"Keep smiling, Anne. This is for science," Elliot said.

She rolled her eyes, drew in one corner of her mouth. "I have a tan, boys. Melanin . . . lots of it. And I have a tan because I've been in the sun for a month. You do remember the effect of light colors on dark surfaces . . . that's why your mummys told you to wear a white shirt when you went bike riding at dusk, right? You recall the camouflage of the lowly spider crab. Now these teeth are not camouflaged. They would not survive long against this tan."

"She's absolutely right, m'man," Ira said, shaking his head solemnly. "They haven't a chance. In that face they're sitting ducks. Now, your teeth . . ."

It was unlike Ira to tease Elliot. He had been a student of Elliot's and the relationship had never really grown out of that, though Ira had already achieved recognition in his field and was successfully 'on his own,' so to speak. The student still looked up to the teacher, and the teacher, more and more, found certain delight in testing and straining that esteem. Maybe Elliot was tired of the role. Or maybe he considered it his final teacherly duty to rid Ira of any lingering illusions: lately Elliot had erupted with ridiculous theories about morality and evolution, theories that were designed, it seemed, to shock Ira. And his social behavior had begun to erode to a weird combination of imperial bravado and adolescent humor. At the end of the trip Elliot seemed, well, *less evolved.*

"No no no," Elliot was saying. "I'm talking about the teeth, the teeth discrete. Not in any context. Not compared to anything else. And not just white either. I'm talking absolute value here. Two perfect strings of teeny neon lights. Don't you see what I'm talking about, Ira?" and he grabbed Ira by the shoulders and lowered his voice to an awed hush. "What I'm trying to get at is *bioluminescence*."

Ira gurgled down a mouthful of gin and tonic and smiled broadly at Elliot who was wheezing with laughter. "Okay Newhouse. Okay. The next one's on you, it is."

Though Ira's area of specialization was coelenterates, his 'thing' was bioluminosity. One night they found him down in the galley, pulverizing the dried out bodies of jellyfish, a species at a time, making a paste with a drop or two of water and the powder, and painting the tops of his fingers. He was convinced that bioluminosity was a function of chemical compounds, if not exclusively, then in conjunction with some specialized light organ, some photophore. It had already been demonstrated with certain crustaceans. That night, however, not one of his fingers glowed.

Sid had the salmon stuffed and wrapped in foil awaiting the coals when Elliot decided that they had to have oysters to complete the feast. Sid shrugged and poured himself another drink. "I don't have a problem with oysters," he said. He was always game, always 'going with the flow.' He considered himself an instant native wherever he was. When he and Elliot had worked together in Patagonia last winter Sid had emerged one morning from a thatch hut wearing a leather diaper and chewing on a coca leaf. For endurance, he said. He was known also to heed the lyrics of the old Steven Stills song, to 'love the one you're with,' whoever she happened to be. He had even made suggestions to Anne one day when Elliot was in Port Hardy picking up supplies.

Anne and Elliot set out in the dinghy, putt-putting toward the thin, white line of surf. The salt-chuck lagoon in the crook of Spencer Spit was a wintering and spring breeding haven for many species of marine birds. Sid had done some work with nesting Brants the year before, measuring the loss of habitat and the impact on the species by the new state park. The eelgrass and sea lettuce on which the Brants fed were disappearing with increased use; sewage was contaminating the water; beachcombers pocketed as souvenirs the round, buff-colored eggs they found in the nests near the water's edge. Sid knew the area well. He said he'd seen a flock of two dozen Black Oystercatchers on the rocks at low tide.

Turning parallel to the mile-long sand spit, the dinghy slipped along quietly. Anne and Elliot surveyed the rocks for the long red bills of the oystercatchers; in the ashen light and against a rock their black bodies would be invisible.

The air was mink soft. The late lighting had an expectant quality as if a secret was about to be revealed. From the lagoon beyond the spit a briny fragrance drifted off and enveloped them. Anne inhaled, closing her eyes and lifting her brows when her lungs were full. She looked at Elliot. His bottom lip went up, he touched his nose. "Fecund," he said.

"The primordial ooze," she answered.

With his arm bent back, hand on the tiller, his expression relaxed yet alert, he looked as satisfied as she had ever seen him. Elliot appreciated timing. He was a great connoisseur of the right moment. He seemed to be utterly content with where he was and with whom. This is how it should be, she thought, looking ahead and feeling him behind her, like a steady breeze.

Around the dinghy the water went transparent, though no more than ten feet away from them it still cast up soft pastels. She patted the air with her palm, and Elliot throttled down.

Ahead on a rock was a Black Oystercatcher, its red bill prying and jabbing at an oyster shell, its body popping up with each thrust. They put in on the beach opposite the rock and stood arm in arm for awhile, regarding Swifts Bay. The sun had fallen behind Humphrey Head, and in the east a sickle moon hung like a child's ornament in the branches of Douglas fir atop Frost Island, but the light was still pure, poised in that time of clarity before the air went grainy and thickened into night. Beside the sailboat beneath the galley lights a pool of bronze wavered. A man's shadow crossed it. Bluish smoke rose from the barbecue grill suspended from the stern rails. There was no breeze. One after another small waves bowed before them. A pair of swallows ricocheted across the bronzed sky. And up the beach, poking through some driftwood, a lone crow began to caw indignantly.

"Something's going to happen," she said.

"Or has. Just," he said.

"I hope not. I hope it's to come." Through her canvas shoes she could feel the warmth of the sand; in an hour it would be stone cold. But for now it seemed the world had exerted and was nearing rest in a kind of euphoric calm.

"For you, it's all to come. You're young," he said.

"What about you?"

"Not so young," he smiled. "I've passed a few posts, some of them with relief."

"Like what?" she asked.

"Like female companionship." Elliot picked up a rock, turned it between his fingers, then tossed it into the water. "Takes too much out of a body, this being in love. So you're it. My last chicken."

"I guess I can say the same."

He dropped his eyes.

"You don't believe me," she said.

"I want to . . . and I don't know what to do with that." There was a pause, then he said, "You're young. We both have that to fall back on."

"If what?"

He tossed another pebble into the water. "I don't know." Then he pulled his collar up, cleared his throat, and announced, "Oysters."

"Huh?"

"Our mission."

"Yes, right."

"Funny thing is," he said, frowning, on the brink of a smile, "I've never been that fond of oysters."

"How fond is that, Elliot?"

"Oh, not quite fond enough . . . "

"To wade out into that cold cold water?"

"Just so. Just so."

"I'll do it."

"This isn't the *sine qua non*. We don't need them, you know. Not that I don't appreciate the carnal benefits of a few fat oysters before bed, but that water would shut me down for at least a week. Maybe longer. I'm a terribly sensitive fellow," he lisped.

She screwed up her face and laughed. Usually waiting to be drawn out, he was on tonight in one of his silly, mugging moods, and she liked it. She would have done anything for him. She would have been anyone. "You shall have oysters," she sang, stripping off her clothes and crashing into the water. For a moment or two as her lungs contracted, she had trouble breathing.

"Jesus, she's really doing it. Forty-five frigging degrees." Hitching his big shoulders, Elliot trotted in a circle and gave the air a few bumps with his hips. "That's my chicken."

"Listen," she called back. "I'm just going to toss them on the beach. You put them in the bucket, okay?"

"Ten-four."

Up to her rib cage, her breasts floating on the surface, she probed the bottom with her feet, trying not to disturb the sand so much that it obscured the water. Directly in front lay a narrow bed that widened out and down into the deeper reaches.

Even through four feet of water she could see the ruffled configuration of the oyster shells. Squatting under, she swept a pile into her arms, sorting out the large, milky ones before throwing them on the beach, then dunked under again, and several times more. Cold water . . . cold . . . her joints began to ache. If we fry them, she thought, I won't need to get rid of the big ones, there might be enough right here around me.

"How many is that?" she called.

Pause. Hurried rattling through the bucket. "Seventeen."

"Damn," she muttered. "I'll have to go deeper."

He shrugged. It's not important how many, he probably meant. It's your body, and this was all just whimsy to begin with, a gilding of the lily of our last night at sea. Do as you please, he meant.

The bottom beyond reach, she swam frog-like out over the dappled bed of oysters. A quiver of panic passed through her body. Her stomach clenched. Her arms pushed forward, rounded back in, pushed forward. In the darkening water her flesh looked mossy and dead. Down there in the depths were her legs – she could not see her feet or what slippery, cold-blooded thing was about to touch them. Stupid, she told herself. Fish and seaweed. Deeper water.

We don't need any more oysters, she thought. I am always doing too much, especially with Elliot. I am always going too far.

The fear retreated behind a sense of purpose. Diving, she felt her fanny breach and follow her down, then begin to buoy her up. She kicked along the bottom, collected half a dozen, swam to shallow water, tossed them ashore, repeated the process. Elliot sat down in the sand and from one place tried to catch each oyster.

"Hey, there's a sign down here."

"What does it say?" he asked.

"'Dead End.' Isn't that funny? A road sign, out here."

"When are you coming home, dear."

"Last one," she said, tossing the oyster twenty feet to

Elliot's port.

Aware of his eyes on her, her body rising from the froth of an expended wave and shedding water, hair washed back and breasts creamy against tanned skin; she was aware of him wanting her, wanting her just out of the sea, like a new creature, wet and naked and stirring for the first time there in the stalled light.

He opened his jacket and she shivered in against his chest.

"Will you marry me?" he whispered.

Shock. A tingle of victory. "Yes." Then guilt. Then something worse – annoyance. Because tomorrow he was going back. And this was their last night. The question was out of its element. They had been away from everything, they had been whole without that. She wished he hadn't asked her now when it could mean nothing here in this place and could go nowhere in the other. "Let's go back," she said. "I'm chilled."

He looked in her eyes. "Someday."

Very slowly, she blinked. "In never-never land."

A shadow crossed his face. "That's the safe way to see it. You're being smart, kiddo. Sure you are."

"I don't want to be."

There was a lightning storm late that night, up from the south. The flashes shot spotlights through the portholes of the stern cabin, illuminating the bed and their bodies as they made love. In the darkness Elliot rose above her, the light strobed two, three times, and she saw his skin, damp and bluish, and his eyes straining with pleasure. She saw, too, something in the doorway.

Distant rumblings, then silence. The water slapped against the hull, and her own breath came fast now. She heard what sounded like someone closing a compact, or a small case of some sort, perhaps a glasses case. The lightning flickered.

"There's someone in the doorway," she whispered.

"Yes?"

"Watching us."

"Uh-huh."

She stared into the darkness at the place where Elliot's face was.

Six o'clock. Passengers were clearing out of the observation area and moving down the stairs to the car deck. In the cafeteria, the steam trays were re-stocked, the tall coffee urn set to perking, the iced display case packed with yogurts, jello salads, and big Red Delicious apples, the empty rollers lined with hotdogs. Lopez Island was the first of four westward stops, the ferry would then return directly to Anacortes; people who had spent the day in the islands would be boarding at each stop, going home to the mainland.

Anne debated over grabbing one of the vacated booths before the onslaught of new passengers, or going outside to watch the unloading. The fresh air would be nice, she decided, and anyway, if she had taken one of the booths she would have had to accept company.

Outside the air was cool and heavy with moisture; it had a mildly receptive quality as if it had washed up for company. She found an abandoned stretch of railing, propped her elbows and leaned forward to see what was happening below. The wind picked up some of the wavy strands of hair behind her ears and like a lover drew them playfully back around the nape of her neck. She rolled her head. I can still do that, she thought, and almost cried.

"Orcas?" a voice from behind asked.

Pivoting, she said, "How did you know?"

"Wishful thinking." It was the man from the teal Porsche. "You're not a tourist, are you? I mean, you're alone."

"Not exactly," she said.

"Alone?" He wore a pleasantly vulnerable aspect, like a boy asking for a sweet.

Anne hesitated. "Not exactly a tourist. I'm from Washington originally."

"Well, I'm glad you came back. We missed you."

Laughing, she nodded at him. And even though they did not know each other, it was just silliness, a joke, he seemed to genuinely mean what he said. She felt missed.

The man took up residence a yard from her against the railing. From his coat pocket he removed a pack of cigarettes, shook one out, then rolled it between his thumb and index finger before lighting it. He pulled on it a couple of times, held it out, studying its glowing tip, and without looking over said, "You don't smoke anymore, do you? I'd've offered you one. It's only boneheads like me that keep sucking these things."

"I did quit," she said, looking at him. There was an overall mildness about his face, as if whatever he gained slid right back out and had no opportunity to sketch disquieting patterns. A few doodles around the eyes – from squinting, probably – otherwise nothing of consequence had seemingly troubled him. She might have mistaken it for serenity except that his hands were trembling. "*Have we met somewhere before?*" she asked.

Winking, he said, "Now *that's* a line."

Together they watched a stocky, jacketed ferryman, the evening newspaper poking out of his back pocket, unhook the chain at the end of the car deck and drag it to one side. He made a rolling motion with his arms and the exodus began. Ramps clack-clacking, the old ferry punched cars out like colored balls in a giant pin ball machine, shot them one by one past the ticket booth with its cracked window, past the snack bar and marina shop toward a tier of russet madrones that mounted back against the dark forests of fir where the serious arboreal business of the northwest went on. At the fringe of madrone, each car banked left and disappeared through a hole in the greenwood. Hurrying home. Even old Bear McBain, though he had not much reason to hurry anymore, was going home, she thought. Maybe I am too. And maybe I am missed.

The ferry had been filled at Anacortes so that it could not simply reverse bow and stern and accept additional cars in a forward maneuver; they had to back down the landing. A small herd of droning cars waited as a motor home towing a trailer was having difficulty. It jerked forward, slid down for its second try, the trailer canted sideways, and the motor home was obliged to lurch back up the landing. This time the driver twisted halfway out his window; the motor home crept backwards and, as the trailer approached the critical angle in the landing, the driver spun the wheel and rammed the pilings full on. One of the ferrymen dropped his head to inspect the ground.

Anne turned away. She was going to say something commiserative to the man next to her, but he was gone, and she wondered if she had somehow failed to be friendly enough, if she had been rude. Then she asked herself why anyone would possibly care.

From the pilothouse the captain sounded the horn, the nasal *hrwraaaaaaong* of departure followed by two *wonk wonks*. Hurry up, it meant.

Standing with his hands on his hips, the driver of the motor home inspected the jackknifed trailer. Thrice he had tried and thrice failed. It happened all the time. People fail.

It's one of our rights, Anne thought. But what makes us keep trying, she wondered, and what about people who don't try, who have no inner checks and balances, who don't care if a thing is right or wrong so long as it feeds, even gluts a need? What about people who are morally impervious, who have no inborn idea what is right and what wrong and who, in the absence of some entity instructing them, behave exactly as they please, glutting away? What mechanism bred in the blood provided the sight, and how did one lose it? Or arrive without it?

There was an elephant seal pup spring before last that she and Elliot had weighed, a super-weaner. Evidently its mother was one of the first females to arrive at the rookery and give birth, because when she weaned her pup at the end of the usual thirty days, there was a high number of subsequent arrivals still nursing. She spent a few days copulating, then went back to sea. Abruptly abandoned and facing a 2-3 month fast before it was old enough to leave the rookery, this weaner – a male – resorted to milk theft. A "double-mother sucker," they were called. Daily, the weaner re-entered the harem, sneaking up on a female whose own pup was either resting or immediately displaced. To avoid being seen he would nudge her from the rear, and she would roll obligingly sideways, assuming nursing position. Sure, he suffered some vicious bites when caught, but at the end of three weeks he weighed twice as much as the average weaner, a *super*-weaner, so bloated that he looked like a blister with flippers as he struggled across the sand. Now he possessed not only a size advantage – more than mere fat, for mother's milk provided all those elements necessary to muscle, tissue and bone growth – but also a clear statistical edge on his contemporaries for survival and most importantly for breeding. His aggressiveness, his head start meant that he would probably develop into a dominant male and *his* genes, not another's, would carry on. Theoretically, the species would be a little stronger.

But it was wrong in human beings to flourish by impeding another. She had seen her father drive other people out of business that his might thrive. And it was just as unacceptable for her to be with Elliot Newhouse.

She stared at her hands. How, she asked them silently, did you reconcile the natural and the moral? Maybe altruism was just another highfalutin survival mechanism furthering the good of the species, and morality a very nice word for fear. If you stole milk, sooner or later someone else's mother was going to bite you.

Anne buried her hands in her pockets.

Down below, a man in a suit was walking toward the driver of the motor home. They talked a moment, then the man stepped on his cigarette butt. It was he. He was going to help. The Porsche man climbed into the motor home and maneuvered it into the ferry. After turning and offering a large, penitential shrug to the cars behind him, the driver – hatted and head straight – followed his home and his family into the already crowded bowels of the ship.

Anne turned around and gazed up at the pilothouse. From the summit of the ferry the captain in his clean, white uniform was watching the proceedings.

There, she thought. There to you and your impatient horn-blowing and your spotless whites. We do not all stand around watching someone else struggle. We are not all morally impervious.

The man returned, carrying two cups of coffee. "You looked cold," he said, handing her one of the cups.

"That was a nice thing to do," she said, indicating the ramp below.

"They're all friends." He tipped his head toward the landing and the waiting cars. The loading process continued one car at a time, backward and slowly, as if each was being drawn unwillingly into the mouth of a green and white whale. "Friends we haven't met, you know."

"Yes," she smiled. It was a sappy cliché, the 'strangers are friends' line, but it was also apparently quite real for this man, and she couldn't bring herself to impose the standard social demotion for such utterances. She was, after all, one of the strangers he had lately befriended.

He sipped his coffee, holding the rim and bottom of the styrofoam cup like someone used to drinking on the run.

She asked, "Is the ferry going to be late tonight?" so that she might look at him again. Because, oddly enough, he resembled her; that is, under his eyes where the cheek bones neared the surface the skin was fluttered, leaving twin welts which were identical to the *faux* welts on her own face. Otherwise, he was all stranger. His hair was dark, his narrow face a landscape of ridges and hollows, his eyes round brown drops which, in conjunction with the tiny muscles surrounding them, gave an overall solicitous impression, as if he had just posed a question and was anxiously awaiting orders. Though no taller than Elliot, he seemed taller, maybe because he was leaner. It might have been the suit. Elliot never wore a suit.

"Not very late," he said. "You won't miss your dinner."

She smiled, saying nothing, wondering if Joe Sanborn had received her telegram and whether there would indeed be any dinner.

"You've never been to Orcas, have you?"

"That's right."

"I would've noticed you if you had."

There was a long pause. Rain dusted down, making a dewy web of her hair. She pulled up the hood of her raincoat, concealing her profile and blotting him out, the man from the teal Porsche with his round solicitous eyes.

Other men's advances amused Elliot. They flattered him, his taste, his success. He was so sure of her. In the beginning she liked the compliments – the start of a smile, a deferential, half-hinted bow – but in the end she felt bad. She was not interested and there was power in that, and there was someone inside enjoying the power, using it occasionally. Sometimes it depressed her. Sometimes it did not, and that was worse. Their attention seemed to obligate her even when she had nothing to give. She would have liked to please men to keep them liking her and that made her mad. They went away inevitably. There was nothing else they wanted. The power she had possessed was hollow and unsatisfying.

It had been that way with Paul, her old friend with whom she had gone through the University and who became a fellow worker at the marine lab. Last year he asked for permission to kiss her, he asked as if he was arranging forgiveness in advance and Anne, without a word, left him dwindling there in the vestibule of the lab, his eyes morbid, his face as white as the smock he was wearing. She was crying.

Elliot felt sorry for him and utterly bewildered by her reaction. "What did you expect?" he asked, cradling her head.

"I don't know. He was a friend, a good friend."

"He's still a friend."

"No." More tears.

"Why not?"

"I don't know. He ruined it."

"Look Anne, sooner or later every healthy guy, even an old friend, is gonna float one. It seems to me he showed a lot of restraint. You've known him, what, five years?"

"Six. Six years and that makes it worse. I feel set up."

"Christ, I don't understand. Most women would be flattered. He didn't exactly rape you. He asked politely if he could give you a kiss. All you had to say was 'No, thank you.'"

"But he was a friend. What does that mean now? What did it ever mean? So he took his time, so what? We still ended up at the same place. God, I can't believe it, even Paul, sweet, lanky . . . he volunteers down at the Y, did you know that? My friend Paul."

Elliot shook his head. "I guess I don't think what he did was so bad."

"Well it was. It undid everything. The friendship was something . . . the rest, the rest means nothing. Nothing."

"You're being awfully hard. I mean, look here, I floated one, too, and my balloon just happened not to bust."

She stared out the window. "He tricked me." And that was the end of the conversation.

It still did not make much sense to her. None of it did. There was no evidence that the man beside her was doing anything more than passing the time being nice to a solitary human being stuck on the same ship of fools. She had become suspicious. Maybe the events of the last week had worn bare patches in her psyche.

As the ferry groaned away from its island slot, a flock of gulls kited up off the quay and followed the ship out into Harney Channel.

Brightly she said, "Next stop, Shaw," and peered around the edge of her hood. But he was gone. The promenade deck was empty. She was alone. With the ferry's departure from Lopez, that end of the ship had become the stern and all the passengers had moved forward to see where they were going. Even the seats in the observation area behind the sweep of big windows were deserted.

Alone. Everything gray and white – the deck and railing, the water and sky, even the gulls squalling above were gray and white. A chaste world. No rain now, but out in the channel away from islands the wind waxed free, and she dropped her hood to let it grab her hair. She tried to think of dying, but the wind for all its disregard was exciting, and it seemed after all to be going somewhere, *she* was going somewhere, to Orcas Island, a place that was in time both in front of and behind her, like the ferry that reversed bow and stern at each stop.

Now, though, she was aft, her gaze, too, swept back and down to the wide wake of the ship that carried her inexorably forward. Underneath, the great props roiled the depths, and the wake lengthened out, like an abandoned highway. A wake of memories, she thought, that would boil up in another place, another time – changed, but wake all the same. Onward went the past, for wake it would.

TWELVE

The landing at Orcas Island was deserted. A couple of dozen cars, including the teal Porsche, departed the ferry, roared up the hill, swung left at the cafe, and disappeared. They were fifteen minutes late, but most of the Tuesday night commuters would probably make it home in time for the 7:00 o'clock news and a quick cocktail before dinner. Anne pulled off to let them pass. The tourist map she had purchased on board was rudimentary, but on Orcas every byway was an offshoot of the Horseshoe Highway which mimicked the shape of the island, and every byway led eventually to water. Shaking out the map, she heard the ferry sound its horn as it withdrew from the slip, then a dusky silence settled over the landing. A tear in the cloud cover sent shafts of yellow light into the trees at the top of the hill. Bright and hypnotic, full of hope, that sudden outpouring, and she let her gaze and her mind melt into it until the yellow light began to fade to gray and the breach in the clouds closed.

It was seven miles west to Deer Harbor where she had reserved a cabin, and twenty miles east, all the way up and around East Sound, down to Doe Bay and Joe Sanborn's place. There wasn't time to check in and change. Sanborn was her father's contemporary which meant he was in his late seventies and might retire early. Still, she didn't even know if he had received her telegram, and there might be a message at the resort.

No. You're alone. The cabin will be cold and empty. It's too early to call Elliot.

The truth was, she didn't know if Joe Sanborn was alive, as Elliot had tried to warn her. Elliot would go to the cabin first; he would not let himself be surprised.

She pictured the cabin: pine walls, flowered bedspread, painting of a wet Paris street screwed to the wall above the bed, the smell of air freshener and cigarette smoke – neither dominating the other – hanging in the still air, ambiguous stains on the carpet, no TV for romance's sake. They were always fun with Elliot, the nights in quaint cabins, or seedy motel rooms – it didn't matter. They would pick up some fried chicken and a bottle of wine, and picnic on the bed while they watched the news or one of those smart westerns – *Little Fauss and Big Halsy* or *Five Easy Pieces*, or *High Plains Drifter* – then make love and fall asleep, tangled in the thin white sheets, to the sound of the air conditioner. If it was a nice room, if he was giving a paper somewhere, all expenses paid, then they would turn off the lights in the bathroom and climb into the big tub with a couple of whiskeys and maybe they would talk about dressing up and going out to a fancy restaurant, but in the end, usually, it was the fried chicken they preferred, and quibbling over the salt packets or the last Lorna Doone. In the end their own giddy world was world enough.

The rental car rattled up the hill. As a child she had been through the islands many times, but they had never stopped on Orcas. Her father was not particularly sentimental about his homeland. He mentioned facts, probably more facts than existed at the time, because in content, Malcolm McBain was a flamboyant thinker. He aimed to do everything and make a lot of money and keep moving. He was especially proud of successful short-cuts. Anne found it difficult to draw from him any stories of the years he spent growing up on Orcas. He was evasive. He seemed embarrassed by the poverty and near amnesiac when asked to describe the daily rural life of a family living on the remote end of a (then) remote island in the middle of the depression. His accounts consisted mostly of hunting bravado and secondhand smuggling tales. What this family of eleven discussed on a Sunday morning around the breakfast board, what they did on a winter's eve, what they dreamed in spring – such memories Malcolm McBain sloughed off deliberately; they could not co-exist with who he had become. He wanted more than to orphan himself, it seemed; he wanted (and felt he deserved) absolute credit for the man he had forged. He considered himself impervious to influence, and others utterly susceptible to the least flicker of his will. Often, he was right.

She reached over to adjust the box containing the urn and her father's ashes. It was knocking against the window, but – ridiculous – she wanted him to be sitting up as she drove the loop to Doe Bay, though he had no eyes, he had only his presence in her mind. Maybe that was all any of us could hope for.

The island was a misty quilting of shades of green, not in the least wild or unassailable . . . domesticated, she thought. Obliging. The mountains in the distance were low and rounded, the land itself either orderly plantings or thinned woods or open fields taking the year off. The twisted black bodies of dead fruit trees showed here and there in the deep grass. There must have been a kind of tyranny in all this plenty, this ease, she thought, especially for a young man. They want adversity, don't they, young men do, something to go up against? And young women . . . what do they want? What do I want?

She thought of Elliot; of the job at Waddington Marine Station in Vancouver and her dream to work again with killer whales, to finish her dissertation. Waddington was the first to distinguish the 'dialects' particular to families of orcas, and whales and whale languages continued to be the focus of many of the biologists attached to the Vancouver station. She remembered with a kind of crazy panic the pregnancy. She wished she had the time and the money to spend a month in the Bitterroots or the Brooks Range or even the Wind River Mountains, just hiking, just being there. She pictured her mother without makeup. She imagined her father as a father.

The roads were slick, the rental car not very stable on the curves, and she took her time winding north, stopping at Snyder's general store in the village of Eastsound to buy a bottle of Chardonnay, then she headed south on the Horseshoe Highway, feeling nervous and lonely. The island was seeming like a giant grave mound on which she was about to tread, and it made her feet feel funny. She wanted to get it over with.

At Olga, she turned east and the road shot out of the woods into the open, rose and dipped, feeling along the hills cat-like, until it fell to the edge of a quiet, glassy bay. In a cypress hedge to her right was an archway and, hesitating, Anne rolled through it, shut off the engine, and stared. It was an enormous house – two stories of yellow clapboard, four dormers, and a great porch littered with padded willow furniture. Every window was lit and, though it was a cool evening, the front door hung ajar, the mercurial harmonies of a Keith Jarrett concert escaping through it, unsettling the leafy sleep of the grounds. A man emerged.

"Are you comin' in, girl?" he called. White white hair; slight, bow-shaped frame; tenuous voice, like the scratchings of an old minstrel recording – it was Joe Sanborn.

"Hullo," she said. She was going to leave the urn in the car, but she needed a drink and the wine alone seemed inappropriately festive; in company with the urn, it would become consoling, she decided.

"I'm not sorry about Mal," he said as he ushered her into the house. "He had a big life, big the way he saw it and wanted it, he did, and there's not much to say after that."

"I guess not," she said.

He nodded at the box. "Is that him?"

For some reason, she withdrew the urn and handed it to Joe who walked over and set it in the middle of the dining room table, moving a pitcher with a spray of leaves to the window sill. The table, she noticed, was set for six – white cloth, no plate like another, at either end a jar of apple butter, two porcelain cowboys, a white hat for salt and a black hat for pepper – and now at the center sat her father. The urn seemed to please Joe. He stood back to admire it, as if it was a trophy.

Outside, beyond the bow window a black man was practicing T'ai Chi on the lawn. Dressed in dark clothes, his movements silhouetted against the silver sheen of the bay were slow and dreamy. His presence was not in the least bewildering to Anne, part of Joe's 'congregation,' was how her father once put it. Young revolutionaries, old widows, drifters he'd met up in Alaska when work on the pipeline ran out, dock alkies, a shoe salesman from Hanover, a redheaded woman from the social security office in Bellingham, strays from the mainland, friends from the smaller islands – all of them at one time or another had passed through the Sanborn place. Joe had been a salvage diver and, until the depths took their toll and his ears gave out, he knew the underwaters of the Pacific from San Diego to Bristol Bay. Probably he was the same way with people, she thought. Parts of all of us are salvageable, provided they can be brought to the surface.

"That's Charles," Joe said, opening the window. "You want some dinner?" he called.

Breaking the flow, Charles made a '1' with his finger which segued at once into a downward spiraling, while his left knee floated up and his shoulders rolled back and his neck went limp, like a marionette suffering the whimsy of a child.

Mostly to himself, Joe said, "Awfully pretty, that," and skated over to a door behind the table. He was wearing white wool socks which slid along the hardwood floors, though one had bunched down and was flopping past his toes. He yanked it up as he hollered incoherently into the hallway. Distant creakings. Doors slammed. Behind Anne, the sound of water rushing inside the wall – old plumbing. And a baby crying.

"You like pork roast?"

"Yes," she said. "But I was going to take you out. I hope no one went to any trouble."

"No trouble to eat well, it isn't. They like to cook, they do."

'They,' apparently, were the two women entering the dining room, carrying platters and bowls and a pot of tea. The younger one departed, the other wiped her hand on a greasy apron and extended it toward Anne. "Rose," she said, then nodding at Joe, "He's my brother." She had a rough voice and a hard grip, hair cropped like a man's, black going gray, and a face as weathered as a prairie fence post. "You look like him . . . sad in the eyes. I swear it didn't matter if he wasn't, he might'a just won the derby, Mal was sad in the eyes and man, the gals loved it. Went for it every time. Those sad eyes." She practically slapped her thigh, then took off her apron and flopped into a chair at the table. "Sit," she said.

The younger woman, an attractive, long-faced blond named Carla, with a cool voice and a baby on her hip, came in. And then Charles, who shut off the Keith Jarrett concert before pulling up a chair. And then, still wiping his hands with a paper towel, the man with the teal Porsche.

Starting, Anne quickly covered astonishment with a wry smile, holding it as long as it took for a few elementary thoughts to rally in her brain. "You knew who I was," she said. "On the ferry."

"No," he said. "But for some reason I thought I might see you again."

"It's a small island."

"Maybe that wouldn't have mattered."

"This is Vinny," Rose said. She popped open a beer. "My son. Only these days he don't like to be called Vinny. Vincent."

Vinny issued his mother an indulgent frown – they had obviously been over this before – then he turned to Anne. "I have a new job," he said. "It's an important position and they want me to sound the part. Not too casual, you know."

"I understand." She felt the others watching them.

Joe patted the air for Vinny to be seated, and he took the chair opposite Anne. Between them the terra cotta urn rose like a tiny tower with an onion dome over which Vinny with his height could peer. Anne was obliged to stare directly at it.

There was the happy clatter of dishes passed around, light exchanges as the first few bites put out the hunger, and the assembled relaxed into the meal. The baby, gurgling from the chair next to her mother, was obviously Charles's – a beautiful mulatto with honey curls and a toothless grin that would have bedeviled the devil, and Anne found herself briefly hypnotized by the infant's expressions which moved and changed like clouds across a fair sky.

"She's pretty," Anne said.

Carla glanced at Charles, then back at Anne. "We think so."

"Do you like babies?" Vinny asked.

"I don't have any." She thought about what she said and added, "So I guess I can't honestly say."

"I'm a sucker for 'em." He laughed.

This was easy to believe, in part because his own expressions were like the baby's – mild and unstable – and in part because he seemed so gentle, the kind of guy who could stand a squalling child with equanimity, perhaps because it genuinely would not bother him.

Joe leaned forward, a fork full of yam waving over the table cloth. "Mal came to visit me this year, he did." There was pride in his voice.

"He mentioned it," she lied.

"Stayed a month. Just showed up, he did, on the. . .the. . . " Nodding, grinning, his mouth full of food, he rose and went to a stand in the entry hall and brought back a large red book. Opening it, he dragged his finger down several of the pages, stopped, tapped the page, and announced, "January the eleventh. It's right here in the book."

The book?

"I was here in January," Vinny said over the urn. "Spent some time with your father, actually quite a lot. We hit it off nicely."

"You must like to fish then," she said. "He wouldn't have spent that much time in the islands without trying his luck."

"There was fishing . . . but I meant more than that."

Pouring herself a glass of wine, she offered some to Vinny, hoping to distract him from the subject of Mal McBain, though it occurred to her that that was likely impossible, given the circumstances. People would feel obliged to talk about him, because here she had come to Orcas, and there he was in the middle of the dinner board. It was just that it wasn't the first time she had heard younger men celebrate her father. He often had that affect, because there was a fearlessness about him which he threw out as if it was something everyone naturally possessed, like an arm or a leg, as if it was nothing to risk money on this or that venture – their money – to pick up the ball and run it in with Malcolm Kroeger McBain calling the plays. (That horrid fellow from Dallas, she remembered, in his white suit and pea green shirt. The cocktail lounge at the Holiday Inn. They were putting together a deal, something to do with Teflon magnets and scalp implants, mens' hair pieces, wasn't it? That fellow from Dallas lost a bundle of money in praise of Mal McBain. Harvey Wallbanger was his drink, so Anne and her father drank Harvey Wallbangers that afternoon, and every time Mal went to the restroom or to the bar, the man in the pea green shirt told her what a brilliant *enterpreenoor* her father was, until he was so drunk he didn't wait for Mal to leave the table, he slathered it on in person. And Mal let the man dance with Anne in the dirty light of the cocktail lounge. "She's only fourteen," he kept telling the man. "Can you believe that?")

"Some men are never relegated to the past. Men like your

father, maybe," Vinny said.

"That may not be a very desirable fate."

He let out a frustrated laugh. "I meant that they make such an impression on the people they know during their lives that you don't forget them. You don't want to. I learned something from him."

"I'm sure you did," said Anne. "He probably made certain of it. He always considered himself a teacher."

It was true: Mal McBain often wrote 'professor' (a loftier title than he had, in fact, ever earned), on forms asking for his occupation, even though that period of his life lasted no longer than two years and was, as he himself recalled it, reluctantly passed among the stubbled lava plains and wide coulees and seed-heads of eastern Washington at a high-school in Moses Lake.

"Do you believe in reincarnation?" Vinny asked.

"I do on a good day. That is, I'd like to come back when the sun is shining and I'm bopping along in a bright world. I'd wish it was possible to stay around, in some form or another."

Nodding, Vinny reached over and lifted the lid off the urn. It was plain to Anne that he did not know what it was. He was listening with some absorption to what she was saying, while rather unconsciously exploring the depths of Mal McBain's penultimate quarters.

"But on a bad day," she said, "I'd consider reincarnation impossible, simply because I didn't want to come back, again and again. Religious beliefs may be just that, don't you think? Big wishes about the big sleep."

Replacing the lid on the urn, he glanced across the table at her. "I can feel him here" – Vinny knocked on his chest with a fist – "your father's spirit, and other people's, too, people who made a difference in my life." Above the urn Vinny's face loomed, as if it had just risen from the ashes within, the eyes strangely incurious, like a large animal's, an animal that knew no enemies. For one horrible moment, she felt as if she was gazing at the reincarnation of Malcolm McBain. The very word sent shock waves rippling up from her gut and hammering into the ceiling of her skull. Re-in-car-na-tion, *bang bang bang bang bang*. She dropped her eyes.

"Of course I didn't know your father well. It was just a month."

Rose was passing her the red book. "Here's where Mal signed," she said.

There indeed was her father's heavy signature in the guest register, and paper-clipped to the page itself was his business card – "Realty: Homes * Land Development * Investments" – with the notation 'just in case' scrawled beneath the type.

Trying to sound detached, just curious, nothing more, she leaned forward and asked, "'Just in case' what?"

"Could'a meant anything, knowing your pa, but I guess it just meant maybe." Pausing, Joe inspected the palm of his hand and placed it carefully on the table, the fingers spread open as if he was going to make a tracing of it. "Maybe if I wanted to sell off some of the upper orchard land that's gone bad, the way he did for his ma when she needed the money."

"You wouldn't sell this place," Anne said.

"No, I don't think I can, no. I was born here, how about that? The old man planted the orchards in 1889, and they're still the best apples in Washington."

Rose snorted.

"Oh, not the big shiny kind, but they've got more flavor than any of Yakima's, they do, more character. If there'd been a cheaper way to get them to Seattle and if folks hadn't cared so much about how things looked, they'd've got their money's worth on Orcas apples." He sipped from his beer, burped, and gazed out the bow windows where night was lying down on the little bay. Then turning to Anne, he gave her the warmest smile. "No, I can't sell this place," he said. "Nice of your pa to offer, though."

My pa, the philanthropist, she thought. And what did he have in mind for his old buddy Joe Sanborn? A nursing home? A rooming house in Anacortes? Because it's obvious what he had in mind for the land.

During dinner it became clear that it was assumed Anne would stay at the Sanborns' while she was on the island. It was a wet night, a long pitchy drive back to Deer Harbor, and anyway, Vinny had offered to take her across the bay the next morning to see the old McBain place on the point, and it would be easier to be ready if they were starting from the same place. She telephoned the Deer Harbor Resort Cabins to apologize and cancel the reservation, and the proprietor – Max – said that if she'd known Anne was having dinner at the Sanborns', she could've told her to hang onto her bag. "Joe's the toughest competition I have," she laughed. Anne hung up the phone feeling like a statistic, one of Joe's strays. She glanced from the entry hall into the living and dining area. Rose and Charles were clearing the table, Vinny was flying the baby above his head, and Joe had just placed the urn on the mantle and was stepping back once again to consider it. Anne was relieved that it was not expected she keep the urn with her in her bedroom: it, too, had a place at the Sanborns', although she found it odd that each time Joe had selected the most obvious place, the center of activity, in fact – Death on exhibit.

Carla showed her to the east end of the second floor, to a small room with flowered wallpaper, a pine bureau, a double bed covered with a thick, white comforter, and in the dormer niche, a writing desk facing out over the lawn toward Doe Bay and beyond to Peapod Rocks and the Strait. Over the bookcase next to the bed was a painting of a young woman with a full bosom, pale and bodiced up like a couple of warm buns in a basket. She was reading a book that lay open upon and was no larger than her hands, probably a pocket bible. The expression on her face seemed peaceful. She was the kind of young lady every woman wishes she had been, or fancies she still is. A natural, not a pro.

On the opposite wall were some of Monet's water lilies. There was a rocking chair in the corner behind the door, and a vase full of flowers on an oval doily gracing the bureau. Anne dropped her bag. "They're beautiful," she said, smelling the flowers.

"Vinny must have just cut them." Carla turned on the lamp above the rocking chair. "He has a big garden. Rose keeps trying to get him to plant vegetables, you know, but he says a flower'll make you smile and a tomato is just a tomato." Carla had a deep, easy laugh, and she swung around the room like an old friend, paying no attention to her manner, letting her thoughts seemingly spill out as she opened the heating grate and checked the window sash and concluded her readying of the room by leaning against the doorjamb, arms crossed, head cocked, eyes brightly amused. "I don't know how he makes it through the day. It's a good thing Rose is here. You can't eat smiles."

"I guess we need a few romantics."

In the mirror, Carla was watching her. Anne shifted her gaze to the dozen or more picture postcards of Europe which were tucked inside the frame, along with a black and white snapshot of a teenaged girl. Her dark hair was squared about her face and lined up exactly with her jaw: the effect was rather severe, because she had a wide, blanched face and black beads for eyes. She held a cigarette. Cradled in her arms was a plucked chicken – head, feet, and all – typical of the rudimentary way Europeans prepared meat for sale. The girl's expression was as fiercely blank as a door slammed behind a fight no one could hear. "Who is she?" asked Anne.

"Joe's daughter, but that picture's eons old. No one knows where she is anymore."

"What happened to her?"

"Rose says she was probably a schizophrenic, but she disappeared before they could firm up the diagnosis and do anything for her. Audrey. Every now and then he gets a post card. They all say the same thing . . .'Wish you were here.'

Creepy, huh?"

"Really."

"I'll let you get some sleep."

"Is there a phone up here?"

"In the hallway." She held Anne's eyes. "It's not very private."

"That's okay," she lied. "Thanks for everything."

Carla was already headed out the door when she twisted around, her straight blond hair settling on her shoulders. "Did you like him?"

"Sure. How could you not. He's so sincere."

"Vinny, yeah. No, I meant your father."

Anne felt her face flush hotly. "I don't know. That's hard to say. He might still surprise me."

Carla shut the door behind her and Anne sank onto the comforter. She was beginning to feel that it really didn't matter why she had come to Orcas Island. Here I am, she thought. Except here I am and I want to call Elliot. It would be wonderful to be around him enough so that I didn't notice him.

She waited a few moments to let Carla disappear, then got up and peeked out her door. There was a green and gold upholstered chair and a small table for the phone in the middle of the hallway, a swag light adangle over the pleasant grouping. Apparently Vinny was a frequent user, because his brown cigarettes were sprouting out of the bean bag ash tray. His office, she figured, if it was true that he was in the same kind of business as her father – real estate and development, enterprises that relied upon the phone call and the daily reminder that there was something out there someone simply couldn't pass up. In the next room a man cleared his throat. She hoped it was not Vinny, so close and able to hear her movements, to interpret them for his own entertainment. Maybe it wasn't fair, except that he had implied that they were supposed to meet somehow, and she could not help guessing at the purpose of that meeting, a purpose he seemed to fancy. Another sound. Glancing behind the open door, she stood very still and watched the wall, the Monet hanging on it, and Vinny behind, beneath the water lilies and the lavender blue water, his dark, angular face like a piece of metal in the depths. Silence. Had he gone to bed? She looked back at the phone and down to the end of the hall where a steamy sheet of light slid out from beneath the bathroom door. There was the sound of water running into a tub. A baby giggled: Carla was probably giving her a bath, and the thought of that honey-colored baby in the water, fat and splashing and happy, was a good, uncomplicated thought, a thought outside and beyond Anne, like a flower growing past the walls of a troubled city. Over the green and gold chair the light was softly anticipatory.

She went to the phone and dialed Elliot's study number. It was late, but she figured he would still be there. Seldom had they been so far apart, the tie between them so taut, ready to snap; but to talk, to plan for the next call or the next meeting would slack the line. Elliot would know that. If he had missed calls in the past, one of their nightly goodnights, he would not miss this one. She decided to make it an amicable conversation, not mentioning the pregnancy or the deadline. She would be supportive, reminding him that he had needed her before this trouble and he would need her again when it was over. The thought of her life before Friday afternoon and the news of her condition, the thought of going back before that, even going on with Elliot and those old complications, was almost appealing. Just put things back the way they were.

No, he would be there when she called: it was funny, but that was still an unbelievable concept. Elliot was as steady as breath.

"Where are you?" he asked.

"Orcas."

"But at Deer Harbor? Because I called several times when your mother said you hadn't arrived . . ." He sounded rushed, concerned.

"My mother?"

"Let me get your number first, while there's time. Then I'll explain."

She found the number on a piece of masking tape and read it off to Elliot. "I'm still at Joe's," she said. "It was getting late and it seemed expected that . . ."

"Look," he interrupted. "Jill's been out here twice already. I don't know how long I can talk. Your mother dropped by today."

"At the University?"

"Here. She heard about your father somehow and was in a tizzy to find you. 'I have business with Dr. Newhouse,' she told Jill. Christ, she was rude. She wouldn't give her name, and when she got me alone, she acted as if she and I were great allies conspiring against my wicked wife. The whole thing's already bad enough, and then to have your mother *drop in* hauling her psychoses behind her like a sack of old garbage . . ."

Anne heard herself groaning into the receiver. She stared at the door to the bedroom opposite the phone, wondering if Vinny (or whoever) was listening.

"What did you tell Jill?" she asked, half hoping he had told her the truth (as he had promised he would), and they could all go on from there. They could all *go*. Move forward. *Move*. What a fantastic, frightening thought.

"I told her your mother was the disgruntled parent of a flunked student. She couldn't have been convinced."

Slumping deeper into the green and gold chair, she found herself responding in the old way to the old concerns. "I'm sorry, Elliot. It never would have occurred to me. If I'd had any idea, I would have told her on Sunday at the restaurant."

"I know, I know." Elliot let go a sigh. She could tell that he was worn out, and she wondered if maybe he was nearing defeat. At least until the next morning, she thought, when he will likely revive the pretense as he has in the past, revive it until the day comes when it will be beyond saving. "It's not your fault," he was saying. "It's this impossible situation. And now with you pregnant . . . I don't know. She looks at me, Anne . . . it gives me chills. She just looks, and it's not a blank stare, you know, there's something guileless about it. She doesn't want an answer. She looks but the look has no conclusion. It makes me feel my blood's been drained off, that look. Christ."

"Some part of her must know. She lives with you, after all."

"It's hard to say with Jill."

Then, despite her resolve to keep the conversation loving, to not press him anymore than he was pressed already, she heard herself say, "I thought you were going to 'clean house,' Elliot."

A small, weighty silence dropped like a stone between them. "I am," he said. "But I don't want her to *find out*. That's a pretty lousy way."

Down the hall Carla emerged, carrying the baby wrapped in a white towel. She smiled as she tiptoed past. The baby let out a soft, back-of-the-throat gurgle, waving her arms toward her mother's face.

Anne was about to go on, but there was a low, muffled "Sorry" on the line, followed by the *click* of the receiver. Jill had come into his study.

For half a minute she left her eyes focused dumbly on the spiky bouquet of cigarette butts in the ash tray. She could feel her heart throbbing at the ends of her fingers, which were still clutching the receiver. Her ears were stinging with anger, embarrassment, shame – shame most of all. He had hung up on her. Elliot. He had just hung up on her. Sure, he had done it before and maybe before it had been necessary, but she had never gotten used to it, never.

In her ear the droning of the dial tone seemed to grow louder, more insistent, like an approaching siren. A terrible emergency coming her way.

But not now, she thought, not anymore. He can't hang up

on me anymore. Decent people don't do that. They don't. He hung up on me. *Elliot*. Why did he hang up on me? He shouldn't have done that, not anymore. I don't deserve that, do I? *Do I* ? Is that what he thinks I deserve? *Oh god.*

Across the hall, she heard a doorknob turn and, glancing up, she saw herself seated in the green and gold chair under the swag lamp, her reflected face in the brass knob ballooning, distorted, as the tall figure of Vinny materialized behind it. Wearing only a pair of gray sweat pants, he stepped out into the hallway and, as Anne watched the smooth, brown, perfectly confident V of his back move away toward the bathroom, she said into the droning receiver, "Well, I'm glad I phoned. Things'll work out, don't worry." It almost seemed she was comforting herself.

He would call back. He always did. Ten, fifteen minutes. As soon as he'd had time to deflect his wife. Which he was still doing. And still hanging up. Clean house, he had said at the airport. Right. So far nothing had changed. Nothing was going to change, she realized. It didn't matter that she was pregnant, that she had been devoted to Elliot for years – *devoted* – her time had not come, her need was not greater. And her father dead, too. *Damn it all.* Sure, he would call back, he always did. To talk. Elliot was a great talker. But Elliot was not going to *do* anything, it seemed. She just wasn't enough, was she? She just wasn't worth the doing. He had been putting her off again. But how could he hang up on her? When she was down, when she was in trouble? You just didn't do that, no, *no*, not to people you loved. Not if you really loved them. It was not nice. He didn't love her enough. She simply was not enough, not good enough for Elliot.

He would call back.

I've been such a fool, she thought, swallowing a sob.

Vinny strolled back up the hall, paused at his door, turned. "Everything okay?" he said.

"A distraught friend," she said.

He nodded.

"They're calling back."

"Can I bring you some wine?"

She shook her head. "Thanks." His kindness about tore her apart.

Five minutes passed.

The phone rang. She lifted the receiver an inch or so, then very quietly replaced it.

In its sounds and smells, the house was still offering up a genial impression, and at the moment she was exceedingly grateful for that. Not fussed over, yet not forgotten, like a member of a family, she closed the bedroom door. It was her room tonight. And tonight was all she seemed to have. She might have wished that Elliot was sitting there in the rocking chair with a newspaper and a glass of wine, imparting an occasional glance or a smile of small consequence that said they had been together awhile and no longer needed to apply unrelenting attention to each other's moods and activities, as new lovers often feel required to do. She might have wished him to her side. But this anger, this humiliation lurking low inside was new, and it scared her, because it was somehow familiar, too, a childhood nightmare coming true. And it had to do with Elliot.

There above the rocking chair were the water lilies, dallying like spring hats upon an idle pond. There sat the chaste young lady, still reading her bible, looking rather wistful now, as if someone dear had disappointed her, too. And there was poor Audrey with her dead chicken. Anne slid the photo from the mirror frame and turned it over. It had been addressed and stamped as if it was a postcard and read, indeed, 'Wish you were here.' Audrey had signed it with a very small, very solitary 'a.' 'A' for Audrey. 'A' for Anne. Very small. Very solitary.

THIRTEEN

Deep under the comforter Anne lay caught between sleep and wakefulness, a patient rising out of a sea of ether, rising, then slipping, sinking, rising again only to waver and repeat the delicious descent. She was aware that she did not really care which way it went. Finally and irreversibly swarming up, she awoke – *pop* – a bubble breaking the surface of a mirror-flat lake. There was no going back, going under. Sleep had perished.

Moving her hand to her stomach, she thought *crackers*, and remembered the packet in her purse which Loretta had instructed her to carry at all times for nausea, in the event she was one of those women who suffered morning sickness. It was Loretta taking charge – not her customary role with Anne – but she apparently felt it necessary in view of Anne's condition and her uncharacteristic indecisiveness. "Don't even stand up, go to the bathroom, nothing," she had said, "without a few saltines under your belt." Loretta's authoritative tone sounded across the miles, and Anne did not think to question it, though she figured she was hardly pregnant enough to detect even the earliest physical signs. Also, it was comforting to have something she should do, an order to obey. Reaching over, she pulled her purse into the bed, found the cellophane packet, and sprinkled the crumbled remains into her mouth. She was pregnant and that really did make her special, at least for awhile.

Through the dormer window the sunlight sliced in, bright and sharp as sheet metal. It was late: in the lower right corner of the window the sun itself was beginning to creep diagonally across the panes. She squinted over the edge of the comforter, half expecting (or wishing) to see Carla standing at the foot of the bed with a breakfast tray, the strange room and the late hour and the purpose of the crackers suggesting an infirmary.

Sounds from below fluttered up against the floorboards. The hallway was cold. She trotted down to the bathroom, hoping that everyone had already used it and that she would not have to conserve hot water for the next in line. A long shower, a strong cup of coffee, a ride across Doe Bay to the point with Vinny – things to look forward to. Everyone needed that.

Someone had left a mess of the bathroom – dabs of blue toothpaste on the counter, dryer cord dangling across the sink, bottles of shampoo, mouthwash, bronzer *(bronzer?)* cluttering the work area. She shoved it back against the wall. "Bronzer?" she said aloud as she stepped into the shower.

A knock at the door. "I'll meet you at the dock in an hour." Vinny.

"Okay," she called back.

"Does that give you enough time?"

"Sure."

He knocked twice to end the conversation.

Anne closed her eyes, letting the hot water follow the contours of her face. Vinny had told her that he jogged, and she tried to picture him now, a tall animal loping along the shore, a native of the islands, a Lummi Indian warrior stalking a doe at Doe Bay. With each footfall the sand flinched. The water was a creamy blue and as harmless as a virgin. He had a sweetheart back in the woods, this warrior (they all did), gathering huckleberries, and an uncomplicated life behind and before him.

Probably Vinny was a good athlete. Not a swimmer, but then most people couldn't tolerate the special brand of boredom swimming induced. In truth, it wasn't boring to Anne: *inward* was a better word. She wondered if Vinny had ever been inward, had ever emptied his mind and found something more valuable than language. He said that he liked to read poetry. Of course, she thought. Flowers, not vegetables; Porsche, not a pick-up truck; poetry, not the morning rag; Vincent, not Vinny; and strangers are friends – jeez. Was this guy for real? And he liked babies.

Fishing a pair of khakis and a red turtleneck from her suitcase, she slipped into her topsiders and, squinting at the light dazzling against the windows, decided a cotton sweater would do, a navy blue Shaker with elbow patches. Plain. Elliot was always urging her to wear more flattering outfits, but she had yet to grow out of buying clothes to grow into, one of Nellie's earliest budget-cutting devices. Almost everything she owned except her jeans was a little too big. In the mirror she inspected her profile, adjusted her posture and, turning her head, tried an open, expectant smile, as if someone had just called her. At the last minute, she dabbed perfume behind her ears and headed down the stairs.

"Good morning," Carla said. She was standing in the parlor to the left of the stairs, a spool of indigo wool in her hands, and a wooden loom before her.

"Hello," said Anne. "You're a weaver."

"Of sorts," she said, tapping down the last strand. "This is amateur stuff."

"Well it doesn't show. I'd call that handsome," Anne said, indicating the rug. It was a complicated design, blue and green geometrics on a white background, and so dense it was difficult to separate some of the shapes. But Carla had not deceived herself, for it was not exciting.

"You slept well," Carla said. "Everyone does in that

room."

"I'm ashamed to say that I barely hauled myself up out of the sack, and it was 7:30. Not the standard I'm accustomed to, really."

"It doesn't matter here," Carla said. She was chewing gum, snapping it now and then between her molars. "But I believe you," she said, smiling.

The room was dark, the curtains drawn on both windows. Metal desk lamps had been clamped to the loom and provided the only illumination to the work. "It's a beautiful day," Anne said, but both she and Carla heard the question in her voice.

"I have to use artificial light," she said. "For the colors, you know. Sunlight tells lies." She adjusted one of the lamps. "One day it looks blue, the next day it's black as a hole." *Snap*, went the gum.

"I was only about to lure you away from your loom, or try to. Vinny is taking me across the bay to my father's old place, and I thought maybe you'd like to join us."

"Thanks anyway. I have a buyer for this one, I'd better keep at it." Her hands fluttered about the loom, pulling this lever, tucking in that, threading the indigo wool. "The Institute's out there, you know, on the point."

"The Institute?"

"Hanuman Institute, yeah. It's a meditation center. Charles works there. That's his thing."

"Hinduism," Anne said. She knew of the Hanuman Institute. It had a place south of Santa Lucia on the coast, and one in Sedona, Arizona, another just outside Jackson Hole. And Orcas Island discovered, too. These people seemed to have a knack for buying up some of the most delicious property in the west, and she wondered now whether their business was indeed enlightenment, or glorified real estate. There was probably some tax break, separation of church and state, that sort of gambit.

"Will you be having a memorial service?" Carla asked.

"I hadn't thought about it."

"Joe's talking about one. He says a ceremony'll put a nice finish on things."

"Sure. I guess I should have one. There are more people here than I expected who knew him and . . . I guess I just didn't think about it."

Carla kept at her loom. "Rose left you breakfast on the kitchen table. She took the baby out for a walk." As an afterthought, she added, "There's some old photos and papers, too, in a packet on the counter. Joe's been saving them. They're for you."

Wandering off toward the smell of coffee, she decided before she even reached the kitchen to save the memorabilia for later. There was a basket of biscuits – still warm – and a dish of peaches placed at the head of the broad kitchen table facing a window. The urn, she noticed, had been moved from the mantle, and now sat at the center of the breakfast table, awaiting her, it seemed. Mal McBain was always the first up and the first to eat and not at all patient about stragglers, but now he had nothing to anticipate except his own dispersion and could afford to be indulgent. Pouring herself a cup of coffee, she sat down to eat, wanting to hurry through the meal so that she would not be found dining alone – the solitary feeder had always struck her as pitiful.

She looked at her peaches swimming like goldfish in the glass bowl, at the perfect pats of butter on the bread plate, the neatly arranged silverware, the five empty chairs tucked in and the silent plank of wood they defined, and the even more silent urn containing Mal McBain. Once again, like a member of the family, she had not been forgotten, but nobody had stood on ceremony, either. The kitchen had been cleaned up, and the members of this household had gone off about their business just as members of households all over the country had done this May morning. Except for Mal McBain and his daughter. They had business with each other – memories to file, doors to close, bad debts to write off – but neither seemed in any hurry to dispatch the job.

From the faucet, water drip-dripped into the sink. The smell of chicken fat and celery steamed off a large stock pot which was simmering on the stove. The house was still. Outside, between the trunks of ancient apple trees, strips of morning mist lay like abandoned wedding veils in the spring grass. Across the western sky a small plane tracked silently.

Maybe Elliot would call.

Abruptly, she returned to the parlor to ask Carla if anyone had telephoned for her.

"Nope," she said. Something in Anne's expression must have told Carla that more was needed, because she added, "I was first up. With the baby. I'd've known."

"It's important," Anne said, by way of explanation. "Elliot Newhouse. If he calls while I'm out on the point, will you tell him I'll be back at noon?"

"No problem."

He would have to call back, wouldn't he? despite her retaliation with the phone. There was too much at stake. She wondered if he missed her, or if he was using her absence (maybe welcoming it) to catch up on some of his domestic responsibilities. She had not begrudged him this in the past. Throughout their first year together he had let everything slide. But with the second year came sanity, he said, and much lawn mowing and deck building and gardening and they even put in a hot tub – *a hot tub*. It had been clear to him, she realized now, that he could relax, take care of the homestead, even neglect her some, without jeopardizing his relationship with her. These responsibilities included dinner parties – social debts, he called them – though she knew he enjoyed them. Elliot was no recluse; he liked a good party, even the war wounds of the morning after were somehow satisfying to him. They told him that he had had a fine time. She could see the Newhouses, host and hostess, beaming from either side of the entry as Dr. and Mrs. Blah-blah bustled into the whiskey light of another soiree among the cognoscenti. And later, out came the cognac and the dope, maybe even a dunk in the hot tub with the professor of philosophy and his witty wife, or better yet, the artist and his *um* who modeled, natch. A sour projection, but the notion of being a hostess for him made the whole thing seem hopeless. Because if, by some spasm of sentiment, McFate let them be together and the quarantine was lifted, how could they as a couple ever venture out into the world with their heads up, among his friends; and if they could not or were not invited, how long would it take for the exquisite isolation of their passion to become a poison?

Elbows propped on the table, she sipped her coffee and stared at the urn. What do you think, daddy?

I know, Elliot'll never leave, and I'm a fool, and this baby is bad news, coming and going. Just as I was, right? Except you dug a little gold between the coming and the going. Capitalize, that's what you'd've called it.

The peaches slid down her throat, cool and sweet reminders that there were things inherently good in this world, like fresh fruit. Indivisible things. Dare to eat a peach, she thought. Dare.

Oh Elliot. I wish you were here. I wish . . . I wish you could believe. I wish I could believe.

From the sink she heard a *plop.*

She wished he would call. Just a few words, like a hot meal, to start the day, a few words from Elliot and she could be free to . . . well, free.

Before her the urn stood, feminine in its symmetrical curves, a small, headless statue. She reached out and touched it. The clay was cool, not damp, but seeming so. I guess you are company, you and your last wish. I guess I am not dining alone this morning. My father and I, she whispered, dared to eat a peach. Dared to make a wish. In the presence of statues.

The faucet dripped into a container, a pot or a bowl, *plop*, like a penny into a wishing well. His last wish, she thought. *Plop.*

Plop.

Make a wish. Did you make your wish?

Yes.

What was it?

You're not supposed to tell, daddy.

You always do, and I always make them come true, don't I?

I shouldn't have told you. It's not fair.

Even if they come true? he had asked.

I don't want them to come true.

What kind of wish is that?

I don't know. My wish.

She could still see the reflection of the white statue recoil as her penny pierced the water and settled to the bottom among the other wished-upon coins. She could still hear her father standing behind her, jingling the change in his pocket.

It was considered a swank place, the Panache, one of the first of the 'theme' inns – ancient Greece or Rome, they did not make a distinction – though the name had nothing to do with its theme and was chosen (probably) because it sounded foreign and flamboyant. Seven massive statues lined the drive, each with a wishing well at its feet – Venus de Milo, Apollo Belvedere, Lysippus, a few Delphian virgins. Between the statues grew cypresses, the kind seen in Renaissance paintings, shaped like tall feathers. The cocktail waitresses wore mini togas trimmed with gold lamé, and high-heeled sandals, and some of them had painted their toenails with sparkly polish. There were narrow, raised columns framing the doors, simulated marble tubs in the bathrooms, and paintings of the Parthenon and other Greek settings hanging on the walls. For a decade or so the Panache offered the most expensive accommodations on the San Francisco peninsula. It was where Mal McBain stayed whenever he had his daughter to himself.

Anne was attending a boarding school in a wealthy area known as Chamberlain Heights, one of several 'bedroom communities' south of San Francisco. Malcolm McBain agreed to pay the expensive tuition so that Anne would have "the finest education," he told Nellie; to keep her away from her mother's "neurotic influence," he told Anne; and the truth – so that he would have unlimited access to his daughter without Nellie's foreknowledge or presence.

As usual, she had been called from study hall and told that her father was downstairs. And as usual, they had driven to the Panache after some shopping, and he had placed the seven pennies in her hand for each of the seven statues and their wishing pools. Though she anticipated this evening to resemble, down to the dinner mints and the bedroom games, previous visits, there was something different about this time, this afternoon. She had just turned fourteen and, like any of her muscles, the intangibles, too, had matured, so that they could resist, like the muscles in her arms or her legs, greater and stronger forces, could even accept a certain amount of pain in order to achieve a desired end, which was very adult indeed, she thought.

No, this visit was different. She had not expected it to be so when he picked her up at school, when he bought her the purple dress with the V-neck. Her mind had been on getting her homework done, on what Julie had said about Sister Gordon, on what she would order for dessert – things of that trivial nature. Yet when she stood before the first statue, squeezing the seven pennies in her hand, she felt inside something hard, like a good skipping stone, something that could take her places, and all she needed was the power in her arm and the correct flick of her wrist and a fine, fine aim. Somehow, quietly, while moving one day after another through her life, it had all come together – the power, the aim, the correctness. She could hardly have been more aware of it than had she simply grown into one of those big dresses Nellie was always selecting for her.

She tossed the seven pennies into the pool beneath Venus de Milo.

"Why did you do that?" asked Mal McBain.

"It was a big wish, very expensive." She knew she was being a smart aleck, but she knew also that he would put up with it because he was going to get what he wanted later on.

Mal McBain squinted up at the naked statue. "Maybe you're too old for this now."

"Not for wishing."

"You'll always be my princess."

From behind the glass doors leading into the lobby a bellboy watched them. His arms were crossed and he was arched backwards slightly in a contemplative pose.

"I know," she said. Flipping her hair to one side, she looked away. The bellboy had disappeared.

"Still won't tell me your expensive wish?" He jingled his change again. "I might be able to help it along."

"No, not this time. I can't."

In truth she had wished for nothing. She was tired of their little rituals and she was hoping that in the final analysis her father would sense this and disregard her words. Why did parents think that the same things were endlessly amusing to kids? But you couldn't hurt their feelings; you had to lie and hope that they figured it out or grew bored with it themselves.

The bellboy was older than he looked from a distance and shorter and he had an ugly birth mark on his right cheek. He was waiting beside Mal McBain's rental car when they returned from the statues.

"Both bags," said her father as he tossed the keys to the bellboy. And out came the black suitcase and her small blue duffel, a pink yarn bow flopping off its handle, so clearly belonging to a girl. A child.

But on the way up in the elevator, the bellboy said: "Shall I make dinner reservations for you and Mrs. McBain, sir?"

Inwardly, Anne groaned.

"Seven o'clock," said her father, and he gave the man three green wads for his trouble. And for the question.

When Mal closed the door to the room, he spun around, half bent over, and practically giggled. "He thought you were my wife, honey. That's how grown-up you are."

"He didn't really."

"Yes, yes." Throwing his jacket on the bed, he held out his arms. "We're going to have a wonderful night. Come give me a kiss." He was obviously pleased with the bellboy's mistake. It seemed to give him permission to behave openly the way he always wanted to. To deny him now, to hesitate, would be difficult. The world in the form of a bellboy had pronounced them husband and wife. Ironically, she realized that she was almost old enough to be that – a wife – for someone, at least in some cultures, and that realization seemed to make what they did together all the more improper. If it was confined to her childhood it could be tolerable, relatively speaking; if it did not spill over like a toxin into her adulthood.

She looked down at her loafers, scuffed and broken in at the heels – a girl's pair of shoes – examined her bare legs, the new purple dress that revealed not actual cleavage, but the shadow between her breasts. They were bigger than any of her friends'. One of the boys at school stared at her chest whenever she was talking, just to unnerve her. Anne ran a finger up her shin, as smooth as the bone it sheathed. She had only begun to shave her legs two months ago during one of his visits. He had given her his razor, and Nellie was angry about it because Anne was too young for 'that sort of thing.' Maybe if she had worn knee socks . . . but it was a warm day . . . if she was wearing socks, the bellboy wouldn't have thought she was his wife. Socks, that's all it would have taken, she thought hopelessly.

Rising from the edge of the bed, she pursed her lips and kissed him.

"Soften your mouth, honey. It's nicer that way."

Relaxing, she felt his lips press into hers, felt the slippery warmth behind them; she smelled his breath – Tums, coffee, and something faintly caustic, like floor cleaner – and pulled away, bouncing onto one of the beds. "I'm starved," she announced in her best little-girl voice, to remind him. Always to remind him.

When he was in the shower, she turned on the TV, went

down the hall and brought back a bucket of ice for his drink – a CC-Seven – found his money clip on the dresser next to a pile of change, and counted out the twenties. There were 12, along with 3 tens, a five, and several ones. She put one of the twenties in her shoe, and four quarters in her change purse. He would never miss it and anyway, after he did what he wanted, she deserved it.

The shower stopped, but the fan was still running. She glanced from the TV – a circus act with a man balancing two women atop his head – to the money clip, then back to the TV screen. The highest woman jumped off and bowed.

Always one twenty dollar bill and some change, unless there were no more than five twenties, then she had to pass, confining her theft to the change, but that didn't happen often. Though she doubted he noticed it, now and then she wondered if he knew all along she was stealing from him, but was not saying anything in order not to jeopardize their "special secret."

The second woman jumped down on the other side of the man, and the three of them sank to a deep and final bow.

Anne stood up.

From the bathroom, she heard the whirring fan, the faucet turning on, off, on again. Shaving, then he would brush his teeth, gargle, and emerge wearing only his briefs. There would be sweat on his upper lip, and sweat twinkling in the dark hair of his back. He would want her to sit on his lap. He would offer her some of his CC-Seven and she would gulp it down like pop, feeling the rush, and letting herself enjoy him, enjoy even his adoration of her until it wasn't possible, until she couldn't pretend anymore that he was just behaving like a doting father.

Picking up the money clip again, she fanned the bills: 11 twenties, 3 tens, and the smaller stuff. She could hear him gargling, that horrible medicinal wash. Any second and he would swagger out, his hips low and slung forward and seeming to precede the rest of his body as a gunfighter's might in order to present firstly his wares; any second and he would appear with his, his, with his penis pushing against the nylon between his legs, trying to get out. And he would smile of things to come. It was a nice smile actually, a shy boy's, a hint of loneliness, and the merest shadow of a shadow suggesting danger in contradiction. He did not smile much: he used his smile as one might an expensive tool whose effectiveness was subject to dulling. He had wintry eyes – not a winter of postcard cheer, but winter hard and bleak – and there was about those winter eyes a pleading quality, as if there were things unspeakable he needed and would simply have to take. Any second now, and the nice smile and the eyes that took. *Take*. Quickly, she re-folded the bills in her right hand and clipped them. In her left hand 6 twenties remained, which she jammed into her duffel just as he appeared.

"I can't find my toothbrush," she said, trying to cover.

"Use mine, if you want."

How could he not know now that she had stolen from him? It was stupid, a stupid stupid thing to do. Why? Why did she do it, what would she say when he found it half gone? A hot wash of panic, and she fled to the bathroom.

The white noise of the fan and the impersonal room seemed to separate her from what she had done. She put the theft out of her mind. It was like a stray dog: it was sick and it was hungry and it was a troublemaker. She just didn't want to care about it, or about anything to do with him. She was fourteen. She wasn't his wife and she wasn't his daughter, she was nothing. Nothing to him. Nothing. And she told herself that she wouldn't care if he never came again. She put it out of her mind – what she had done, what she had been doing, the possibilities – put it out, and only an hour later, trotted ahead of him down the hallway to the elevator, counting the red and black diamonds in the carpet as she went and telling herself that if she stepped on a line, someone would die, and stepping, *oh* stepping on one line after another.

Dinner, like staying at the Panache, like the seven pennies, like the new dress, was the same. She ordered prime rib. Though she wanted chicken, her mother told her always to order the meat entree because it was the most expensive, and he was paying, and they couldn't afford it themselves. Similarly, her father wanted her to choose an expensive item, because it put her deeper in debt (along with the new dress), a debt on which he had never failed to collect. So there it lay, a slab of meat wading in blood, and on the right corner of the plate, a scoop of horse radish turning pink and pulpy as it soaked up the *jus*. And a fruity Fog Cutter full of concealed alcohol, delivered to his side of the table, but meant for her. "You'll like it," he said. And she did: it came in a tall brown glass molded into the face of a Tahitian idol, a tiny paper umbrella and a toothpick-sized spear heavy with chunks of pineapple and maraschino cherries rising from out of its head.

The cocktail waitress in her mini toga dropped some change next to Anne's father, and when she bent to pick it up, she whispered something to him. He gnawed on his knuckle – something he did whenever he was nervous – and grinning, said, "Sounds expensive." Below the waitress's toga panties, longish dark hairs had escaped. She wasn't wearing any stockings, Anne noticed.

"I think she was asking me for a date," he said. He sent Anne his shy needy look. "But I already have one."

She was aware that she had smirked, and looked quickly away. Everyone was always asking him for a date. Was he that handsome or did he do something to invite it?

He did it, she decided, surprising herself.

A familiar voice reached Anne and, searching the adjacent tables, she saw that it belonged to her piano teacher, Mrs. Worthington. She was seated with a man (her husband?), and Peter, her son and Anne's classmate. He nodded Anne's direction, and she pretended not to have seen him. But it was too late; here came Mrs. Worthington.

"Hello hello," she said.

Anne's father stood up. They bussed each other, having

met before at one of Anne's recitals. Mrs. Worthington had introduced Anne (the first performer), and as she was walking up to the stage, she saw her father gesturing toward Anne's empty seat. Later, the two of them now side by side, he said something, though he did not look at her, and Mrs. Worthington tipped her head forward as if in agreement. She was wearing the most peculiar half-smile. Neither appeared to be listening to Anne's playing, despite their enthusiastic applause at its conclusion. It was her favorite, too. Mozart.

"It's wonderful, isn't it?" Mrs. Worthington said, making a point of glancing around the room. "The Panache never fails."

"That's why I keep coming back," said Anne's father.

"You've been here before."

"Once or twice."

There was that peculiar half-smile again. "Are you in town for long?" she asked.

"Just tonight. I have to get back, I'm afraid. The business." Looking suddenly awkward, he cleared his throat. "It needs me more than I want it to," he added.

There was a small hole in the conversation. Under the table, Anne rolled and unrolled her napkin. Mrs. Worthington's eyes were directed toward the slab of prime rib, though she did not seem to see it. She was wearing a simple knit dress which exaggerated the curves of her hips; they swelled outward, then slid back in and down to her calves. Her square face with its faded freckles, and brown hair which she always wore up, and her fingernails which she kept clean and short for the piano keys were ingratiating, Anne thought. Except for her figure, everything about her was measured, like the music she so loved, and Anne had grown to depend upon Mrs. Worthington as she might have a favorite aunt, sometimes confessing to her troubles at home, or quarrels with her friends. She once told Anne that she was 'spirited', and let her learn a waltz instead of a sonatina or a 'folk dance' for the Christmas party. Spirited . . . Anne liked that.

"Anne's playing is so lovely this year. She's developed a

sensitive touch," said Mrs. Worthington. "Quite mature."

"She's a smart kid," he said.

"Yes, yes she is." Her voice was drifty, preoccupied. "Peter said to say hello to you, my dear," she said to Anne.

"Say 'hi' back."

"I'll leave you to your dinners. Goodnight now."

Then Mal McBain said, "Goodnight Tori," and Victoria Worthington – that was the name Anne had read many times off her briefcase – winced, blinked up at him with alarm, turned, and rushed back to her own table.

It occurred then to Anne that perhaps Mal McBain had not gone back to Seattle the day of her recital. He was supposed to have caught a flight out that night, but maybe he didn't, maybe he and Mrs. Worthington . . . Tori . . . Stopping herself, she stared across the room at Mrs. Worthington's brown bun atop her head, hating its teacherly neatness, its steadfastness, hating her for that flamboyant figure, so incongruous and such a betrayal of the rest of her, of the things that mattered most. Of Anne.

At the end of the meal, the waiter brought the check and Mal McBain reached into his pocket for his money clip. He opened the bills, counted them, paused, looking up and across the room as if seeing someone he knew, counted them again. Very faintly smiling, as if it wasn't a smile but only his recollection of one he had tried years ago, he placed 3 twenties on the tray and said, "We're a lot alike, princess, you and me."

Did he know? How could he not know? Feeling sick to her stomach, Anne ducked into the ladies' lounge, rinsed her face with cold water, stared at her eyes in the mirror. They looked frankly back at her, like the eyes of an imaginary older sister who had 'told her so.'

At the elevators he was waiting, a toothpick dancing between his lips. "You'd let me know if you needed anything, wouldn't you, Anne? Even if your mother put you up to it, and believe me, I know she does that now and then, if you need books or clothes or *money*, just ask. You might want some money that she doesn't know about, money of your own, and that's okay, too. Every young woman needs her own spending money."

Money, he said, money four times. Nellie wanted it and he had it and Anne stole it. And she didn't have the faintest idea why. She just did it.

He knew now.

Well, good. Fine.

"Okay," she mumbled. "If I need some." She tried to hold his gaze, but he had those sad eyes going again, and she faltered beneath them.

He knew. She had stolen from him, but he wasn't going to punish her, he wasn't going to say peep and mess up his evening. And she realized that that was likely why she had taken the money – to make him mad, to stop him. What else would he let her get away with? Smoking, that was already permitted, and Fog Cutters, and he had taken her to a club once in San Francisco where men dressed up like women. She really wasn't sure she wanted all of it, at least not all the time. Maybe occasionally so that she felt grown-up, felt important, but she didn't want to *be* grown up, not yet.

The elevator doors opened, and she jumped in, defiantly pushing every button on the panel. Behind her he stood, saying not a word, and at that moment she was aware that she could do anything – anything – and he would say not a word.

"I'm not like you, dad," she said.

"Dad?"

Not turning around, not explaining her use of the more formal address, she said, "I'm a girl and I'm not like you anymore."

"Sure you are. You're smart, you're . . . "

"No," she interrupted. "No I'm not. Not as smart as you are. And anyway, you don't even like Mozart."

"Mozart didn't just buy you dinner."

"I only meant that we like some different things. I'm fourteen, you know."

"I pay for your piano lessons, for Mrs. Worthington, and *I'm* the one who gave you Mozart. You can look at it that way." He cleared his throat. "I know what you like, too." There was a certain threatening lilt to this last assertion that brought the blood to her cheeks.

Just above her head the lights blinked on and off as the elevator rose and stopped at each floor, opening to no one and nothing, and she seemed to feel the flashes as if they were pieces of a large thought that was trying to form. A very large, complicated thought. When they reached the sixth floor, the thought pieces coalesced, and she stepped out of the tiny room away from her father and into the empty hallway with its many many doors, saying to herself, I don't have to be like anyone.

In the swank hotel room at the Panache he removed the baby-blue woven shoes he had had made in the Bahamas, then the ultra suede jacket, slacks, the thin, feminine socks, the gold cuff-links with the tiny diamond centers, leaving the white shirt still unbuttoned to the middle of his chest.

Anne tried closing her eyes. The alcohol was particularly strong this time. Along with the usual sensation of downward pressure, as if she was in a plane that was plummeting faster than the pull of gravity – it was called negative G's, she had read somewhere – she felt that she was spreading out beneath it, but each time she opened her eyes before the crash. Negative G's, she thought, closing her eyes. Negative.

"I feel funny," she said.

"Oh?"

"Like something's pushing down on me."

"I'll be there in a minute."

She put on her nightie and crawled onto one of the beds. She heard him gargle, rummage through his suitcase, double lock the door.

"Is it your stomach, princess?" he asked from around the corner.

"Not this time."

"Because I have something that might help it," he said.

"It's not my stomach."

She was always having stomach aches, usually just before bed, but it was okay tonight. He had got her drunk, she realized, he had got her drunk so that she would be easier to manipulate, that's what she had heard men did, and here he had done it to her. Her father.

On the back of his hand was a plastic box held in place with two thin straps that ran under, across his palms, and back to the opposite side of the box. He pulled up her nightie and laid his palm on her abdomen, then, touching a button on the side of the plastic box, his hand began to vibrate. He moved it in circles for a minute or two, watching his hand as it paused to massage, his fingers like roots stretch, spread down toward her legs, curl back, only to reach further the next time.

"Does that feel better?" he asked.

"My stomach's okay, daddy. I think it was the Fog Cutter. There was too much alcohol in it, I think."

"It should've relaxed you."

"I guess it did." Under his vibrating hand her skin was jiggling in a frantic, almost comical way. Conceding to his fiction, she added, "And my stomach's okay now."

Not seeming to hear her, he circled her stomach again, and when he made a pass far beneath her navel, his middle finger dropped between her legs, gently probing, re-emerged briefly, then plunged again. Uncomfortable, embarrassed by the noise of the little machine, by the feel of it, by his skew-jawed expression, and squirming backwards against the headboard, she was, nevertheless, not surprised. Anymore, very little surprised her, and that was not good. No good. When his other hand went to himself, she reached to the nightstand and shut out the light.

She remembered when he fell asleep that night and the snoring began, loud and sloppy-sounding, she remembered waiting for it. Because she could not sleep next to him. She just could not sleep next to him ever again. The bellboy and the money and Mrs. Worthington in her knit dress and that awful little machine's buzz-buzzing as if she was a thing, some thing you put machines to, like a car, and the seven wishes she had wasted, *wasted* on Venus de Milo with her one arm and her stone nipples, because what good were wishes when you were fourteen and you couldn't believe, what good was nighttime if you couldn't sleep, couldn't dream, what good, what good?

The curtains were closed, but every now and then the cold metallic light of a car slid along them, like a giant probe, and the room was thrown into icy shadows, and the sheets became a stark, white pool in which their bodies were lost, their heads floating, like buoys. Danger, they said, dangerous waters, danger below. She waited an hour maybe, to be sure. Then, very slowly, she eased herself over the edge of the bed, rolling lengthwise onto the carpet between the glass balcony doors and the bed. Don't move. Listen. Still snoring. If he woke, she would tell him that she must have fallen out of bed, and to ensure credibility, she left the pillow and the trailing sheets and blanket above her, next to him. On the floor against the glass doors it was cold. It was long and narrow and hard as a coffin. But it was her place for the night. And she let the lights of the occasional lonely automobile move along her body, like a giant probe searching for life.

The next morning when he was shaving she returned the money, including the 4 quarters. Then she sat down at the table with the Panache stationary and a pen, and drew dark Egyptian eyes, and wrote her name as fast as she could, the way adults did when they were signing something important, until the page was crazy with great staring eyes and her name, barely legible, circulating between them. She felt that she had made a decision, though she didn't know how to say it yet.

Outside, down below, people were loading up their cars. The statues in the morning sun were too white to look at, but the troughs beneath them were a cool, alluring blue, the coins at the bottom shimmering, like fallen fish scales. Overburdened bellboys wobbled out to gaping trunks, then tarried conspicuously as the ladies settled themselves in the car and the men dug in their pockets for a tip, and the children disappeared among the sculpted shrubbery for one last go at hide-and-seek. They had all had a nice time, Anne figured, here at the Panache. In their petty comings and goings they could not imagine the secret world she was living in, nor the cell from which she peered this bright morning. She was forever beyond them, a foreign body, a cancer so tiny that she didn't even matter and wouldn't affect them or their lives or the way the day went. They would not glance up and see her. They would not feel her miserable presence behind them. They were invincibly normal. Normal. But she was inside a cancer, it was inside her. She was fourteen. It had to be stopped.

She heard her father clear his lungs and spit the mucus into the sink.

Arm in arm, a young couple strolled the path between the statues. Late spring, and the lady was wearing a sleeveless white dress. Her bare arms were brown and pretty and she reached up and let them float gracefully down, like wings. To Anne, it did not seem impossible that the lady could fly.

"What are you doing?" her father asked.

"Nothing. Just doodling."

"You could doodle off a few more letters to me, princess."

"I write you every week."

The soft swishes of clothes started up behind her as he sorted through his suitcase. She wanted to wait until he was dressed, when there wouldn't be naked skin between them.

"You wrote your mother every day last summer."

"She's used to having me around," she said, startled by the coldness in her voice. "I was just trying to cheer her up. It was kind of a joke, anyway. Not enough happens to write every day. You'd be bored."

"I don't think so." He was picking the pennies out of a handful of change, which he did every morning, leaving them on the dresser for the maid, or, when he was home, for his wife, Marlene. He checked the alarm on his watch and unbuttoned one more button on his blue Hawaiian shirt. "It's going to be a hot one." Already, there were crescents of sweat under his arms.

"I have a boyfriend now, dad."

"You do? What's his name?"

Not anticipating the question, the only name that came to mind was, "Peter, Peter Worthington." A smart boy, terribly shy, and kind of nice looking, despite the glasses and the perpetually half-tucked in shirt, she had to admit that she had never really thought about him until this moment and certainly not in any romantic context.

"Your piano teacher's son?"

"Yes. He's really smart," she added, trying to behave as if she wanted him to like her boyfriend – as any teenaged girl would with her father.

"I'll have to meet him some time." Something was wrong: he did not sound in the least bit hurt or jealous or even concerned. Maybe she had better say more.

"I guess I have a crush on him," she tried.

"He's a lucky fellow, princess."

"So daddy, so . . . " The eyes on the stationery watched. "It'd be better if we weren't together in bed anymore, you know."

"What?" He had been combing his hair in the mirror, but abruptly he dropped his hand and studied her, his expression moving from confusion through anger and arriving (somewhat worse for the wear) at relief. "Look, honey, I think I know what you're trying to say, but it's okay with me. I want you to date boys and have fun. I didn't do enough of that when I was young, I was always studying or working. It was the depression, and that was what you had to do to survive. I was bashful, too. That didn't help matters. But we have something special, you and me, something most fathers and daughters could never have because they aren't smart enough to understand it, they don't have big enough minds for it to fit into. But we do. It's very special." He paused to smile. "At any rate, it won't bother me if you date."

"And we would still . . . "

"Make love." Another smile, tender, reassuring.

"But I have a boyfriend, daddy."

"That's fine, fine. Peter, was that the name? Peter will only reap the benefits of all that I've taught you. I'm just happy it was me who taught you about love."

"I can't . . . I can't do that. I have a boyfriend now," she said, unable to think of anything more convincing than simple repetition.

Slumping down on the edge of the bed, eyes watering, he said, "It doesn't matter to me, princess, don't you understand? That's how much I love you, how much it means to me. Marlene has problems, I've told you that, and our love relationship is empty. She can't, well, she hasn't slept with me for years, and making love is like food or water to me, I have to have it. I'm a healthy man. She doesn't understand the way you do, she never has. She's not like us. Nobody is."

Anne heard herself saying, "I know."

"I love you so much. You're my princess. In my eyes, you can do no wrong. Your mother used to criticize me for that, she was afraid I would spoil you, but there was nothing I could do. It's how I feel. And our little visits mean the world to me. I don't know what I would do without them, without being close to you, princess. There is no one else. I don't know what I would do." He was crying.

The many eyes on the Panache stationery were still watching her. Some of them were almond shaped with fluttery eyelashes – a woman's – others were narrow, scrutinizing, full of intelligence, or round and foolish, the pupils unaligned, or squared off behind glasses, but they were all watching her, waiting for an answer, the eyes of people she would meet someday, maybe even the eyes of the man she would marry. And the answer was there among them, it seemed, in her signature, fast and illegible, like an adult's. Very adult.

He was still crying, trying to hide it, but not really. She went to him, resting her arm across his broad shoulders. She said, "Please don't cry, daddy." His hands were dangling off his knees, but he turned them upwards briefly in a gesture of helplessness, as if he couldn't resist the weight of the sorrow she was bringing to him. "I'm sorry, please stop," she said. "I know what we have is special."

Snuffling, he looked up at her, that weak pleading cast to his eyes she had seen so many times before when she would tell him she didn't feel well, or was too tired, or that she just couldn't 'pop' for him, her legs shaking with the effort, the rigidity inside too much. "We're so much alike," he said. "I'm so proud of you. You know that, don't you?"

"Yes, I know. And I don't want you to cry. I think it's neat that you want me to date, to have the fun that you didn't get to when you were my age. And we can still sleep together, it's okay with you, that's neat." She paused, took a deep breath. "But I don't think it's okay with me. I mean, I have a boyfriend now, and it wouldn't be okay with Peter. It wouldn't be very nice, probably." He was pulling away from her, standing up. His back loomed upward, and she added in an almost gay, matter-of-fact tone, as if this last would clinch her argument, "Anyway, I want to be a virgin when I get married." He had always told her that what he did did not mean she would not be a virgin. She could only lose her virginity if he pushed it all the way in. Plus, he was her father so none of it really counted.

Mal McBain swung around, his face red, his hands like clubs. "What is this boyfriend crap?"

"Huh?"

"Who cares if you have a boyfriend? Or not. I don't think you do. I think this is a smoke screen."

Her mouth dried up, her heart jumped. He was like a monstrous rock before her, hard and dangerous, ready to let loose, to crush her. She tried to sound calm, innocent. "I don't understand . . . what's a smoke screen?"

"A lie."

"I'm not lying. I do have a boyfriend, daddy."

"So what. What difference does that make? You know it makes no difference."

"But it does. I'm fourteen, and it all matters now."

"Get your stuff. You're going back to school."

"Aren't we going to spend the day together? We were going to spend the day together. Weren't we?" Ridiculous, impossible, but she thought to diminish the argument and pacify him, even enlist him in the fiction by pretending that it wasn't a big deal. He had to be careful because he didn't want her to tell; maybe he would ease up. Though it was a big deal. It was everything. Now she knew that. For him, it was everything. Which meant there was nothing else, there would never be anything else.

He was throwing clothes in the suitcase. "You're just as neurotic as your mother. I should've known better. You won't hurt me anymore, Anne. No more."

"I didn't mean to hurt you, daddy. Really. I love you. You're my daddy and I love you."

"As far as I'm concerned, I don't have a daughter. And I have news for you, Anne. You're no virgin."

FOURTEEN

From the kitchen window Anne discovered Vinny down on the dock, skipping stones across the pale blue satin of the bay. How long had he been waiting for her?

The stones danced off into the rising sun, leaving pin pricks in the satin, until each in its turn pierced the fabric and sank beneath it. Jumping down from the dock, Vinny bent and gathered up additional stones, examining each for its flatness and weight, testing its shape in his throwing hand, its contours against his fingers, and he even crouched low once and pretended to flick one across the water. Climbing back on the dock, he resumed the sport. One stone ran out particularly far and must have touched down at least a dozen times. Vinny made fists of his hands and shook them once, triumphantly, then he glanced back at the house.

A big kid, Anne said to herself as she rinsed her breakfast dishes, just a big kid. And again she realized that she was looking forward to spending the morning with him, an uncomplicated excursion with someone who considered a stranger his friend. How easy, she thought.

Taking her hand, Vinny helped her into the skiff, saying something gently sarcastic about women never failing to do dishes just about when it was time for people to leave.

"Sorry," she said. "I kept you waiting."

"You did," he said, but he was smiling, and it was clear to her that it was not that he had been kept waiting, but that he had been deprived of time with her, because he seemed to be in no hurry as he aimed the skiff southeast over the slack water, following the curve of the shallows to the point.

"You don't work today?" she asked.

"This afternoon. I thought you might like to use my car. I'd need a ride to the landing, is all."

"Are you sure you want to trust me with it?"

"Porsches are designed to make driving easy." This sounded like something the salesman had told him. "Anyway," he added, "that rental of yours looks sick."

"It blew a water pump between Seattle and Anacortes." Reporting this fact gave her great satisfaction. She had always enjoyed confirming other people's suspicions; it was a little like giving them a gift.

"Then you have to use my Porsche."

The bow did not even bounce as they crested a few low swells – a "set" in California terms, but of laughable dimensions for surfing. It was that way in the islands: fantastic tidal fluctuations and knee-high waves, exactly the opposite of the southern coasts. It had to do with relative exposure to the open ocean, and the shape of the adjacent ocean basin. In Washington the ocean floor was a deep bowl, while along the California coasts great shelves extended sometimes miles out before dropping off. On just such a shelf Gina had been hit by the shark last weekend.

A pang of guilt. She shook off the memory. Anyway, Elliot hadn't blamed her for Gina's death. He was a biologist; things happened. They had lost a mature male last year trying to weigh him. Drugs had induced near complete paralysis, and he had gone into shock. But females were used to submission. They could be handled. Even some human females went around half-sedated, like Jill Newhouse – she had to know her husband was up to something, but she kept quiet, letting him handle her. Sedate her.

How any self-respecting . . . Anne cut off the thought. It was catty. Anyway, she was just as sedated as Jill Newhouse who had every reason to say nothing, a whole history to preserve, stuff that was worth a little self deception, a little waiting-it-out. So let her study Elliot's face and try to guess, *is he? could he?* Unless he hangs a neon sign on his forehead, she might not ever answer the question.

We are all waiting for a sign, she thought.

And what was Anne's excuse? Nothing so noble as history. Love. *Luuuuuuv*, she sneered. What a word. It had been used so much there was nothing left of it, it was a dull, shapeless thing, people had wrung the life out of it, so that now when she said it – *luuuv, love you Elliot* – she found that it had to be revived with just the right tone, (a hint of melancholy seemed to give it a certain verity), or propped up with adjectives – desperate, utterly irresistible – or heightened with snippets of poetry – there in the foul rag-and-bone shop of the heart, *luuuuv*. Love on the radio, love in the Chevy jingle, love every Christmas from Aunt Eloise whom you've never met, tru luv carved into benches, love boats and love bugs, God loves you, love for sale, first love, then marriage, and squalor, love nests, love lives, and love from you to the old friend who betrayed you more than once and whom you hate really. Hate – now that was a word. It had edges, and its color was black-red, it was dense like lead, and it had a weight you could feel in between the muscles of your back, it smelled like burning weeds, and it didn't ever need the right tone or a string of qualifiers or poesy to convey itself. Say 'hate' and everyone knew exactly what was stirring in the air.

I hate.

Trying to remember the last time she had used the word 'hate' and coming up empty, she vowed to say it at least once before year's end.

Yet it was love that drove her. And love was using itself

up. A cannibal for the cause. She felt like the fellow in the old cartoon – on a train trying to escape the bad guys, the coal runs out, and he begins dismantling the train, board by board, to keep going, until there is nothing left but the very plank on which he stands and this, too, he throws into the fire. For the cause. Anne figured she was down to a handful of boards.

Maybe it's not impossible, she thought. I could learn to leave him. And after a year or so of no one, of putting that part of me to sleep, I'd let some nice young man in, a big kid like Vinny who keeps a flower garden, someone who wouldn't know how to leave me.

The outboard grew louder. Now the skiff etched a thin, white V in the water. Vinny touched her arm and pointed to a rock in the shallows. On it perched a jet-black cormorant, its wings hung out to dry, presumably too sodden from a dawn feeding bout to lift him off the water. He fluttered them regally as the skiff passed.

"Means herring," Vinny yelled. "And good fishing."

She nodded.

"Maybe tonight."

Nodding again, she added a smile. *That would be fun.* Fishing in the islands. She and her father had wound in and out of these over-sized rocks since, well, since she had memory. The smell of gasoline, kelp beds, salt drying on her skin, and fish if they were lucky, and the thermos of coffee he always saved until they were headed back to Roache Harbor or Friday Harbor or the mainland, until they were headed back anyway, and he realized with a flicker of desperation in his eyes that he had hoarded the coffee beyond desire – smells. *Smells.* Old smells right here. Now. She dropped her hands over the sides of the bow, trailing them through the cold water, then laid them on the wooden bench to dry. Later, she would lick the salt off their backs, taste this place, this bowl of ocean, this good memory.

The point jutted due east out from Orcas toward the collection of rocks and toy islands known as Peapod Rocks, about a mile offshore. No fringe of surf defined them – the water was too placid – and they seemed to be sailing away, like a lost regatta.

Vinny slowed the engine, and they chugged through the shoals into the shadow. Off the end of the point was a gravelly spit which waves had gradually thrown up as they angled around, trying to get into Doe Bay – a common phenomenon in an archipelago. The spit was arched, its tip curling back on itself, and the water inside qualified as a lagoon, even though at its west end it opened into the bay. Along the inner waters salt grass grew – tall and graceful – and the even taller bulrushes, and buttercup reaching up through the water. A rocky beach followed the point inland, sweeping around toward the Sanborn place. The beach was littered with driftwood – great trunks – bleached, smooth, light as balsa, she guessed, and terrific for leaning against as the flames of a beach fire, barely visible in the dusk light, rose in time for supper and midsummer dreams. She could remember times with her father and his friends and their kids before such a fire, a whole salmon wrapped in foil and ready for baking; she could still hear the night they sat on one side of a tiny anonymous island, knees up before the campfire as marshmallows were loaded on long twigs, the fog huffing off the water like the breath of a sea monster, she could still hear the fantastic call of bagpipes drifting in the fog over the island, sad and eerie, some Scotsman lonely for the moors and chancing onto the same island, and no one thinking much of it except Anne. No one falling through a hole in Time. Because in that tiny timelessness it had all seemed to converge, what being was about. And it meant nothing. That was its beauty. She just happened to be there, a part of the convergence.

Before we all flew apart and found out about love. And hate.

Up the rocky shore young rabbits hopped among the driftwood. A gull swooped down and sent them bobbing off for cover into the elderberry bushes.

"Watch your ankles," Vinny said.

The rocks were softball-sized and well-rounded from eons of beating about in the surf. Tottering inland, she retraced evolution, and spotting the base of the trail, turned to Vinny. The northwest was behind him, green and blue and empty, not a boat or a building in sight, not anything to do with their real lives. No evidence of California, no sign of trouble.

"I feel like a brand new creature," she said.

Vinny selected a rock, stepped, selected another, stepped, then apparently becoming impatient with the routine, he said, "Forget this," lifted his head and trotted forward, ankles intact.

Stretching her arms out to her sides, she sang, "I could be anything."

"I know how you feel," he said. "Now. I've kept moving, changed jobs."

This had nothing to do with what she meant, but it didn't matter. She would have said it regardless: the company was nothing, part of the scenery.

On a beached log they rested.

"It must be hard, if you have a family, to move around." For some reason it was easy to picture Vinny with children, clean domesticated children.

"I was tied down once," he said. "Really tied down. Wife, two kids, budgie birds. The wife was into birds. And she was a good mother, too, I couldn't complain, not about that. My boys love her. But I needed things, everybody does, excitement, you know. I needed to feel alive, and after awhile, she lost interest. I didn't feel loved, and that's what's important. She just didn't mind the way our lives were going."

Anne murmured sympathetically.

Vinny got up and began hunting about for a walking stick, testing each prospect against a boulder. "Every Saturday morning, pancakes, every Sunday afternoon, barbecue with the Austens, horseshoes, beer, the works, and once a week, a tiff about the boys. Even our fights could be predicted. She would run off to her mother's which was less than a mile away – that was a big mistake." Vinny whacked a length of fir against the boulder. "And they'd sit in the garage smoking cigarettes because the old man had allergies, until I came along and got her. I mean, I just couldn't live knowing *exactly* how my life was going to be, day in and day out."

Anne was startled by Vinny's confession, despite its over-rehearsed quality; it sounded a little like a sales pitch. That's unkind, she thought. He probably has talked about it a lot. Everyone does that, to work it through. It was perfectly healthy, she decided, though she still didn't know what to say. "It doesn't have to be that way," she tried.

"Right. Right. That's what I kept saying. Let's spice things up, travel, whatever. She didn't know what I was talking about. She was happy, she said. *Happy*. We were in a truck-sized rut, and she was happy. One weekend I bought her a new outfit, took her to the fanciest hotel in town, champagne, the works. And she . . . well . . . you just can't hurt a man that way and expect him not to look around. She got all steamed up about a wig. I bought her this blond . . . " Suddenly he looked embarrassed. "Hell, it doesn't matter now."

Anne was beginning to feel sorry for Vinny. She didn't know many women, but of the ones she liked only Loretta seemed capable of the monotonous, because she was so excruciatingly disciplined. But she was not insensitive.

Moving past her, Vinny started up the trail.

She heard herself ask, "So how did it end?"

"In a pretty typical way, I guess. I had an affair. When it was happening I figured I was the worst human being on the planet, that no one else had done what I was doing, or could ever feel the sick guilt I woke up with every morning of my life. And it went on a long time until the wife found out. And you know what she did?" He stopped, turned around. "Nothing. It was a Friday night. Saturday morning, there were the pancakes, every one exactly the same, same size, same color, and stacked up like the years of our marriage. 'They're getting cold,' she said. 'Better hurry.' Not 'you bum.' Not even a tear. That was it. They're getting cold."

"I guess you don't eat a lot of pancakes now."

They smiled at each other.

"Not on a regular basis," he said.

The woods were quiet, their steps springing on the thick humus. The air was damp and shaded. Several times she caught the burnt sugar scent of balsam, like a child's Christmas, and she wanted to find it, stand next to it, inhaling. It was time she stopped passing things up. The funny thing was, she was sure that if she asked Vinny to indulge this silliness, he would, and with the same glee. She didn't ask him.

Ahead, she could see blue sky filling in behind the boughs of fir. They were almost on top. She made a very small prayer that the Institute buildings would not be visible, not at first.

"There's a road out here, isn't there?" she asked.

"Sure," he said. "But it's not as fun."

"I was just wondering how Charles got to work."

"He probably wonders himself."

Usually she would have let this sort of slighting intimation pass, because she wasn't interested in Charles – he seemed fairly self-explanatory – but she was curious what Vinny thought about ambition, given his admiration of Mal McBain, and the decidedly romantic slippages in Vinny's personality. She said, "Charles isn't exactly goal-oriented?"

"Not unless you count sitting around cross-legged and breathing weird."

"Pranayama," she said absently.

"What?"

"Breathing meditations. It's a Hindu practice."

He was helping her past some large boulders that had collected at the base of the final incline – an act that would not have been allowed with Elliot, because it had obviously always pleased him that she made her own way in the world. And she wanted to please him. But here with Vinny (what was his last name?) the opposite seemed natural and, as she accepted his hand she realized that already the relationship had evolved some rough contours. Pausing, his tone incredulous, Vinny said, "You do these things, too? Practice breathing?"

"A phase," she answered. "Years ago. It was useful at the time. I needed calming down."

"Now you're all calmed down?"

"That depends," she said.

"I won't ask on what."

Emerging from the woods, they stood at the edge of a meadow, the grass a dusty green and thigh high, wild flowers straining up. To their left the point of the point was shaped like an arrow and filled in with trees.

"Is it in there, the Institute?" she asked.

Vinny nodded. "Incredible piece of property."

She didn't need to ask about her father's house. Small and boxy with one of those bungalow style roofs, like a dutch hat, it sat in the middle of the meadow on a slight rise, commanding a king's view of paradise. She ran to it, grass slapping against her khakis, air sliding in and out easily. Vinny caught up with her at the house, bent double, hands atop his knees, his Reebok tennis shoes a harsh white under the midday sun. Gasping, smiling broadly, he said, "I haven't done that in ages."

There seemed something vaguely inappropriate about a huffing, puffing Vinny.

"You're a beautiful runner," he said. "A doe, a long-legged doe."

She smiled and turned away toward the house. "It's smaller than I imagined," she said. She peered into one of the windows; on the other side was a face, a face with large, amorphous freckles. Anne jumped back, and the window flew open.

"I'm sorry," said freckles. "I didn't mean to scare you."

Her name was Lisa, and she and her friend, Arbind, who came around the corner with a coffee can in his hand, were 'sort of caretaking,' or at least they had been during the winter when the Institute wasn't so busy, was, in fact, empty a lot of the time. It was May and they were supposed to be out, but it was so special now, the wild flowers and the berries – her friend held up his coffee can, filled with red currants – that they just hadn't been able to move on.

Arbind was a dark, wiry fellow, with deeply set eyes magnified by his old-fashioned spectacles, and a thick, brindle beard. He looked hungry. He looked like a vegetarian. And Lisa was his opposite: a wedge with strawberry-blond hair, leather shorts, serious hiking boots. Anne pictured her with power tools in her hands.

Vinny hung back, looking awkward and antsy. Anne explained their presence. The couple exchanged glances and practically bowed.

"Please have some tea," Arbind said.

It was Chai tea, a blend of herbs and honey and cloves, a slosh of hot milk, all boiled on the stove in an open pot until it was the color and consistency of a southwestern river, reddish brown and just past transparency, the spices swirling, like unsettled silt. On the low cushions and pillows lying about they sat cross-legged, talking about Orcas and the locals, about the Institute with which they had a failing relationship, somewhat like expatriates. "It's a business," Lisa said. "The people in charge have lost touch with what it was supposed to be about. They have attachments. They're not centered anymore."

"Maybe they aren't in touch because that wasn't ever the point. They own a lot of fancy real estate," Anne said.

Arbind pulled on his beard. "Yes. We were troubled by that when we found out."

"It's just not necessary," Lisa said. "Not for yoga, not on the path to enlightenment. They could have built ashrams in Nebraska or Texas, it wouldn't have mattered. The worldly is not where it's at." Pausing, she looked at Arbind, as if to obtain permission. "I think they're planning to build something. Not a spiritual center. A resort or something."

"I hope not," Anne said. "But I guess I wouldn't be surprised."

"You know," said Vinny. "Last week I was standing in the middle of this beautiful green field, there were cows even, and I knew an office building was going to be there where I was standing in less than six months, and I felt sad. I stood there and felt lousy. I mean, development has to happen, I guess we all know that. We need the units and the company I work for will do a first class job, I know. But I tell you, I grew up hunting and fishing, and I love the out-of-doors."

No one quite knew how to respond to this.

Units, Anne thought.

Lisa passed the plate of nut bread around for the second time. Vinny was the only taker. The couple finished their Chai tea, insisting that Anne have some time alone in her father's old home, and off they went in the direction of the orchard.

"Centered?" Vinny said. "Does that mean you live without electricity and plumbing?"

"It's easier that way," she said, not trying to be understood.

"My knees are killing me." Unkinking himself, he stood up and began poking around the house.

Between the scatter rugs, Anne made out the old linoleum, its loose pattern of flowers, its thinning patches, rough wood emerging through a red petal, like pentimento. Water stains wavered across the ceiling, around the sashes; nicks showed here and there where a chair had leaned, a pail had bumped, an angry fist struck. In the kitchen a small, pot-bellied stove stood, and judging by its condition – the broken mica windows, the missing leg replaced with a couple of end cuttings, the tarnished nickel – it probably was around when Mal McBain was a boy. Two small bedrooms peered into the kitchen. No toilet.

In the door jamb between the front room and the kitchen she noticed a series of notches, an initial beside each one, many of them M's, mostly M's, in fact, toward the top of the jamb. M for Malcolm. While the others had lost interest or only occasionally bothered, Malcolm McBain had measured himself regularly, and in the end his notches appeared unsurpassed. The last one, the highest, had been dated June 1927.

Vinny came over and inspected the marks. "Must be sixty, seventy years old," he said.

"Yes. My father . . . " But she didn't know what she meant to say. What was there to say in the face of such hopeful looking forward, these notches, like tallies, a young man's measuring up, and that man, that future gone now, become a small drift of ash? She felt Vinny's hand on her shoulder, and wanted to cry. But he said, "He was a terrific guy," and this seemed to quench the desire. No he wasn't, she wanted to say. But he *was*, and here are the marks to prove it, carved with his own hand nearly three quarters of a century ago.

"Lot of books."

It was not true, not by her standards. Brick and board shelves lined one side of the parlor and at eye level, girding the room, was a single shelf, the books facing out and spaced as if on display. Before several of them small candles stood, or metal incense burners, or a few dried flowers. *The Tibetan Book of the Dead, Satsang with Baba, Desert Solitaire,* something by Aldo Leopold, Emerson, *Autobiography of a Yogi, The Snow Leopard.* It was likely she would feel more at home with Lisa and Arbind, with people who asked questions, than with Vinny, even though she considered herself a scientist, not a philosopher, and therefore justifiably responsive to the empirical only. She could not deny that she had read some of the books on display and many more of their ilk not present. But biology was safe. It could be verified. It could be counted on. Unlike people.

Still, there was something about Vinny, a willingness to . . . well, a willingness. It was endearing. In that respect, he was indeed like Mal McBain. He would try anything, no questions asked. He was game. He had exhausted himself running across the meadow trying to keep up with her when he was so clearly not up to it just to . . . *there, that was what was wrong with what he had said earlier* – I haven't done that in ages, he said. But he was a jogger.

Out on the porch Vinny bent down and brushed off his tennis shoes then, straightening, he peered back into the dimness of the old McBain place and offered an uncertain smile to what must have been an uncertain impression of Anne. Would she like to walk down to the south cove before heading back?

"Okay."

"It's hard to leave," he said.

"Not really. I don't think of him in this context." Hotel rooms, restaurants, airports, big cars – they were more often the circumstances of their meeting.

Vinny chuckled, a wisp of self-consciousness lingering around his neatly drawn lips. "I meant I was enjoying being here with you."

FIFTEEN

They were silent on the drive to the ferry landing. It had nothing to do with the visit to the McBain place, or with Vinny's little deception about his daily jog. In fact, in regard to the latter, Anne decided that he had said it to impress her, as if a small boy had bragged on himself and hadn't enough guile to remember what he had said and not go about contradicting himself later. Meaning Vinny was not a frequent liar, and his sin was therefore, somehow, flattering to her.

No, they were silent because when they walked up from the dock, they caught Rose squatting in a wallow, urinating, all the while reaching forward to pluck a handful of wild daisies which were thriving in the low, muddy areas of the field.

Red-faced, Vinny veered off. "My mother, she doesn't care how things look." This was not the first time he had apologized for Rose, it seemed. Jaws tense and eyes averted, he rushed into the house. Minutes later when he re-emerged suited for work, and they climbed into the Porsche, he gunned it out of the driveway.

Anne wanted to tell him that she didn't care much about how things looked, either. That she lived on a ten-acre piece in the high hills above the ocean, and that now and then, on a summer evening when it was still light, when she was comfortably flopping around the property like any of its inhabitants, like the jays or the quail or the gray squirrels or even Holmes, she would squat down herself and for a few moments admire the peeling bark on a nearby madrone, or a wild iris coming up through the decomposed granite. Not to say, this is my territory. I'm here too – that's all. Too. She wanted to tell him that she liked to shower outside, especially on cold mornings when the hot water made a wild contrast; that now and then on clear nights she slept on the deck with Holmes; that she enjoyed the smell of drying sweat and burning cedar and Acacia blossoms after the rains have beat them off the trees and they've begun to rot sweetly under foot. But she didn't tell Vinny. He seemed at home in his three-piece and his Porsche, his brand name tennis shoes, his brand-name being. He had set himself apart from the natural world – a hunter, a seller of unreal estate, a dealer in units.

In spite of this she noticed that she was happy around Vinny. He had sincere, straightforward understandings, even if they didn't have much staying power. She found herself reverting to archetypical behaviors with him: she let herself be helped up the cliff, she accepted the only cushion, the last soda, his childish fib. She seemed to need the simplicity here on Orcas Island, here in her mess of a life. Archetypes were easy, like masks. Like lies. He was so very different from what she knew. And what she knew was falling apart.

They had skipped rocks, and Vinny's stone had won. This was fine, as it should be. Imagining a shining yacht anchored in the south cove, they gave it a name – *Seamagic* – and sailed it to Hawaii, though she cared nothing for pleasure crafts or cloying tropical islands. The wish belonged to Vinny, but the game was theirs. They had discussed the memorial service, where to scatter the ashes, and Vinny had comforted her as men are supposed to, and it had felt good, illusion or no. His comfort didn't need to *mean,* it only needed to be.

Vinny was returning at the same time she had arrived the night before, and she would meet him with his car. The next five hours were hers.

Joe Sanborn hitched across the drive as Anne pulled in, his white hair surprisingly exotic from a distance, like the crest of a rare bird. Male plumage. The sign of a survivor, that white hair. Desirable genes. Joe was a venerable old fellow, she decided, and he probably had not felt the need as Mal McBain had to cash in on all of his talents and qualifications, to live off principle. Interest only – that was Joe Sanborn. A saver, a man of moderation. The salvage diver.

A hammer dangled from Joe's hand, and from the other a rubber flip-flop. He stopped, squinted her direction, removed a nail from between his lips and dropped it in his shirt pocket. "Have you seen my wall?"

"No," she said a little reluctantly. Her plan had been to swing back by the Sanborn's for some recent periodicals on whale communication which she had picked up at the University library the morning of her flight, along with the packet of old photos and papers, and a thermos of watered down *vin ordinaire*, then to drive up to Cascade Lake where her father spent time as a boy – a favorite spot, he told her once – for a light afternoon hike, some preparation for the next day's interview at Waddington Marine Station, and if there was time before Vinny's ferry returned, maybe even a snooze in a sunny glade. The plan had been to forget Elliot and the pregnancy for a few hours. To try to, at least. But as she crunched through the pea gravel behind Joe, she heard herself ask for the second time that day if anyone had phoned for her.

"No," he said. "Except if Carla took the call and she's sleeping." He lifted and turned his head to the side, and she watched the smoke of his gaze drift out over Doe Bay. "My wife used to do that, she did, when Audrey was new. She got so she could sleep any time of the day, like that," and he snapped his fingers. "Like a baby."

Anne hung back, digging the toes of her moccasins into the gravel.

"She's been gone," he said, as if Audrey was simply on an extended holiday from which she would return any day, full of gay stories and art books and baubles. "They kept saying she's not right. What does that mean?" For a moment, it seemed a genuine question. He glanced back and smiled broadly. "That's her room you have. She'll like you, yes, I think."

Rounding the southwest corner of a small barn, they came about before a twelve foot wall. Hundreds of flip-flops, not one matching another, had been affixed to it, toes down, neat rows, and each flip-flop with a single, flat-headed nail – a roofing nail probably – sunk through at the narrow juncture between the heel and pad. The nail heads had rusted, and against the flip-flops the rust showed – a brown orange halo, like old blood.

"They wash up on the beach," he said. "They float."

"So many," Anne tried, not knowing what to say, not at all. The idea that Joe Sanborn might be, well, a little *off*, blipped momentarily across her mind.

"That's just our beach. Folks have tried to give me the ones they find from other places, but I only hang the ones that come here to Doe Bay, just them." He knelt down, pressing the recent arrival to the weathered gray wood, the last one now in the bottom row, and pounded in the nail. "You see that one up there." Standing, he pointed to a small green flip-flop – a child's – terribly corroded, at the upper left corner of the topmost row. His finger was shaking. "That's Audrey's, it is. I remember the day she lost it. We were fishing on the far side of the Peapods, and she had her feet in the water. She liked her feet in the water. She was eight that summer. And happy, oh boy, you could feel it sitting next to her in the boat. Happy." He let his hand fall. "You could," he said quietly.

What was there to say? Stick to facts, to the measurable measures. "When did you find it? Soon after?"

"Oh, years later," he beamed, his pinched, minstrel's voice sounding pleased and proud and sad, as if verging on a hymn. *Years later, oh yes, alleluia, alleluia, yes, I found it, alleluia.* "After she went."

"It must be hard with her gone."

Nodding, eyes wide and vulnerable, he admitted, "I do miss her."

She touched his shoulder.

If Audrey were to step out of the surf now – one foot bare, the other wearing the mate to the founding flip-flop on the great wall of strays – she would see an old man with white hair, white like something new, not old, something untainted, undefiled, like his love, and a young woman wishing very hard that she could be Audrey for Joe Sanborn, that she could be a daughter cherished in absentia, and coming home.

They walked back to the house together.

Behind her the screen door banged shut. She looked for and found the urn back atop the mantle now, commanding from its high place: you will go to Orcas Island, you will carry my ashes, you will scatter them in a fitting manner and in a felicitous place, in my memory. Because I am your father.

"I have a picture." Joe reached into his shirt pocket and held out a sepia photo. "We were eighteen, we were, because that there's a '27 Ford."

In the photograph on either side of the Ford stood Joe Sanborn and Mal McBain. Strapped to the front fenders were two young bucks with their heads posed so that the antlers curved skyward. His hat back, young Joe smiled genially across the hood at Mal, while Mal McBain, with the butt of his rifle resting on his thigh, and his hat angled down over his forehead, like a gangster's, stared straight out of the photo, out of the scene, out of that black-and-white time, as if he thought someone important might be sizing him up. He looked comfortably tough.

"That was the only one on the island, not figuring in the orchard trucks. Mal bought it brand new himself. A '27 Ford."

"But they were poor," she said.

"Poor, oh boy, sure, we all were. That was the normal state of affairs. But not dumb. Dumb like a fox, Mal was. Smuggling was the game then for plenty of folk, good folk, too. These islands are dang close to the border, you couldn't not see that during prohibition. Your pa," he said, as if to remind Anne. "He was always one to see a big opportunity when the rest of us wasn't looking." Squinting at the photo, Joe let go a soft chuckle. "'A handy place to get lost,' he used to say."

She passed the photo back to Joe as they went in to the kitchen. He pulled two beers from the refrigerator, offered her one, and replaced it when she declined.

"I'm going for a hike," she explained, "up at the lake." She held her thermos under the tap, then added a couple of long sloshes of red wine to the water. "For flavor."

Over the rim of the beer can Joe raised his eyebrows.

"It's very French."

He smiled agreeably and peered at the photo again. "Yuh, he bought the Ford in Bellingham and gave it to his Ma on her birthday, and she never asked. She never asked and she never would ride in it, neither. Hooch money, she knew right off. Your grandpa liked to drink, I'm sorry to say. It was a hardship for the family, I'm sorry to say, his drinking." Pausing, he took a sip of beer and swirled it around in his mouth. "He always said you looked like his ma. They were real close, Mal being the eldest and in charge of the place for a long stretch. I don't see it myself. Selda was a mannish sort of woman."

Anne stood up.

"Lake's not far," he said.

"Good," she said. "That'll give me time to do some reading for the interview before Vinny gets back."

"We'll have a ceremony to say good-bye to Mal."

"Yes. Friday, before I leave. Is that okay?"

"Fine, fine. Always liked a show, he did," Joe muttered. "A big show."

It was six miles to Cascade Lake, back along the Horseshoe Highway. She was ready to be alone.

Inland, the road swept along the eastern slope of Entrance Mountain, dipped, rose sharply, then fell against the long edge of the lake. Pulling into a campground, she shut off the engine and waited as the trailing cloud of dust enveloped Vinny's Porsche and swarmed on, into the shallows. She would try to hose down the car before returning it. Several small boats bobbed on the water. It's too early, she wanted to tell them. You won't catch much now. Dusk, when the bugs come out and the wind rests and the knifing whistle of an osprey can be heard off above a tranquil cove slicing through the silence cleanly, astonishingly, as the lovely speckled bird lifts heavily away from the water, a young trout held between its claws, and very much alive as it points like a shiny metal rudder toward the osprey's nest. Dusk, when the small disturbances on the surface of the water tell all – the tracings of a long-legged skater, the nick of a dragonfly, the penny-sized hole where a trout kissed its ceiling, the comings and goings between two, sometimes three, (if you included land), great mediums – that is the time to fish.

Then, fish is not what fishing is about, she thought. Just as daddy has little to do with my coming to Orcas.

An aluminum dinghy went by, its outboard gurgling softly in the water. On either side two boys held rods, the lines and poles forming sharp angles so that the small craft seemed to have spread transparent wings on which the children rode. Father in his fishing hat manned the rudder. They were trolling. Trolling, the way Mal McBain liked to fish. Some people simply had to keep moving.

Vinny had suggested they troll some that evening: it was still an appealing idea, provided she talked to Elliot first, put her mind at ease.

The photos and papers Joe had left for her, together with

the thermos went into the daypack she had brought along. She slung it on one shoulder and locked up the car. The campground looked full. There were children wading at lake's edge, women in lawn chairs outside the doors of their campers, some teenagers throwing a Frisbee, a girl in a straw hat, the smells of burning charcoal, outhouse chemicals, citronella, and the vaguely metallic under-aroma of the lake itself.

A man approached her. His skin was as pale as jack cheese, and he was wearing army green shorts, gym socks in street shoes, and a cockeyed pair of black rimmed glasses, thick as Coke bottles. Behind, at the bottom of the spiraling concentric circles in each lens, she found the small black BBs of his eyes shining kindly.

"Excuse me, miss. Number seventeen's open. We, my wife and I, we try to save seventeen for the tenters. It's level, and all grass." He pointed over Anne's shoulder. "Up there, last one."

"I won't be camping. I was just going to take a short walk, maybe an hour or so."

He seemed disappointed. "We get mostly RVs anymore. They need hook-ups."

"Are you the . . . " she searched for the right title, "the camp custodian?"

"Host," he corrected her. "Nancy and me. I'm Norm, and that's our trailer there." He gestured toward what looked like a metal boxcar, a torn awning hanging off the far side, and a set of jerrybuilt stairs listing away from the door. With the flat of his hand he shoved his glasses back up his nose. "Now, do you know how to get to the falls?" It was the official camp host's voice he was using now.

She shook her head, not knowing of any falls on Orcas.

He drew a map in the dirt. There were four falls, the first less than a mile from where they stood. Norm offered to keep an eye on the Porsche, and walked off toward the boat launch.

Cascade Falls, a long white rope of ice water, was a popular spot because of its proximity to the campground. Not stopping, she picked up the trail to Rustic Falls and, finding people there, resolved to keep going through Cavern Falls, hoping to shed tourists the further she got from the lake. At Hidden Falls she would stop regardless. The approach led along a gravel service road hemmed in by shrubbery which exposure to sunlight had encouraged to grow unchecked. Dense and head-high, these bushes, and after the filtered green lighting of the woods, the service road promised a far less appealing route back to the lake than the way she had just come.

Within a hundred yards she began to hear the falls off to her left behind the greenery. Angling down, she checked her watch. Several hours before she would have to meet Vinny, though she had decided she would try Elliot from the pay phone at the landing, which meant arriving a little early. She ached to talk to him. Ached. She would not see him until the day after tomorrow, and already that seemed far away. Between now and then were veldts of time. And Vinny, Vinny would be . . . well, he would not be absent. It was hard to say whether or not she was glad for that.

Tucked in behind a tumble of boulders was Hidden Falls, much smaller than the others, dark and grotto-like and, inside the bowl it had carved, as cool as a rainy dawn. A young couple moved off when they saw Anne, and she made no attempt to excuse herself. Emptying her daypack, she dropped it in a crevice, and leaned against a jutting slab of granite. The water flowed evenly over the lip of stone so that with the wall behind, the falls were as black and shiny as lacquered wood. A contemplative place.

Shivering, she began sorting through the papers Joe had left for her – several photographs, Mal McBain at around ten wearing a boy scout uniform, saluting, the smile sweet and unsure, the eyes squinting up; the entire McBain family except for the old man, Mal standing in the back next to his mother, his expression posed, looking both solemn and wounded, (if that is possible), as if he wanted to be taken seriously and taken care of, by whom Anne couldn't say, maybe his mother; then Selda McBain, a tall woman with a muscular face, holding a baby; and a copy of Joe and Mal and the bucks strapped to the Ford. There were some school transcripts – all A's – receipts from a Western Avenue fruit company, an envelope from a boarding house in Bellingham, 'Geo McBain' the return, (circled), and 'Malcolm McBain' of Orcas Island the addressee. And there was a story written in 1929 for English IV by Mal McBain. The pages were thin and browned, the lengthwise fold almost worn through. Beneath his name, a large E had been penciled, E for excellent, she supposed. The story was called "Jimmy's Courtship."

"Jimmy Bales," it began, "was one of those bashful, retiring, unassuming young fellows" who was "afraid to talk to a girl" and had resigned himself to bachelorhood. "He had poor will power," it continued, "and could be swayed to do anything or to admit whatever another desired him to admit." "Poor Jimmy," as he was frequently designated, was placed next to the town's old maid, Miss Sourleigh, during the July 4th picnic. "Surely they did not class him with the useless, the drones, the backnumbers, and the tattered ends of society," Jimmy worried. From there, the young man stumbled and stammered and yessed his way into matrimony, for Miss Sourleigh could not help but interpret his bashful agreeableness as proof that their souls were "in harmony." "And a happy pair they were," the story ends, "if you could judge by the happy Mrs. Bales. Jimmy, of course, replies 'yes' to whatever she says about the matter."

Anne shook her head, smiled. What a funny story . . . for him of all men. He was twenty when he wrote it, and if he understood this fellow's predicament or imagined himself to be like him, then he had changed a very great deal. He had developed, as they said nowadays, he had gained confidence and stature: this was what young men were supposed to do. Maybe it began with a little success with a shy lily, a girl of his own ilk, then a woman of experience perhaps took a fancy, a taste of desire and of desire satisfied, more women, more success, success exclusively and the sense of power that that fathers, the illusion of rightness that *getting* conjures up, and finally he might have asked for appearance's sake only, or on some occasions not have bothered to ask at all. Making assumptions, he might have taken without resistance, with impunity. As he did with Anne.

He took the way Holmes rolls his catch between his teeth, she thought. Not biting down, savoring the prospect, the small twitches of resistance backed up against the assuredness of his eventual success. Confidence and time were his, he held the softest of birds between his teeth, possessed it, possessed her, her heart and her humiliation. She could *not* say no. Could not, from the beginning. Because there were those tender teeth about her, and in them the feel of a great need, his pleasure . . . and her power, the only thing he gave. Power was the victim's pay. She knew she could hurt him and she knew too that she would not, not for a long while.

When it was clearly over between Mal McBain and Nellie Gallagher, it started with Anne. The business in bed. (Later, Anne considered this timing to be curious, but she left it at that. Much of what he did could not be explained, and anyway, there was always the possibility that the answers would be worse than the riddles.) They had been in California over a year, and still he had not joined them, though Nellie knew the divorce must have been finalized and that there was ostensibly nothing preventing their union. He was in New York City and had big doings, he said, involving the world's fair. It could 'set them up,' he said. She had to be patient, think of the future.

Of course Nellie was capable of neither. It was in the past with Mal where she had lived, while the present in California represented inertia and doubt. Nellie's dream of the future meant regaining the past. And as for patience, the year in California had exhausted what meager reserves she possessed.

They went to New York.

It was a long flight, Anne remembered – six hours – one for each of her years. She knew her mother was excited, she kept ordering CC-Seven's, and when the stewardess came by to say that they were about to land, there was a tidy row of the miniature bottles on the tray, which Anne had made into soldiers, saluting them before she put them away.

Her father met them in a new turquoise Cadillac: there was some discussion about it, a funny look on Nellie's face, a nervous smile on his, and another funny look with a shake of her head when Nellie ran her hand over the black leather seats.

"My," she said. "My, my."

He chuckled. He roughed Anne's hair. He seemed not to want to pay much attention to the new car, except that Anne could tell he was proud of it by the way he stood back from it, as if it was royalty, something you gave a lot of room to.

"I never knew you liked turquoise," Nellie said.

"It was a good price."

"Doesn't everyone take the subway in New York City? I thought everyone took the subway." This was Nellie's first time east.

"I guess a lot do, have to. But these investors . . . the limited partnership I told you about, they all drive 'em. I'd just as soon go without a tie as not show up in one of these." He bowed slightly toward the car. "You have to look rich to get rich in this business."

"Oh," said Nellie.

Walking around the long hood to the back end, he slid the Cadillac emblem up to the side, exposing the key hole, and opened the trunk. It was lined with a soft black fabric and shaped like the inside of a Jacuzzi with a deep hole in the center and higher, bench-like sides. A set of barbells clanked in the center well, there was a bottle of windshield cleaner, some maps, and a pink umbrella. He threw the suitcases on top of the umbrella and slammed shut the trunk lid. "At any rate, it was good price."

Nellie said, "It'll be such fun to drive back to California," and she said it so that he would notice *how* she said it – eagerly, the way a child speaks, eager and innocent and impossible to disappoint, and yet daring him to do just that. Daring him to hurt her.

Mal was silent.

They checked into a hotel because he had lent his apartment to a buddy, he told them. Anyway, a hotel would be more fun, he winked. Anne was sent down to the lobby, equipped with a box of crayons and a coloring book. "Don't hurry," said her mother. "Stay inside the lines. It's not how fast you finish each book, it's how well you color them."

They rode to the top of the Empire State Building, though it was foggy below and they couldn't see the tiny cars and the specks of people, and they went to the world's fair, and if Anne hadn't gotten lost walking ahead of them and ended up in the police station, they would have seen the Pietà by Michelangelo which had come all the way from Italy, and Nellie wouldn't have developed blisters in her new high-heels, looking for Anne. And it all would have been fine, a nice visit, if a little tense because he wasn't ready to come to California, he had business, he said, and he wanted Nellie to understand, to be patient. She was trying – Anne could see that – she was wearing makeup and her coat with the fox collar, and she was terribly cheery around him, as if it was her last chance, saying how much Anne was like him, how clever he was whenever he talked about business, how wonderful the places he took them, what a pretty little family they made sitting on the picnic blanket in Central Park. At night when Anne was supposed to be asleep, she could see them bouncing in the next bed, and in the morning they passed secret looks across the coffee shop table. Anne figured they were happy, or at least that her father was trying to be nice and her mother was trying to believe.

It would have been okay if Nellie hadn't hired the taxi to take them to his apartment the afternoon before their flight.

She found the address on an envelope in his coat pocket, and while he was in the shower, she copied it onto a piece of the hotel stationery. He would be working that day and would meet them later at the restaurant. Nellie bought a greeting card – one of those poor children with the big sad eyes on the cover, 'I miss you' in tiny typed letters within – and she was going to slide it under the door where he would discover it tomorrow after Nellie and Anne had already left, after his buddy had moved out. Anyway, Nellie thought it would be "interesting," she told Anne, to see the building he lived in.

"We'll hurry," Nellie told the cabby.

Shrugging, he said, "Meter's running." Despite the rain, the cabby opened his window as the two hurried to the stairs under the awning.

The building had a locked lobby, but someone had wedged a folded piece of paper between the door and strike plate. Nellie removed the paper as they slipped through. "That's dangerous," she explained. "Anyone could get in."

His apartment was on the seventh floor. Number 79. On the way up in the elevator, Nellie licked the envelope flap, puckered her lips, and kissed it. She was all dressed up for dinner – they were going to Le Pavillon, the finest, he told them – and her makeup was fresh, so the kiss left perfect peachy lips on the flap.

"You smell good," Anne said.

"Thank you, dear. It's Christian Dior. Your father likes it." She sounded calm, assured. The trip to New York had been a good idea. It would be easier now in California. Maybe she would even take down the blankets which she had hung over the curtains in her bedroom. Maybe they would go for drives again.

"What about daddy's friend? Won't he be there?"

"We're not going to knock, honey. It's supposed to be kind of a surprise. I'm writing 'Mal' in big letters on the envelope, and tomorrow when he comes home, when he's already missing us, he'll find the card and he'll know how much we love him. I'm sure your father's friend will leave it some place obvious."

Number 79 had to be away from the window at the front of the building where the numbers were lower and where the elevator doors opened, it had to be at the far end of the hall in the corner, but they could see the umbrella as they stepped off. They could see that it was pink, and they both must have realized then that it was the same umbrella they had glimpsed in the trunk of the new Cadillac, glimpsed without comprehending, without seeing it really in its incongruity, and mother and daughter both must have known for fact that nailed to the door the umbrella was now propped against were the numbers 7 and 9.

Forgetting Anne, Nellie walked steadily to it, picked it up, held it away from her body, glanced up at the numbers on the door, looked at the umbrella again. Water was dripping from it; its owner had just arrived apparently, and was inside, behind his apartment door.

"Pink," said Nellie.

By then Anne had caught up with her, though Nellie did not seem to be aware of her.

"Be patient?" Nellie asked of the pink umbrella.

And the voices began: His voice, Malcolm McBain's, Anne's father in New York City who was coming to California to be with them when his business was all done, coming to California in the turquoise Cadillac, his voice, "It's just one more night. They'll be gone tomorrow morning." That was what he said. They'll be gone.

Then a she voice, she of the pink umbrella. "Did you tell her yet?"

Turning, Anne walked toward the window at the other end of the hall, her black patent leather shoes moving of their own accord, like the plastic feet of a wind-up doll, until they bumped into the wall. She touched her forehead to the cool window. Outside it was still drizzling, still, as if it had always done so. The empty wet street, the buildings of stone seeming to lean inward as they peered dourly below, and the drab sky made the day seem pointless. Even the prospect of dinner with her father did not cheer her up, though she did not understand why. Maybe it was the way he had said 'gone' . . . 'they'll be gone tomorrow,' as if it was something he wanted. She looked out the window again. The only color on the street was the bright yellow of the cab, everything else was gray. Everything else was bad looking. But the cab was yellow, yellow like the sun, like something happy and alive. *Don't hurry, we'll hurry,* said Nellie. *Meter's running*, said the cabby. He could take them away from here, back to the hotel where Anne could fetch her coloring book and sit in the red leather chair in the corner of the lobby where no one would notice, and she would color very carefully, she would be very good, keeping inside the lines, while happy dressed-up people came and went before her. *Hurry, oh hurry, the meter's running, and stay inside the lines, you must, stay inside the lines when you color in your book.*

Down the hall was Nellie, a rag doll about to crumple to the floor, her head tipped downward, her eyes painted on, staring lifelessly at the carpet. She was listening to the closed door. Seeing Anne, she straightened. Then she did something funny: she opened the pink umbrella, propped it like a shield before the door, and sprinkled some of her Christian Dior on the pink fabric.

As they drew away from the curb, Anne saw in the gutter the 'I miss you' card with its sad-eyed little girl on the cover floating toward the drain.

From there the memory was fragmented. There was the ladies' room at the restaurant – Anne could definitely say that that occurred next – with its marble wash basin and gold couch, and all those fancy ladies, lipstick tubes in hand, trying not to hear Nellie sobbing, and one finally asking if she could do anything, though it was clear she didn't really want to, while Anne stood off, embarrassed and helpless. But after that the sequence and the explanations went screwy, the images colliding, like drunken birds. When was it, for instance, that Nellie fell to her knees before him and begged him not to leave, and he kicked her off, was that before they went back to California the first time, or the second time? And how was it that he was in Anne's bed while Nellie slept alone in the next one, and why did he choose then, when Nellie was so upset, to start the funny business with Anne? And how was it that Nellie did not see, did not protest? Because Anne could remember vividly him putting her hand around him, and the whispered instructions, and the slippery feeling when it was over, she could remember wondering if her mother was awake, and what these things that had no names could mean, and knowing instinctively (as she washed it from her hands) that there was no one safe to ask, no one to tell, not even in secret.

There was the airport in California where they waited for the very next flight back to New York, though Anne wanted to go home, she was so tired, and they had just left New York, they had just walked off the plane 15 minutes before. It was all so crazy. There was her mother telling her, "it'll be a surprise, it'll be fun," though Anne saw that she was trying not to cry. And the stewardess bringing them pillows, the hotel man smiling as if there was something wrong with their clothes when they came back, even though he was a friend of her daddy's. And there was the nighttime. Nighttime when everything seemed to happen – the restaurant where they found him, the deep, curved booth, the lady he was with calling for a cab as he dragged Nellie by the elbow around the corner of the building. There was the shouting. There were his big hands clenched and hanging at his sides, like stones, Nellie in her new blue dress hugging the wall, the black sky behind him. Nighttime. The dirty slush along the sidewalks. The honking horns. The Roquefort dressing that made her sick. The crowds at the fair. The smell of warm whiskey in the hotel glass. The muffled clanging of the barbells in the back of the Cadillac. The way that Nellie cried, with her whole body. The way he moved when he was mad, fast and jerky, like a trapped animal.

The background rush of the falls seemed to mount *fortissimo*. Anne eased away from the granite slab and pulled the pack onto her lap. She poured a cup of the watered wine, sipped, sipped again, watching the lightless sheet of water flow over the edge above the pool. The sound of the falls was comforting, the grotto they formed promising things eternal and reducing somehow the size of her memories – the childish violence of her mother and father, the endings that never quite ended things, the other airport scenes.

Airports, for some reason, seemed to bring out the worst in Nellie. Maybe she simply wished she was going some place herself. Maybe she had her own memories – airport memories – even while she was making memories for Anne. The worst was in the summer of Anne's sixteenth year at the San Jose Airport. Regrettably it was Anne herself who precipitated the incident by finally 'telling on' her father in what seemed an almost accidental way: during her annual summer visit, Marlene had simply asked – no one else had ever just asked, flat out – and Anne had answered in kind. What led Marlene to suspect, Anne never knew, but yes, he did do that, she said, yes. Yes.

Nellie's reaction was not simple.

"Did he penetrate?"

Anne remembered staring across the table in the airport cafeteria, and picturing her suitcase, which Nellie had shoved into a locker until she could 'get to the bottom' of her daughter's behavior. Evidently, the suitcase was not going home; it would remain imprisoned in a metal box until warden Nellie released it on good behavior. At least it was a novel reception. But where did her mother think she would send Anne if her behavior turned out to be unacceptable? Back to him? No, he wouldn't take her. To the family in Vancouver? How would

Nellie explain it to them? No, it would be much too embarrassing for Nellie, too messy, this talk of incest. Still, maybe it would put Nellie in a more favorable light with them, if he turned out to be a bad person, and she (by way of Anne) a victim. So there was a chance that Anne would not be going home, that this suitcase-in-the-locker routine was not just meant to scare her.

Her head was still spinning from the flight. And now to be asked words like *penetrate* . . . so clinical, so specific. She felt sick to her stomach, irrevocably forsaken. To be separated from her suitcase, from her clothes and things – that worsened it, as if she had been made to stand naked in a doctor's room while silent onlookers judged the operation. *Penetrate?*

"I don't know," said Anne.

"You understand me, don't you?"

She shook her head. She wasn't willing to admit what she understood, not until she could establish Nellie's sympathy.

"You're not going home until I find out whether you've made this mess up. And if you have, I'm sending you straight back to Los Angeles to apologize to your father. I've tried to mend things these last years so that you would have a father, so that there would be some money, some help . . . for you," she said, exasperated. "And that woman . . . Marlene, how could you tell her? What possessed you to . . . to betray me that way?" She leaned forward. "I know that you smoke with her. He told me when he called. Don't try to lie about that."

Even though Anne knew he was angry, it surprised her that he reported the smoking. Because he never said anything about it when she was visiting. He never cared at all. That had bothered her too.

Studying her mother, she tried to gauge how much the business with her father would offset the smoking. Nellie was in one of her sloppy periods – hair unwashed and pulled back from her face in a taut, angry way, the pony tail itself still ratted from the last time she had gone to work and had had to wear it up in a bun. Her eyebrows needed plucking. Her neck was puffy and dimpled – the weight had come right back on after the last diet, Anne saw – and above her lip a fine mustache of sweat was growing. The black stretch pants with the brown plaid shirt, along with the tough expression of the cross-examiner, (she was awfully good at that), made her look very much like a man.

Nellie set the corners of her mouth. "If you're lying young lady . . . about something like this . . . "

"I'm not lying." Somehow, she had expected her mother to hug her, to cry, to say, 'oh darling, why didn't you tell me when it started, we would have put him out of your life for good, you poor poor thing, and what a wicked man he is, how frightened you must have been.' Well, probably she didn't expect that; probably it would have been nice, this imaginary reaction, but not really what she expected.

"Did he push it inside you?" Nellie pursued, her face twisting, her lips flattening and disappearing among the freckles and flesh.

It was difficult for Anne to keep looking at her mother. She felt ashamed, yes. But there was Nellie, the sight of Nellie, so, so *ugly* – really, it was terrible to admit – and the cafeteria hot and smelling of steam trays and grease and dead vegetables, and the table so dirty her arms stuck to it, and she wanted a cigarette but knew she wouldn't get a chance to have one, not for a long while, and the summer ruined, and all in all everything seemed so awful, so ugly, as if the color had faded away and would never come back, that she just didn't care. She just didn't care what happened. It would have been a nice summer – the pool, the fishing boat, the shopping malls. He hadn't done anything for a long while . . . since the Panache. A nice summer, then there would have been school and new clothes, all her dorm friends. If Marlene hadn't asked, if Anne hadn't said 'yes.' Yes, he did, and please pass the lemonade. Still, it was the first time she had seen her father nervous, scared actually, though he tried to hide it, and Anne had to admit that she didn't mind seeing him that way. It made her feel strong inside, untouchable. Except that her mother didn't believe her, her mother seemed to be mad at *her*.

Anne glanced down at the cheeseburger on her plate: the thought of having to eat it made her stomach go clumpy.

"His *penis*," Nellie said, and her head dropped and shot forward like a striking snake when she said the word 'penis,' the word itself a poison, each syllable a drop of deadly poison. Nellie looked disgusted that she had had to say the word.

"It's hard to remember, he hasn't done anything for a couple of years. I guess he . . . rubbed it around. But I don't think it went in. I don't think so." Would this make it better, Anne wondered, that he didn't actually *do it?* The other things he did were just as bad, as far as she was concerned, but *penetration* had always been the most important to him, and now it was important to Nellie, too. It all seemed beside the point to Anne, the gory details; except that she couldn't say what the point was, either. It had to do with love – she knew that – she had wanted her father to love her, and she thought that he wouldn't if she didn't. And there was definitely something wrong with that. The weirdest thing was, it seemed to be for Nellie, too, what had happened, though Anne couldn't work out the configuration.

"My God," said Nellie. "The way you talk."

"But you asked."

"How many times did this happen, tell me."

"When I would stay with him at his hotel, all those times. Summers too."

"And you let him . . ." Nellie said, her brow creased, her eyes aimed at Anne.

"I had to."

"He forced you? Where are the bruises? Show me, prove to me that you fought back."

Of course there were no bruises now or ever, and of course Nellie would have concluded that there hadn't been any struggle, because if there had been she would have known about all of this long ago. She was demonstrating . . . something. It made Anne feel weak and dirty, that it hadn't even occurred to her to fight back, and that Nellie expected her to have done just that. Or did she?

"Daddy said . . . " Anne thought better of recounting what daddy had said; it would have sounded hokey and embarrassing, the stuff about their "special love" and the "secret project" and how much alike she and her daddy were. Especially now when it was beginning to look as if he didn't mean it; it was just a way to get her to . . . Oh forget it, she thought, forget about it. It was all too complicated to explain. She didn't want to talk about it; no one would understand. She said simply, "I couldn't fight."

Nellie shook her head. "All those years, his monthly visits, and you just let him. God. What were you thinking? He's a man. What do you think he thought, if you just *let him?*" Idly, she picked up some french fries and fed them to her mouth as she regarded Anne's face. She did not seem surprised by her daughter's news; she seemed annoyed that she had to deal with it, but strangely prepared to do just that, as if she had known all along and was now using it to instruct Anne in the prescribed manner. Because she had to. Because Anne had had the bad taste to expose it. They had never had one of those mother-to-daughter conversations, and Anne couldn't help wondering where Nellie figured Anne was supposed to have learned things about Men, like what they thought.

There was a wall of glass next to the booth, and beyond it airplanes rolled up to gates, loaded, and rolled away. A man wearing an orange vest and earphones directed traffic. Compared to the great silver tubes lumbering above him, he was small and alive, his tiny arms moving fluidly, making patterns that had meaning and order. In the roar of the world out there, Anne thought, nothing he said could be heard, nothing, while everything he did was important to the big planes turning about him, going away. More than anything she wished she was in one of those planes, going somewhere else, not coming back.

"All those years," said Nellie.

"I was afraid. I thought he wouldn't give us any money."

"Don't you dare try to blame this on me."

Anne clamped down on that line of argument, even though it was the truth. He *had* stopped giving them money when Anne said *no.*

"All those years," Nellie repeated. "He was touching you, the only thing he left me, and he spoiled it. My little girl . . . " Her voice began to wobble. "And he spoiled it. Tainted," she announced, as if she had suddenly discovered the word on her plate. "Tainted."

"I didn't know what to do."

"What to do? You're supposed to tell me, tell me everything. I'm your mother. That's what you do. Not her, that woman. She's the reason you don't have a father, Anne. You know that, don't you? She's the reason."

This made no sense, since Marlene met her father long after he had left Nellie. Maybe she meant any 'she', all 'she's.' Except he had told Anne it was her mother's neuroses that drove him away.

Anne said, "From now on I'll tell you." It was the standard penitential response, promises of future reform, she had mouthed it at least a hundred times – from now on blah-blah – but when she caught the look in Nellie's eyes, she saw instantly that it was the wrong thing to say.

"From now on?" cried Nellie. "If you think you're going to see him, if you think you're ever going anywhere without me . . ."

A busboy came and cleared Nellie's empty plate. She eyed him as if he was offending her, his very maleness.

Anne swallowed against the lump in her throat which seemed to be getting harder, more implacable and painful, yet she didn't cry. In fact, she realized with surprising certainty that she wasn't going to cry. Not this time. Not in front of her mother. No, she wouldn't give her that.

"What else?" said Nellie, as the boy left.

"Huh?"

"What else do you know about now?"

"Can't we go home, mom?" People at other tables were listening to their conversation, Anne was convinced of this, but she didn't dare look to confirm her fears, to meet other accusing eyes.

"Not until you tell me everything."

"I don't know what you mean, everything?"

"You know how to do things now, don't you, Anne? You know how to *do it*. We'll just stay here until you figure out how to say it."

Powerless and trapped, trapped in the San Jose Airport cafeteria where it seemed she would spend the rest of her life, she glanced around, as if looking for her one last chance out. The busboy was leaning against the tray dispenser, tossing a red apple up and down. There was a crop of pimples on his chin, and oily stains on his busing smock, but he seemed ambitious when he grinned at her, as if he too knew how to do it, as if he too was waiting for her answer.

So, Anne told her mother everything, and that was the last time they ever talked about it.

At age 27 Anne figured she still didn't have many answers. Some, but not many. It seemed likely, fairly conspicuous actually – a given – that what happened with her father was in large part responsible for her involvements with older men, the crossed lines of lover and father. The stuff of Psych 1A – not too insightful. Why they had to be married men complicated the straightforwardness of the case study, but not much. Probably it had to do with Nellie. Probably a lot more had to do with Nellie than Anne was willing to figure out.

Rolling her khakis to her knees, she slipped out of her shoes and waded into the pool beneath Hidden Falls.

The problem was Elliot Newhouse. She was in love with him, sure, that was easy, anyone could stumble in up to their ankles, back out, dry off, and move on – a standard, 90 day romance. And you went your way relatively unchanged – same clothes, same side of the lake, same way of looking at things, same dirt you started out with, the sun still high in the sky. But she loved Elliot. She had fallen in, all the way, they had swum a great distance together, and it had altered them. Now it seemed they were further from where they started than where they were going, that regardless, they could not go back. Too many clothes had been shed. Too much time had passed.

The surface of the pool was dark and depthless. There was a place like this in California, a pool beside a river, dusty cliffs surrounding it, and she had climbed to a ledge and jumped feet-first, for him; alone she would never have tried it. She sank so fast her heart jumped toward the greenish light that went small and black as she descended, the pool like a funnel. Toes still pointing, her feet took her down. Was there a bottom, would there ever be a bottom? With desperate longing she watched the light diminish, and lucky *lucky* bubbles rise into it, and she fixed in her mind the image of Elliot standing on the bank, tracings of worry about his smile as he encouraged her to leave the ledge. *Elliot*, said her mind. *Elliot*, just to fill it up, to keep everything else out, the things she could not know, things that would not comfort, *Elliot*, *Elliot* because he was a good safe place to rest her mind, a place she knew. On her way down.

Yet she rose, was rising, arms and legs climbing, lungs on fire, heart beating like a crazy fist inside the walls of her chest. Her head burst through the surface, she cried, "that's so scary," cried the way a child cries, with amazement and honesty and a clear sense of death.

And Elliot bent over, laughing, relieved maybe. "You should see your face."

She stepped further into the pool. Muddy clouds blossomed above her toes, the water lost its clarity, and the memory of that afternoon sank away.

In spite of everything, they had good memories, she and Elliot Newhouse. They had called upon each other to be better, as if to somehow counterbalance the great weight of deception upon which they floated their relationship. It seemed to draw them closer together, the wrongness and the effort against it and the failure. The failure especially. They knew that one day someone would not fail. Someone would leave. And until then each had found a home in the other, and neither was willing to give it up.

Maybe home was coming apart. And maybe the interview in Vancouver would provide the easiest out.

Behind her the outlet trickled into the woods, down toward Cascade Lake where there were other people, Norm and Nancy, boys fishing the way Mal McBain had fished seventy years ago, a girl in a straw hat. Under the trees on the ancient granite, patches of sunlight lay, like children's clothes abandoned for a summer swim. The dogwood was blooming. A small ribbon of water slid around her bare feet, leaving the secret grotto, going places. There was her daypack resting in a warm crevice. There a coppery fish making loose S's in the gentle flow. And from somewhere above the falls, an anonymous bird *klee-wheeed, wheeed.*

She was not unhappy, it occurred to her. A nice place, Hidden Falls. It had been here hundreds of years, she supposed, and would be here hundreds to come. She might not have the baby, and she and Elliot might not be together in the future – that was probably how things ought to go – but this place would still be here. It made things less ominous, a place like this. It made going on without Elliot somehow faintly possible.

Voices approached through the trees. It was time to meet the ferry anyway. She went to her things and stacked the photos and papers Joe had given her. A telegram slid out; "Western Union," it read. It had been sent in care of 'Sanborn,' and when she tore it open she saw it was from Nellie.

VANCOUVER WEDNESDAY. CALL ME
AT JUDITH'S ABOUT MAL. LOVE MUM

Wednesday. Today. She was already there, making yet another visitation to what she called "the family," though the idea of Nellie as "family" was ludicrous to Anne. *Christ.* What timing. Obviously news of his death had been the catalyst. And who could say what craziness it had triggered? Did she have some misguided notions of coming to Orcas to take part? To intrude? Anne would have to head that off. She wasn't about to sponsor a reunion of the little family that never was. Nellie was not to be trusted.

SIXTEEN

From a distance the ferry looked small and friendly, a toy boat full of matchbox cars and tonka trucks and painted people with painted smiles, incapable of sound and action without a child's imagination, incapable of sin. But it came closer and grew, swiftly inflating itself – beamy, graceless, Goliathan – against the sky. The few sallow clouds that had gathered that afternoon scudded off. A dark line of wake emerged, long and whiskered back. Against the vastness that was the auto deck, a yellow dot tracked west to east, east to west. Someone's hat? A rain slicker? Finally shoving forward chest first, like an angry man, the ferry bellowed, a vainglorious chilling bellow, and another.

Anne picked up the receiver. There was time to try his number; she would probably not get an answer. There was time to be disappointed. That was what she expected, that he would not be there, and that she would go away disappointed, to wait, to plan for the end. It had always been that way.

The phone rang.

"Anne?"

"You're there," she said, startled, and at once profoundly relieved to hear his voice.

"Yes."

"How'd you know it would be me?"

"I didn't know. I've been waiting, I guess. I wasn't sure you would still call, after last night."

"Of course." She watched the ferry move closer.

"You've put up with so much," Elliot said.

"I love you. That's my only excuse."

"I guess you do," he said. "I guess you really do." His voice was deep and absolutely smooth, without intonation.

"Are you all right?" she asked.

"Just tired." He paused, clearing his throat. "I've figured things out a bit, Anne."

"Things?" But she knew. She was ready.

"My life. Us."

"Us?"

"I'm a slow learner." He let out a sardonic chuckle. "Yes, us, our situation I mean."

A low microsound escaped Anne, and she recognized it as the sound a rodent makes when caught, a rodent who cannot theoretically make sound.

"Anne?"

"I'm listening." She could feel the precipice beneath her toes, could sense the space ahead, predict the downward speed, the rush, she could hear the unheard-of words behind her, approaching, about to push her off even before he uttered them.

"Well don't sound so lugubrious," he said.

Not lugubrious, she thought. *Being brave*.

"I'm trying to tell you I want to make an honest woman of you."

"Me?" A fusion of wonder and elation and an awful fear mushroomed inside her, massively instantaneous, a personal nuclear reaction, only to cave in abruptly, the center giving way, as if something irresistibly heavy was pulling it back down. But what?

Elliot was silent, maybe to appreciate her response, then he went on. "I can't move out instantly, there's still things I have to do here. But I told her. That was the first step."

Doubt. That was what pulled down.

"Yes," was all she could say.

"What's wrong?"

"I guess . . . I'm overwhelmed, I had no idea . . . It's just so surprising."

"Is it that surprising?"

"I don't know." The question confused her, the news, the idea that Elliot might be 'hers' – it was all enormously confusing. She had been preparing for everything but good news.

The ferry drove for the landing, reversed its engines suddenly, and crushed into its slip, rocking and swaying like a dozy giant, and jostling the pilings so violently that they screamed back, as if about to burst their steel binds. She could see the first rank of cars bouncing comically, like circus cars. She could see passengers on the decks clutching the railing. She could see Vinny. *What was his last name?*

Elliot was talking. "'Believe,' you always told me. 'Have faith.' 'Make it happen.' Well it took awhile, but . . . well, it never occurred to me that it might not be what you wanted."

"It is what I want. You just knocked me off my pins, that's all. Oh Elliot . . . please don't think that I'm not happy."

She heard him sigh. "Sorry. I was up all night. I'm a little frayed around the edges."

"Sure," she said. She tried to picture Elliot up all night, talking about *them*, an official subject, Anne and Elliot, a reality suddenly; she tried to imagine the words he used, but her mind would not stay in focus. It ricocheted, touching everything and sticking to nothing. "You said you had things to do?"

"To try to explain . . . to resolve things with Jill," he said. "Not about us. It doesn't have anything to do with us. There's so much stuff between me and Jill that needs to be hacked through. The irony is that I was using my relationship with you to make my marriage more bearable, and when I finally realized what that meant . . . " But Anne had stopped listening.

More talk, she thought. She had spotted Vinny who, she noticed, looked a lot like Malcolm McBain in the old photo Joe had given her, that same injured look around the eyes, that same bravado. He was walking down the forward stairs onto the gangway in his hat and suit, a tall distinguished-looking figure among the summer flotsam of the islands, and he was scanning the waiting people, the parked cars. "Elliot," she finally said. "I want to believe you. I'm really trying to believe . . ."

"Trying?"

"Well, you should hear yourself, sweetie." She meant to be gentle. She just wasn't sure about anything. Because what if it wasn't the same old resolutions? What if it was true this time? "I hate to say this, but from here it sounds like more talk to me."

"It isn't," he said, obviously hurt.

"Then why aren't you moving out?"

"I can't just dump it in her lap and leave."

"No?" she said. "No, you can't just do that."

"This is not exactly the reaction I expected," he said, almost as if to himself.

Vinny was standing alone by the side of the road, searching.

"I'm going to have to call you back," she said.

"What?"

"The ferry," she said, as if this would explain.

"Where are you anyway?" Elliot said.

"At the landing. I'm supposed to pick up Vinny," she said.

"Who?"

Malcolm redux. "Vinny. I don't know his last name." The person in question took off his hat and spun it self-consciously.

"Who the hell is Vinny?" Elliot said.

"If you had any idea how much I want to believe you . . .

all the years, Elliot, all the waiting. It's so late, and I'm so tired. It scares me to believe anymore, do you understand that? It isn't safe. I need to see you standing on my doorstep, a physical fact, that's what I need. The present is falling apart, and I need you with me now. I don't know about the future, I don't want to hear about your marriage, how important it is, how careful you have to be, the things you have to resolve. Before. Before us. I know. Don't tell me about it anymore, please." One by one, cars rocked off the ferry and sped up the hill past the phone booth. "You know," she said, "I always wished you would act . . . that would have said something, oh boy. But you didn't. You reacted, in the last year to my disintegrating happiness, and now to this pregnancy. What does that say about us? How careful have you been with our relationship? How important am I?"

"That's a ridiculous question," he said.

"I never asked it, Elliot, because every day I waited for you I heard the answer."

"It's a ridiculous question in view of what I'm telling you now," he said.

"Yes, it seems like good news. Wonderful news, Elliot. The best. But you're still there, and I'm sick of being relegated to the future. I just can't think about the future," she said, though trying hard to think about their future in fact, to concentrate on Elliot's news, while watching Vinny whose bewilderment over having apparently been forgotten inspired in her both concern and coldly sadistic pleasure. Keep looking, sucker, she thought, and immediately wondered why the words occurred to her. She hardly knew Vinny . . . Vinny whoever he was. From the pay phone at the cafe she could see him clearly, but he would not be able to see her or his Porsche unless he gave up waiting and came up the hill. Or she stepped out . . . into harm's way. She frowned. What was happening to her mind? What was happening?

"Christ Anne. Don't you think I realize that things are different now, with you pregnant?" Elliot said.

"Are they?"

"I'll do this as fast as I can," Elliot said. "That's all I can promise."

She watched Vinny check his watch, pull his hat down across his brow as if to hide under its narrow brim, and start up the hill toward the cafe. A teenage girl walked by; he said something to her, she shook her head and, both laughing, they resumed opposite courses. The girl was wearing tight blue jeans. Vinny managed four or five steps before he turned and looked back.

"I've really got to go, Elliot. I love you, but I'm going to have to call you back."

"What is going on, for Christ's sake?"

"I borrowed a car. I've got to return it. I'll call you . . . " When, when would she call him? Not from that hallway at the Sanborns'. "Tonight if I can. Because I've got to go now, I'm sorry, Elliot, I've just got to go."

Vinny stopped when he saw her and spread his arms. With his raincoat on and standing as he was on a downward slant, sky mounting up behind him, he looked impressively like a large gray bird who had just landed before her.

"There you are," he cried, and when she came down to him, they hugged. At the moment it seemed the natural thing to do; anyone watching would have presumed they had known each other a long time and had endured an acutely unwelcome separation. His torso was firm, she smelled the tea-like aroma of expensive fabric. It was not at all like hugging Elliot.

"I was worried," Vinny said.

"Why?"

He shrugged, and put on a sheepish grin. "I guess I'd *like* to worry about you. I have a feeling you don't let that happen much."

Obviously Vinny had a knack for saying the right thing at the right time. Yet even while she considered the possibility that he was simply highly skilled at gaining an entrance – a pro – even while she remembered the teenage girl whose behind he had been admiring moments earlier, she felt herself respond to his concern, real or not. Because what did it matter whether it was the shadow, or the thing itself? In a desert, both were welcome.

"I don't need worrying over," she said. "Anyway, no one has offered lately, not for the duration. When it's convenient people say they care. When there's a payoff." This wasn't true, at least not of Elliot (maybe, always maybe), but she said it anyway to encourage Vinny to worry about her.

"I'm sorry," he said. "It shouldn't be that way, not for someone like you."

"I'm no more needy than the next person."

"But you're special," he said. "I can see it."

She glanced off, neither accepting nor dismissing the notion that she might be 'special'; everyone liked to fancy that about himself. Special to *whom* was another matter altogether. Anyway, it was a self-serving opinion, what Vinny said. Except he seemed genuinely concerned, a sensitive man sensing turmoil. After all, her father had just died, and here she came a thousand miles, alone. Maybe he had no romantic interest in her. And then maybe he was a pro using the unusual reversal-with-a-twist mount.

He removed his raincoat, folded it inside-out, and hung it neatly over his arm. Though it was the end of the day's labor, he had not loosened his tie; beneath the neat Windsor knot, a gold collar bar was still intact, executing its small impeccable job. Vinny was a very different sort of man from Elliot, an altogether different sort of man. Still, he was a man, and he was unhesitatingly here with her.

He crooked his arm for her and, when she took it, she saw that her hand was shaking.

They walked up the hill to the Porsche which was now visible, parked in the lot above the cafe. Beside him she felt like a child who had just taken a nasty fall, and was still dizzy, still afraid of the possibilities.

"You seem upset," he said, opening the passenger side of the Porsche and helping her in, then squatting to bring his eyes level with hers. He seemed to be waiting for her to tell him something, something serious and personal.

"I'm scared," she said. They were the first words that came to mind. And a compulsion took hold of her to tell everything about her and Elliot, to throw down the pick-up-sticks of her life and say 'tell me what to do.' She felt she could trust him with her exposure, though the feeling vaguely impressed her as containing some of the elements of a seduction.

Once she'd started, it didn't take long. Summarized, the circumstances which had always seemed irreducible, the history that was so convoluted nothing could honestly reveal it, even her feelings for Elliot became somehow two-dimensional and mundane, like an amateur painting – no depth, lost perspective, uninteresting use of color. When she mentioned the pregnancy she heard a voice from the back step of her brain wonder if it occurred to Vinny that Anne was thus contraceptively 'safe.' A second voice asked if she might have revealed her condition precisely in order to let him know this. She might have wanted to throttle the voices, but she was curious in a perverse way what else they would observe about her behavior or motivations, none of which so far she was too terribly surprised by. When your boat was sinking, it was natural to look around for one that wasn't.

As if having heard it a hundred times before, Vinny nodded at regular intervals while she told her story. His left hand was draped confidently over the small leather steering wheel, his right shoved the stick shift into higher or lower gears, though not smoothly, she noticed, and in an increasingly rough and testy manner. Twice he gnashed the gears, then red-lined it before shifting up, as if to eclipse his mistake. At one of these piercing junctures, he turned to her and shouted, "A good engine likes to run hot. Designed that way. Not many people know that."

By the time they reached the rolling hills above Doe Bay, she was describing the telephone conversation with Elliot at the ferry landing, explaining that he had told her he was leaving his wife.

Vinny said, "And you don't believe it."

She stared at his profile.

Expressionless, he watched the road ahead.

"He seems to mean it," she said. "I know he does. Maybe that's why I'm scared, if that makes any sense." She said this as much to convince herself as Vinny; the whine in her voice was unmistakable.

Vinny pulled the car to a stop at a vista point along the road. "Look," he began, stretching his arm out across the seat back and looming paternally over her, "I've been in his shoes, Anne, and I know exactly what he's feeling. I hope I'm not out of line, but he's not gonna leave his wife if he didn't do it when you two first got together. He's stalling."

"Why would he stall now, when I'm . . . "

"That's why. Because you're pregnant. If he can convince you that he's going to be with you *definitely*, then you're not going to balk about an abortion now, not with that carrot out there. Any businessman knows that, you give up a little something today for a better return tomorrow."

"Elliot doesn't operate that way," she said coldly. She was outraged by Vinny's crude appraisal, his blunt words – at the same time there was something she wanted to hear in them. Confirmation, maybe. Because in a way she was desperate to be released from hoping, from the not knowing: it was too painful, it had worn her out. Still, in Elliot's defense, she said, "He wouldn't lie to me."

Vinny let out a sigh that seemed to indicate she was pitiful in some way – had terminal cancer, had been left at the altar, didn't get the job. "I'm sorry, honey."

Honey? In this man's presence she was beginning to feel very young and naive, and also very much in need of care. "I guess I don't understand what you're getting at."

"He had this deadline you gave him, right? So he was already scrambling. Then wham-o, you show up pregnant and that really balls things up. *Then* you back up the deadline."

"He loves me."

Vinny gave her a charitable smile. "Sure he does, of course. Who wouldn't? But he's stuck, and he knows it, and you're probably the main reason he gets out of bed every morning. He doesn't want to lose you. He's desperate. Desperate men say things."

"I can't even imagine . . . he's never lied to me before. He's always meant what he's said, even if he didn't succeed."

"I'm sure he doesn't think he is lying."

"He said he told her everything. Why would he tell her everything if he wasn't serious?"

Vinny lit up a cigarette and, as an afterthought, tipped the pack toward her; when she accepted, he removed the one from between his lips and handed it to her, filter-first, then lit up another for himself and pulled cautiously on it. "You said the wife already knew."

"Years ago. I think she figured it had ended."

"No," he said, with mock incredulity.

Anne dropped her eyes. "I guess she must have known it hadn't."

"So when he told her 'everything,' he really didn't tell her anything."

"In a sense, no."

"When is he moving out?"

"He said not instantly."

"What does making an 'honest woman' out of someone mean? A trip to the altar? Marriage?"

Opening the window, she turned her face away from Vinny. The word 'marriage' conveyed to her just how foolish she had been, how absurd her hopes. Marriage – *hah*. Even in her own mind the image did not qualify as a dreamable dream; it was impossible, it was something other people did – marry. Better people.

To Vinny she answered, "I'm not sure what he meant."

Vinny let the ensuing silence wrap up his argument.

They smoked their cigarettes. He held his in an effete manner, she privately observed, with the cigarette reaching languidly across the back of his hand. Even in the old days when she smoked she would not have held it that way. Like a tough kid, squeezed between the thumb and index finger, discarding the ashes with a flick of her ringless ring finger, and Elliot . . . she could not picture how Elliot had smoked.

She thought about when they had quit a few months after meeting, she and Elliot – soaring high on each other, feeling invincible, one day they simply agreed to stop smoking. That was that. At the time the feat seemed to endorse their relationship, to corroborate its inherent rightness, that a habit so foul and tenacious had been so easily thrown over. By the two of them. Together.

Maybe everything had been a fallacy. A big shuck. Maybe he was a lecherous philanderer, she was his bimbo mistress, and what they had had was no Grand Passion, just a cheap trifling affair with a statistically predictable whimpering end. There would be a messy, back alley abortion by a German experimentalist. The patient would die – the patient being whatever it was she and Elliot fancied they had together – and everyone would go away caring a little less about a great many things. So it went. Eventually you stopped caring altogether, you died.

The cigarette was one of those long narrow brown numbers laced with some artificial scent, and not nearly as harsh as the old-style brands. Camels had been Elliot's brand. The macho jerk. She took a hard pull on the cigarette, forcing the smoke into the walls of her lungs with stinging vengeance. She imagined millions of her bronchioles withering, turning black. Oh well, she thought. Oh fucking well.

The setting sun had transformed Doe Bay to a glaring shield of hammered bronze. Eyes blinking against the light, nevertheless she gazed at it, as if she was seeing Truth for the first time and would not stop looking even if it blinded her; a blazing hole in the center of her vision formed, spread outward, eating through reality. From the woods a red-tailed hawk swooped down across the fields, pursued by a smaller bird who bobbed and jabbed and finally jerked away, flitting back for a nest somewhere. He was probably not even interested, thought Anne. In your nest, little bird. He was probably just toying with you. The hawk banked east, its wings set vertically into the bronze shield until, tipping ever so slightly, it slid off the sky and out of sight.

The engine started up. With a quick casual gesture, she knocked the pools of tears from her eyes and crushed out the cigarette.

"I'm sure it'll happen soon," Vinny said. "You'll be that honest woman."

Now he could afford to lie, she thought, to pretend to pretend along with her, having planted weeds in her garden.

He patted her hand. "A baby . . . your baby especially . . . any guy with half a brain would figure having a baby with you would be too good to pass up. I'm sure Elliot will . . ."

"No," she said. "Please." She leaned into his chest. The crying came easily and lightly, like a summer rain, and ended similarly, lifting from her as from warm earth and moving quietly away. She could hear his heart beating, the Porsche purring in place, and the two in her mind became interrelated – made to run hot, a good engine, a good man.

"Don't worry," Vinny said as he shoved the gear shift into first and pressed the accelerator.

SEVENTEEN

After dinner when the water went pan-flat, Vinny nudged the skiff and it coasted eagerly out across the empty bay. Once they had cleared the rocky shallows, he plunged the mini props of the Seagull into the water, leaving the big Mercury jutting straight out off the stern. It would be too much engine for trolling. He gave the pull-start a smooth and decisive yank; the response was immediate. Straightening, he nodded as if to acknowledge his success, and aimed the boat toward the point where the salmon sometimes swung in. Anne turned to face the wind.

Vinny had invited the others to join them. It did not seem to disappoint him, however, that there were no takers. Carla was a safe bet with her child. Charles, being a vegetarian, was likely not a killer of fish. Joe and Rose, well, they were old and it was late. So probably Vinny knew it would just be the two of them.

Anne began rigging the lines – a half-pound weight, then a 5-inch flasher, the lure – a greenish minnow – and attached to its underside, the triple hook. The hook seemed enormously brutal, hardly sporting. It had been years since she had gone out for salmon – that time on the sailboat, but it had been Sid with the rod – no, probably since the last time she had been in the northwest with her father; and she had forgotten the hooks.

Elliot was a fly-fisherman. Barbless hooks. Almost everything he caught he threw back. Occasionally, if they were camping in the intermontane desert between the Sierra Nevada and the Whites where the fishing could be too good, he'd keep a nice rainbow or a brown for dinner, and she'd throw it whole into a pan with butter and a handful of sage torn from a nearby bush. A white Graves, lean and flinty, and cold from the hours it spent buried in the shallows of the stream completed the dinner. Elegant fare, Elliot would say. She could still smell the sage on the dry air, still see the barren mountains in the east go purple at dusk, the stream whispering by like so many dreams she had only to reach out and grasp. And she could still feel the delicious postponement of a night with Elliot. Now it seemed there was nothing left to postpone: the debt had come due.

Hanging his knee over the tiller to steady it, Vinny let out his line, counting 10 arm lengths, then he gave the reel a reverse turn to flip the bail into place.

"Beer?" he said.

"No, thanks."

He rummaged through the cooler and brought up a can. Rod in one hand, beer in the other, he steered with the crook of his knee: it looked as if he'd had a lot of practice.

Before dinner he had changed into a pair of jeans – Calvin Klein, the label said – a yellow cotton sweater, and the new Reebok tennis shoes, no socks.

Très sportif, she thought. Vinny could easily have been advertising any one of the items adjacent to his person – beer, shoes, jeans, even the diminutive, British-made engine, the Seagull, which Anne knew was not inexpensive, and which had been designed for trolling or as a back-up to a larger engine. Its top speed was probably no more than 5 knots. It was quiet; would not scare the fish away. It could be relied upon.

Yes, Vinny was an effective ad, and maybe not for a thing. Maybe without knowing it he was selling an idea. *"Make a change,"* read the copy. *"For the best."*

She probably shouldn't have told him so much. About himself he had revealed nothing of importance. The imbalance annoyed her. She felt she had placed herself at his mercy. And maybe he wasn't really so nice, didn't really care. Why should he? What did he want? And what did she want him to want?

Behind her Vinny sat, relaxed and patient, the picture of confidence, a man who knows he has won and who has all the time in the world to collect. Or not to collect. He sipped his beer, adjusted his sweater cuffs, leaned back against the black metal casing of the Mercury outboard, his legs falling loosely open.

She resolved to sidestep any future conversations about the state of her life. She decided that if she and Elliot were finished, if Vinny was right, if she was just worn out with the whole thing, she would have nothing to do with men for a long time. At least a year. She had wanted to be happy, had tried very hard, and she had failed. Maybe it was not possible for her, this thing called happiness, and neither effort nor time nor discipline led to its attainment. It was an inner environment. There was something wrong with her, a vital place inside had been razed, the soil stripped, and no sweet thing could now grow. Plants with spines and shallow roots, tough hides, and poison in their veins – they would take hold. One day she would go mad: this she honestly expected. Already it had happened – the cold light, the crackle of hypocrisy, the thunder in her ears, the world outside enshrouded, as if the very blackness in her mind had eclipsed the light, and what remained were shadowy impressions, paranoiac undertones, the chilling hands of memory, palpating, palpating. Is she still alive? Good God no, man, she's mad, quite mad. Man mad. Anne McBain.

One day she figured she would turn away from the life she had managed to create; after all, it was not so grand a life by comparison, a small life, shuffling dinner plates, sorting species, a cabin, a dog, a friend or two, inappropriate love, inaccessible dreams, inescapable history. A mind unraveling. Still, considering all, she had done okay – her best. She had kept going, kept being. She had given her life the benefit of the doubt.

Across the still water the boat moved quietly. Vinny seemed content not to talk, and she was grateful for that. She wanted to figure it out, why what she wanted was never possible. Or why, on the verge of getting it, she was filled with fear.

Even with Elliot and their situation she had always sought a place inside where she might enjoy relative peace and a limited happiness, but happiness nonetheless. It had been her way, finding pockets of happiness, like some precious metal trapped in cold stone. Within any great mass of one thing, she believed, there was bound to be its opposite: air trapped in water, water vaporized in air, a little hate dissolved in love, hope at the bottom of Pandora's box. Even when she was as young as five or six, she tried to be happy, and she seemed to know what it was then, too. When her mother left her that summer with the sisters to go with Mal McBain to Europe, and all the other children had gone home except for one boy, *he* was happiness. He stayed in the boys' area; the nuns would not allow them to play with each other because she was a girl and it was not right. From the long windows in the stairwell, she used to watch him down on the playground, bouncing a ball off the side of the brick building, or pushing toy trucks through the dirt, or sometimes he just twirled in circles, his face skyward, his eyes closed, his arms stretched out. In his red sweater, she could always find him, even when he wandered into the thick of the blackberry patch. When she was tired of playing with the doll houses or watching television – an evening treat – or seeing how fast she could get from the sixth to the first floor, scuttling down the marble stairs *lickety-split*, she repeated to herself, *lickety-split, lickety-split*, her shoes clacking out the syllables; when the cook didn't have any peas for her to shell on the back steps, or apples for her to gather behind the grotto of the Virgin Mary, when boredom was stifling and too real to imagine away, she twirled round and round in the dorm as she had seen her distant friend do, twirling twirling between the iron beds, dreaming of fall and friends, twirling, the dizziness a narcotic that altered the world until she began to tip and totter and, finding a wall, she would slide against it down to the floor and watch her shoes until they stopped dancing before her, and the stillness with its invisible audience moved back in. You're alone, said the audience.

Hans was his name. He had yellow hair, and he sang while he twirled. From the sixth floor window, from a distance his voice lifted up to her, a light chirping: then he was a red and yellow bird, singing a little song, or a prince calling to Anne in her dark tower. His twirling was slow and graceful, not the dizzy escape that ended near nausea on the floor. Even alone he seemed happy. He was a boy. He was outside.

One day she did not see his red sweater on the playground. The cook – a fat woman with soft white facial hair – told her that he was gone to the hospital to have his tonsils out. A week later she reported that the 'boy' was back, that in the hospital he had eaten nothing but ice cream and sherbet, that he had stayed in a room with lots of other children, and that Roy Rogers had come to visit him. Such happiness! To possess it never occurred to Anne; she wanted only to be near it, to hear Hans describe his adventure, and to keep his story, like a secret penny in a secret pocket, proof that it was possible – happiness. She begged the cook to let them play together.

Not long after Hans' return, all members of the community (that was what the nuns called themselves, a community) attended a lengthy evening prayer in honor of a Saint's feast day. The cook was left in charge. "You can play with the boy when you're finished eating," was all she said, and she placed the plate in front of Anne and went about her kitchen chores.

Ground meat, beans, boiled potatoes – so much. Hardly able to bear her excitement, she put the food in her mouth, one forkful after another, as fast as possible. Not to jeopardize cook's goodwill, she would clean her plate. She would keep it as her best secret, she promised, this visit with Hans, this happy gift. Perhaps there would be another.

But there was not another, not even one, because when she climbed down from the kitchen stool and ran to the door to await cook's instructions, her knees began to wobble, and up came her dinner, the beans astonishingly green against the white tile floor.

Cook shook her head sadly. "Too fast, little one, I'm sorry. You've made yourself sick."

To the sixth floor Anne was sent, to the room full of beds, none made except the one in the corner by the window.

You've made yourself sick . . . trying to be happy . . . too fast.

I am still doing that, Anne thought.

The tip of her pole nodded regularly as the boat slid along, nearing the point. Salmon poles were heavier and more rigid than trout poles, but even a one pounder on the line could make that tip dance a jig. Watching the rhythmic bobbing, she dreamed up the sequence: the telltale vibration – *don't move*, her father would warn – the sudden hard pull, the pole jouncing wildly while the reel clicked out the alarm as a sockeye or a coho or a big, flashing king ran the other direction, fighting back. Usually, while she horsed the straining rod, she was aware of him reeling in, rummaging for the gaff, spinning the boat to follow her line so that it would not go crosswise underneath them, or tangle in the props, so that they wouldn't lose her wonderful fish. And always she was aware that he was excited, and she would have in an instant wished that fish onto his line to see his look of gleeful, boyish concentration. To see him innocent. Simple-hearted.

In the glassy water of Doe Bay her line traced a fine and infinite V. It was the kind of water she liked to swim in, water that came back together just beyond her toes, not damaged by her passing. People should be more like that, she thought: vulnerable, quick to recover. Lots of give, she thought.

Leaning out, she touched the water. Too cold. Anyway, there was Vinny. He wanted to fish. He didn't know her. And as much as they had talked, she didn't know him. Did she want to? was the question. Did it matter whether they knew each other? Vinny seemed to be, indeed, The Perfect Stranger. What did she have to lose? She had never *had* anything to lose.

He was watching her as she drew a fish-stained rag from the creel and dried her hand.

"Have dinner with me tomorrow?" he said, taking a sip of beer.

"I can't." Peripherally she saw something, a shadow, a movement. "I've got an interview in Vancouver at the marine station. I don't know what time I'll get back." There would be Nellie, too, to deal with, and Anne was at a loss to predict how 'Mal's' death was affecting her. Nellie might be toughing it out, which an absence of any surviving feeling for him would make entirely feasible, in which case Anne's meeting with her would be brief, a demonstration (for Anne's benefit) of stoical concision. *Or* Nellie might sink into a swamp of maudlin remembrances and regrets, in which case they would 'struggle' with the knowledge of his death all afternoon. She just didn't know. With Nellie, extremes were the rule. One had to be prepared for fire and ice.

"I work in Bellingham," Vinny said. "An hour's drive. There's a great place in North Van, if you like to dance."

"What woman doesn't," she said, thinking that Vinny sure had a knack for pushing the right buttons. Elliot had always been too diffident, and in a funny way too polite for dancing. "I don't want to offend people's aesthetic sense," he would say, begging off. It was an endearing excuse, but they couldn't dance to it.

"When do you get off work?" she said.

"I can leave anytime."

"We could meet there, I guess. I could call you when I'm finished." A shadow again, nearby, in the water, something, there. Did it move?

"It's easy to find," Vinny said. "The biggest hotel in North Van. They just finished it last year. The Liongate. I had a hand in it, you might say. You'll like it."

"Okay," she said.

On the port side she spotted it then, an enormous deadhead, dark and algal, trailing kelp, and five times the length of the skiff. It was barely clinging to the ceiling of water. She pointed to let Vinny know; they veered and skimmed close by it, watching their lines. It was frightening to look at, once a lovely Douglas fir, no doubt, but now something else, something transformed, lurking just below the surface. Vinny kicked at it, and it rocked in monstrous slow-motion, not seeming to budge, not giving them any more room. A few more ounces of saltwater absorbed, another pound, another month, maybe two, and it would let go, sink to the bottom.

"Don't they flag those anymore?" she asked.

"What they find. That old boy's been around awhile. The worst kind," he added.

"I wonder why it hasn't washed up on a beach. They're so pretty when they bleach out, smooth and white. Like bones," she said. "Dinosaur bones." She thought of the 15-million-year-old whale skeleton Elliot had found on Año Nuevo. He had probably gone back out to the island by now to deal with Gina. Elliot was not one to neglect his work, no matter the condition of the rest of his life.

"It'd take a pretty good storm to throw that one out. It must weigh ten tons," Vinny said. They were coming up on its narrow end. Drawing the tiller in against his ribs, he aimed the bow for the deadhead and, using his heel, pushed it under hard; this time it began to decline, a long dangerous shadow bending down toward oblivion.

"It's going," she cried in disbelief.

Vinny was beaming. He hung his dripping Reebok over the side, jammed his rod under his thigh, and grabbed the tiller commandingly to avoid the wide end of the deadhead as it rose, bobbing, one last time before following its tapered length down for good. "Needed a little help, that's all." He might have just dropped an elephant with a BB gun.

The base went under – it was maybe 4 feet in diameter – and the brief hollowing of the water, and a tail of swirling foam was all that remained of the great tree. A pang of sadness and behind that, a cold wash of fear. What had they done? "Do they ever come back up? Can they?"

Vinny shrugged. "I guess so, with the right conditions. It was almost totally saturated, but who knows? Maybe in this calm water it'll float back up."

Now the thought of swimming with that deadly thing down there scared her. What if it rose into her? Into the skiff?

Her reel began to click. "I've got something . . . no, wait, I've got it, I've got that damn tree!"

In an instant, her pole was wrenched down against the boat, and the two foot section that extended beyond the edge was bowed violently, the line unwinding itself steadily, the clicking crazy in her ears. If she could have she would have pulled it up, she would have tried to save it, that damned old tree. It had probably been around when her father was a boy, it was probably about the same age. If it would just wash up on a beach, she thought, it couldn't hurt anything, it couldn't hurt boats or swimmers. Turning white, it would dry out peacefully. The sun would warm it. Children play on it. Time erase whatever damage it had done below the surface of the water. Below the surface. If it would just come out of the water, it wouldn't hurt anyone. He couldn't hurt her.

Water was pouring in over the salmon rod, and the skiff was beginning to heel onto its side. Vinny reached over and threw the bail on the reel, the clicking stopped, but the line continued to loop out. For a moment, the pressure eased, then it resumed. The line had snarled, was beginning to tighten, cinch. Her hands were jammed against the inside wall of the boat: she was using them as stops to keep the pole from dragging her in or slipping away.

"Let go of it," Vinny yelled.

Peripherally she saw him press his body against the high side of the skiff, his hand still clutching the tiller, though the props sputtered free in the air. It was clear to Anne, even in her confusion, that the angle and weight of the Mercury would very soon flip them over. But she wouldn't let go of the rod. Her knife was in her pocket but she couldn't let go to get it out. To cut it loose. To let the old boy go.

Vinny thrust his hand into the tackle box. "Here," he said, waving a boning knife at her.

She glanced away.

"Cut it if you won't let go."

"I can't."

And then the line snapped.

Still. Stillness here as if nothing had happened, ever. Between them in the boat sat the Present, like another passenger, demanding attention. There was no past, there would be no future. They were here and it was palpably still about them. If she opened her palms she could touch it, this stillness, and it would feel like satin coming down, almost heavy, almost cool, but not. It would feel like death, and not. Smooth silver water surrounded them, held them. The water appeared to be as it appeared, depthless and immaculate. The boat did not move. The air was a hollowed thing where a passing had been and was no more. Space and time were not relative, they were the same. It was all the same. It was all different. They were alone with the Present. In the boat on Doe Bay. Still.

Vinny kissed her. It was then she noticed that her hands were bleeding. It was then she realized he was dead, her father, and not dead. He was here with her, in the boat, inside, palpating, palpating.

And undoing her mind, she let him.

God man, she's mad. Man mad.
Still.

When they got back to the Sanborn's she tried Elliot's number. She tried it a dozen times, hanging up and dialing again immediately, hanging up, dialing. Finally, surprisingly, a woman answered.

"Wrong number," Anne said, and felt bad, felt worse.

Then she went to her room.

Elliot, help me, please please help me, she whispered, entombing herself beneath the covers.

EIGHTEEN

The interviewer – Ms. Julie Dumont – was a delicate woman with thin, colorless hair drawn up into a wispy halo about her head. She wore no stockings, no jewelry, and no detectable scent. She did not carry a notebook. While walking across the grounds of the marine station, they exchanged no pleasantries except to mention *El Niño* whose effects had been the focus of the spring work at Waddington. When they entered her office, she placed two straight-backed chairs directly opposite each other, and there they sat, kneecap to kneecap, as if about to engage in a child's pat-a-cake game.

The questions began – lightly uttered, precisely aimed. She had anticipated a general conversation about her education, experience, and the subjects of projects in which she had participated. Instead, she was asked to comment on Dr. Nemeth's hypothesis concerning the unusually aggressive behavior of the transient pod of orcas sited in the central coastal waters of California; to briefly speak to an index of parental investment in sea lions; to discuss her role and ambitions if hired at Waddington. Was she familiar with Carefoot's piece on intertidal invertebrates and patterns of distribution? Had she worked with Newhouse at the Año Nuevo preserve? *Ah yes,*

yes. And throughout, the feathery voice, the needlepoint questions.

After some initial foolishness in which Anne tried to sound like a confident, 'empowered' (as they said nowadays) woman of the late eighties, shaking Ms. Dumont's hand vigorously, Anne gave up. She saw herself as Ms. Dumont might have – loud, oafish, blathering nervously, her palms sweaty, her expressions parodies of expressions. She was not confident, and the notion of female 'empowerment' struck her as the worst form of sloganizing. Everyone was just trying to make it through the day. Maybe it got easier, maybe not. The days changed, if you were lucky. So she wound up just answering the questions. Probably the job would go to someone else. She would be relieved of having to choose to take it or turn it down.

"You seem to know this area well," Ms. Dumont said, to conclude the interview.

"There's much to learn," Anne replied.

If it had been a man, she might have had a chance. A man was easy to impress, a woman like Ms. Dumont impossible. She reminded Anne of a very strong, very fine stainless steel tool: eons from now it would still be around, a tool such as this.

And yet, as Ms. Dumont walked her to the parking lot she offered her the job. "Take a week, think about it," she said. "It's a big move."

"All right."

"Of course we'd want you up in Johnstone Strait this summer, with the killer whale group."

"That would be ideal."

Ms. Dumont nodded. "Your dissertation, yes."

Stopping at a gas station, Anne rang up her mother's cousin, Judith, with whom Nellie had indicated she was staying.

Nellie had moved to the Georgia Hotel in downtown Vancouver, Judith told her, because she needed the 'space.'

Judith was one of the more upbeat Gallagher relatives, or at least had become so over the last decade, and Nellie was not altogether pleased with the transformation. 'Bohemian' she called it. After her divorce Judith became a marriage counselor, a jogger, and a free-associating nonstop talker. When she started in on "Mal's ending" being a beginning, and an opportunity to "process submerged feelings and get centered," Anne told her someone was waiting to use the phone.

Nellie was on a diet and did not want to go to a restaurant – too many temptations – Anne would understand, of course. They agreed to meet at Stanley Park. A few low-cal items from the corner deli would do for lunch.

"Sure," said Anne. She bought a bag of peanuts from the gas station snack counter, and headed north toward the Lion's Gate Bridge. *Diet*, she thought. *Another diet*.

It was a lovely May day, but Nellie was sitting in her car with the windows closed when Anne pulled into the lot. This was what Nellie did if she was the first to arrive, which did not happen frequently: she stayed in her car, staring ahead. She did not want to appear too eager by getting out, or by having waited long. The interior of the car constituted an extension of her territory. Outside on a picnic bench she would have felt exposed, alone, vulnerable – the one who needed. Vulnerability was not Nellie's strong suit.

Anne knocked on her window to get her attention, though she knew Nellie had already seen her. "You beat me here," she said.

"I know a few short-cuts." She gave Anne a hug – a real hug – and Anne broke away, stutter-stepping off into the park as she tried to collect herself.

They followed a trail through the woods until it emerged onto a sunlit, grassy expanse overlooking Burrard Inlet. To their left in the distance were the graceful suspensions of the Lion's Gate Bridge, and down the slope to their right, a shallow, salt water bight separated from the Inlet by a stone wall, and presently alive with children and lap swimmers and, in the far corner against the wall, a circle of elderly people chatting as they kicked slowly in place.

"I always liked this park," Anne said.

"But not the water. 'Freeeeezing,' you used to cry."

"I went in, though."

Nellie smiled. "That was the funny thing about you, the way you would do things you didn't like." She began unpacking the luncheon items, then stopped, a bag of dill pickles in one hand. "Why?"

"Why?" Anne repeated. Nellie was definitely not herself.

"Yes. Why."

Anne blinked away the present, remembering those gray autumn days in Vancouver, the emptiness of the park, her mother waiting on a bench for him to come, a bright scarf around her hair, the other swimmers – usually only one or two young men pulling hard through the water, back and forth, 'training,' she was told – and the great ships beyond the wall, the tugboats towing barges, the tankers, trawlers, ocean liners all leaving Vancouver, going north before the ice, or south through the Canal, or west across the Pacific to Japan with a load of Douglas fir, or just out, up into the fjords, up through the Queen Charlottes until the holds were full. A chill wind rustled through the trees. If she closed her eyes she could tell which kind of tree was disturbed: the *clackle* of the stiff Arbutus leaves, the *whish* through the pines and firs, the soft sounds of the maple leaves, like a woman's skirt. With a quick glance back she dove in and stayed in, making up games, holding her breath under water as long as she could, beating back the impulse to give up, and in her mind begging them to call to her, those two warm people on the bench, to release her from the effort to please.

"I guess I just felt bigger afterward," she told Nellie. "Like something else, someone stronger. If I could still do it, and not want to."

"It was one of the funny things about you," said Nellie, not seeming to have heard Anne's response. She rummaged in the brown paper bag. "Turkey," she said. "Turkey's not naughty, is it?" Smiling conspiratorially, she passed the cellophane package to Anne.

"Turkey's just fine." It was more than she had expected, a sandwich.

They ate in silence for awhile.

"I'm sorry about the telegram," Nellie began.

The opening line, Anne thought, her heart beating faster. This was Nellie's show, this meeting in Stanley Park.

"But you wouldn't understand," she went on, "about telegrams. You're too young. They give me a fright, ever since my brother died, and daddy too I guess. Daddy most of all. His cancer came by telegram from the Mayo clinic. In Rochester, you know. I was 12, but I can still remember Donny Olson, the clerk from the train station, standing on our veranda with the yellow paper in his hands, and mother behind the screen door, refusing to go out and take it from him. We didn't have a phone, of course. There were a few party lines, but they weren't very private. Everyone listened in." She chewed thoughtfully. "Telegrams were always bad news. Those clipped sentences, so cruel. You could hear the death in them. And the getting on, too, as if there just wasn't time to say it slow or to mourn. Dreadful, mum used to say." Nellie stared at the insides of her sandwich. "Now mourning is important, I hear. That's one of Judith's big things, mourning. I wish you had known her before she had her problems."

"Judith?"

Nellie flashed Anne an impatient frown. "No. Mum. She needed help . . ." A man with a dog strolled close by, and Nellie lowered her voice. "Psychological help, I've told you that, but in those days you just didn't talk about your problems the way people do now. Stiff upper lip, that was the way. You'd've liked her before daddy died. You have her hair."

Anne did not think she would have liked Grammy (as she was called) ever. The few contacts Anne had had with her as a child were striking for the singularity of the impression they left: that of a fierce distaste for anything to do with life. Grammy dressed perpetually in black. She was small and squarish, though not heavy, and she always wore a cape-like coat and a hat. Even the lanky feathers bending from her hats were black. She had a restrained way of talking as if she would have yelled if not for her extraordinary control, for which all present sinners were to be grateful. There was some problem with her tongue – cracks and fissures having to do with malnutrition – and it was always swelling out and receding, especially after she had delivered an opinion. She carried an umbrella, rain or shine, for "protection." About her rooms there was a sweet dusty smell, like an old sachet. The place was tidy but not clean. To Anne, Grammy spoke of her 'hubby' who was dead, her 'privates' which were burning, and the 'Scotswoman' next door who was watching.

Anne studied her mother as she bit into the turkey sandwich, a blop of mayonnaise landing on her chin. Without thinking, she reached over and wiped it off, then recalled with the force of a cold wave the protectiveness she had always felt toward her mother; at some critical point, it seemed, the roles had been switched.

"They're messy, aren't they?" Nellie said shyly, holding out the sandwich.

"Very."

Her eyes glazing, she went on. "Mummy used to be as chipper as a little girl. I try to remember her that way . . . it was a long time ago. I wonder if I imagined it, her old happiness. Everything changed when daddy died. He was a good man. You know, he tried to wait. My brother told me. He tried to hang on until spring for mummy's sake. Winters were so hard anyway, so bleak in the prairies. But he couldn't. It had taken his liver by then, and his eyes had turned that awful yellow. Two weeks after Christmas he died. Died and left us alone. Everything changed then." Nellie laid her hand over Anne's. It felt warm and dry and soft, like a sick bird, and Anne experienced a sudden urge to wash. "You know I heard about Mal," she began, "and, and I want you to know that it's okay, Anne, that you didn't tell me. Really. You don't have to explain. You were being nice because it was Mother's Day. You were always being nice when you were a girl. Very sensitive. I used to worry about that. I just hope you're all right, Anne, that's why I wanted to see you."

"I'm fine."

"It's okay, isn't it, if I worry about you?"

"There's no need."

"I have to wonder sometimes, darling, if you want even that from me, even just a mother's natural concern for her only daughter."

Anne didn't know what to say to this: she doubted Nellie understood the meaning of half the words she had used – mother, natural, concern – although it was pleasant to think of Nellie in a genuinely selfless mood, and genuinely worried about someone else.

"Have we ever talked about him?" Nellie asked, her green eyes looking small and faded under the noon sun, looking old, Anne thought, and a little desperate.

"Not for a long time."

Shaking her head, gazing out at Burrard Inlet, Nellie said, "I couldn't, you know. You knew that. You knew so much it seemed. Too much. But really darling, what could I say? Afterward, I mean. I was angry with you – you didn't know that."

Anne heard herself say, "Yes, I did." Not consciously, no, she thought, but I could feel it, the condemnation, the withdrawal.

"It wasn't your fault, of course I had to believe that, but it happened, it happened to my pretty little girl. And there you were, still happy, going to school, doing the things girls do, and I was torn up. It killed me. He did it to hurt me, to destroy me, I was sure of it. I did think about taking him to court, you know, but that would've have been messy for us. I would've had to bring in the paternity letters. You'd've had to say everything, I mean *everything* out loud – you know that, don't you?"

"I guess so."

"Out loud," she repeated. "You do understand why I didn't take any legal action. It was to protect us from the humiliation. And besides, he'd've just sat there with those eyes he had, and they would've believed him, I'm sure of it. He was so easy to believe, wasn't he, darling?" She made a dispelling gesture, releasing Anne's hand in the process. "But you know this, the way he could lie. That's not why I wanted to see you, to talk about his, what should we call it, his faults. It's just that now he's dead, and I don't know what it means to you, that he's gone now. Isn't that funny? I don't know what you feel." A small, anxious laugh sputtered out. "Maybe we should've talked more," she said, her face struggling with the possibility that they had not talked enough, that she might have failed somewhere in Anne's upbringing. "I just hope you're all right. I guess you are, I mean, you have been, haven't you, all these years?"

It seemed incredible to Anne that her mother had asked such a question. She thought she could hear the guilt in it, and the fear; she knew she could hear the faint call for truth. "I don't know about the years, mom," she said very gently, protectively, "but probably not."

"No," Nellie said. "No, of course."

"Probably I wasn't really all right inside. I should have seen someone, though it wouldn't have made much difference."

"Really?" Nellie sounded relieved.

"What could they tell me that I didn't already know? It wasn't knowledge I lacked. It was something beyond knowledge, something to believe in." She paused, trying to remember what the question had been. "But about him dying, well I'm okay about that. I'm okay."

"I just didn't know what to think." Squeezing Anne's hand, she returned to her sandwich, took a bite, chewing haphazardly, as if she kept finding more of it in her mouth and, with a final, hasty swallow, swung her head toward Anne. "If you want to know the truth I'm a little sad about it myself, even though I haven't seen him since then." She searched Anne's face. "I was always careful not to show any, well, any feeling for him in front of you. I wanted you to know I was your ally. He used to call me now and then at the shop and leave messages with the girls. I never returned the calls, I want you to know that."

This was not true. Nellie had called him; she had merely forgotten reporting it to Anne. But Anne would not expose her; it was too easy. It was too late.

"I was always on your side," Nellie said. "But I couldn't help missing him. I'm sorry, darling."

There was a lot you couldn't help, Anne thought. *The combat mentality of sides and allies, and the notion that he was a battle lost because of a tactical error, because of me.*

"If you had only known him before California the way I did, a girl just off the prairies, just a girl in her first city, her first real job . . . he was so dashing in his black suit at the restaurant, and the grand way he greeted people, and that softness he had with dogs. Oh, there were lots of things a girl would fall in love with. Lots. He could do anything, fix things, make things. We traveled. We danced. He was always giving his money away, friends took advantage of him, his family even. We used to run into people who knew him, or just knew of him, all the time, in Seattle and Portland, Vancouver, and I was so proud to be with him, to be his gal. It was the most exciting time of my life. We were in love, we had dreams." She wagged her head emphatically. "But Anne, darling, if you could've seen him when he came to the hospital after you were born, oh, the look in his eyes. He cried, you know. He tried to get his brother to take you – Louis, the one with all the boys – and, oh, I guess it was a month later when it was clear Louis wouldn't, I could see, Anne, that Mal was, well, he wasn't unhappy about it. There you were, this perfect little baby, his baby girl. And from then on you had him wrapped around your finger."

"I didn't know about Uncle Louis . . . "

"I was so confused," Nellie said quickly. "Of course I desperately wanted to have Mal's baby, I wanted to keep you, but he had such an emotional hold on me, he was a powerful man, and you know when you're pregnant you're up and down anyway, and there's post, postpartisan depression . . . well, I was terribly confused. He was threatening to leave me. You understand, darling, the confusion. It was not a time to raise a child out of wedlock. Things are different now."

"Yes," Anne said. She gathered up the paper bag and cellophane and shards of lettuce wilting on the sunny park bench, and carried it over to the trash barrel. She could see Nellie brushing the crumbs from her blouse. Today her hair was pulled straight from her face, producing a moony, scrubbed appearance, though in back it was a snag carelessly bound with a red rubber band – Nellie in a difficult mood. Her darkish clothes – obviously expensive – were mismatched and awry in some indeterminate way. Was the blouse hem down? were the slacks too loose? were the colors not quite, quite. . . ? Anne dropped her eyes. In general Nellie seemed frantic and exposed, like a mental ward patient on visiting day, and if Anne could have steeled herself, she would have walked to her car and driven away.

From the salt water pool she heard children squealing, the pool she used to swim in when the park was empty and it was safe for them to meet, her mother and her father, when it was autumn and the leaves talked back to the wind, and dreams were easy to believe, and it was possible to be bigger than you really were. Under the Lion's Gate Bridge a trawler silently slid, riding low in the water. Coming back in, she thought, coming back heavy and needing to unload.

Nellie appeared beside her, clutched her arm. "Please darling, please come and sit. I need to tell you."

Anne let herself be led back. At the moment her mother's

touch was almost painful; she sat with her hands tucked under her thighs, her feet moving deliberately, coming together, separating, coming together, then separating. "I'm listening," she said.

"Years ago I told you that I wouldn't call him 'your father' because he wasn't to you. It would be easier I thought, for both of us. I don't know if that was right." Nellie paused, as if waiting to be told whether or not it was 'right.' "But it wasn't fair to him. Oh, he didn't deserve fairness, we both know that. And anyway, at that point it was easier not having to be fair, not separating things like who he was some of the time, the nice times. It was easier just to say he was bad and he was gone. We would cut him out of our lives like a cancer. We would forget him. That was our right because of what he did being so awful. I thought we both needed simple solutions then. So I called him Mal whenever I had to. Period."

Glancing away, Anne watched a lap swimmer paralleling the stone wall. He stopped, coughed vigorously, then resumed his workout. Probably he had breathed in some water; it happened, usually when you were tired, careless, you took in the wrong thing.

"But when you got older I decided that some kind of formal relationship would be appropriate, for your sake, believe me. Maybe a couple of brief visits a year with what's-her-name there of course, maybe a Christmas letter, a birthday card with a newsy note attached, but keeping it light, if you know what I mean. On the surface, no heavy discussions."

Again and again the pale hands of the lap swimmer cut the water, mirror images of each other, both preceding and succeeding, never meeting, never touching, but moving forward. Down. Then back.

"For your sake," Nellie repeated. "So that you wouldn't have any regrets if he died someday. And you don't now, do you? You said you didn't."

"I said I was okay about his death."

"Yes, darling, and I'm so relieved. Really." Nellie frowned, trying to find where she had left off. "Anyway, what I was trying to say was that it was never to forgive him for what he did, don't misunderstand me. It was unforgivable, don't you think? My life has never been the same since."

What are we talking about here? Anne thought. *Whose life? By default you participated, by proxy you chose. If your life was ruined . . . well you were the adult. I had no say, mom. The kid had no say.*

"Still," Nellie continued, "he was your father, Anne. He felt things a father is supposed to feel. He used to look at your toes, just look at them, like they were tiny pink jewels, when you were a baby. And when you graduated from kindergarten, from *kindergarten*, we drove all the way to Tacoma in a hail storm to buy you a blue dress, one you had seen. He would take your report card to his office and show it off. And I remember when we first visited the Convent and we were waiting for the Reverend Mother – Baldwin was her name, wasn't it? – there were all those old tapestries, and our footsteps sounding in the hallways, and while we were waiting in the visitor's parlor I shushed you for laughing – I can't remember what it was about, some little thing, nothing – and he was furious. I had to stop him from leaving. 'I don't want her to come here if she can't laugh,' he said. Do you remember that?"

"I think I do."

"He was really worried that it wouldn't be a happy place. It was so quiet, and there were all those nuns dressed in black. It must have scared him. He couldn't understand a woman wanting to do that, be a nun and give up . . . well, give up so much."

Sex, Anne thought. *You can say it in front of me. And sure he was scared; how could he begin to relate to a celibate woman?*

"Anyway, he wanted you to be happy, darling, just happy, the way any father wants. Any father. He paid for your schools, expensive things, piano lessons and riding lessons, do you remember that watch he gave you? It was a real Swiss watch."

Anne nodded, trying to think of some way to stop Nellie, stop this, this manic recitation.

"The point is, even when he stopped sending me money, he kept paying for you, for your school, for whatever you needed. And every time he saw you his eyes got sparkly and he became the silliest man, giggling and playing with you. I used to kid him that he was making me jealous. But you were his princess," Nellie sighed, sounding disappointed. "There was no changing that. You could do no wrong – we got into a few fights about that, oh my. It wasn't easy trying to discipline you with Mal around, I mean it made me look bad. I had to play the heavy. When you have children you'll understand, it isn't easy to say no. I had to be both parents to you. I did all right, didn't I? I mean, look at you, you're beautiful. And we made it without him, that's what's important." She leaned around, catching Anne's eyes with a pleading, childlike expression. Her lower lip was trembling. "You think of me sometimes, don't you Anne? Your old mum."

"Sure."

Nellie's face quivered into a smile, eternally grateful. "Remember the walks on the beach? They were such fun, weren't they, the walks we used to take at sunset, and you running with your long hair, full of life, reciting Shakespeare, wasn't it? Yes, it was Shakespeare. My beautiful daughter. I wanted you to have all the things I didn't. You were going to make up for it, for the loneliness, for the mistakes. You would be the life I didn't have. But then he . . . well, I thought we could erase it, you see. We would be happy, that's the best revenge, you know, that's what they say. You remember the walks, don't you Anne? You do."

Anne said nothing; she dug up a clump of grass with the toe of her shoe and laid it aside. The walks she did remember, and running ahead of Nellie, pretending she was free, unkinking the kinks, and letting the salt air blow off the house smells in her hair. Living with Nellie was like living in a closet – dark, confusing, cramped, a place where all is oppressively well known and any erratic movement is painfully answered. She remembered Nellie sitting in the sand, drinking cheap bubbly wine. She remembered how elated she felt at the beach, how hopeful, not because she thought there would be an end to the life she was living, but because of the space and the clean air and the other people there. Normal families represented the *fact* of happiness, not the possibility; it never seemed that her life could actually *be* a happy life. The fact of happiness out there, surviving – that was enough.

"I guess I could've done better on the dating, but you didn't seem to want to go out. I don't remember you ever asking, did you? No, no I don't believe you did ask."

Because it wasn't possible, mom. Not possible. Because by then I felt so abnormal, so utterly beyond it, I could not have asked. And you could not have dealt with it if I had.

"There was that one boy, Robert, his father was a doctor. I remember you went on a picnic with him. Maybe the long skirt seemed a little old-fashioned to you, but you said you liked it, you did say it. And darling you know that really, boys prefer nice girls. To marry, I mean. Why didn't you see him again?"

"I don't remember."

"You looked so wholesome, that was how you looked with your picnic basket. It reminded me of the prairies when I was young. As soon as the crocuses came up, we had picnics. Lavender crocuses. Oh, they were wonderful, a carpet of them. And the people, the farmers and town folk coming together. There was none of this every man for himself. People helped each other in those days. There were barn raisings and bonspiels and socials. We tried to do a good turn every day. Oh, I guess there were a few rough types, ruffians, daddy used to call them, but mostly there was innocence. That was what Mal liked about me, I think, when we first met in Seattle, my innocence. I was only 20 and oh my, he dazzled me. We had something special, he always said."

Yes, he always said that. When he wanted something, it was always special.

"He was a daddy, Anne, that's what I'm trying to say."

A daddy to whom?

"He was the other, too," Nellie continued. "And I don't mean to make that seem unimportant, but Anne, none of this is easy. He wasn't easy to figure out. A complex man, I used to tell myself. You broke his heart when you told. You should read some of the letters. It was crazy, I know, for him to be so hurt, but aren't we all?"

"Aren't we all what? Hurt or crazy?"

Nellie flinched. "I'm not trying to excuse him," she said hastily. "Nothing like that. He had a sickness, a terrible sickness. I only thought that now it might be important for you to know more . . . well, more of the nice things. What would it hurt, I thought, if she just knew some small nice things she could hold on to, things she could tell people if they ask about her father. About Mal." Nellie stopped, as if she'd lost her place along with her pronoun. "You don't have to tell people the truth all the time. I know you like to do that, darling. It's fashionable, I guess, to talk about things with strangers, but it can put people off, knowing so much of the truth."

"It certainly can."

"Just a few nice things to hold on to," Nellie repeated. "That's what you need."

Anne felt her jaw clench. "The last thing I need is a few nice things. A few nice things aren't going to cut it now and they sure as hell didn't cut it then. He was a liar, and a moral troglodyte, and he was guilty of incest, many times over. Many times," she said, wanting to cry but not, grabbing hold of the anger, grabbing hold for the first time, it seemed. "If that's what you mean by a complex man, then yes indeedy, he was a complex man."

"You know that's not what I meant," Nellie said coldly. It was the voice that used to scare Anne, but not anymore, she realized with a raw sense of freedom.

"Then you must mean his intelligence, right? That seems to excuse him for you, his intelligence, that he could think and sin simultaneously. But that doesn't cut it either, it condemns him, because he was aware, don't you understand that? That's what condemns us, the awareness." Abruptly she stopped, for in the light of that bad moon of awareness she saw the faces of men before Elliot, her own desperate service of desperate needs, her own mistakes and, beneath the lurid glow, the dark topography of memory lay exposed. *Awareness*. And she might have – for an instant – forgiven her father if she could have forgiven herself. Except that he had never been sorry, not even the first time. Never said he was sorry. "If he had a conscience," she said, "which is doubtful, but if he had some misshapen little remnant of a creature up there muttering about right and wrong, then he could talk it into things just as smoothly as he talked you and me and everyone else he used to feed the black hole of his needs and inadequacies. And you know why? Because he didn't care, he could not care, did not know how. Was not able. *He* was the misshapen creature, the cripple. And I bet he knew it. I bet he knew it deep down inside. *That* was his weapon."

"He loved you, Anne," Nellie said, her control an obvious effort. "He made mistakes. We all do."

"Mistakes? He made mistakes? A little boo-boo? Please, please don't trivialize what he did. You don't have the right."

"All I'm trying to tell you is that he did love you, and he loved me, too, in the old days, the way he loved you."

"Obsessed. The word is obsessed. And you knew it, you knew that I was what kept him coming to California, and sending checks. I was what kept *you* in his picture. That was your piece of the action."

"Oh, you know that's just not true, Anne. That's ridiculous. You're not making any sense, none at all." Frowning, Nellie scanned the park, as if she was expecting someone, someone who was coming to explain, to stop things, to help, and they were late. Terribly late. "I was just trying to be smart about him," she said. "Play his game. He was always playing games, Anne, you remember that, don't you, the games? We needed the money. I had to raise you by myself, give you a decent home. And I knew he would help if he saw you, if you wrote him. You were his prin-cess. That was why I had you write him every week. For your sake. I thought you needed a father, even part time. Every girl needs a father." Her voice cracked. "Every girl. And I knew he would come for you. Not me anymore. You."

"That's right. When you weren't enough, and a daughter wasn't enough to hold him, you offered a lover. Me." She saw Nellie's eyes go skittish, then added finally, "You were my pimp."

Nellie slapped her across the face, gasped and slumped back against the bench.

"That's always your response," Anne said.

Crumpled hands held before her lips, Nellie said, "Why are you so hostile?"

"You never cared about me, you never even asked how I was. Not once."

"But you didn't want to talk about it."

"I didn't want to? And now that he's dead, you ask if I'm all right, and you've collected a few small 'nice things' to hang on the daddy tree, and we're all supposed to step back and say 'ain't he pretty.' We're supposed to remind ourselves that the devil is a gentleman and a scholar, and what the hell, he's an angel, too, right? Well, I don't want to do that, *mum*. It's a lie. It's like putting makeup on a corpse – no one believes it. It makes it worse. It makes me sick."

Nellie's face was red and pinched; she began to cry.

For a few moments Anne watched her, indifferent. "I don't know how much you knew then, and I don't want to ask how you could possibly not have known, but I definitely do not want the few things I can bear to know and understand and live with to be whitewashed by you, simply because the old deuce is dead and you want to forget, or primp up, or be absolved. I want to remember everything. I *want* to remember. That is my legacy. My hope."

Nellie was sobbing heavily now, her body bent, her arms crossed over her chest, as if she was trying to keep it from ripping open. "Maybe I could've done better, is that what you think? That I should've been a better mother?"

To Anne, the question was surreal; she sighed, worn out. "I think it was too big for you to deal with. Too complicated."

Nellie leapt at this explanation and, for the moment, her tears abated. "Yes, that's right. Complicated, much more complicated for me, because, you see, I had known him other ways, before. That's what I've been trying to tell you. Yes, yes that's exactly right, darling. Thank you for understanding, it's so important, that you understand."

A couple of boys made a dash for the pool past them, their mother hurrying after with towels, inflated toys, a basket of food. She glanced around, saw Anne, and smiled a tired smile.

"We should've never gone to California," Nellie said absently. "California was the mistake, but I was so sure he would follow me, you see. Sunny California. You know how he felt about warm weather."

Anne said nothing.

"You still love me, don't you? We had some really nice times together when you were growing up. I think about them often. You remember them, don't you, the walks and the, well, you know, all the nice times."

"I know."

"We made it. That's what's important. We survived. We believed in each other and we survived. I've always been so proud of you, your grades and things, the way you keep yourself up. I have a new friend, Vickie, I've told her all about you, about your dog and your truck, your little cabin, and that big, strong man you've got. He's kind, I can tell. If I ever think about getting married, that'll be the one thing I look for, kindness. Daddy was that way. I still miss him, you know, all my life I've never stopped missing him. Vickie's husband is a grammar school teacher, a good sort, as mummy would have said. She reminds me so much of you, Anne. You'll like her. She washes her hair every day, too. I used to get a little cranky about the hot water, I know, but, but you still do that don't you, Anne? Wash your hair every day?"

This has got to stop.

"Forgive your old mum. She did her best, but it was too much." Nellie spread open her fingers; her hand was shaking. "Too much."

"It's all right. We did what we could do. And it's a beautiful day." Anne stood, but Nellie grabbed her hand, pulling it down and back toward her. She tipped her head to the side and made a pouty, little girl face. An old routine, too old, too late. Anne took a deep breath, knowing exactly what was expected. "You want me to tell you I love you," she said.

"*That's* what I needed to hear." Anne tried to extract her hand, but Nellie squeezed and pulled it down again, speaking against it in a lowered voice. "I'll be all right about Mal. It'll just take a little time. Don't worry about me."

They walked past the pool on the way to the parking lot. The two boys were pushing each other up and down in the water, while mother lay on the grass with a paperback. The water was probably still cold, Anne guessed, the warm May air deceptive. It would never be comfortable, not even in the middle of summer. Suddenly Nellie halted and gave a wild gesture at the water.

"What?" Anne said. "What?"

"Freeeeeezing," Nellie shrieked.

The woman with the paperback dropped her book and glowered at them.

"It was one of the funny things about you," Nellie said gleefully as they continued along the path.

Reaching over, Anne touched her mother's tangled hair. "Yes. It was one of the funny things."

NINETEEN

They were an unlikely couple, and in Anne's case, an unlikely patron of The Liongate Hotel disco scene. Vinny wore the three-piece suit she had seen him in the day before, and he fit in nicely with the rest of the men in the bar – successfully slim, tailored, and coiffed. His shoes were so shiny you could've chopped a line of coke on them. In fact, cocaine seemed to play a small, but clearly supporting role at The Liongate: there were frequent pilgrimages to the restrooms. Not Vinny. Vinny was a clean-cut, true believer of sorts, (though his beliefs might shift in the breeze); he would likely not ask questions, at least not ask the ones that had no answers, so he would not need to run from that abyss. No, Vinny would do lunch but he wouldn't do drugs, she figured.

After her meeting with Nellie, Anne had changed into some faded Levis, an oversized white shirt belonging to Elliot, and a well worn pair of Noconas she had had made in Galveston a few years back when she and Elliot were involved in a Gulf Coast project. This was who she was. Anyway, she thought Vinny needed exposure to a natural woman. Though she had to confess that the other women in their gold chains and silk pantaloons and 'styled' hair that scarcely moved as they jiggled around the dance floor made her feel, well, un-adult and unfinished. The raw material of a woman.

A rapid song began, and the dance floor cleared except for one couple – a tall woman in a red jump suit, and a tweedy fellow with a gray terrier beard and a collins glass in one hand which he held low, against his thigh, as if trying to conceal it.

"I've got two hundred thousand in my book already," Vinny was saying. (She had asked him about his work.) "And with the new complex in Bellingham, that'll make it over three fifty."

"Three fifty?"

"Square feet. The money's in the millions." Vinny chuckled in a proud, satisfied way; she could almost hear the suspenders snap. "Per month," he added.

Lifting her brow and tipping her head, she tried to look impressed. "Millions," she echoed.

"The anchor tenant signed on today. The rest'll fall like dominos now, I've seen it happen before. All you need's one good draw and you've got instant eighty percent occupancy. And you know what did it?"

"What?"

"Trim," he said.

"Trim." She hadn't the faintest idea what Vinny was talking about, but she thought she should be agreeable to him, to someone. After the phone call to Elliot, after the afternoon with Nellie, she needed very much to find some safe harbor, and tonight Vinny seemed a likely candidate.

"Yeah. I had them paint all the trim purple, and the guy loved it. 'Daring,' he called it. The kind of image they want to project. He signed the lease before lunch arrived." With his index finger, Vinny stirred his scotch, nodding, starry-eyed into its swirling depths, then sucking his finger, he murmured, "Daring." Glancing up, he searched her face. "You gotta be creative to make it anymore, don't you think?"

"That could be said for most occupations, except maybe

accounting."

Though not appearing to register her attempt at humor, nevertheless he nodded again. "Creative marketing. You gotta think in technicolor."

She smiled back at him. "Sometimes that's all it takes, I suppose, a small thing like, like your trim, that makes a big statement and reveals what you're truly about." Blather. Pure blather. But it mattered to Vinny, this business. That she cared not a whit about developments and creative marketing had no bearing. Safe harbor, she reminded herself. And stormy seas out there. She could simply tuck herself in here with Vinny, hide with handsome Vinny. Because it was too rough out there. Too real. Crazy real. Because now what difference did it make what she did, Elliot would never be hers, he had never really considered her a viable option, he would keep hanging up on her, the less important one, the worth-less one. He would keep making false promises. Besides, Vinny required very little energy on her part. Vinny was shallow water, a pleasant wade. Vinny was the control in a failed experiment. And Vinny was here – that was seeming very important. She was going backward where she belonged. She was going crazy, and Vinny's was the face of craziness.

The woman in the red jump suit gyrated around the tweedy fellow, thrusting her hips at him in a suggestive manner. The music became more frantic, the harmonies tormented, winding up to an ugly pitch. Raising her arms, jump suit shimmied in, touched her pointy little breasts to his chest, and shimmied back out. Anne did not think her particularly alluring; she tried too hard. Mannerisms, no makings. Elliot had always liked Anne without makeup, without trying. "You don't have to," he said. Now she wondered if that was true. It had been awhile since she had been 'available;' she might not have what it took anymore, she might need a little help.

"She's good," observed Vinny.

"At what?"

"Good at whatever."

"Whatever," she said.

He tilted his head and winked, and she realized then that it was the same sort of wink – playfully lewd – same sort of look as of someone who knew how to get away with things, a boyish man, to all appearances harmless. It was the same look she had first seen on the ferry, and it had most definitely been meant for her. She had been Vinny's mark from the beginning. And there was something, well, something provocative about that . . . under the circumstances. She did not feel so powerless around Vinny. She had some weight, some small and desperate value.

The cocktail waitress came by: Vinny switched to beer, Anne ordered another Jack Daniel's, but when it arrived she decided not to drink it. She was just drunk enough to . . . to what? she asked herself.

Forget, maybe. No, not to care. Caring too much – that had been her undoing.

"Anyway," Vinny said. "Managing property for a firm like mine is exciting. There are big opportunities. In a few years I could be running the whole western region, I could be in Hawaii. With profit sharing, which'll kick in after I've been with the company a year, I'll be tipping the scales at six digits." He gulped down his beer. "It's exciting."

"Sounds like it."

Vinny laid his hand across her thigh. "So are you."

A dizzying rush, and she had to find and focus on a small carpet stain; at the same time she experienced a strange fatigue, and a desire to let things go blurry and slip away from her, to let things happen. Just happen. She heard herself say, "Good."

For years she had been Elliot's, only Elliot's, and what good had it done her, where had she gotten? Maybe her mother had been right: Anne wasn't fit for marriage. Damaged goods. So she would have to take what was offered. The damage couldn't be repaired. The experiment had failed. She had failed.

Vinny chewed on his lip, then he put on a candid, unsure face. It was instantly endearing. "You're not interested in my business, are you?"

"I don't know anything about it. It's a completely different world. That makes it very interesting," she lied.

"You're just being nice."

"Not at all. I'm being honest," she lied again. She was sorry she wasn't interested, sorry she had let it show and, trying to look earnest, she frowned as she said, "I wish I had what it took to do well in business. Not many do, I suspect. It sounds as though you're one of the few."

"We'll see. You can't hide from the numbers." He was smiling. "I get the feeling I'm not the type of man you're used to, but . . . what I mean is, do you think you could like me, Anne?"

"Too late. I already do. And anyway, occupations have nothing to do with it." Actually, she didn't believe this, at least not in the long run, but she thought it was what Vinny wanted to hear. So she said it. *Safe harbor, safe temporary harbor.*

Seeming reassured, he gave her leg a shy squeeze. "I've been saving something," he said. "For the right moment. It's kind of a present."

"Vinny . . . "

"Wait. Let me tell you. Because it's not exactly from me, and it's not exactly to you. But I think you'll like it, I know you will. You'll see it as a kind of gift, like I do. And your father, too."

"My father?"

"I almost told you at dinner the other night. But then I thought 'no, wait till she sees it.'"

The blackest dread swept up inside her. Wasn't it over yet, would she ever be done with him, would he ever really die? Out of the mouth of babes, she thought, of babes . . .

"Malcolm and I had something special up our sleeves."

Malcolm? Seldom had anyone called him 'Malcolm.' It

made him sound like a different sort of man, a better human being; to Vinny, he probably was just that. A better man.

"Like I said the other night, we clicked, and in more ways than one. Now it's up to me to bring the whole deal off."

He was dragging it out, she could see that; he was clearly so delighted with the prospect of her imagined happy reaction that he hadn't perceived that so far her reaction was one of uncomprehending fear, uncomprehending fury.

"Bring what off?" she said. "What are you talking about?"

"Let's dance." Already half up, he began tugging on her arm.

"No, tell me now Vinny. I'm not very good at waiting, believe me." She tried to conceal her impatience, to make it over as girlish anticipation, but her voice ended up sounding kittenish and phony. "What were you and daddy up to?"

"No good," he laughed.

"Please Vinny."

As if he'd been a naughty boy, he put on a serious face. "A resort," he whispered.

"Where?" Though she had already guessed. It was obvious. It was utterly in keeping with her father's remarkable ability to destroy what he should have cared most about.

"That's the best part."

"That's the part I want to know."

"Doe Bay. All of it. The whole bay from Uncle Joe's out to the point. Malcolm had the investors before he even got there, before I met him."

"My father," she said, to remind herself.

"It was amazing, Anne. I mean, he arrived with most of it already put together – backing, blueprints, the works. That's how sure he was. And he did it. He talked the Institute into a limited partnership, and these are people who, who meditate." Vinny made a prissy expression. "They wouldn't have the faintest idea what to do with a prime cut of land. They didn't."

"I doubt that very much," she said, keeping her voice as cool and level as ice. "They own other property, Vinny, just as stunning as Doe Bay."

"And they're just sitting on it, that's my point. It took a man like your father to show them what could be done, the possibilities."

"A resort."

"Executive retreat," Vinny corrected. "No garden variety tourists, not there. It's classy land," he explained. "Classy land demands a class act."

Anne wiped the condensation from her glass, slowly turning it and drawing her thumb from rim to base until the glass was clear. "Of course," she said. "An executive retreat. For executives. America's brand of nobility."

He frowned. "You're not happy about it."

"I actually like unused land, Vinny. I actually do."

"It's going to be beautiful, honey, trust me."

Why was he always asking her to trust him, damn it? How could she possibly trust him? He couldn't even see what he was going to destroy, he couldn't see. How could she trust him? To begin with, he was male.

"Maybe it will be . . . attractive, in its way," she said. "But that has nothing to do with what I'm saying. The land is beautiful as it is, it doesn't need our help."

"You don't understand, it'll be *the* place to go. *The* place in the northwest. Five hundred units, and lots of them suites. There'll be conference rooms, a game room, exercise rooms, stables, tennis courts, shops, even an indoor swimming pool. Every room will have its own refrigerator and bar, fully stocked. Every room. There's nothing else like it around here." Again he slid his hand across her thigh, and despite her anger, maybe because of it, she let him leave it there. Also, she took a certain perverse satisfaction in knowing that what was giving him pleasure, she could in any given instant reject. His desire was her power, the only thing it seemed she had.

Vinny was still talking. "I know this sounds crazy, but I half hoped . . . well, I had this crazy fantasy about you and me carrying on your father's dream, making it go . . ." He dropped his eyes, peering furtively up at her. "I guess I shouldn't be talking like this. It's just that I felt an instant closeness with you." He jerked his head sideways. "Oh hell, maybe I'm getting ahead of myself."

"Are you?" She stared at her glass; it was fogging up again. "Carrying on my father's dream, huh?"

She thought about her job at the Bella Vista, shuffling dinner plates, collecting tips, and her other job at the marine lab, doing grunt work for big shots with grants and endowments and Ph.D.s. She would probably never get her dissertation done, never be more than a well-appreciated underling. In the books and periodicals, the journals of thises and thats, her name might be found in the 'acknowledgements,' no more.

She thought about Nellie's attempt to unlock the door between them – a momentary spasm, Anne supposed. Anyway, she wasn't sure she wanted that door unlocked. Wasn't it too late? Did she care anymore what might have been there between a mother and a daughter? Was it really worth it anymore, caring, trying? *Could* she stand caring? No, she didn't think so. No. There was nothing left, except charity. The basket itself was woven of charity; the rest she had spent years ago.

And she thought about Elliot and the pregnancy, about her years as the other woman, *the other*, and she wondered if what he had told her was true, that he was leaving his wife for her and that they would have children later when the timing was better. And after that, she wondered about herself, if she had the energy to go through the mess, to keep believing when it was so obviously unbelievable. She wondered if she wouldn't rather tell him 'forget it, just forget it, you took too long, you wore me out.' Just to beat him to the inevitable punch.

She thought about Vinny's fantasy of living on the island, managing a swank resort (swank, that was a word he would like) catering to men like her father; and to a part of Anne this sounded inevitable, exactly what McFate had in mind for little Miss McBain who sat on a tuffet – to become a docent for yet another of her father's monstrous webs. And to live with a replica – not so smart, not so bad, Vinny, but a replica of her father nevertheless. Maybe, if you weren't careful, they were all replicas, and she was making them over to be so.

Her dream of marrying Elliot Newhouse and having a rosy cherub, a house with lots of windows, *oh* lots of windows and friends and laundry on the line, a life out of which she would rise, not crouch beneath – a dream. All dreams. Trifling, trifling, trifled dreams.

Her throat tightened. Everything seemed broken and wasted, and she was so very tired of trying to believe and of not believing, she just couldn't believe anymore, no more. And she was so sick of hope, it was choking her, a sweet pathetic wad of hope, all her life she had hoped that what was wasn't, that what could be would be, that what others enjoyed she too would enjoy someday, and that when that day came there would be something left of her – that was important – to *save* something for the day when she would be there, standing intact, full of readiness. When the normal, the fantastically unexceptional came knocking. But no. She had not saved. She had thrown it all into the fire for the warmth, the love, and now she was tearing apart her being and burning that up, too. Anne McBain was on fire. Helplessly on fire.

"Are you still with me?" Vinny asked. He sounded genuinely concerned.

Wouldn't it be nice if he was, she thought wistfully, if he really was concerned. For the time being, because she needed to, she decided to accept him as real. From across the small table she regarded him: despite his question, there was no apparent curiosity in his eyes – they were round and lightless, and against his tanned skin, like two pebbles half buried in the sand.

"Anne?"

"Right here." *Where I've always been, will always be.*

"I'm glad," he said. "I like you here with me."

Handsome, sincere looking, full of great expectations,

great schemes, Vinny meant no harm. Not to her, not to the pristine bow of land and sea called Doe Bay, and not to the species to which he belonged. Nevertheless he was a danger. In the evolution of higher consciousness, he was a nanoweight pulling down, backwards, ever so slightly and ever so surely. And in her own evolution he was an earlier, recognizable and comforting form of life.

Neither did Anne mean any harm. But she would probably kill the little life within her. And if she wasn't careful – and why should she be? why try? who gave a damn? – she might sleep with a fool tonight, denying it even as she did so, enjoying it only for the sake of the most ephemeral sense of order in a life blown apart. And though she should not, must not, in the morning she would probably cry when she sowed the Pacific with her father's wretched ashes. They would disperse, disappear. It would be a painfully bright day. She would have to squint just to see them go.

"Are you okay?" Vinny asked.

"What about Joe," she said. "How does he feel about a resort?"

"Oh, Uncle Joe, he won't care."

"Then he doesn't know yet."

"Well, it's a little tricky, legally speaking. The place'll be mine after my mother dies, and she's older than Uncle Joe, but they don't have to die for it all to happen, that's the beauty of this deal. I mean, your father – and me – we didn't see any reason to wait."

"No."

"All they have to do is sign a paper deeding it to me in name only, right? Then to sweeten the deal, we make them limited partners in the whole project, and they just go on like they have, living in the house."

"And when they are gone?"

He shrugged. "I guess I'd demo the place. It's turn-of-the-century stuff. Put up something new. Anything you like," he added, and he was wearing the kindest smile. "Anything at all."

Trying to ignore his innuendo, nevertheless she couldn't help a small nod of thanks, (it was such a pleasant thought, that a man would build her a house), though of course she would never want the place destroyed, if she was to live there, which wouldn't happen anyway. She didn't want anything to happen to Doe Bay; having only just seen it for the first time, she didn't want it then irrevocably changed, destroyed. It was a little like meeting some terribly nice person the day before they died. "You don't need the Sanborn land," she said. "What the Institute owns is enough, isn't it?"

"Well, no," Vinny said. "Uncle Joe's land runs almost all the way out to the point. His land is Doe Bay."

"So you need the access."

"Right. For the marina. It's a good bay. And the cove on the other side of the point is too small, too rocky. Plus, the way the waves and currents crisscross there, well, it'd be rough, especially for sailboats. Doe Bay is protected."

Not hardly, she thought. None of us is protected.

"Part of the plan was to have executives sail in," Vinny added.

"I don't think your Uncle's going to go for it."

"Well, my job was to get him to go for it."

"Your job?"

"As GM. Malcolm needed me as General Manager."

"I think he needed you to solve the only problem he might have had." By now she was feeling sorry for Vinny; her father had suckered him, had made of him a glorified footman.

"It's a good idea anyway, you know, as your father was the first to point out, to avoid inheritance taxes. If the property's going to be mine anyway, what difference does it make if Uncle Joe deeds it to me now?" Downing the rest of his beer, he held up the empty bottle to catch the waitress's attention.

Speckled lights circled above the dance floor, changing color faster, slower, keeping time with the music. Behind the window in the corner of the lounge the DJ placed another record on a second turntable, gave it push and, as the last song faded out, he announced the next. “A slow one.”

Vinny stood up and bowed. “May I have this dance, Miss McBain?”

She thought: Elliot never asked me to dance, not once. It never surprised me, either. Why didn’t it ever surprise me?

Because you knew you weren’t good enough, said a voice.

Vinny was standing there with his hand out, and she took it the way someone starving might accept donated food – with terrific gratitude and terrific hatred and a terrific sense of failure.

The DJ had on a pair of pink, mirrored sunglasses, and an orange, double-breasted blazer with chartreuse spatters. When he grinned in the broad, theatrical way characteristic of night entertainers, she imagined they were trapped in the lounge, that some maniacal godling had taken over the control booth, and was manipulating their lives for his own amusement. “A slow, slow one,” said the godling. “Keep it clean, folks.”

Inwardly, she winced.

“That won’t be easy,” Vinny said, his voice low, so low.

A tacky scene, The Liongate Hotel disco lounge. Another world altogether. Elliot would’ve run from a place like this. He had done just that one Saturday night in San Francisco (though the place by comparison was all elegance and taste) when they decided to go out and ‘put on the dog.’ After cocktails at Cherry’s, while hunting for a parking place near a place called the Isis Room, he was overcome by urban claustrophobia, and before she knew it they were rocketing up a freeway ramp, bolting from the city. Forty miles down the coast at an all-night convenience market he finally stopped, and bought a can of toffee nuts and a screw top bottle of burgundy. Somewhere near Bean Hollow State Beach they pulled off the highway. A sliver of moon, stars twinkling, and the surf rolling in, (a reliable old friend, that surf, and open 24 hours, no tie required, no cover charge, and no trouble finding it, either, no trouble at all), and they had had to conclude it was the best idea all day, worth dressing up for. Hitching her gown, she walked through the sea foam, her hand in Elliot's. The world seemed to rush up to them, the world in the smell of night cliffs, in the feel of fine spray on the wind, wet sand between her toes, the world from the black sky prickling with stars – yes, the world rushed to meet them. Now it was rushing away, an ever-widening diffusion of parts.

The under-lit plastic of the dance floor was done in a psychedelic design; Anne watched her boots move from lipstick red to blazing yellow on across a cool, candy purple where Vinny apparently determined his spot was and there they teetered slowly round, two wind-up dolls whose batteries had just about run out.

She could smell the scotch on his breath, a hint of yeastiness from the beer chaser. Oddly, it was both seductive and repulsive, his breath, and the cologne he had sprinkled onto the lapel of his fine suit, the flashy lounge, a plasticized version of the sixties scene developed no doubt by someone in creative marketing. In this place, with this man – so opposite . . . *opposing* all that she could like and believe in – she was a whore. And yet it was near to her, near and understood and in her veins.

"My princess," he would say from the darkness. Daddy's princess. How she came to loathe the sound of that word – prin-cess in-cest, it sang in her mind – no term of endearment, but need honeyed over. For his princess. A term of imprisonment.

The DJ cranked up the volume, and she began to feel the music as if it was being injected into her veins, a compelling warmth, like a strong drug coming on.

No, she thought, what Elliot had said was just another delaying tactic. It had to be. She would never be 'an honest woman.' Hers could not be a real life. He would keep stringing her along until she couldn't stand it. A mistress, worthless, god-forsaken . . . well, if he thinks I'm worthless, if he can just hang up on me, if he can lie to me now, when I'm . . . then I may as well *be* worthless, be the way everyone has always treated me, this person they see, they want. Not me. It isn't really me, is it?

As good be hung for a sheep as a lamb, she thought.

Vinny nuzzled her neck. Low down in her stomach, the heavy, liquid music stirred.

The thought of having to go back to California to her old life, but without Elliot, the thought of a day without talking to him, even when there was nothing to say, was almost too much to bear. Bleak and frightening. It would be easier to get out, to take the job and come north. Cut her losses. Vinny would approve of that, cutting losses. It was sound business advice.

The lights dimmed to reddish tones, and the mood on the dance floor became more intimate, more sensuous. Shadowy couples revolved slowly around them, figures in some lurid vision of hell, their eyes closed, their bodies melting against one another, disappearing down a chasm of passion and sin. Vinny held his hand on her lower back, pressing her in toward him, and his entire presence became focused in the weight of his hand.

Again, she felt the strange fatigue.

"What's your last name?" she asked.

His chest vibrated against her face; he was laughing softly. "Whatever you want."

She closed her eyes, losing balance, as if she was caught in a terrible undertow, had struggled and struggled against it, reached toward the shore, and if only Elliot had put out his hand, if he had stopped *saying* he would and just grabbed her, then she wouldn't be so tired now, it wouldn't be pulling her out, away, into the deep water, and sweet Elliot still standing on the shore, talking from the safe warm shore, and the undertow so very strong, so very very strong.

Another couple bumped them, and she blinked into the murky outskirts of the dance floor. From soft chairs people watched, their faces remote, their postures indifferent. Against the ceiling the smoke gathered ominously.

It was perfectly natural, this place, this man who had no last name, this relief over not having to try anymore to be better than she was meant to be. The old undertow could carry her out, down. This was what happened to girls with histories like hers. This was what happened.

They missed the last ferry. The landing was deserted except for scattered cars parked in the overnight lot belonging to people who had walked aboard – commuters with wives who picked them up, tourists with bicycles, whatever. In the shuttered window of the snack shop they found a schedule. The earliest ferry departed at 7:10 the next morning, which would get them back in time for the memorial service Joe had planned.

So okay fine, Anne thought.

A thick fog had tucked into Horseshoe Bay and settled on the landing, damp and vaporous and, beneath the lights down by the water's edge, ghostlike as it darted here and there before the onshore gusts. But it did not seem especially cold as they walked back to the Porsche, as they paused in the murk and kissed. Not especially. Because there was a fire inside. His hands slipped in, running quickly over her, and over again, like twin hounds who had caught a scent and were determined to hunt down its owner. Around them the fog swirled, ghosts crowding in to watch and to judge, excited by the antics of the living. And they in the pit, as it were, a woman and a man, feeling the dank breath of the past, of the physical world.

Fantastically overcome, fantastically alert as he pushed her backward, she perceived the instant it had gone too far; it was in his eyes, a kind of faltering followed by a taking aim. It excited; it did not frighten; and it triggered something distinctly familiar, setting into action a series of responses as ordered and as finely tuned as the movements of a precision machine.

Vinny was spontaneous, decisive, here. And utterly hers.

Elliot was not.

Behind Vinny, dim fog, and the ghosts – Elliot, *oh* Elliot, she thought with dreadful wonder; and her father, tenderly grinning; other men along the way with their habits and hands; and far back, hardly there, hardly believable was Nellie's face, a look of grim satisfaction set about her green eyes, whispering *good work, daughter, good work.*

Suddenly against her back was metal, cold and smooth and unyielding. The hood of the Porsche. *A good machine likes to run hot,* Vinny had said. A good machine does, she thought.

He struggled with her jeans, and she saw as she always had – from a safe distance – that she did not stop him. He said something rough and meaningless, and she heard herself answer with the appropriate murmur to convey a modicum of wantonness. He lay his palm on the exposed skin of her abdomen, surprisingly still warm, and she felt the obscure mechanism of her hips lifting automatically, lift the emptiness deep down, and the fear and the confusion, the anger, the sadness too – heaviest of all – lift it up to him, the him of salvation. Any hymn would do for so lost a soul. Deliver her, fill her, keep her going.

She thought: I have a weakness, my father's weakness. A tragic flaw. Sex.

She thought: Oh hell, there's nothing wrong with sex, there's nothing wrong with Vinny. A healthy male, that's all. That's him.

This is not sex, she thought. This is . . . something else.

A loss of nerve?

A form of death.

And Vinny?

Vinny is . . . well, who Vinny is doesn't matter. Vinny is mine. That's all. Mine, now. Really, Vinny is nothing. Generic aspirin – cures your head but makes you bleed internally.

So stop.

I can't, it's too late, it would hurt him.

Who?

I don't know, him, Vinny.

Not Vinny.

No?

No, okay no, so what.

So why can't you hurt him?

Because, because, *damn it,* because I can't, I can't hurt him because I wanted to hurt him, and I couldn't. Because he was my father who couldn't care, and I wanted him to care to keep him. It was the only way to keep him, you see. *She* couldn't. Nellie couldn't. Nellie failed. And it wasn't so bad, was it? A small price to pay, sex. Really. To keep him tender, to keep him needing next to me. And I needed his needing. It was the one thing I could count on. I needed something to count on. I needed to count on him coming to me, next to me. Because he was my father and it was my right to have someone to count on. Because he had muscles and I did not, but when he touched me they were mine, and I was strong and he was not. It was my duty and my infinite bane and my bitterest will to lie with my father as they wished me to, and keep it all together. Our little mortal triangle, our de-loved family.

That strange, unspeakable fatigue again, and for the first time that evening she recognized it: it was the way she had always felt afterward with him – voided, as though who she was had simply been erased. And she had done it, not him; Anne had blotted out Anne. To survive. There was no Anne. Like dying, a small measure of death but enough to fade colors, obscure edges, enough to leave her feeling flat and lost, the victim of a holocaust inside her, intimate, secret, relentless.

She saw with some surprise, as if it did not belong to her – and it really did not, could not – the naked flesh of her thighs, and Vinny's long fingers curled around her panties.

"Help me with these," he said, snapping the panties playfully.

Prin-cess, breathed the ghost.

And she saw that she did help him; that she tugged down the panties and let them drip off her toes, like blood, to the ground; that unflinchingly she took him with both hands sure, one on the curving muscle of his buttock and the other on his swollen flesh, and drew him in, because everything was lost, everything else was beyond her control; she took in her hand the one thing she knew she could always count on, and felt the world disappear behind the intrusion.

He tried to look in her eyes, and she saw that she would not let him, that she closed them as she always had with him.

He tried to kiss her deeply, and she watched as she gently – so as not to trouble or disturb him – turned her head away. Eyes and mouths were not allowed: the rest went on remotely of its own accord. The rest was authorized, impersonal.

Tender and steady, he began driving it all back, the emptiness, the fear and confusion, the anger, the sadness, too – hardest of all – drove it all back down, his hips with the knowledge determined, thrusting, and her hips, she saw, meeting madly, desperately. And when it was all shoved back down, when her mind had pinched off thought, and she was not feeling herself feel but was *feeling* wholly and only one thing, one bright, tiny, overwhelmingly sharp thing – *hope* – she whispered her cry, "Please give me . . . "

And he did.

She watched his face straining against the pleasure, eyes squeezed shut, lips loosely parted, as the desire drained away with the hope, with all. Gone.

Slumping down, he pressed the damp skin of his cheek against hers, and gave a short, soft laugh. "If he could see us . . . "

"What?"

"Your father." Again the little laugh, too genial, too easy.

Maybe it was that she could not see his face, that she felt only his weight above and the cold steel of the machine behind, against her back, and the ghostly fog swirling and surrounding, like death come too near; maybe it was just the word invoked, the black magic of *father*; or maybe it was only the little laugh, blithely foolishly composed and sounding in her mind like the first of a funereal tintinnabulation. Probably it was all of these, all of everything, the past that could never be, and the future, the hairline crack of chance she might have; probably, maybe. But at once all the parts of all the world underneath broke the surface, an explosion of pure instinct, and she cried, "Get off me," shoving him as hard as she could. "Get away from me, *get away, AWAY.*" Feeling for the ground under her feet then, grabbing her clothes, her boots, and running from him. Running for her life.

A long while later, the longest while yet, she slowed to a walk and advanced without thought, her breath coming hard, her body a moving presence in the night, and so far only that – absolute determined movement.

Vinny pulled along beside her. "It's too far to walk," he said.

She gazed up the empty road, slashed here and there with moonlight, at the imposing banks of Douglas fir mounting either side. There was a strange comfort in the emptiness, the unmistakable way rising toward . . . she didn't know; but the way, she knew the way there, and she was not afraid. It was a place called the way.

"You'll be out here all night. I can't leave you," he said, tossing his cigarette into the ditch.

Saying nothing, she got in, and Vinny drove off slowly, cautiously, like someone leaving the scene of a bad accident.

After a while he asked her what happened 'back there'.

"You wouldn't understand," she said.

"The slam-bam?"

"Go to hell."

He drove the Porsche in silence then, until they reached the lighted roadways of North Van. "Look, I'm sorry. Did I come on too strong?"

"It has nothing to do with you." She would not look at him.

"Should that make me feel better?"

"Feel nothing. That's what you should feel."

"I can't. I like you too much," he said, almost touching her hand, but in the end not daring to.

"Forget it, Vinny. There's no chance."

"We were having such a nice time . . . " he said wistfully. "I don't understand."

"I'm through with nice times."

Shaking his handsome head, he said, "I guess I really blew it."

"Somebody did."

By the time they had returned to The Liongate she was once again feeling sorry for Vinny, but this time distantly, as if she was no longer personally implicated. He kept combing his hair in an utterly pitiful way, and it kept not doing what he wanted it to do. She didn't see why she should hurt him anymore than she already had. Vinny had so little to do with so much.

Back at The Liongate they took two rooms.

Vinny had with him a shaving kit which he always brought to work in case he ended up stuck on the mainland after a late business dinner – or so he told Anne when she glanced quizzically at it as they road the elevator up to the ninth floor.

She did not feel that bad, she realized, watching the lights on the elevator panel blink on and off as they had half her lifetime ago in the elevator at the Panache, her father looming behind her. No, she felt shook up, tired, confused, but not *bad*, not oppressed anymore.

"I didn't mean to ruin things," Vinny said apologetically.

The elevator stopped at the sixth floor, the doors opened. There was no one there. The elevator continued up.

"There was nothing to ruin," she said.

"I've been thinking about your father," he said. "How much I admired him, even for that short time. You must have really loved him, a man like him."

"I must have," she said.

"After the memorial service would've been, well, better? Is that what was wrong back there? I said 'if he could see us,' and it reminded you."

Anne said nothing.

"I guess I'm wondering if we could start again, over, you know. Because it should be nicer with you. I mean different. I'm the one who blew it, I mean, I pushed it, didn't I? I'm really sorry," Vinny said. "I've been with a lot of women. Sometimes just to get it over with, if you know what I mean."

Ah, the confessional tact. Still, she knew what he meant about getting things over with.

"Do you want anything to happen between us now? Anything long-term?"

"No."

"If there's a chance . . . that's all I want."

"Vinny . . . there's no chance. Forget me. I'm bad news." They were the same words Elliot sometimes spoke to her.

"I don't believe that." And *they* were the same words she had always said to Elliot.

At 3:00 in the morning, Anne got dressed, and went down to the lobby to find a pay phone. The hotel was so new that the phones in the rooms were not operative yet.

She had had a dream. A woman, a big, handsome woman wearing a toga, white with gold trim. The woman was sick and in pain. Mythical looking, with broad hips and a man's strong face, but stark feminine eyes, she lived alone in a house with countless stories and stairways, some going nowhere. Many of the doors were locked. All of the open rooms were empty. The sickness was inside a hump on her back, which was so large now she could no longer hide it. It was there because she hadn't washed behind her neck, that's what Nellie had said. Now even when she gazed straight at the mirror she could see it rising behind her head, growing, like the belly of a pregnant woman. In fact, it seemed to have something to do with a baby, but she didn't know where the baby went. Down on the first story she discovered a circle of naked boys sitting cross-legged on the marble floor and eating from a basket of fruit. A boy with a knife sliced off some papaya. Papaya is good for the stomach, he told her, and to please him she ate it. They were such lovely boys, there in the empty room, and the papaya so sweet, with its slippery texture. Then, with the tip of the knife, the boy traced the word 'love' into the taut skin of her hump, and she screamed, terrified. Instead of blood, millions of tiny transparent snakes gushed out until all that was left was a loose sack hanging from her shoulders, and the letters of the word 'love', shrunken and scabby. Dazed, she wandered off, up through the hollow house. Some of the boys followed and, one by one, she pushed them out the windows, such lovely boys, too. Doors swung open as she passed. People stood around, happy people drinking and talking. Where is it? she asked from the doorways. Have you seen it? They shook their heads, they shrugged, they looked confused, and beckoned her in for a drink. They were well dressed, and the woman knew she could not go in wearing a toga which had suddenly become a nightgown, she could not join them because her feet were bare. No, she said, I am looking. You must tell me if you have seen it. But what have you lost? they asked. Why do you care? Come join us. No, my pain, said the woman. Where is my pain? Oh, how can I live without my pain? she cried. Who am I without my pain? And it was true, for now in the mirror she had no face at all.

Anne slid into the phone booth – a walnut and red leather revival from the era of the Grand Hotel, with a hinged seat and, though narrower, a standard door. Private, she thought, dialing the number.

She got a recorded message: "Elliot Newhouse may be reached at . . . " There were pencil and paper in the booth provided by the hotel; she scribbled down the number and dialed it immediately. He was probably attending some conference, still not letting anything interfere with his work. And not 'resolving things with Jill,' since he wasn't even home. What a chump I've been, she thought, as she listened to the phone ring. On the fifth one, he picked it up.

"Hello?" a groggy voice asked.

"Is it true, Elliot? Just tell me if it's true, damn it. Once and for all, tell me what's true."

"Is what true? Where are you?"

"Vancouver. I'm in a hotel in Vancouver. We missed the ferry."

"We? You and Vinny. That was his name, wasn't it?"

"He met me after my interview. He was here already, on the mainland."

"What interview?"

"I had a job interview at Waddington Station."

"You didn't tell me you were looking for a job."

"No," she said. "I was only trying not to be such a fool. It was your advice all along, not to count on anything, on you."

"And afterward Anne, when Vinny met you?" She could hear the anger slicing through his voice.

"He's a nice guy. That's all."

"They're all nice guys. They put you in debt every time, how nice they are. You keep trying to prove the same bloody point."

"What point?" she said. "What point?"

"So after Prince Vinny took you out?"

"Tell me what point."

"Then what'd you do?"

"Nothing," she cried.

"Bullshit." Elliot's voice was cold like some impenetrable metal, like the hood of the Porsche against her back.

"Well I don't believe you, either," she said. "You wore me out and I can't believe you anymore. I don't have the heart for it, Elliot. I don't believe anymore."

"Nice timing, Anne. Vinny is, no doubt, a compelling part of this transformation?"

"Vinny isn't part of anything. And I didn't time this, you did. You took too damn long. Why should I believe you now? What's different about now? What makes *you* different?"

"Nothing."

She was all twisted up inside, twisted tight, and tighter; a sob tore loose. The way they were talking, the things they were saying to each other . . . "Oh Elliot, I wanted to, I tried so hard to last, but the time, it scared me, I began to feel like, like a foolish child. I love you too much, I think."

"Too much for what?"

"I do things for you, Elliot, things I shouldn't have done. There was something wrong with me. I kept wanting to believe in us, and you told me not to. It wasn't healthy."

"I told you that I couldn't make any promises." There was a pause, as if he had just remembered something important. "Just to satisfy idle curiosity, what *did* you do tonight, Anne?"

She was furious. It didn't matter, it couldn't possibly be significant, couldn't ever stack up against the years she wasted waiting for Elliot to come to her, to demonstrate that he loved her the way she loved him, to prove he was real, that it was true. "I fucked him, Elliot. That's what I did. We fucked. The way you and I do, to get it over with. That's what it was about, wasn't it? You never wanted anything real. You never expected us to last. I was never quite worth it, was I? I was expendable. You never really wanted us to last."

At the other end of the line there was a sigh, a tired expulsion of breath too much and too long held, an expurgation and, for Anne McBain, it was the sound of eternity, that sigh, an eternity without Elliot.

She stared at the phone number she had scribbled hastily on the hotel pad, and it occurred to her that it was a local Santa Lucia number. He *had* moved out. And she knew then it was too late.

"I did want us to last, Anne," he said quietly. "I confess to filibustering my way around the question, because of the massive pain and confusion it was going to bring upon my wife, not to mention my life, and because I was afraid of you – any sane man would be – but I was prepared, Anne. You can take that away with you, at least. In the end I was prepared to disprove your hypothesis, that we're all nice guys you have to throw a piece of ass so you can feel sorry for yourself. Or whatever it is you want to feel, or confirm, or expunge. So you can pity us males hanging from the nether side of evolution, us animals." His voice was agonizingly calm. "It's easy not to care then, isn't it, when we're so beneath you? We're pitiable and weak because we want you. Sex is your reducifier, reduces us to your old man's level. And you understand that. What you can't get around is that you like men . . . it's a pisser, isn't it? And some of us aren't so nice, Anne, some of us are mean enough to take you on, for the duration. Love is what you don't understand, not when it comes your direction. At least one of us loved you. Now it's hard to remember why."

The thing winding up in her suddenly sprang into jagged fragments of emotion, every kind of emotion, and she didn't know what to grab, where to start, it was all so desperately broken. "Elliot . . ."

"I'm going to go now, sweetie," he said.

And then he was gone.

In the corner of the lobby she found an over-stuffed chair and sat, tucking her hands beneath her knees as a small, disappointed child might. She did not cry: she felt she did not deserve to. Through the soles of her boots she could feel the heavy, regular thump of the music from the disco lounge, still open at 3:00 a.m.; it seemed to mock her heart which beat languidly, as if it could hardly bother going on, hardly bother pumping that foul blood around the same cursed circuit, as if it couldn't possibly compete with real hearts, good hearts. Good people.

Blear-eyed, she stared into the emptiness of the lobby – red carpets, wood columns, deserted couches and chairs, matchbook tents in each unused ashtray, an abandoned glass upon a low table, and the black wall of windows keeping the inside from the outside. Even the registration desk had been left unattended, though she imagined someone back there, reading a magazine, a book, someone who might have been a witness.

Yes, I saw her, she was here.

What had happened that she was here?

He died.

He did die, didn't he. But that is not all. He was only a beginning. I have perpetuated my father, and I have made of his deeds, permutations, and of his victim, my victims.

Outside, under the lights of the porte-cochère a yellow taxi drew to the curb. The driver did not emerge; he was waiting for someone, he had been summoned.

Was it only a week ago she had been with Elliot in his kitchen, sipping red wine as they waited news of her pregnancy? And those poor birds crashing into the windows where the sky was not real, lying stunned beneath the awful reflection? Only a week ago . . . an illusion, the windows, and all the while all the world was about them, those pretty little waxwings, and the blue sky rising forever above, if they had flown that way or this, if she had seen the difference they might have survived.

Fleetingly she considered phoning Elliot back to tell him that it was not true about Vinny; or that she was desperately sorry, or just desperate; profoundly regretted, etc. etc.. But of course it was beside the point. Utterly beside the point.

Oh God, what I have destroyed . . . Elliot, you were real, I could've been your honest woman. They would've taken a picture of us together. 'There we are,' I would've said, pointing.

There.

We are.

We were.

Maybe it was bound to happen. Like *El Niño* and the rookery at Año Nuevo destroyed. Losing Elliot seemed a terrible price to pay. She had to wonder if she had the strength and even if that was what it was called, what it would take to go forward from this wasteland.

From the disco lounge a couple wandered, still shouting as if the loud music had followed them out, but to Anne their words were merely the unintelligible sounds of life going on, leaving her behind as it had always done. In a similar corner chair, in another lobby years ago she had watched people come and people go, and the morning came and the morning went while she bent to color in her book, *stay inside the lines, you must, stay inside the lines when you color in your book,* and they were upstairs, her parents, in her head, while she colored in her book, and turned the pages, and colored more, in the chair in the corner of the lobby, until there was no more to color.

I have been here long enough, said Anne, though there was now no one to hear. To care.

A woman passed by. The red jump suit. Alone, Anne noticed, with a commiserative pang of self-pity. Sober-faced, the woman strode through the glass doors and vanished into the cab, which, from where Anne was sitting and for all she could see, had no driver.

I am so sorry, she whispered, don't let it be too late to be sorry. Now that I have driven everything away, because I could not bear to believe I deserved, let me have remorse. Don't let it be too late for remorse. If I have that then I am still alive. I am still. Please let me keep remorse, she prayed, keep it tight. And the prayer rose up, like a white vapor, spreading out against the ceiling, and there it lay, above her, a harmless stratus, waiting for the glass doors to open that it might escape homeward.

At 5:45 Anne McBain took the elevator up to the ninth floor of The Liongate Hotel.

"Wake up," she called to Vinny through the door. "It's time to go."

From a smiling waitress she bought two cups of coffee, then she returned to the lobby to wait for Vinny. The hotel was beginning to come alive. She could hear a vacuum cleaner running somewhere, smell bacon from the kitchen. A man left his engine idling as he filled the newspaper racks under the porte cochère, then drove off in a hurry to make his appointed rounds. The outdoor lights had been extinguished, the sidewalks were hosed off. Beside her the glass doors swung open and a guest passed out, suitcase, raincoat, attaché, yellow tie; while he waited, he bought a newspaper, tucking it under his arm for the flight home probably. Home to a family. A lovely, loving family. A home. A dream.

She sipped coffee, recalling some old lines, "*. . . and yet when all is said/It was the dream itself enchanted me . . .*" There was more, the last lines . . . frowning, dropping her gaze, she studied the tips of her boots . . . *'now that he's gone,'* no, *"Now that my ladder's gone,/I must lie down where all the ladders start,/In the foul rag-and-bone shop of the heart."* Yeats, she thought, I still have Yeats. And memory.

Vinny arrived: they found the Porsche and headed for the ferry landing.

The early morning air was raw, the sky anemic gray and cold seeming, like the skin of a dogfish you always threw back. Across Burrard Inlet, the city of Vancouver carved a geometrical range in the southward view. Before them, to the west, inky stands of Douglas fir blotted out the Strait of Georgia. It was dawn, but she could neither see its yellow eye nor sense its hopeful intimations of warmth inside the impenetrable dome of clouds. The light was absolutely flat, and the world stood exposed, shadowless, its colors true, its flaws visible, its face unreflected and unreflecting. The car made its way through the suburb toward the water. She opened the window, letting the wind catch strands of her hair and comb them back, letting it rustle intimately under the heavy fall at the base of her neck. She was out for the first time, it seemed, out following a prolonged convalescence. Her senses were ultra keen, susceptible to the least and to all details – there a heap of rubbish (something coppery near its peak) against the side of a brick wall, and a man eating a donut at the bus stop, his pants sagging at the knees, blackbirds on green grass, an arch of water over a row of identically grinning new Chevys, the smell of bus exhaust, the explosive first taste of coffee, like brambles and pepper and burnt chocolate, Vinny's skin where he had not shaved the color of blueberry batter, and the knowledge of what she had lost like a bad hole in her gut, and who she had been spilling out that hole, washing away. It had been through Elliot, the washing away, but he had washed away, too.

She pictured him on the beach at Spencer Spit while she dove for oysters; she saw him on the island with his tanned legs walking in the sand before her; and standing on the bank of the Rio Grande – "you can do it, you'll feel like a million bucks," he had said. Well. She had done it – that was something, that was everything now – but he wasn't standing on the shore anymore, and she didn't feel like a million bucks. She felt broke. Once again, she tried to tell herself that Elliot was gone, but the words were stark and unreal, and she figured they would likely always seem so, alien things the heart would reject.

Dawn light, and she was moving in it, a part of what she saw, and okay, she supposed, just for that. In some measure blest even. It was not beautiful, this world, not today; it was coarse, frightening, it did not apologize, and it was exciting.

TWENTY

After a year and a half, Holmes was still not used to the rain on the north end of the island, but Anne figured he'd rather be with her in the field than back in Vancouver where the apartment cramped his natural style. She reached down and scratched behind his ears; he lifted his muzzle – more please – beleaguered but willing to be placated.

Aiming the skiff east out of Telegraph Cove, she slowed crossing the tide rip, then picked up speed in Johnstone Strait, heading for the research camp Waddington had maintained for almost a dozen years. Grant would be there, first one up at the spotting scope, waiting. And what remained of the crew – reduced to Noma and Ian now – there to the bitter weather end. Fanatics, Anne thought. Grant too – it was hard to say with him – but maybe in his worker bee way he was another sort of fanatic.

She smiled, shook her head. She could still see Noma standing on the tube of the Zodiac she had just beached, a dip net in one hand, her other raised high – almost a religious gesture: "These fingers," she had announced, pausing. "Today these fingers touched a whale."

"Bring them up here and touch a few pots," Anne had said.

The precious, awestruck attitude of some of the assistants at the camp had about worn her out, even while she recognized a younger version of herself behind Noma's unruly enthusiasm. She remembered once asking Elliot what it was like to swim with seals, and he had told her that it wasn't a spiritual experience, as her question obviously implied, because the "bastards" could bite you at any minute.

In the two summers of heading up the killer whale project, and the rest of the time at the station in Vancouver working with the hard data people, Anne admitted she had toughened up. The abortion had left a callous, but not so bad that she regretted it. She wondered if Elliot ever thought of her.

She stared blankly across the water to Cracroft Point, her gaze drifting south to the Sophia Islands, no more than ghostly stepping stones leading nowhere.

She and Elliot had been completely obliterated by her departure, no geography to trip up resolutions, no chance encounters. And now seemingly no trace of those five wonderful terrible years. It was the right thing to do, taking the job at Waddington Marine Station, getting far away and leaching out the impurities in her life. Yet memory had been kind to their relationship; she found she had to remind herself of the mess they had gotten themselves into, the desperate complications, the nights alone; she had to resist the nostalgia of old sweet times piercing the present, like shafts of yellow light on a gray day . . . Elliot presenting the puppy Holmes to her, Elliot going goofy on her when it was clear he couldn't whip her at tennis, Elliot calling out to her to keep pulling on the oars when she rowed her first big rapid, calling out that she could make it. *Ah Elliot*, she thought. I wish you could at least see that I became the person you envisioned. I wish you could know that the hypothesis was sound, only the methods flawed.

Low clouds wedged inside the point and the pretty little Sophia's were blotted out. Easing off port, she let the skiff move away and drove right down the middle of the Strait.

All that's behind me now, she told herself. Now she had a

working career, she had friends and . . . possibilities. Like Grant. Grant was different – not an Elliot, not a man always pushing the envelope – but that was good. Sure, he dodged the big, reckless questions, taking one step then another, but he could tell at any moment exactly where he stood. Still, she wasn't sure what to make of him.

It had been raining only since last night, a light rain, but as she reached behind to tuck the tarp back over the boxes of supplies, she saw the clean line of demarcation between the current in the Strait and the mineral waters washing down from the Franklin Range into the cove. And they think clear-cutting the Tsitika watershed won't hurt the rubbing beaches, she thought, won't drive the whales away. Christ. A small deadhead poked through a swell just off the bow and dunked back under. She veered to port, softened the angle, and maintained a long easy tack across the Strait, away from a seiner – probably the last of the season – working the kelp beds along the starboard shore. The wind came broadside now, skimming salt water off the surface, seasoning her lips.

Holmes snapped playfully at the yellow flag hanging off the stern, and it dipped, snapping back. She should have taken it off, she thought, since she was just dropping off supplies and picking up the latest data and a few instruments. Saying good-bye. There wouldn't be time to follow any whales today, no need to identify herself. They were mostly gone anyway. Still . . . she flipped the radio to the whale band. In the summer when there was high observer effort, voices crackled dawn till dusk, reporting the locations of various pods, direction, number of animals. But today . . . she left it open for a full minute, listening to the empty static – so desolate sounding – and was about to shut it off when someone said, "Hello!" She throttled down.

"Hello with the yellow flag. Seen any blackfish?"

Which told her instantly three things: that it was the fisherman from the seiner, monitoring the whale band, since the whales followed the salmon and salmon paid his way, that he was old – only the old timers (like the local Indians) called them blackfish – and that he wasn't having much luck along the kelp beds.

She told him no.

"You got a flag," he said.

"A supply run to Mookwa Cove."

There was a silence. The skiff knocked about between the swells, the engine gurgling low and steady. Elbow clasped over the windshield, she stood, squinting through the drizzle at the distant spot of color behind the window of the seiner, the pink face of another like her, making contact this wet gray autumn morning in the Strait.

"Say," he said. "*Aboot* how much salmon do blackfish eat?"

She smiled, grimly, mildly self-satisfied. He's alone, she thought. His buddies can't hear him. It's safe to question.

"All whales, or just one?" she said.

"The lot of 'em."

She tried to sound nonchalant, informative – nothing more. Not accusative. Not defensive. She tried to read the name on the seiner's bow. "Less than 20% of the available Chinook, pinks, sockeye, chum. Even less of other species."

Another silence. She waited, thinking, *please believe me*. It was only a month ago a fourteen year old male washed up on Hanson Island with a large caliber rifle slug lodged in his brain.

"That's a small boat," he said. "Storm coming in this afternoon. Spose you know that, too, eh?"

"I suppose I'd ought to," she said.

She heard him laugh, and in the background the big diesels revving up as he said, "I'll try north in the sound for the other 80%."

"Good luck," she said.

"Right-o."

The rest of the way to Mookwa Cove she ran hard. The swells in the Strait were fat and lazy sprawlers, without obvious direction, and she made good time, the skiff cutting a true course.

As she approached the beach, Grant left the spotting scope and dropped down off the cliff to meet her. She figured he'd been watching her for the last mile, and it occurred to her that she could not imagine what was in his mind when he did so. Any latent desire for her? She let out an ironic snort. Probably do him good, she thought. Definitely do me good at this point, to be desired. It's been so long. But who could say, Grant might just be observing. Gathering more data. *General Life History Parameters of the Anne McBain.*

"I had the band open," he said.

She tossed him the bow line. "The guy in the seiner was all right. At least he was questioning some of his assumptions."

Grant looked at her and nodded pensively. From the skiff she could see the bluish, transparent skin pull across his brow and along his temples, the plates of his skull seeming to shift ever so slightly as they accommodated new thought. His ash-blond hair fell straight back from his face, as if he had just stepped out of the water; he looked clean and disciplined and a little fierce except for the frail veneer of his skin, and the blue veins – his inner workings – so dangerously close to the surface.

Sloughing her life jacket, she buckled it to the bar across the stern, then straightened and paused a moment to gaze back up the Strait, to try to paint in her memory the scene she was about to leave. The high mountains above the opposite shore sailed in and out of the clouds, and the water had a smooth, swollen, expectant quality, as if it was about to tear open and give violent birth. She realized she was ready to go, ready for a visit to California and all the wineing and dining that would accompany the annual meeting of the American Cetacean Society. Then there would be a winter of work in the laboratory at Waddington, and in the spring field studies north of Tofino would start up, an energetics project involving the local fisheries. The dogwood would be blooming. Grant would come over from Nanaimo to join her. That was the plan. She thought maybe she would ask him for Christmas, get him off the island and out of the inlets for awhile. It was a cloistered sort of world. Maybe they'd go up to Manning Park, do some skiing, or make a real expedition of it and head into the Rockies to elegant Lake Louise. She could wear a dress.

Wading into the water, Grant pulled the supply boxes from the stern and carried them to the beach, then returned to the skiff for Holmes.

"You know, Grant," she told him, her mind still on the seiner and its captain, "maybe all it takes is for everyone and everything to back off every now and then, and I don't mean just people, researchers and fishermen. I mean the salmon gone, and the whales gone with them. I mean back off so that we can hear each other, and this other thing out there bigger than us, coming in; the storm and this place asserting itself."

"You're speculating," he told her. He was on his knees, examining the contents of one of the boxes.

Now it was Anne's turn to stare. "It's my last day up here, Grant. It's a proper occasion to speculate."

"Sure." He peeled a banana and bit off the exposed end. In his mid-thirties, Grant was both strong and wiry, absolutely fit, and attractive in the way ascetics attract, the very intensity of their convictions magnetizing. The trouble was, if you swung around to the wrong side, you sometimes found yourself repelled in equal measure. Repelled and exhausted.

"Hey Grant, let me give you some advice. After the log hours and data sheets and acoustic recordings, after the brown rice and bagels, *there is more*. You add it up and analyze and see that maybe it points somewhere, and if you get enough stuff pointing in similar directions, you begin to get a view of life. That's what it's about. *A view of life.* A paradigm for understanding animals and humans. Not just killer whales, not one animal, *all* animals."

"Reliable data," he said.

She supposed he was trying to annoy her. Laughing, she said, "Yup, that's where it starts. Maybe the trouble with you is that that's where it ends, too."

"*You* make something of it," he said, lifting his chin. "That's why you're in charge." His calmly intense exterior seemed to falter for an instant. She saw again the bluish skin, the hint of sickliness and, drawing close, gave him an impulsive kiss, pulling away before he could respond.

"I'm sorry," she said. "It's just that you're so good at all of this." She made a sweeping gesture to include the camp and the Strait. "And meticulous. And you've been here forever. *You* should make something of it."

"Like what? A field guide to killer whales?"

"Why not?"

His back was to her. He was tramping up the beach to a small grill parked under the edge of the kitchen tarp, a slab of salmon hissing away. Yanking a handful of salal leaves from a bush, he poked them carefully into the fire; it was an old custom around these parts. And it never failed to remind her of Elliot, poking sage from a sage bush into the fire under a broiling trout, in the purple haze of an Owens Valley dusk.

"It wouldn't be accurate. Aquatic mammals aren't on stage." He turned and fixed his eyes on her. "And I *like* it on the ground floor. What I record can be depended upon. I'm not interested in hypotheticals."

"You're limiting yourself, don't you see that?"

"I *like* my limitations."

She looked at him in his olive green army surplus wool pants, the big pockets sagging from the memory of too many notebooks and tools and oversized cameras, the Norwegian fisherman sweater with its smell of lanolin, the rubber boots – his habitual cold weather outfit; she noted his hair combed in the same way he combed it every day; she found his expression the same modulated intensity she had seen when they first met; and she understood that he had made a premature peace with himself. Also that she was beginning to sound like a reformed smoker. She watched him squat next to the grill and eat a hunk of salmon with his fingers. "Okay, I'll drop the subject," she said. But when he finished eating and rose, and went down to the water's edge with the greasy grill, washed it, and plodded back, wiping his hands against those surplus wool pants she had seen so many times before, she couldn't resist. "Even killer whales evince an enjoyment function," she said dryly.

"Inference," he replied.

"Okay, okay."

Unpacking the food supplies, she used the boxes to load up the material that was to return with her to Waddington, checking each item off a list. The morning was getting colder, the rain more audible. Holmes tucked himself between two of the big metal kitchen boxes and stared accusingly out across Mookwa Cove, as if waiting for someone to blame. Eventually, Grant went up to check the spotting scope and, when he returned, they hunkered down together to go over some of the log books. It was 8:00 a.m.. At 8:30, Ian and Noma emerged from the same tent.

"What's this?" Anne said in a low voice.

"A reproductive female and a sub-adult male."

"Naturally you don't infer anything, like hanky-panky, right? That would be hypothetical."

"Yes," he said, raising his eyebrows. "Off-stage and therefore speculative."

She gave him a small push, and he put on a self-composed smile. She was glad he had forgiven her. She had a great deal of respect for Grant, for his work, and for the most part found him pleasantly comfortable to be around, even though he often vanished completely from her thoughts. Perhaps he was attractive *because* he often vanished completely from her thoughts.

"What a yucky day," Noma said. She was braiding her long, black, frizzy hair as she headed for the kitchen area, not seeming the least chagrined about her new sleeping arrangements – unlike Ian, the La Jolla boy with the soft face and close cut, pastel stripes down his shirts, and the polite, unsure manners of a civilized youth seeing the world for the first time. Ian zipped up the tent, re-positioned the rocks anchoring it to the impenetrable ground and, in a fussy, embarrassed manner, indicated in non-words that he would run up and check the spotting scope.

"Brownies," Noma announced, pawing through the supplies. "And tempeh. Where did you find tempeh?"

"It wasn't easy," Anne said.

"Tempeh," she repeated, dropping down next to Anne and clasping her hands in mock prayer. "Totally hectic."

Noma was hardcore vegetarian; she was also endlessly, infuriatingly cheerful. And her preference for calling the whales 'orcas' because of the negative vibes associated with 'killer' whales – particularly on the data cards – had become a problem. "They're the top predator in their world," Anne had told her. "Face it, they *are* killers."

Ian came skidding down the cliff toward them. "Two blows," he called. "Right off the south shore. *Right here*."

"What?" Anne stood up.

Grant shoved past her and cranked up the volume on the hydrophone. The four of them gathered under the speaker box lodged in the crook of a low branch. The underwater mikes had a four mile capacity, and the south shore was no more than two miles off. Saying nothing, scanning the water, they listened. Nothing. Five minutes passed. Noma picked up the binoculars and almost immediately said, "Blow."

Finally, faintly, they heard several low burps and an attenuated whine.

"Transients," Anne said. "Not much vocalization."

Grant nodded. "Has to be. The Residents are gone with the schooling fish."

Anne glanced at her watch, even though there was no question in her mind what she would do: Transients were a rare opportunity. She would simply have to leave later and drive straight through to Nanaimo to catch the ferry.

Everyone began loading the skiff. Ian caught Anne's arm. "One boat, or two?" he said, making no attempt to hide his petition to go. Generally they tried to diminish their impact on the pod by limiting the number of researchers and boats, but the camp would be shut down at the end of the week, Ian was a bright young man, competent with the Zodiac, and the Strait was still relatively calm. Hell, she thought, holding up two fingers, it's a Transient pod.

"Oh wow," Noma said.

In ten minutes they were off the beach, cameras, notebooks, nets, the precious theodolite piled haphazardly in a plastic milk crate jammed between the seats. She told Ian and Noma to trail; she didn't want to create a herding presence with the two boats. It wasn't clear which direction the whales were moving, but they traveled at a speed of three to four knots, and they were so close that Anne was sure they would catch up with them.

The seats were wet, and she stood next to Grant as the boat sheared across the Strait, her knees absorbing the smack of the keel, a breezy rain prickling her face, like tiny injections of life. "A lucky last day," she hollered.

"So far," Grant said.

About 300 yards from the south shore she cut the engine to an idle. No whales. Ian hung back about 15 yards and made a palms-up gesture – where? She shook her head, put her finger to her mouth. Transients were known to dive longer than Residents, sometimes for 15 minutes. They would wait quietly, watch for dorsal fins, more blows. She dropped the hydrophone in the water; maybe they would hear something.

Suddenly, *behind* the Zodiac they saw a blow, and simultaneously a second whale spyhopped not 5 yards off the bow of the skiff, regarding the newcomers with what seemed to her a cool, almost nonchalant intelligence. They had stopped right in the *middle* of the pod. And something was up, she could sense it, something was definitely *up*.

The whale dropped under, apparently having determined they were inconsequential.

Grant was already on his knees in the stern, shoulder brace and camera strapped on, waiting. A whale breached – an adult female with a clean dorsal fin, which made her difficult to identify – and then another surfaced and dove, the sleek black and white coloring dazzling against the matt gray water. And this time there was no question who it was: M1 with the distinctive quarter moon gouge at the tip of his dorsal fin – the result of an old bullet wound. Which meant, since killer whales are matriarchal, the males remaining with their mothers or closest living female relative until death, unless they were breeding, that the female was probably M2, the bull's mother.

Two more females surfaced.

Anne could see Noma writing in a notebook, Ian reporting the behavior in 10 second intervals. Good, good, she thought. This is all perfect. This is good stuff. The M1 pod hasn't been seen for years.

The whales were milling between the boats in confusing patterns. In no pattern, she thought, which was odd because typically the oldest female initiated behavior and the rest followed, the pod moving in relative unison.

"What *is* this?" she said to Grant.

He kept his face behind the camera and answered in a low, controlled voice. "I don't know."

She glanced over at Ian. He flicked his thumb backwards, cocked his head: should they move off? For half a minute she made no sign. By rights, they should be at least 30 yards away from the whales, traveling parallel and slightly to the rear of the pod. The trouble was, the pod wasn't going anywhere, and she kept expecting it to. She shook her head, and made a T with her hands to indicate they would wait a little longer.

Another five minutes of erratic swimming; then, as if some silent strategic signal had been issued, the four whales submerged simultaneously, and there was a horrible, fleshy thud as one of them surged up and out of the water. There, within the crater of splash, were the rear flippers of a Steller sea lion, a young male. Again and again the whales rammed him, sometimes lifting his body wholly from the water; sometimes diving over and slamming him with their flukes, their dorsal fins vibrating from the blows, their conical teeth seemingly bared and bristling in a grotesque smile. At one point the bull clamped down on the sea lion's flippers, slung him 180 degrees, and bashed him against a rocky outcropping, the gross slap, the grunt maddening. *Maddening.* There was a savage, military quality to the attack, the sea lion having no single opportunity to escape from the moment he had been rediscovered. *This* was what the boats had interrupted. Temporarily having lost their prey, the whales were not going to abandon it just because an audience of hominoids had shown up.

The attack lasted forty minutes. Now and then Anne had to remind herself to breathe. Awareness seemed concentrated and intensified to sound: the tiny mechanical whine and precipitate click of the camera, *whiiiiin-click*; and the relentless eruptions of water around the sea lion; and the strangely interior silence of the whales during the attack that was somehow *not* a silence but a vibration Anne could feel in her blood and which the hydrophone dutifully broadcast and recorded; and at the end when the sea lion made a last fatal swim for the shore and the bull rammed him just under the throat, and the sea lion went unconscious, the whales shoving him down under, drowning him, and the first one brought up a great gory hunk of flesh, she heard Noma scream from the Zodiac. Sound. And sight – except for the vestige of loyalty to her work which kept her noting in routine fashion on the back board of her brain the sequence and details of the event – sight went sharply white-black and double-visioned, the four killer whales like some nightmarish Rorschach come alive.

The sea lion was swiftly dispatched, each piece of him brought individually to the surface where it was hardly chewed before being flung back and gulped down the maw. A rusty stain dispersed across the water. And above, like litter caught in an errant wind, gulls flapped and swooped, one darting down and crumpling over a pale rag of meat, then laboring up and away before another could steal his prize.

Soon enough, the whales moved northward, accelerating, slapping their flukes playfully.

Grant pushed himself up, and she thought: *he's been on his knees the whole time.*

For a moment they stood looking at each other, avoiding language. It seemed to have nothing to do with what had happened, and she knew that they were occupying together a kind of Jungian rift in which they were the sea lion and the sea lion's death, the whales and the full bellies of the whales, the watchers in the boats, the water underneath, the dark cherty beach, the storm coming in, the drop of rain hanging from the end of a nose. Finally when someone reached out – who could say which of the two? – and a hand clasped another, the rift closed up, the words toddled awkwardly back in. And they were separate again. Back in Time.

Grant slid his eyes away. "No less than 1200 pounds," he said.

She stared at him, disappointed.

"Just a guess, naturally, based on length relative to M1." He bent, fished up the theodolite, and began tinkering with the instrument. "They're probably headed for Blackfish Sound. And if I can just get this damn survey transit to work . . . " He sprayed some WD40 on the side lever. "We can estimate speed, and that'll tell us if they're still foraging or settling into a synchronous swim/rest pattern." His eyes flicked up, then back to the transit. "I want to get some dialect recordings before they rest. For the acoustic similarity study."

She turned away. It was pounding down rain.

"What's the matter?" Grant said. "Aren't we going after them?"

"No."

He came forward abruptly and peered at the gas gauge. "We have enough gas."

"We have enough of everything."

"So we're not going?"

"No." A sudden sense of bleakness, like a flat wind come up off a flat land, blew over her. She couldn't put her finger on it. It was as if she had discovered something terrific and had no one to show it to. She thought about the whales, how splendidly beautiful the attack was, splendidly terrible, and the small peephole it seemed to have opened. A view of life. And for the third time that day she found herself thinking about Elliot.

It was almost 11:00. The sea was cobbled now, the swells no longer flattened and sprawling like lazy animals, but showing muscle, rippling heavily down the Strait – a flowing tide. They would have to buck it all the way to Telegraph Cove.

"A view of life," she said aloud as she throttled up.

"Of a sort," Grant said. It almost sounded like a curse.

She glanced over, then looked ahead to the Zodiac and took up position in its wake. Ian and Noma had their arms around each other as they huddled down for the wet ride back – a nice picture. Killer whales took care of each other, too, were known to support sick members of the pod to shallow water where it was easier to breathe and recover. They stayed together, never abandoning each other. We sociobiologists call it *reciprocal altruism*, Anne thought. Christians call it *The Golden Rule*. Psychologists have all manner of clumsy and undecipherable coinage, most generally implying that to help oneself is to help others. Scratch an altruist and watch a hypocrite bleed, someone once said, but Anne did not agree that animals helped solely to receive help themselves at some later date. Not all animals, at least. The play between morality and biology was synaptical, she thought, too intricate and too blurred to be seen by the human mind's eye, and far too ticklish an issue for a sociobiologist, or a behavioral ecologist, or a marine mammalogist, or for anyone paying homage to the

Lord Gene.

Grant touched her shoulder and pointed. The whales, still engaged in almost childlike percussions, gamboled up the Strait toward the Sound where the seiner had gone. And seeing them, the fisherman would take their presence as a good sign, an omen; he would not know they were Transients, a different race than the Residents, or that their diet consisted primarily of marine mammals, not salmon. Different habits, she thought. Adaptive dispositions.

The Lord Gene. *Thou shalt act only so as to increase thy fitness.* Who wrote that? The wheel slipped, and she tugged her cuffs over the backs of her hands, numbed in the cold wet wind.

Douglas Boucher, a Canadian, wrote that. *Thou shalt covet thy neighbor's wife, and house, and field, and ox, and ass, and everything else that is his; for with these thou canst reproduce more, and he less, and thy fitness shall increase over his.*

Climbing an oversized swell, the boat sheared off its crest and went airborne a moment, then landed hard and flat in the nautical equivalent of a belly flop, and Anne felt the blow shudder up from her heels to the base of her spine and settle there, like a thrown rock.

"A rogue," Grant said.

She cinched the straps on her life jacket. "I hope so," she said vaguely, still thinking of Boucher. When it came to human beings biological explanations tended to slip and slide, and if they found footing at all it was of the crudest sort, the effort showing. If, for instance, philandering in humans could be biologically explained – males were increasing their reproductive success without any of the work, and a male who was a philanderer would pass on more genes and, theoretically, the philandering gene – then why the hard feelings? And what of forgiveness? What of theology? Maybe morality was a chemical, but she wasn't convinced. Maybe the behavior humans call 'moral' was at some distant point in the past *advantageous*, and that moral man survived over others, and his genes survived, and that moral behavior became a predisposition, evolved into a genetically mediated behavior, and achieved finally gene status.

Sitting down, Grant flipped on the radio, turning it until he found the weather band and, together, they listened for the marine forecast in the North Vancouver Island and Johnstone Strait areas.

Whatever the explanation, she thought, whatever the source and the essential nature of it, it is in humans to care, and often to love at their own expense and to their own detriment. It is in humans to see *out* while peering in. Has the gene gone too far? Is it now *dis*advantageous? Maladaptive?

A dull *clunk* under the bow; in the next instant the props broke the surface, a large branch bobbing into the wake. She went back, reset the Mercury, and staggered forward, blowing on her fingertips. "They're as dead cold as that branch," she said.

"Here." Unzipping his slicker, Grant pulled up his sweater, took both her hands and clamped them under his bare arms. He never flinched; he looked steadily, intensely at her face, not as if waiting but as if they had had some clear understanding all along and needn't speak. It was a cold sort of understanding, purely biological. *Reciprocal altruism*, she thought. Feeling trapped, she watched the water over his shoulder. If earlier she had felt the impulse to share, she knew now that that impulse had everything to do with the company; that it was a crummy feeling, but somehow Grant had an impeccable way of *diminishing* experience to examined parts. The boat tilted and dropped under their feet; her hands, as if caressing, shifted and she stiffened them against his skin. The Zodiac, which had initially paused, disappeared in the rain and mist, another point of gray in a graying world.

Finally she said, "They're beginning to sting," and heard the awkwardness in her voice.

"Sure?"

"Yeah. It's a good sting. Thanks."

Grant was standing next to her, legs slightly bent and braced for the rough water, hands gripping the top of the windshield. Right next to her, and yet when she gazed to starboard she could not feel his presence. Maybe she had forgotten how, or had shut down those mechanisms which allowed for subtler communication. Maybe that was the only way to have gotten through the last year and a half. Cautiously, she studied Grant; again she thought of Boucher's spoof on biology . . . *whosoever doth not always look upon woman with reproduction in his mind, shall fall behind in the race of fitness* . . . and she said, "Why do you think nothing ever really happened between us, Grant?" In asking, she knew that nothing ever could.

"I couldn't say."

"Did you ever want it to?"

"Yes." He looked at her, and she smiled gently. There were plenty of moments when she had been genuinely attracted to him, his intensity, and the clean simpleness that a life with him – or someone like him – proposed.

"You never tried," she said matter-of-factly.

"It wouldn't have lasted."

"Is that so bad? A summer romance?"

He nodded. "With you it would be." The engine was loud, the wind sheeting past them, and they had to shout at each other, though it seemed perfectly fitting that she and Grant, engaged in their first and only intimate exchange, would have to shout in order to be heard.

"Why bad with me?" she said.

He closed his eyes and shrugged. "You'd've been trying out a theory." The noise forced a cut-to-the-bone reply, and she felt it.

She put on a thoughtful face. "What do you want, romantically speaking?"

"Reliable data." It wasn't funny, it wasn't meant to be funny. He sounded bitter, and she felt misread. "Besides, I *did* try. You missed the signs. You weren't looking for them."

"Grant . . ."

"Missing signs is answer enough."

"I resent the assumption . . . "

"We're different," he said, staring at her as if checking and recounting those differences. "I thought that might be good, but it isn't, because I'm happy here, looking at what's at my feet. You're looking away. Even what you do here you take away, like all Americans, to 'make something of it' as you say. I'm staying here."

"I'm not going anywhere," she said, deliberately simplifying his meaning.

"You're going back to California," he said.

"A visit, that's all. To deliver a paper to the American Cetacean Society. You wouldn't begrudge me my glorious return."

They were entering the cove, darkened by the high-sided bowl of Douglas fir, and she throttled down across the shallows, weaving around the kelp bed. In the tarnished water she saw a reflection of their faces tangled in the kelp, and their expressions clear and unwavering – friendship. They didn't have to shout now.

"I like having film in the camera, Anne." His voice was soft, his attitude, faintly bemused resignation. "Something tangible to show for my time."

"Yes, I see that. I only hope it isn't simply more data, more IDs. I hope that you don't always need to know what it is you're looking at, have a name or a word for it."

"Not entirely."

The Zodiac was beached, and Ian had a fire going already, the sappy smoke of green wood drifting down across the water. Grant began looping the bow line from hand to elbow, making a neat coil of it.

"I want to stick up for the things in life that leave no trace," she said. "That can't be photographed. I want to stick up for the wild ideas and dreams and the old-fashioned good time with its bad news morning after. For the delicious failures."

Reaching over, she grabbed hold of the knotted mess at the end of the bow line, forcing Grant to stop his measured hand-to-elbow-to-hand operation. "Maybe you should get involved in something utterly meaningless, or make a mistake, or at the very least develop some endearing foible."

"Maybe." He smiled and frowned simultaneously. "Of course that wouldn't have been possible with you."

"Thank you. I think."

"I'm not sorry you missed those signs," he said.

"No," she said. "We'd've lost ground." Still, she felt a little of the old hurt.

Cutting the engine, she let the skiff coast in. Bow line in hand – neatly subdued now – Grant jumped into the water and started for shore, then he turned and said almost flippantly, "You know you're still in love with whoever it is in California."

She couldn't think of a single thing to say; not yes, not no, nothing came to mind. He tied the boat off, she handed him the crate of instruments, and they went about the usual camp business, his comment hanging like a rope in the air she had no intention and no ability to grab. She thought about Elliot, their time together, and how within the imperfection there had been something true, a glint in the shadows, and that only at the end when the imperfection blackened around them, did they, she, lose all sense of that perfection. Now she had, indeed, nothing to show for her time with Elliot save perhaps a new behavior, a predisposition. The makings of a gene.

TWENTY-ONE

Island Highway 19 between Port McNeil and Sayward is a 100 mile stretch of the wildest wilderness. Until recently, when the road was finally completed joining north to south, it was known as the Incredible Gap. The old logging railway climbs directly out of Telegraph and Beaver Coves, and the highway follows the rail lines inland and up along the Hankin Range then, swinging southward, it traces the Nimpkish River, cuts left, crosses the Tsitika River and its dozens of tributary creeks which are rivers by any other standards, and finally angles back down toward the east coast of Vancouver Island, toward Sayward and into the Salmon River valley. In every respect it is an imposing length of blacktop. And driving it alone during a storm, it is worse than imposing: it is a kind of biblical trial of Nostradamusian proportions, or a Donner Party – of one – or the whole of the soul's long day's journey into night compressed into two hours of 120 minutes, each an eon long and lengthening. Or so Anne began to think as she stared at the windshield, waiting for the metronomic instant when she could see *through* it, when the wipers pushed the water aside and there was a brief wake of visibility behind them. Her eyes burned with the effort to focus. Not on the road – a gray line parting mile-high mountains. She focused on the water sheeting down either side of the crown, on the water rushing along the gullies and, where the gullies had backed up, on the water that flooded out across the road. How deep was it? Did she have time to brake before sliding through it? And if it was flowing, which way was it flowing? Should she angle the wheels? Should she stop?

She pulled off the road, shoved the gears into four-wheel drive, got out and locked the hubs, then climbed back in and onto the ribbon of water that was the highway.

A logging truck passed, and the land cruiser was momentarily blinded – it was almost a relief, seeing nothing. Then the mountains reappeared, or at least her peripheral sense of them looming about, like sulky gods, resumed. Now and then when she glimpsed a safe length of road, she stole a view of the surrounding wilderness. On the right side of the road were massive clear cuts coursing with muddy rain, like blood from a raw wound, the occasional spiked remains of a tree that had splintered rising up above the slash, pale and bony. And on the left side, forests, the ones that local environmentalists were trying to save in order to save the rubbing beaches, in order to keep the whales in Johnstone Strait, and so on in order. Almost purely Douglas fir, these woods, some of the tallest trees on the globe. The Doug fir was neither an unusual nor a beautiful tree with its thick gray bark and needles always green, a somber cast. But it was big and straight – very important – its taper almost imperceptible. And it's here, she thought, here *en masse*, here a-plenty. A two-by-four rookery.

The tires slipped, then abruptly grabbed the pavement, jerking her body forward and back. She decided that despite the prospect of oncoming traffic – which was beginning to seem unimaginable – she would let the left wheels ride the crown of the road where it was least likely to be flooded.

The green digital numbers on the clock caught her eye. Five minutes later she deliberately looked at it. Her fingers were stiff and bloodless, her palms damp: she opened and closed them several times, not daring to lose contact with the steering wheel. Then she looked at the clock again. Three minutes. Three lousy minutes. Well, don't look, just don't look at it, she said aloud. Later, she reasoned hopefully, if she happened to see the clock, a lot of time will have passed and she would be pleasantly surprised. She would be almost there. But nine months of minutes later she looked at it and groaned. Finally she shoved her wallet in front of the small black window and, after glancing at the wallet several involuntary times, gave up on the first dimension altogether. Which left her with space – inside of the land cruiser, outside the land cruiser. And the *muchness* of the outside very soon reduced the inside to claustrophobic proportions.

Rain beat down. Not the airy, spitting rain of the southland. A noise. A weight. A glowering twilight. A massive display of water that in its unrelenting excess took on a phantasmal quality, like a drugged state, and she had been called back from within it's very heart to perform some small critical real task. Write her name. Or drive from Telegraph Cove to Sayward, British Columbia. Alone. While all around the raining drug came down, trying to overpower.

If there was a radio station, some numbing oldies music, it might relax her. But creased inside these forbidding mountains no human sounds reached her.

She couldn't say how long it had been since the last, but another logging truck grew in the rearview mirror, and she experienced a foolish spasm of hope. Slowing to let it pass, she gripped the wheel and held her breath. Mud and road water blasted the side of the door as the great trunks swam by amidst a fanfare of torn bark and flying fir. Holmes lifted his head to watch the thing barrel away, engulfed in spray. A ghost truck. She could see a distance now, the truck pulling along the knife edge of a long grade, walls of granite behind it and, above the walls, the endless gray quilting of rain clouds drawing swiftly in over the mountains from the west. In the valley beneath the grade, low clouds twisted over another clear-cut, like smoke from a war zone.

Just a glimpse of the driver would have made it seem less . . . *frightening*. It was fear binding up her chest and hollowing her gut, she realized. And the spasm of hope – that she was not alone here – was rubbed out as the driverless truck disappeared around a far bend.

A taste of bile steeped upward into her mouth. Probably she should have brought some food along. A full belly would ease the tension, distract her body, though she was admittedly too clenched for eating. There was an ache in her lower back; her trapeziuses were petrifying; her right buttock had gone to sleep. But even if there was a place to stop and stretch, she knew she wouldn't. She knew she just wanted to get south of the Gap, south and off the island, and keep going south. Because if before the lure of California had lain in a mixture of intangibles – curiosity without object, wispy nostalgia, and some misapplied prodigal son-ism having to do with her profession – now there was something *driving* her south, *not* intangible, something appallingly blunt. Rain. And she didn't want to die in it, not here, a place where the land did not know her.

Now the road followed the Nimpkish River, which meant she was headed south and up over the steepest part of the Gap. Halfway there and still no cars coming north. Was the road open? With a defiant flip of her wallet, she checked the clock. An hour and a half had passed, longer than it should have taken to reach this high born stretch of the Nimpkish. There was a ferry at five, two more after that if she missed it. It didn't matter what time she got into Vancouver, there was no one waiting up. But she was determined to make that five o'clock, though at the moment it almost seemed impossible – not getting there and seeing the mainland again, but getting *out* of this place, out of this nihilistic presence, this unreality that insisted upon itself to the utter erasure of everything else. The rest of the world had gone extinct. This *was* the world. She *was* its population. What then did anything mean?

It means something, she said aloud, because it *is*. And *I* mean something because I am. *Je pense*, she chirped in the silence. Yet she couldn't help wondering how long it would take for the whole of civilization contained in a single isolated being to break down.

Opening the window, she let the rain splatter against her face. *Je suis*, she whispered, and resumed her vigil.

Switching and climbing, the road crisscrossed the Nimpkish, which was running mad over its banks, flooding low lands, boiling between stumps. In every direction, down every slope, waterfalls volunteered.

They never stop the ferries. They're equipped with stabilizers for the big Pacific swells. They always run, she told herself.

Many times she thought of Elliot. So many that she gave up her habitual resistance, the way someone on a diet will eat during a crisis. Because he was good in these kinds of situations. He drove the way he hiked – slow and steady. While she sprinted ahead and stood huffing beside the trail, he measured his steps toward her and, in passing, smiled a Cheshire smile. If called to react, he was quick and firm, having prepared himself. She was nervous and reflexive, having imagined the worst.

There was something to be said for leaping, too, though.

Rain-pocked mounds of snow. Debris on the road where flooding waters had surged across and drained. Creeks that were rivers, and rivers like the Nimpkish and Tsitika and the Davie swollen to runaway lakes. She crept across a number of creeks that had taken the road. She watched the speedometer, and the effort not to vary, to be a steady ordered presence in the midst of fray was exhausting. She was beginning to feel that while the few acts she had been reduced to were of immense and increasing importance to her and to her life, they were in like measure increasingly meaningless in this place. She was a blip of warmth on a blank screen. And who cared? What gopher, what god watched?

The windshield wipers ticked back and forth, the defrost vents blew cold air, the rain drummed on – an eerie monotony of sounds closing in. And oblivious, Holmes let out tiny dream-born yips from the back seat of the land cruiser.

Swinging around a bend, she climbed a mile or so, crested, and started down another precipitous grade between granite walls, easing intermittently on the brakes. The walls on the right soon vanished down into a vast muddy valley trenched with water rushing in and out of the Nimpkish, which was again directly below the road. The current tugged at small bowed trees. Slash washing in from the clear-cut on the far slope swirled and snagged, accumulating in mini-dams. A sure place to drown.

She heard it before she saw it, the way you could hear rapids in a river canyon minutes before reaching them. The sound and the long wait had become a part of the ritual of preparation. And hearing that same sound now she had an urge to cinch her life jacket, check the tie-downs, stash whatever consumables were scattered about the raft. She felt the old urge to look across the water for Elliot and the eddy-out signal that meant they would scout.

Then she saw it. A great waterfall. Ahead, on the left. All white and wide and as far as she could tell through the veil of rain, the water was making a sheer fall off an overhang and piling up in the gully that had been dug out and was a ten foot wide gorge flowing both directions.

No problem, she told herself. A big, bad sound, that's all. It had even waked Holmes who raised his muzzle and sniffed. But approaching, she saw the worst of it. She saw that the gorge had swamped at the base of the fall, and that a river the size of a southwestern river, the size of a Dolores or a San Juan, and the same chocolate color, too, was rushing across the road and dropping another 500 feet into the Nimpkish.

At the edge of the river she stopped, shut off the engine, and got out. Stopping was so much of a relief, and this new obstacle such a wonderment in an old-fashioned sense, like one of the many obstacles westward settlers had to face, that initially she found herself dispossessed of any feeling as she studied it. There was no angle to the flow, despite a gradual decline in the road. Then it's deeper at the far edge, she thought. As if in confirmation, a good-sized log shot up out of the gorge and, alternately dragging and floating, moved ominously across the road and over the brink. The falls boomed in her ears. She stood for a long while, not thinking. No one came, no logging trucks, no other cars. No one was going to come, she realized. And she felt a sudden bolt of fury at this ultimate reality. That it should come to a bastard river borning itself in the middle of her way, in the middle of her life. Her new life. Tomorrow when the storm was over this River Styx would be gone. *And me?* Her eyes followed a clump of uprooted fireweed as it curved over the edge and vanished.

Branches, leaves, small bushes, like fragments from an exploded dream, traveled across her vision. When a long willow switch tilted up out of the gorge she counted in seconds the time it took to snake its way across to the brink on the right. Then walking the distance herself, she missed the time by a third. So, it was slower than the Dolores, faster than the San Juan. Good news, bad news.

She listened to the falls, its familiar sound and the memories it quickened – of Elliot, of the best-loved times. When *they* were a chaos, a fray, an unreality in an ordered world. She listened to the falling water, and she knew then that she wanted to see him again. Just to look at him, happy. In much the same way a note repeated frequently enough begins to sound as one note held long and insistently, the year and a half of wondering how he was had simply become the need to know.

Down her neck an icy trickle of rain started, picking up tributaries from her collar and hair and continuing into the warm valleys of her back. Shivering, she hitched her jacket and grasped the hood under her chin. It was true that sudden and complete submersion in frigid water confused the body. It didn't notice the cold. In ten minutes hypothermia set in. That was always the danger of running snow-melt rivers: if you ended up in the water you didn't notice that you were dying. She turned and walked back to the land cruiser, reaching through the open window to give Holmes a pet.

"The possibilities here," she told him, "are not many. We make it across; that's one. We are swept over the edge and killed in the fall; two. We survive the fall and end up in the Nimpkish, trapped in the land cruiser where we swiftly drown; three. We manage to get through a window, but have the water to contend with. Cold water. Fast water. A lot of downed trees, a lot of strainers. And not much left of the banks. There's hypothermia, too, let's not forget the fiend hypothermia – fifteen, twenty minutes before the muscles begin to fail."

Holmes licked her hand.

"As for options," she went on, "there are only two, m' boy. The grand old two of Time. Go on, or go back."

Walking across was not a consideration. Never underestimate current, any current – river credo number one.

She collected rocks. Varying her aim, she tossed each into the river. With one exception at the near edge, every rock disappeared, even a heavy chunk she had to lob two-handed out into the center of current. Gone.

But the land cruiser is high, she thought. And it's wearing snow tires.

Nothing in her wanted to turn back. Nothing, and yet she had to consider it now. Back into the teeth of the storm. A cinderblock motel in Port McNeil. A day or two, maybe. But getting there, *driving*, staring at the windshield, and the grisly tedium . . .

And what of the trucks? Had they gotten through? Or had they cut off somewhere, up into the veinwork of logging roads to wait it out at a staging area? Maybe she had imagined the severed trees passing by, the whining diesels; maybe she had merely heard the phantom pain of a whole country. Or her own phantom pain.

The roar of the falls enveloped her. And in the twilight that was not twilight, at the edge of a river that was not before and may not be again a river, Anne felt about for her future. Then she climbed back into the land cruiser and started for the water.

Windows open, just in case. Wheels at a ferry angle up current. She hung her head out to see more clearly and, as the water rushed under the floorboards, she heard herself erupt in crazy defiance. "You may be a river *in fact*, you bastard. But you're not the real thing. No sir-ee *bob*. I've seen a real river." Inspired, Holmes began barking wildly out the other window. Directly to their left the falls were deafening. She was still shouting, "You bastard, I didn't come all this way just to . . . you bastard, I'm going to California, that's what *I'm* doing."

The back end of the land cruiser swung out loose, and there were several moments in which she *lived* the helpless, slipping sensation of nightmares. Another minute and they would be floating. Water spilled in under the doors. She punched the accelerator and the brakes, but they were still slipping back toward the edge. She heard Elliot, his serious voice – *let the current work for you*. Maybe she could. Maybe there was enough room for a downstream ferry angle. Maybe not. "What the hell," she said, spinning the steering wheel. Abruptly, her right front tire got a bite of something – pavement, rock, whatever – and it was just enough bite, though she knew it couldn't hold. Not hesitating, she ran the front end up on a branch and used it to launch the vehicle closer to the opposite shore, jamming the accelerator and angling the wheels downstream. The current *was* pushing them.

"I'm finished up here," she cried. "I did it and I'm done, you bastard."

Every rock, every branch, every snag of brush she aimed for, anything that would offer traction and lessen the depth of the water. Despite the awful *clunks* and *cracks* under the chassis, she kept on the accelerator, leaning into the precarious momentum. The land cruiser bucked and lurched, now plunging in deep, now spluttering forward in a cloud of steamy spray. A cough. A squealing wheel. A bone-rattling jolt. They were almost across. Almost to the brink, too. Fast current, here. *Means deep*, said the alarm in her head. And she rammed a log, a big log. They were hung up.

For a full minute nothing happened. Then the back end of the land cruiser floated up and, like a great ballerina, began a slow, graceful pirouette. There was nothing to do but wait until they were facing exactly the wrong direction, then shove her in reverse. She tapped the accelerator. Some purchase; not much. A few more taps. Had they moved? *Put some English on it*, her mind said. Tap. *Tap*. And they were coming loose! Enough time to punch it, that was all. Holmes pitched onto the floor as the vehicle leapt back, wallowing almost immediately in the current.

Well, she thought.

But one rear tire had grazed the edge, was skidding sideways; then, seizing open pavement, both rear tires pulled the land cruiser free, and it bolted backwards down the road.

She was crying, laughing – there didn't seem to be much difference. Not much difference between anything. *No sir-ee bob.*

Thirty minutes later at a truck stop in Sayward she used the restroom, bought some juice and a stale cupcake and, just to be saying something to someone, asked the girl at the cash register if the road was open south to Nanaimo.

"South, sure," she said, looking puzzled. "But I heard it's closed north."

"It's closed," Anne said.

"You just came over?" the girl asked.

"I don't know how."

"I've never been up there," she said in a faraway voice.

And though to Anne it seemed odd, almost ridiculous that the girl hadn't been north on her own island, she understood how faraway the Gap could seem, even when it was so near.

Driving south on Coast Highway 1. After Vancouver Island, after the rain, even after the coasts of Washington and Oregon which were lesser imitations, California was like a cartoon paradise, and she a refugee from beyond. Just above Año Nuevo, where the land begins to curve out, Anne pulled off the road to let Holmes run in the wild oats. It had to be at least 80 degrees out. A red-tailed hawk sat sleeping atop a fence post, his beak tucked in under a wing and his coloring so close to the old wood that he might have been a carving. At land's end, in a breathtaking leap of vision was the sea, a soft, twinkling blue sea. She shook her head and laughed out loud. "Twinkling . . . *really* now."

Compared to the northwest, California had few islands, a dozen maybe, and she had to admit that it was a relief to see again the fluent space of open ocean and the old friend of the horizon unequivocal.

She reached into the land cruiser for her sunglasses, and walked out into the yellow field. The light was as brilliant as blown glass; she felt if she reached up and flicked it, a single, serene note would vibrate out. Holmes, reduced to a snaking rustle through the high grass, was apparently after something headed for the coyote bush.

And there was the island . . . almost two years since its devastation, but from where she stood she could see the valance of white sand, the beaches fully restored. She could hear the elephant seals – November, she thought, males. In December females would arrive. The breeding season would commence.

The lazy buzzing of insects made the air seem even warmer. She bent and broke off some yarrow, twirling it, like a parasol, between her fingers, then she looked across the fields and over the twinkling sea to the island again. It seemed different.

Driving straight through Santa Lucia around the bay to the

south peninsula, she located the Plaza Hotel where the American Cetacean Society had reserved a group of rooms. It sat at water's edge and was only a few blocks down from the Aquarium where some of the talks had been scheduled.

In the elevator the bellboy told her she could bring her dog in during his shift and he wouldn't "say peep." She smiled and thanked him. With freckles and a blond forelock which he hid behind when he spoke and, at the conclusion of speech, flipped back – a tick – he had nevertheless a nice manner, like a nephew playing the host. "There's the ice machine," he said. And nodding toward the end of the hall, "The stairs. No one uses them." *Flip* went the bangs. She understood that the stairwell was the route by which Holmes should be smuggled in.

At the door to the room, she tried to give him a lavish tip.

"Oh no," he said. "That's not why. I've got two. They're just mutts, but . . . " and he shrugged off the rest.

"It's not for my dog," she said.

As if he ought to do more, he pointed out the honor bar again, and the Jacuzzi controls and finally at a loss, retreated behind the forelock which had overcome his face.

Anne flopped back on the bed. The boy had drawn the heavy drapes but left the white linings across, and the breeze off the bay made spinnakers of them. They luffed and snapped, withered and luffed again. She turned her head toward them. The blue sea was just there, behind, peering around the edge of the white linings now and then, like an anxious lover. After awhile she got up and went out on the balcony.

The hotel was cantilevered over the water between a small inlet and the wharf on the right, and a restaurant to the left. Directly below, five stories down, the waves slid in between jagged rocks – small, untroubled waves that seemed to moderate her pulse. Watching them, she let time go. When the breeze dropped, the sunlight swarmed up, quiet and penetrating. It was a late sun, and it conjured from her skin the sweet, salty smells of a long day. A fishing boat trailed past the hotel and around the pier into the harbor. In the space between the souvenir shops and fish stands lining the wharf she glimpsed people strolling by – it was the kind of weather and the time of day for strolling. She put her hands on the rail and sighed deeply. She had come a great distance to be here. It was good to be here.

At the end of the wharf a man poured out a bucket of fish cleanings, and the flat sea underneath humped and rolled with seals. In moments, gulls listing on a thermal high up above the bay canted sharply sideways down to the feed, pulling up abruptly just over the water, their wings flat and seesawing, clashing like knives above the gore, their sound shrill, chaotic.

She left the balcony.

When she returned with Holmes to the room the red message light on the phone was blinking. From a distance, unpacking her books and toilet kit, she noticed it as it performed its job silently, persistently. Then she went into the bathroom and turned the tub faucets, holding her hand under the column of water – cold, warm, too hot – making several adjustments before straightening. The towels were expensively thick, and seemed to endorse her decision to use the Jacuzzi. She read the instructions on the wall, glanced sideways in the mirror, pinned up her hair, and read the instructions again. *No high sudsing agents, such as bubble bath. No glassware. Do not block suction inlet.* When the tub was full, she shut off the water and went out to undress.

The message light – still blinking – now seemed almost to be making a sound, a piercing signal she could feel inside her head. Probably John Devlin. Or one of the other conference coordinators. Probably Devlin, she thought.

She sat on the edge of the bed next to the nightstand, touched the phone and, instead of lifting the receiver, pulled a menu card out from under and read down several of its offerings – Poached Salmon with dill sauce, Seafood Fettucini, Calamari Parmesana – then she walked across to the bar cabinet and made a bourbon, neat. She wasn't ready to talk. She would lose it if she talked. The clear hard feeling. Losing it was the last thing left to be afraid of.

In the steamy twilight of the bathroom she slid into the Jacuzzi and finished emptying her mind. The emptying was a kind of death, like the space at the end of a breath, only the space opened up and everything in it was keened and quick and sheering through her so that she knew and then didn't know the secrets in the least of details. The pink islands of knees. White tile. Shining knobs. The miraculous green of a tub full of water. Against the soles of her feet the jets worked, while her chest rose above the water, subsided, rose and cooled, then sank into warmth. She watched steam lift from an index finger; at the time, it seemed to be the only thing she ought to be doing.

Behind the white noise of the Jacuzzi was the whiter noise of the sea. She felt white inside, too, like a clean linen canvas. It was a dangerous feeling, but she knew that whatever happened – the first brush strokes, the last – it would be okay. She held the bottom of the bourbon glass in the bubbling water, warming it as if it was a fine cognac, then passed it under her nose and sipped. It was sharp and exciting in her mouth, and hurt a little going down in the way that she liked. This was what she was left with – small, savory hurts of her own making. The ones that didn't belong to her were gone now.

She stayed in longer than she would have in the past, because it was nice: nice things weren't so difficult anymore. The sun was almost down, a red ball melting into the edge, and fishing boats scudding in made black toy shapes against the burning sky. As she dialed Devlin's number the lights at the tips of the boat rods blinked on, so absurdly wonderfully small and ready now for the coming night.

"McBain?" a woman said. Then, "John, it's Dr. McBain."

It was the first time anyone had called her that.

Devlin picked up the phone. "You've made it in time for the reception," he said.

"Reception?"

"Cocktails and hors d'oeuvres at the Aquarium. Six thirty."

"Okay."

"There's a fellow from Newfoundland who wants to meet you, been collecting ID's for ten years. A couple of students from the Gulf, too. It should be a fair crowd."

"Lord, will I have to be official tonight?"

"No, no, this is fun. A drink with old friends." John had been her dissertation sponsor, was a good drunk and, whether they wanted or not, everyone's favorite uncle.

"Which old friends?" she said.

"Willets, the lab crew, all the whale people from the University of course, even some refugees from your first command."

"Not crazy Crawford."

"He's in."

She smiled at the phone. "Okay, I'll be ready."

"Newhouse, too," John said, as if he'd just remembered.

Music and voices strayed downwind from the wharf. There was one of those end-of-a-breath spaces again, only this time it didn't open up, it closed in, and she felt herself take two, three breaths in quick succession, without release. "Why is he here?" she said finally.

"I suppose he's drumming up support for the new whale center at Davenport."

"I hadn't heard."

"It's a big project," he said. "Blues, grays, humpbacks, killers. Supposed to be the nerve center of Pacific cetacean research. He's got plans to rebuild the old whaler's landing, run a pier straight off the rocks. It's damn deep there. They can draft a ship the size of the Ellen B. Ironic, isn't it? I wager that's half the attraction, too, building a research center atop a graveyard of whales."

She stared through the balcony doors out at the bay. It was a black void now: the last fishing boat had come in, and the moon wasn't up yet. "He never had much to do with aquatic mammal research," she said vaguely, more to herself than to Devlin.

"Excuse me?" Devlin said.

"The seals were right there on his beach, he could see what they did and he knew what they *would* do. He liked things that way."

"Oh, he hasn't quit seals," John said. "Newhouse calls himself a behavioral ecologist, you know. Gives him the right to shift about, he says. Shuffle the cards."

"Yes," she said, and something in her voice, maybe only the sound of the weight of memory drew John in close.

"Was it that rough?" he said.

"At times." Then she realized he was asking about her day, or the drive down from Vancouver: Devlin knew nothing of Elliot and Anne. "I had some trouble getting off the island," she murmured. "And my back is still paying for the cheesy motel in Oregon."

"Well, pour yourself a drink."

She smiled. "I already have."

"Pour yourself another, and get over to the Aquarium."

"All right," she said. "By the way, John, did you leave a message for me at the front desk?"

"Not I. One of your other fans."

The air had cooled some, and she called Holmes in from the balcony, then closed the french doors. He went over and nosed at the bag which contained among other things his food. She poured some of the kibble into the ice bucket, along with sandwich scraps she had saved and, when he was finished, she filled it with water and told him to be quiet while she was gone. He circled several times and with a pleasant sigh, settled next to the overstuffed chair in the corner. Holmes knew how to be at home.

Of the clothes layered in the suitcase, she selected unhesitatingly the ones on top, purchased a month earlier in Vancouver – a sleek silk skirt, midnight blue, a draping linen blouse, black belt and pumps, big silver earrings, no rings –

then tried her hair loose, pulled back in a tail, and finally she rolled it up neatly with a couple of black lacquered sticks so that from the front she looked like a fair-faced boy, and in the back like an elegant older woman. But not a girl. Not a girl anymore.

"There's a message for me," she told the man at the front desk. She gave him the room number.

"Anne McBain," he said, handing her a folded piece of white paper. She put it in her pocket, still not wanting to know, and still a little afraid of the first brush stroke.

The Aquarium was built at the end of Cannery Row on a small promontory, the road making a sharp left turn at the main entrance and continuing up the hill into the town. Most of the old canneries had been either converted to restaurants and shops, or had been burned down by arsonists hired by property owners frustrated with the local historical societies who were bent on preserving the past; in their place inns and parking garages and hotels had been cast up, each straining for a view of the bay. But you could still see the crumbling seawall, a piling or two standing alone in the surf, and up along the sides of the buildings, strings of tiny, broken-paned windows and the pentimenti of family names once the dons of the sardine industry – Aneas, Hediondo, Ventimiglia – painted on tin and brick. In a queer turnabout the reemergent signs were gaining on time.

It was fresh out, not cold, the day's warmth clinging just behind the leading edge of night. There were a lot of people on the street. Shop doors had been propped open. Smells of fish and wine wove through the crowded vestibules of restaurants and out across the sidewalk where several times couples walking in front of Anne paused, then turned to go in.

Halfway to the Aquarium she stopped in the orange light sliding from the doorway of a tavern and opened the note.

Welcome home. It was signed *Eliot:* the operator who had taken the message had misspelled his name, and Anne felt that this small remote crime committed against him had been committed against her too.

She put the note back in the pocket of her evening jacket and continued along the sidewalk. Her hand was in her pocket, around the folded piece of paper. She thought it was just right, what he had said. Just right.

At the main entrance to the Aquarium three women seated behind a table wrote out name tags for the incoming guests. Anne slipped past them behind others who had already received their names, and found the portable bar stationed in front of the enormous kelp forest tank. She had not, as John Devlin suggested, had a second drink. Several acquaintances nodded in passing while the bartender poured her a bourbon on ice, then she made her way through the clot of people at the hors d'oeuvres table, around the kelp tank and into the winding hallways lined with exhibits. They were backlit and colorful, and lent an eerie watery quality to the otherwise unlit hallways.

Several former assistants came up, Crazy Crawford among them, and Anne exchanged overly enthusiastic greetings and inquiries. Crawford was subdued; she wondered if it was because she would be giving one of the talks, or if he was still sore with her for sending him home two summers ago. The isolation had laid him open the way a sharp knife lays open salmon and, at the end of a month, he was psychically filleted. Crawford was into Indians, shamanism, the works. When Grant and some of the others arranged logs around the campfire in the shape of a square, Crawford threw a fit. Squares are spiritually incorrect, they were told. He wanted a circle. Anne took him into Telegraph Cove the next morning.

Moving off, she stopped before one of the habitat tanks, watched for awhile, sipped her bourbon.

A woman in pink approached. "I'm looking forward to your paper," she said.

"Hello Carol." Anne took her hand; it was as soft and dry as a tame bird.

"I read the abstract this afternoon," she said. "And I've got a number of questions about it."

Tipping her head, Anne smiled gently. "I'm sure you do."

Carol Phillips had been at Sea Park for twenty years and had a twenty-year-old perspective. Anne always figured she didn't have the stuffing for field work, or the imagination for hard research, and was now in the business of forever defending her chosen stasis. She was one of the animals held in captivity at Sea Park, a live capture and another 'ambassador for the species,' as she liked to call them. And Carol Phillips would not be the only one with questions.

Most of the work done with killer whales was limited to the recording of general life history parameters, but Anne's paper concerned the development of sex roles in the Resident population of whales living in Johnstone Strait – a lot to ask for in terms of information from an aquatic mammal. She had looked at other species with similar behavior patterns, maternal groupings, a social order distinguished by family dialects, and she had speculated and interpolated and had come up with what she believed was a fairly sound theory. It would be challenged. That was part of everyone's job here.

We are each other's checks and balances, she thought, and if we ever achieve that vision of life we're all looking for, the peephole will be smallish indeed, and through it a kaleidoscopic scene, changing with each viewer and inextricably placed between two facing mirrors, the sublime symmetry of birth and death.

"I know I'll have some backtracking to do," Anne said. "I was trying to see how far it would reach theoretically. I realize it pushes the data."

"Well, it's very interesting," Carol chirped, by way of retreat.

Anne thanked her and excused herself. She had seen the bald pate of Borovich nestled like a large, prehistoric egg inside a group of admirers. His name was in the Conference brochure next to *Mysterious Mysticete*, a paper detailing the results of the study prompted by the 13-million-year-old whale skeleton Elliot had accidentally uncovered two years ago out on the island. Now it seemed to Anne that whatever she and Elliot had uncovered themselves then during that week when events converged so precisely, when her father died and the baby was conceived, when the awful effects of *El Niño* were beginning to be tallied up, and in the contemplative years following, the quiet reclaiming of land and life, she too was here to report on the findings.

She watched Borovich pound another man's back. Male greeting rituals, she thought. And, as if he'd heard her, he turned and glanced up the hallway, tightened his brow, then let it go as the slick of a grin appeared, and he started toward her. She ducked around a corner and ran right into the back of what for a fleeting moment seemed like a bear in a Harris Tweed jacket.

"I'm so sorry," she started to say, and stopped in mid-sentence.

For an instant Elliot looked scared to death. And in that same instant she thought she could retreat, and they could pretend that it never happened, that at least the purity of their separation had not been corrupted. But it was too late.

"You used to be lighter on your feet," he said. His smile was skittish. It reminded her of the bellboy.

She wanted to say his name – she knew that – and so she said, "How are you, Elliot?" The idiotic formality of this greeting echoed in her head.

He made a slight oblique gesture with his head, as if the answer wasn't important. "What about you?"

"I'm well. Very." And she nodded once to convince him, wondering all the while why was she acting as if he was some distant acquaintance, dimly recalled. Did the perimeter wall really need to be that high?

"Yes," he said, then repeated the question. "How have you been, really?"

"I've just been working. It's been good."

He touched her arm as if to be certain, and withdrew his

hand. They were standing in one of the darkened hallways lined with tanks, the anemones and blackeye gobys, the bat rays, the shrimp and shark in their fluid world surrounding them, and the air felt as heavy and slow as water. Neither one of them said anything for a moment or two. Individually they peered into the tank, and she noticed in the glass reflection that he looked younger, thinner.

"I see your friend Loretta in the bank every now and then. She gives me news of you, along with my deposit slips," he said.

"And how does *she* say I am?"

"She reports that you're . . . thriving." He paused, then looked into her eyes. "She also told me you'd gone ahead with the abortion." Turning gently, he took her arm. "I should've been with you for that at least, and I'm so sorry."

She tried to look away. Her throat swelled, but she managed to say, "It was all right. A friend came with me."

"Of course." He sounded momentarily lost. "I just meant I should have been that friend."

"It wasn't a role you could have played, not at that time."

Behind them, people swam by, then they were alone again.

"Was it the wrong choice?" he murmured.

"I guess that all depends on the point of view," she said.

"That's not an answer. Was it the wrong choice?"

"Not really," she said, aware that his insistence rather annoyed her. He had relinquished the right to ask a long time ago.

There was nothing she wanted to ask him, she realized, nothing she wanted to say except his name, and only to hear the way she said it standing next to him. She knew she had loved Elliot Newhouse and that, like some wingless bird perched too high, she still loved him.

"I almost called you last spring in Tofino," he said.

"How did you know where I was?"

"Ah, well, a man of my exalted stature has infinite resources." He smiled. "Among them a former student who works at the biological center in Tofino. He referred to you as 'that stunning broad who's up here doing reproductive studies on killer whales.'"

It was her turn to smile. "Stunning broad with wrinkles and crow's feet. So why didn't you call?"

"Why didn't I call," he mused. "Why didn't I call when you were in Tofino, and when you were up in Prince Rupert, and when you were down in the San Juans, and all the other many times when you were wintering in Vancouver at Waddington and the apartment on Arbutus Street. I could've picked up the phone but didn't."

"You *have* been spying," she said, making no effort to hide her pleasure. "And you didn't answer the question."

"I didn't call, I suppose, because I was afraid of the reception. I suppose I thought I'd better let you be."

"I'm glad for the impulses," she said. "But I'm just as glad you heeded the suppositions. I needed to be let be."

Elliot nodded, though she thought she saw an errant shade of disappointment cross his face. And then they were silent. It was a comfortable, unhurried silence, as if they had both decided it was simply time to rest, to let what had been said filter down and settle on the bottom. To keep the water clear. She felt profoundly at home standing next to him, and homesick too. Because it was all still impossibly impossible. She might have even wished she was back on the island.

Eventually, Elliot leaned away from her, cocked his head, and said, "You do look wonderful, Anne. You've become . . ." He gazed into the aquarium tank. A school of fish flashed by and purled off in unison, like a single graceful creature. "You've just . . . become," he said.

"I guess so," she said.

"Are you happy?"

"Differently. And you, are you happy?" she asked.

"I'm busy."

She remembered her drink then; she had set it on the sill beneath the thick glass of the tank, and she picked it up and gulped. Her hand was trembling. "And you and Jill have . . . resolved your problems?" she said.

He looked at her blankly for a moment, as if he did not understand whom she was talking about. "I think the word is dissolved," he finally said. "As a matter of fact she's getting remarried next month."

Anne dropped her eyes.

"You didn't think I'd go ahead with it."

"It was too late for believing."

"Yes, for you it definitely was too late. And I guess I got to where sometimes I didn't believe I would do it either. But you weren't the cause of my dysfunctional marriage, you were a symptom. The best symptom, I hasten to add, and to me, the only *obvious* symptom, which is why for so long I kept missing the forest for the trees." His expression was tender. "Anyway . . . yes, in a sense we resolved our problems."

She was silent. She couldn't thank him because he hadn't done it for her, he hadn't even called after. And even if he had done it for her, she wouldn't thank him. Gratitude was the start of something malignant. Anyway, she really didn't want to talk about it. She really was finished with those years. And the meaning of what he had said earlier – that he had wanted to call her but didn't, that he was afraid, that even though he had kept track of her he had known he had to let her be, to let her become – the meaning of all this, combined with the sudden realization that his life now was no longer what it had been, seemed to pile into her present, like a sudden fall of water, and she was quite literally staggered by it.

"After the divorce Jill moved back to Chicago where she was raised," he was saying. "The man she's marrying is an artist of some kind. A painter, I think. She said she didn't want anything more to do with biologists and reproductive strategies."

"I don't blame her." Anne lifted her head and smiled at Elliot. "We're a motley crew."

He picked up her hand. "You want to get out of here, go

get a drink, or some dinner?"

"I can't," she said, but she left her hand in his. "I haven't seen John Devlin yet, and there are people I want to say hello to."

He thought for a moment. "Well, I'll be at your talk tomorrow. Maybe we could meet afterward. By the way, John gave me a copy of the plenary paper. It's terrific, you know."

"Don't be kind, Elliot. Not now." The words impressed her. They were not angry; they were not anything but alive and in that alone they seemed to convey a certain endurance. They came from that new immutable place inside, but every now and then the voice took her by surprise, as if she had spoken in a lately acquired foreign language.

He held her gaze and said softly, "I wasn't being kind. I'm just proud of you."

"Okay," she said. "Then, thank you. By the way, I liked your message."

"It seemed safe enough."

"For whom?"

"Maybe for both of us."

Someone was trying to make an announcement around the corner. The sharp reports of spoon against glass preceded directly a noisy crowd of conferees which gathered and crushed back into the hallways flanking the kelp forest tank, and swept Anne and Elliot in among them. Greetings and loud toasts were made. John Devlin spotted her and pushed over, hauling the fellow from Newfoundland. When she turned to include Elliot in the handshakes and introductions, he was gone.

It was almost an hour before she left, but even then she paused reflexively at the main entrance, as if they'd had an assignation and he was late as usual. Several guests departed; one of them said good-bye to her. Prompted by the word itself, she started along the sidewalk, retracing her steps. She did not feel the old regrets, as if she had lost something, and she moved through the night with an even gait, listening to the tap of her shoes and the cool comings and goings of the waves.

There was a weedy lot near the Aquarium and, as she approached it she saw a figure seated on the crumbling remains of an old cannery foundation that ran parallel to the sidewalk. New, taller fortifications had been built atop the other three sides and, though she couldn't tell what kind of structure it would be, she was gratified that the old piers buried deep would be put to some fresh use.

The figure stood. It was strange to see Elliot alone: it occurred to her he probably wasn't very good at it.

"You vanished," she said.

"After twenty minutes at these things I get a tad claustrophobic." He looked at his shoes. "Actually, that's not exactly true. As a matter of fact I'm out here sulking."

"About what?"

"About other people commanding your attention," he laughed.

"Well, you're getting just like that pompous old fool, Borovich. But my attention is on you now, your eminence. Does that offer of a drink still stand?"

"Yes ma'am." He hooked her arm in his.

They found a corner booth in the tavern. It was deep and covered with red vinyl, a world unto itself from which they could view the whole of the busy little room. On the wall behind the booth was a mirror and, when she glanced at Elliot, she caught peripherally the back of his head: it seemed so near and defenseless, and almost too personal to look at and at the same time, she wanted to touch its familiar curves.

"Have we been here before?" Elliot said.

"No, dear, not here," she said, patting his hand. "Every trysting spot in northern California, but not here."

The waiter brought them two glasses of Chianti, and she slid a five dollar bill onto his tray.

"Like old times," Elliot said, clinking her glass.

"Is it?"

"No."

"Because I'm buying this time?" she said. "Is that what makes it different?"

"That's not what I mean, and you know it."

"Yes, I know."

"I'll get the next round," Elliot said. "Then we'll see if it's the same as old times."

"I've had too much already," she said.

The Chianti was young and flinty, and needed food to soften it, but she didn't want anything soft tonight.

Elliot told her about the center for cetacean research, who was funding it, the commitments he'd secured from other scientists. And when she began to describe her work at Waddington and in the islands, he interrupted her, and there was a sort of wobbly note in his voice, as if he was saying something that mattered to him a great deal but was something he was still learning.

"Anne," he said, "would you think about coming back to California, would you consider being a part of this center?"

"It doesn't even exist yet."

"It exists on paper; it takes people to make it happen. You could help put it together. With your help it could really be something."

She raised the glass of Chianti and took a sip. "I have a living to make," she said.

"Your salary, a good salary, would come out of the funding. It could start anytime. It could start now."

She didn't say anything for a few minutes. Elliot put his hands on the table and leaned forward. The glass of wine was between his hands, and he stared at it, picking it up once, then twice to drink and returning it to the same place each time. A holding pattern. Sitting back against the vinyl, she watched the waiter move from table to table, bringing drinks, taking orders. There was a place at the end of the bar where you could get burgers, fish and chips, and a young man in a white apron, a sort of factotum, swung around from behind the bar, delivered an armful of plates, then fetched a busing tray and hurried along behind the waiter, clearing dishes and wiping off abandoned tables. Presently, the waiter glanced inquiringly over at the red booth, and Anne shook her head no.

"Start now," Elliot repeated. "If you want."

"It would look a little odd, would it not, for a novitiate to suddenly become a prioress? People might suspect you of having unsavory motives, Mr. Newhouse. But that's not the reason. I have unfinished research," she said. "All the summer data to analyze."

"*When* you finish, then."

"It's tempting, Elliot. It would be wonderful. And the whole thing sounds terribly exciting, but . . ."

"No rain," he interrupted, grinning.

"No rain," she said. "There's that." She looked wistfully at his face, at its broad strength, at his blue eyes and the delicate upward strokes at the corners of his mouth that always gave his wish away. "I have my own boat now, Elliot, and I'm the one at the oars. It gets me to shore. That's a place I haven't been very often."

"Bring your boat with you, then," he said, "since we're reduced to speaking in metaphor."

"And tie up to the stern of the *S.S. Newhouse?"*

He slapped his hand on the table. "You can have the directorship of the center, you can have whatever you want, you can be the *janitor*, for Christ's sake, I don't care. Just be a part of it."

Again she felt the tightness in her throat and the need to avert her eyes. It was only a moment. The hard place held. "It is tempting. But I do have unfinished projects, Elliot. They're important to me."

He sighed heavily and leaned back against the booth. "Okay. Well, how the hell can I come courting with you up in Vancouver?"

Picking up her glass, she smiled at him over the rim. "I

guess you'll have to figure that out all by yourself."

She put her hand on his, wrapping her fingers under his palm, and they sat like that for awhile. The waiter brought them another two glasses of wine, 'on the House,' he said, and she didn't trouble to question. They drank with their free hands, and the two that were one did not stir.

When they were leaving, Elliot asked her if she still had Holmes.

"Oh, yes."

"Did you bring him?"

"Everywhere I go, he goes," she said, resisting an impulse to propose the reunion of man and dog. There would be world enough and time for gatherings.

"That's great," he said, suddenly smiling, as if this was the best news he'd had all evening. "That's . . . great."

Outside, the breeze had dropped, and now they could smell the water, Pacific water, colder than most, tattered at its broad edges with tidal algae, minutiae living in cracks and cutaways, bore holes, erosion pools, in patches hanging from rocks, midst grains of sand, living in two worlds wedged between time; they could smell the place where they met, land and water, where they lost themselves, not a border but a blending, and not antagonistic, but adaptive. The intertidal zone. It was the smell of history smelled in the present. It was the smell of life living.